KEY HORIZON

GARY WESTFAL

ISBN-13: 978-0-9992220-1-0
LCCN: 2017914644

BOOK DESIGN BY: G-Life Enterprises Corp.
Gary Westfal, Concept
Scott Grinnell, Graphic Artist
Justin Park, Artist

Printed in the United States of America

ALSO BY GARY WESTFAL

DREAM OPERATIVE

This book is dedicated to my son, the real Joey G, after whom the protagonist in the G. Weston series is molded. It has been said that a father is a son's first real hero. While I hope that holds true, I watch in awe at the hero he has become in his own life as he continues to inspire me in more ways than he'll ever truly know.

ACKNOWLEDGMENTS

To write is one thing, to publish is completely another. That seemingly insurmountable feat could not be possible if not for the woman who stood by me through endless late nights at the computer, the call of an author driven to tell a story— her understanding, compassion, love, and ceaseless support made everything possible...my wife, my friend, and my partner...Janeen.

To the men and women who unselfishly serve our country in the quiet and humble capacity of their profession of arms, both past and present, I salute you!

To my characters, the drivers of my visionary story lines, who make it all possible and put it all together in form, fashion, and dialogue; always ready and willing to show me the next scene, to reveal the purpose or intent in a way that delivers valuable content to the reader—Rock on!

To the team at Westfal Publishing & Graphics, LLC, responsible for the artwork, layout, arrangement, and publication processes, I thank you.

To those who inspired me, encouraged me, and believed in me, I am humbled by the experience and am a better writer because of you.

1

He awoke to the sound of running water coming from the bathroom just off the master suite. A smile appeared on his face when he caught the sweet scent of her perfume lingering on the sheets. Drawing a deep breath, he stretched his arms above his head and squinted to allow his eyes to adjust to the morning light. Slowly, he moved to the edge of the bed, where he sat for a moment to clear the cobwebs from his mind. A corner of the bedsheet, covering his lap, was the only thing he wore, which wasn't unusual considering he typically preferred sleeping in the nude—especially when he wasn't alone.

He sat still for several moments, lost in thought, allowing his senses time to come around, attempting to absorb the quality of the moment.

A quick glance at the clock on the nightstand caught his attention for a moment: *3:33...a.m.?*

Hmph, gotta reset that thing, he thought, quickly shrugging it off, realizing it *had* to be wrong.

Scant memories from the night before flashed through his mind when he noticed an empty wine bottle next to the clock—Cayman Vineyards, Cabernet Sauvignon, 2004. Again, he smiled as he recalled her laughing and carrying on about nothing...and everything. What a night!

The room was large and well-appointed in a traditional Mediterranean motif—white concrete walls and tile floors throughout most of the expansive vacation villa. Beyond the foot of the bed stood two tall French doors framing the morning light filtering in through sheer curtains.

The bedsheet fell from his lap as he stood and casually made his way across the room, running his fingers through his hair. The warmth of the morning sun bathed his naked body as he pushed the curtains aside to take in the view. A shimmering private swimming pool lay just beyond the open balcony. From his second-floor vantage point he could see the ocean nestled between two large white concrete homes situated behind a stone wall surrounding the property just beyond the pool. He paused to savor the scene and bask in the solitude of his thoughts. It all seemed comfortably familiar, yet strangely surreal. He closed his eyes and smiled as the images lingered. Everything was perfect.

The serenity of the moment was suddenly interrupted by the muted sound of a closing door, coming from somewhere behind him in the sprawling villa. He shrugged it off, but it was enough of a distraction for him to turn from the tranquil view and make his way to the bathroom.

Steam escaped through the opening of the bathroom door as he approached. Knocking politely, he called out, "Hello…can I join you?"

Hearing no reply, he slowly pushed the door open. "Anyone home?" he playfully called out again as he casually walked into the bathroom.

As the steam cleared, he saw an empty shower stall—the glass door open wide and shattered, the water still running. A crimson trail stained parts of the shower frame, the surrounding marble sill, and tile floor. Looking down, he saw he had walked right through the bloody evidence. His mind raced to absorb the entirety of what he saw, his thoughts quickly returning to the sound he had heard just moments before. His body surged with adrenaline as his mind went into overdrive in an attempt to catch up with the reality of it all.

He quickly turned and darted for the bedroom where he knew he would find his weapon. In his haste, he slipped on the bloody floor and lost his balance. Crashing uncontrollably, he struck his face on the wall and cut his shoulder on a glass shard on his way down to the hard tile floor. Struggling to maintain consciousness, he pushed himself from the floor and made sure to secure his footing before making another attempt. He wiped his bloodstained hands on the nearest towel and quickly moved across the room to the bedside where his clothes and holstered weapon were hanging over a chair. He grabbed his 1911 Kimber Custom II .45 caliber handgun from its holster, chambered a round, and placed the weapon on the bed where he could get to it in one move while he quickly put on his pants and a pullover shirt. His mind seared with the overwhelming gravity of what was happening. He picked up the gun, ran to the French doors, flung them open, and stepped out onto the balcony, determined to find something…anything that would make sense.

Nothing—only the serenity of the scenic landscape.

He quickly returned to the room, grabbed his shoes, and headed for the bedroom door—gun drawn, safety off—the barrel leading the way. He peered around the doorjamb and then quickly back in again.

All clear.

His heartbeat sent the sound of blood pounding through his ears as he stepped into the hallway. His thoughts were at war with one another. Thinking of his next move, he had to anticipate a confrontation. He had to be decisive, and he had to be quick. He wrestled with the thoughts fighting for dominance.

How will I react? Will I be fast enough? Will I be accurate enough? What will I do if I find her injured or…worse? Those bastards!

Rage…fear…determination. *Gotta focus!*

He turned his head quickly left, then right, in search of danger, his eyes analyzing everything, quickly scanning.

Making his way to the top of a gently winding staircase, he pushed the barrel of his weapon over the banister and then followed with a quick glance to scan his intended route.

All clear.

He cleverly dropped his shoes over the rail to see if they would draw the attention of anyone below. He watched as they seemed to fall in slow motion and followed their descent with the steady aim of his weapon as they hit the wood-plank floor one story below with an echoing *slap*.

No reaction…nothing but silence and the deafening sound of his heartbeat.

Another surge of adrenaline shot through his body as he carefully took the first step down the stairs. Trace bloodstains on the steps and banister caught his attention as his mind continued to struggle to make sense of it all.

Focus! Stay focused.

Each step of his descent brought an increasing level of uncertainty and anxiety as he continued to scan his surroundings, his back pressed against the wall and his weapon extended in front of him, both hands firmly grasping the pistol grip. Reaching the first-floor landing, he crouched and pointed his weapon in several random directions. He scanned the floor and walls for a continuing blood trail, but it had mysteriously ended, marked with what appeared to be a faded swiped handprint along the wall, possibly marked by the blood of its victim in one final attempt at resistance.

He paused for a moment to collect his thoughts, attempting a rational evaluation as images of what *could* have happened played out in his mind. He rose to his feet and quickly stepped to the front door, turned the brass knob and opened the oversized door. The world outside was strangely still. No people. No birds. No breeze. No sound. He had opened the door to a literal dead end.

Outside, a white late-model Bentley Continental GT was parked on a circular cobblestone driveway that led to an open gate about forty yards away. Beyond the gate, the street was empty. He stood motionless, enveloped in the noiseless surroundings, his weapon now in one hand and relaxed at his side, pointed down.

The hair on the back of his neck bristled as he snapped his attention and the aim of his weapon back into the house as he heard a faint sound coming from behind him.

Five years had passed since he made the decision—a decision that quite literally changed his life as he knew it. The recollection of his former days had faded as he forged a new life in a new role. The controversy surrounding his "recruitment" had been bizarre, yet all things considered, he felt he had ended up in the right place... even though his specialty, or "gift," as the agency referred to it, often made him feel like one of the loneliest men on the planet.

Word eventually got out that the agency had hired a "psychic," which was about as far removed from the truth as it could get and a stretch of the true nature of his value to the agency—and to the country as a whole. It was just as well though, because one of the provisions of his cover was to ensure anonymity in the form of nondisclosure and the deepest cloak of secrecy. The controversy provided just the opportunity he needed to disappear into the shadows and adjust to his new role in the real world, outside the confines and immediate protection of the agency.

He was told that if he were to remain with the agency and pursue his study and exploitation of dream analysis and manipulation, he would have to become a *NOC agent*. That pretty much meant he'd live a "normal" life of his own, while still essentially working for the agency, but his connection to anything or *anyone* inherently governmental would be untraceable. His *NOC* status, or *Non-Official Cover*, would be the appearance of a normal, independent life, and he would not be endorsed or acknowledged by the agency in any way. But his connection and commitment to them was for life.

Five years—not long in terms of working for a new company... but when that company required such total commitment and the use of unconventional methods and tactics, it can complicate things, to say the least, especially when things are asked that aren't always congruent with personal ethics, beliefs, or values. Such things are considered secondary and expendable when "unconventional" services are called upon in the name of the mission. Those unconventional methods and tactics ultimately led to choices that often meant the difference between life and death, despite personal convictions.

Joey G. Weston preferred things to be simple and straightforward—uncomplicated. But over time, he had learned to adapt to the complicated expectations of the agency in his own way. A former PhD research student and part-time college professor, he was well respected for his intellect and insight into the field of human psychology. He had been on the fast track to tenure at Georgetown University when his life was turned upside down. The event was harrowing, but he had adapted well and was getting used to his new role. In fact, he was actually beginning to enjoy it.

Weston respected the ethic of hard work and the importance of political connections and had learned to apply both inside the invisible walls of the agency. He had even developed some close relationships with certain key people on the inside and knew when and where to solicit their assistance. He fell in love once, or so he recalled. But he had chosen to walk away to protect the woman he loved from the dangers of compromise to a profession they were both a part of. His decision led to a life of independence, free from the commitment and expectations of long-term relationships. Despite this, he had developed an innate ability to connect with people on a personal level. His introspect and intuition paved the way for an attraction beyond his unassuming good looks, which typically served him well, whether he was engaged in casual conversation or in search of clues and information in support of mission objectives. Most people liked him and were naturally drawn to him.

G, as he was most commonly called, spent most of his time on his passion for the study of oneirology—dream interpretation and manipulation—and he had made significant breakthroughs, thanks to the generous funding and accommodations of the agency. Despite these breakthroughs, he had learned to keep things in perspective, not to overanalyze, and to never discount anything as insignificant. In fact, the one thing he kept deeply ingrained was the philosophy that things were seldom what they seemed. The philosophy served him well and often provided the perspective and insight he needed to analyze, interpret, and act when considering an effective course of action or providing a much needed gut check.

G had developed a distrust of virtually everyone, save for a select few he considered to be well within his inner circle. Even *they* were unaware of the true nature of his new skills and increasing lethality. Keeping it all in perspective was a daily exercise in self-control as he managed to project the same cheerful, nonchalant persona he had been known for when he originally signed on with the agency…five years earlier.

In one fluid movement, he spun around on his heel and quickly crouched, raising his weapon in response to the sound behind him. His mind raced as he tried to decipher the source, pinpoint the direction, and assess the threat. He quietly stepped back over the threshold of the doorway and slowly closed the door behind him, careful not to make a sound. Then he waited.

His eyes darted about the room—quickly right, then left…high, then low. His breathing was slow and deliberate, his heartbeat rapid, and his thoughts raced at warp speed.

Motionless, he listened intently, waiting…*hoping* to hear the sound again.

He continued to absorb the details of his surroundings while trying to replay and reevaluate the sound in his short-term memory. Wood-plank floor confined to the foyer area, a stone fireplace in a room to his right, white stucco textured interior walls, high ceilings and archways leading to adjacent rooms. A wrought-iron door on the far wall of the room to his right revealed the corner of a wine rack just beyond its opening. A faucet dripped in the next room, which seemed to keep time with a clock somewhere, ticking with an annoying mechanical rhythm.

Glancing up at the stairway, he retraced his steps in his mind, mentally capturing the detailed, agonizing sequence of his short journey to the first floor landing. Random thoughts reemerged, peppering his mind with images of the horror that had evidently taken place, while his heart ached for answers.

The silence was suddenly broken by the same faint sound he'd heard moments earlier.

Decision time.

He rose to his feet, pointed his weapon, and quietly stepped across the foyer. The wood floor occasionally creaking beneath his weight, he approached the threshold of the room and cautiously peered in—an office adorned with high built-in bookshelves filled with colorful bindings, picture frames, and several varieties of knickknacks and mementos. Papers were strewn about a large oak desk in the center of the room. Drawers were pulled out of place, most of the contents dumped onto the floor.

Another glance around the room revealed one entrance—no exit.

Whoever's in here isn't leaving without a confrontation, he thought, his eyes continuing to dart about the room.

A closet door in the left corner of the room was slightly ajar.

Quietly stepping forward, he positioned himself on the wall just outside the door and carefully poked the barrel of his gun into the opening, then used it to slowly push the door open. He purposefully stepped slightly left of center of the door opening and aimed his weapon chest high.

"Show yourself!" he demanded.

His eyes opened wide in surprise and shock when he looked down to see a child huddled in a fetal position, whimpering and shaking uncontrollably. Reacting quickly, he flipped the safety switch and placed the weapon in the waistband of his pants at the small of his back. He extended his arms while slowly dropping to his knees and approached her in a whisper.

"It's OK. I won't hurt you."

She reached out for him and cried aloud when she saw him. He scooped her into his arms and held her tight. The scent of her soft hair filled his mind with a confusing familiarity.

"It's all right, sweetie," he said again, in a reassuring whisper.

"You're bleeding, Daddy," she said, looking at the cut on his shoulder.

He held her close and assured her he would be OK.

Why did she call me Daddy?

He struggled to absorb the totality of all that had just happened.

What's happening to me?

aul Harriman assumed the position of Director of Operations for the National Security Agency when the former director, Dan Keppler, quietly slipped out shortly after having been awarded the Presidential Rank Award.

The Presidential Rank Award was the government's highest award for civil servants. Typically, senior management officials at various federal agencies nominated executives for the awards, while panels of private citizens selected the winners. The panels' selections then went to the president for his approval. Dan's selection was unique in that it was a unilateral decision, made by the president himself after learning that Dan personally orchestrated the operation that had killed the world's most wanted terrorist, Khalid Abdul Hakim. The classified details surrounding Hakim's demise were never released—not even to the president. The only fact known to the president was that Dan had orchestrated the snare that resulted in Hakim's demise at the hands of one of the agency's own quiet operatives.

Paul's team of professionals conducted, supported, and coordinated joint special missions that others weren't technically cleared to orchestrate. He and his team successfully facilitated the air support and sterilized the airspace for the operation that resulted in the Mohammed Atef kill by an AGM-114 Hellfire missile launched by a Predator remotely piloted drone just outside Atef's home in Kabul, Afghanistan. Dan was impressed by Paul's leadership and his ability to quickly respond to unusual requests by the joint forces commander in the new theater of operation. Paul's rise to the directorship was inevitable when he initially found favor with Dan during an assignment to Afghanistan in 2001, when Paul was the Special Operations Liaison Element, or SOLE, Director for the region.

At sixty years old and the agency's newest director, Paul had oversight responsibility for the security of the entire country, its territories, and international interests. The agency primarily exploited signals intelligence to gain decision advantages for the United States and its allies through various means, to include clandestine operatives, or agents, supporting worldwide operations in cooperation with other governmental agencies in the interest of American ideals and objectives.

"Good morning, Lisa. How are you this morning?" said Paul to his executive assistant.

"Doing well, sir. And you?"

"Lisa, how many times do I have to tell you, you don't have to call me 'sir'? Those days are long gone," he said with the warm smile he was known for.

"Well I know you're no longer a colonel, but have you stopped to take a good look at the title next to your name now? Hello—*director*."

Paul smiled.

Lisa's comment reminded him of a time when he had been assigned to Kirtland Air Force Base as a Pave Low helicopter squadron commander and later as the commandant of the US Air Force Special Operations School. And so the story of the day began, as it typically did most every morning, over a cup of coffee. You could almost set your watch to Paul's stories. Most of them were reminiscent of his days leading the troops, or of an account of a decorated friend or an operation he conducted, orchestrated, or was involved in, all of which somehow typically had value or relevance to current operations. He was a leader with charisma, character, and compassion. These traits, combined with his obsessive-compulsive nature, made for a blend that people naturally gravitated toward.

"Well, enough of my stories. We better get back to work. What does our day look like?"

A fresh scent of jasmine filled his senses as he held her close. He guessed her age to be about nine, judging from her general appearance.

"Everything is going to be fine," he reassured her in a confident whisper, looking into her eyes and holding her shoulders in his gentle grasp.

He stood and glanced about the disheveled room, taking an inventory of its contents. Then he walked to the center of the room where he noticed a set of keys with the Bentley logo among the scattered papers on the desk. He grabbed them and turned toward the front door.

"Let's find someplace safe for you," he said softly.

He grabbed her by the hand and led her to the foyer where his shoes were lying in the middle of the floor. The handgun pressed against his back when he sat down to put on his shoes. The contrast of the cold steel against his skin and the innocent smile of admiration coming from the child gave him pause as he considered the dichotomy of the situation.

"Let's go," he said, grabbing her hand once again, leading her to the door.

Outside, he caught a glimpse of something he hadn't noticed earlier—a man lying motionless on the lawn, face down in an awkward pose. Blood stained the side of his head and the collar of his white shirt.

He scooped the child into his arms, shielding her from the gruesome sight, and carried her to the car, his head purposely positioned near hers, blocking her view.

The doors of the Bentley unlocked as he approached, it sensing the proximity of the key fob. He placed the child securely in the back seat, buckled her in, and made his way to the driver's side where he took a seat in the plush leather cockpit. The gun pressed uncomfortably against the small of his back, so he pulled it out and placed the weapon on the passenger seat. The powerful, 6.0-liter, twin-turbocharged V12 engine roared to life with a gentle press of the start button. He glanced over his right shoulder to see the child smile at him with confidence and admiration. Returning his gaze to the driveway ahead, he placed the car in gear and drove toward the front gate, which opened automatically as the car approached. The community outside the gate was unfamiliar to him. Positioned at the end of the driveway, he had no idea which way to turn. So he made a random decision and turned right.

He approached an intersection, stopping only long enough to consider his next move. Glancing into the rearview mirror, he saw a Renault police cruiser approaching with its lights on. Looking right, he saw another. Two more approached from his left.

He remained motionless, his foot resting on the brake, and his hands firmly gripping the wheel.

Police cars completely surrounded his vehicle as he put the car into park and placed both hands at the top of the steering wheel in plain sight. Uniformed officers emerged from their vehicles with weapons drawn. Desperation gripped his mind like a vice as he tried making sense of it all while the officers took up defensive positions behind their cars.

Glancing over to the passenger seat, he saw his weapon lying there, standing out like a sore thumb, and knew it would only spook the police. Thoughts blistered through his mind while he contemplated his next move.

The rearview mirror framed two uniformed police officers emerging from their vehicle, their weapons drawn. He saw part of his own reflection in the mirror and took note that his face had swollen from the blow he'd taken earlier, falling in the bathroom. He also noticed something else quite odd. The face staring back at him was not his own.

A sleek high performance fishing boat gracefully moved through Hillsborough Bay at sunset. Its three 275-horsepower outboard engines quietly purred as they easily pushed the sleek craft through the turbid waters leading into the channel of East Bay. Such boats were a common sight in the Tampa area, so it easily blended in among the others.

The pilot pulled back on the throttles to slow the boat to idle through the no-wake zone as it passed Causeway Boulevard on the east and South Harbor Boulevard on the west side of the bay. The landscape to the west was marked by the silhouettes of buildings painted against an orange hue of a setting sun, fading into the blue black of a twilight sky. The navigation lights on the boat illuminated with the flip of a switch as the vessel slowed to approach the docks at Barge Avenue.

Darkness had completely fallen when the boat quietly moored alongside the dock. The two men in the boat worked together to secure the dock lines loosely enough for a quick getaway, then quietly waited for their contact to arrive.

Two silhouettes, still some distance away, cautiously made their way toward the boat. One of them illuminated a small flashlight three times to indicate they would be approaching the boat. The men in the boat looked at each other, nodded, and returned three short flashes with the subdued stern light. The deal was underway.

The bright lights of the terminal penetrated the deeply tinted windows of the Greyhound bus as he made his final walk through the aisle after the predawn arrival at the Tampa terminal. He found G still slumbering in his seat. "Yo! Wake up, *mon*. It's time to get off the bus. Grab yer belongins and kindly make yer way to the terminal. Move along now," said the driver, a cheerful, hard-working Jamaican man.

G stretched his arms, grabbed his bag from an overhead compartment, and casually made his way off the bus. His current assignment brought him to the Port of Tampa to serve as an undercover collections agent assisting the DEA in uncovering the source of an increasingly complicated rise in drug traffic activity in the region. It was a low-threat support op tasked to the NSA because of the specialized tools and intelligence-collection expertise employed by the clandestine agency.

He was especially gifted in uncovering details typically missed by even the most experienced investigators because of his rather unconventional methods and unique abilities to discern things most people could not. His cognitive abilities were a well-kept secret. His unconventional methods and tactics were a different matter altogether. He often employed a simple, investigative methodology that worked well, despite the drama and chaos that typically ensued because of those methods. Instead of spending a lot of time pursuing a lead on a suspect or target, he'd gather enough credible evidence, determine the target's vulnerabilities, then turn the tables by "shaking the hornet's nest," effectively drawing a suspect right to him or into a well-designed trap. G knew that an angry, frustrated suspect was typically a careless suspect. A careless suspect was what he had hoped to create for the DEA to determine the source of their problem. The only issue was the limitation of the NSA's orders calling for him to collect and analyze—and to otherwise stay out of the way. He was to report to the NSA through periodic SITREPs, or situation reports, which would be filtered for relevant content and transmitted to the DEA once the reports were determined to be sterile, that is, containing nothing that might negatively affect or compromise the agency or the agent.

He stood on the sidewalk under the pale yellow glow of a street lamp and took a casual look around. The humidity collected on his skin as he breathed in the scent of the thick, salty Florida air. A partially illuminated neon hotel sign across the street caught his attention, so he walked over to inquire about a room.

"It's ninety-nine a night," said the desk clerk, barely making eye contact with him.

"I'll take it," said G, pulling a wad of crumpled bills from his pocket.

"We prefer a credit card," said the clerk.

"Lost my wallet. All I have is cash."

"Need a receipt?" she asked.

He knew if he didn't ask for a receipt she'd keep the cash for herself but wouldn't press him on a formal registration. It actually worked in his favor most of the time.

"No," said G, shrugging his shoulders.

"Cash will do then. Room 357. It's not the best, but it's clean," she said, handing him a key card.

G thought that number was a good omen—357, like the handgun, rugged and reliable. *Should be all I need for now*, he thought.

G walked into the dark room, flipped the light switch, and sat his bag on the floor at the foot of a worn-out, queen-sized bed. He walked into the bathroom, turned on the light, and looked into the mirror.

Visions of his latest dream flooded his mind when he came face-to-face with his reflection.

Paul's direct line rang. "Paul Harriman," he said in a professional but cheerful tone.

"Hey, Paul. Jon McCoy at State. How are you doing, my friend?"

It was typical for other agencies to place calls directly to Paul when they needed to bypass the customary red tape associated with national security operations. Paul was used to dealing with most agencies having a domestic issue or concern that required his attention on such matters. He *wasn't* accustomed to calls from the State Department, however. So this call, although from a known friend and colleague, was out of the ordinary.

"Hey, Jon, how are you? How's Candy doing?"

"She's well, Paul. Can you go secure, my friend?" responded Jon, skimming quickly past the pleasantries.

"Certainly," said Paul, pressing a button marked "secure" on his secure terminal equipment.

"I show 'secure' on this end," said Paul.

"Secure here as well. Thanks, Paul. Listen, we have a developing situation that's got us reaching out to all agencies for assistance. I realize this request is a bit outside the confines of your lane, but we're looking for creative solutions."

"I'm listening," said Paul, as he waited for more details.

"The French Ministry of the Interior and the Israeli parliament have reached out to the secretary on this for counsel. Seems the Israeli minister of defense, Deputy Prime Minister Avigdor Malkinson, has been implicated in the disappearance of his wife while vacationing in the South of France. Both governments are in an understandable turmoil over the ordeal."

"What's his status?" asked Paul.

"French authorities have him in custody and are refusing to extradite him until they have more to go on. They have suspended his passport, and are ignoring his typical high-visibility political status, considering the circumstances, citing investigative due process," explained Jon.

"So he's in jail then?"

"No, he's on lockdown, in slightly better circumstances than an actual jail cell. Call it more of a sequestration than an incarceration. As you know, diplomatic status does not apply since he's not in country on official business. His political status offers *some* level of protection and delicate handling, but, when foul play is suspected, it changes all the rules. But here's the kicker—they have his nine-year-old daughter sequestered as well, currently being held separately from him."

"Ouch…this *is* sensitive. So the United States is acting as intermediary on this?"

"In a manner of speaking. We have FBI on scene in Saint-Tropez assisting local authorities. So far, they have nothing but his side of the story and, of course, the absence of his wife."

"What *is* his side of the story?"

Jon explained the circumstances to Paul, who listened intently for anything he or his agency could provide in terms of assistance or insight.

"Listen, Jon, it sounds as if you have the right people on it, so I'm not real sure what I can provide you with that you don't already have other than say, a focused communications watch and a deep-dive on the networks," explained Paul. "I assume the Israeli consul is on scene providing counsel?"

"The consul is on his way to see the deputy minister as we speak. Look, I agree we have the right people on this from an *overt* perspective, Paul. My gut—*and my boss*—tells me we're goin to need to use all available options and a source we can count on to look beyond the obvious to discover the truth. The longer we wait, the more complicated this gets."

"I understand, Jon. Let me run this by my analysts, and I'll get back with you if I can think of anything at all that can help."

Paul hung up the phone and pressed an intercom button. "Lisa, do me a favor and run a list of idle operatives."

"Certainly. Any specific skills you're looking for?"

"I'm not really sure yet," said Paul. "Right now I just need to see what our agent availability is to help a developing international situation."

"I'm on it. Anything else?"

"Yeah, pull the 201 file on whomever you find so I can review the details. I'm still trying to get to know the remaining few agents

I haven't had the pleasure of interacting with yet. And contact the ops center to see if we can get a wideband satellite positioned over southern Europe, specifically France and Italy."

"There's ten kilos. That's seven-hundred-fifty large," said one of the men in the boat. The other stood behind him, slightly to his right.

"Seven-fifty? When did the price go up?" asked the buyer, standing on the dock.

The men in the boat didn't offer a response. Instead, they returned cold, stoic stares.

The buyer turned to his partner standing behind him on the dock.

"When did the price go up?" asking again rhetorically, posing with open arms.

He turned back to the men in the boat. "Look, Larry never mentioned anything about a price increase. You guys wanna tell me why you suddenly raised your prices by fifty percent? I mean, don't get me wrong, we know the quality is good, but this could almost be considered price gouging if you know what I mean. Tell you what; if you'll take five hundred this time and lemme explain to the boss why he doesn't have a full delivery, we'll let the big boys figure it out. Deal?"

The buyer didn't wait for an answer. Instead, he walked over to a dark corner of the dock and lifted a worn, dusty tarp revealing two hundred-quart ice chests. He wheeled each of them to the edge of the dock while his partner kept an eye on the men in the boat. The buyer pushed one of the ice chests toward the boat while his partner, now a few steps behind him on the dock, kept a close eye on the transaction, his hand close to the side of his hip where his weapon was at the ready—safety off, round in the chamber.

"Here's two-fifty. Other half is in this one," he assured them.

"What's with him?" asked one of the men, referring to the buyer's partner.

"He's cool. He's just here to make sure we're *all* cool."

The man calmly nodded. "We're cool."

The pilot checked the ice chest and carefully counted the bundled cash. He pulled out a small, handheld black light and scanned the pile of bills to determine if they were marked in any way. Satisfied, he nodded to his partner, who handed half the product over to the buyer in a black canvas bag.

The buyer knelt on one knee and unzipped the bag to examine the contents. He broke open one of the sealed packages, jammed a small knife into the side of a cellophane-covered brick, and brought it to his tongue for a quick taste test. He turned to his partner and reached his hand out, accepting a butane torch lighter from him. Holding the knife up to eye level, he scorched the underside to determine the purity of the powder sitting atop the blade. Satisfied, he wiped the blade on his jeans, stood, and pushed the remaining ice chest toward the boat with his foot.

The men in the boat divided the remaining product, placed it into a second bag, and tossed it onto the dock.

"Pleasure doing business with you, gentlemen," said the buyer as he picked up the bag. "If you're ever in town again, give us a call, and we'll do lunch."

The men in the boat weren't amused. The pilot untied the lines while the other remained focused on the buyers. Returning to the cockpit, the pilot pushed the throttles forward and quietly slipped away into the night, lights off until they cleared the inlet.

"Let's get this stuff to Larry's office and call it a night," said the buyer.

Random images flashed through his mind as he stood motionless in front of the bathroom mirror.

Blood-stained floor, winding stairwell, 1911 Kimber Custom II ACP handgun...not really his weapon of choice, but a nice handgun nonetheless...

He subconsciously moved his hand to the small of his back where he found his own weapon, a short barrel Sig Sauer P238 sub compact, comfortably parked in a soft, quick-draw holster.

Well-appointed home, large office, nice car...the girl...the kid who called me...Daddy...

G tried making sense of the dream's purpose by analyzing the fleeting images. His brow furled as he continued pushing his mind to recall more details. Leaning against the vanity, he rubbed his tired eyes, then turned on the water to wash his face. Despair, mixed with anger and determination, unexpectedly welled within him. He took a slow deep breath and focused on the images, continuing to search for meaning and interpretation.

Questions loomed.

Man, what's with this dream? Where are these emotions coming from? Who is this man, and what's this all about? Is it even real, or is it a metaphor of some kind? What about the kid...the girl?

G knew enough about how his mind worked to trust the missing pieces would eventually reveal themselves. He never cared for the waiting part of the process and rarely enjoyed the lesson in patience.

He moved back into the bedroom while drying his face with a hand towel and sat on the edge of the bed. Carefully placing his weapon on the nightstand next to the clock, he froze when he noticed the time—*3:33 a.m.*

G arrived at the docks at sunrise and joined a group of laborers waiting outside a locked gate, hoping to pick up work as a temp hire in some capacity.

"OK, listen up," said a foreman behind the gate, holding a clipboard. "We need six strong laborers, one person qualified to operate a forklift, and anyone with welding experience. Form three lines, and we'll see if we can use you today."

The majority of the group clamored into the line for the laborer positions. G stood behind one man positioned in the forklift line. No one offered to be a welder.

"OK, first six in the labor line…go over and see Larry, and he'll issue you a hardhat and give you your assignments."

Disappointment was written all over the faces of those who weren't selected as they walked off in search of another alternative for a day's wage.

"Only need one of you for the forklift position," said the foreman. "And it's temporary. Our normal operator is out for a couple of days, so make a decision between the two of you."

G was ready to concede when the foreman spoke up once again.

"By chance, either of you got any welding experience?"

"No, but I'm a quick study," G offered.

The foreman sized him up and responded after a prolonged pause. "I can teach you the basics in a few hours if you're up for the challenge. We'll see if Larry will go for it, considering we have quite a few annoying repairs that need to be made. Come with me, and I'll see what I can do. If Larry asks, you have *some* experience, so play along, and I'll see if we can get you hired on."

G joined the foreman outside of a modular, aluminum-sided building that must be "Larry's office." The building was more of a converted storage house than an office. The men walked into an open bay where they met Larry, a lanky man in his midfifties.

Larry sat behind his desk and sized him up while the foreman sold his "welder for a day" pitch to the boss. He told Larry that G had *some* experience but required some refresher training, which he would happily provide, if Larry could spare him for the task.

"Well, you better have some experience, or we'll be able to tell right away, in which case you won't last long anyway. Grab your gear and a hard hat from that bin over there. Find a hat that fits and hang on to it as long as you're working here. You lose it, and we take a hundred bucks right outta your wages."

"Is he always that direct?" asked G of his new friend as they made their way to the supply bin.

"We caught him on a good day. You stick around long enough, and you'll get to see his ugly side."

"Great. I have no idea what the hell I'm doing, and I may have to deal with him on a *bad* day?"

"No worries. A few tips from me and you'll be up and running in no time. Welding isn't rocket science, my friend. But there are a few basics you should know. Hell, if I can do it, anyone can."

"Why are you helping me like this?" asked G.

The man shrugged. "I have a sense. You seem like a good dude. Besides, looks like you could stand to eat. You always that lean?"

G smiled. *Looks can be deceiving*, he thought.

"Keep your hands where we can see them at all times," warned a voice over the police-car loudspeaker. "Turn off the engine, and exit the vehicle slowly with your hands up."

He remained motionless, his hands still gripping the top of the steering wheel. His eyes darted about as he attempted to analyze the enormity of the situation.

Police cars continued to arrive and surround him.

He took note of his close-quarters environment. Resisting would be damn near impossible, not to mention stupid. A handgun lay fully exposed on the seat next to him. And then there was the child—the girl, not quite tall enough to be visible to the authorities outside, sitting still in the back of the vehicle where he and his family typically sat as passengers chauffeured by professionals. For the first time, the lingering fog of uncertainty completely lifted as he knew he had no choice but to react peacefully, to ensure the safety of his daughter.

"Rina, I need you to be brave. The policemen outside wish to take me in to ask me some questions. We will be separated for a time. No matter what happens, know that we will be reunited, and I will never allow anything bad to happen to you. Do you understand me?"

"Yes, Daddy."

He slowly opened the palms of his hands to openly reveal them to the police.

"Daddy…"

"Yes, my love."

"I miss Mommy."

He fought hard to control the overwhelming emotion he felt. "Me too. But don't worry, my little dove. I promise I'll find her, and we will all be together again soon."

He turned off the engine, opened the car door, and slowly exited the vehicle.

Paul looked over the list of available operatives in support of the State Department's most recent request for assistance. The top-secret list was categorized according to specialty and accompanied with electronic links to in-depth personnel files.

"Lisa, when you have a moment, would you step into my office please?" asked Paul, using his office intercom.

Lisa appeared in the doorway without answering the intercom. "You called?"

"Yeah, c'mon in and have a seat. Listen, you've been here a lot longer than I have. What's your take on this group of operatives?"

Lisa raised her eyebrows. "You actually didn't give me much to go on, so I gave you the first twenty on the idle list. If you can be a bit more specific as to what you're actually looking for, I'm certain I can offer you a more comprehensive list."

Paul gave her the surface details of the State Department's situation.

"The South of France, huh? Nice. Listen, if there are any administrative support requirements I can help with on site, I'd be happy to put *my* name on that list," said Lisa, half-jokingly. "Seriously though, we can coordinate with the CIA station chief in Paris to see what their resources are. I know we have a couple of agents who are currently in Europe who may be able to help. If you're not happy with any of those choices—"

"Excellent idea, Lisa. I'd prefer to rely on someone in country who speaks the language and knows the culture, even if we cross-pollinate with the CIA. I'll take you up on your offer for a more specific list of operatives. Bring up a fresh list of available agents to include their current obligations. I don't want to take anyone off of an assignment unless their expertise is relevant to the situation."

"Get down on your knees, and keep your hands where we can see them!" yelled one of the police officers.

He slowly dropped to his knees, his hands raised head-high in a surrender position. The hot pavement seared through his pants as the intensity of the sun beat down on his head.

The police officers cautiously moved in, weapons trained.

He glanced toward the vehicle and saw Rina looking at him with fear and concern in her eyes, her hands firmly pressed against the window. A firm shove from his blind side surprised him and sent him face first to the pavement. He felt the heat of the asphalt against his face as his head hit the pavement and his arms were pulled together to be handcuffed behind his back. He looked up to see an officer pointing a .40 caliber Sig Pro 2022 handgun at him.

"Sir, there's a child in the back seat!" exclaimed one of the officers.

"Rina..."

"Daddy!"

"There's a weapon on the front seat of the vehicle," shouted another officer.

"Take the girl in your vehicle and bring her to the municipal office. Seize the weapon and take it into evidence," ordered the on-scene commander

"On your feet!" ordered an officer, pulling Avigdor's arms convincingly.

"Where are you taking me? I am a visiting dignitary. I demand to accompany my daughter! She's just a child."

"Quiet! The girl will be held in a safe place," said the officer as he closed the door to the police cruiser.

The foreman managed to convince Larry to put him and G together on a repair project on the southeast side of the wharf.

"We have an easy project to start," he said. "Convincing Larry was easier than I thought it would be; he's usually a hard-ass about things. Could be that he knows these projects have to be completed, and I think he kind of suspects you don't know the first thing about welding and wants to see how fast you can pick it up. Assuming you do well, he'll most likely keep you around awhile longer."

"Thanks for the motivational speech," responded G sarcastically.

The men spent most of the day making basic repairs near the water as G absorbed the lessons provided by his new friend and vocational mentor.

"Here, your turn," he said, handing an acetylene torch to G and igniting the tip.

G extended his arms to avoid the blast and squinted to shield his eyes.

"Make your gas adjustments just like I showed you."

With the flame under control, G went to work making minor repairs and welds.

Larry was making his end-of-day rounds to check on his new hires as G was putting the finishing touches on a small gate weld.

"How's he doing?" asked Larry.

"See for yourself," responded the foreman, proudly pointing to new repairs.

Larry nodded. "Not bad, but can he do it by himself?"

"He's meticulous. His experience is evident, and he's improving on every pass."

"Works for me. We have plenty to keep him busy for a while," he said. "I'd like you to return tomorrow if you're available," said Larry as he turned to G.

"Be happy to," said G, extending his hand to Larry.

Larry reluctantly returned the handshake. G held his grip just long enough to discern Larry's more private side. If he were hiding anything, G would know it almost immediately. He looked past Larry's psychological barriers and saw a man mired in deceit and corruption. G's mind flooded with images he didn't immediately understand, but some of the things he did see gave him enough of a clue to indicate that Larry was living on the edge—and a very dangerous one at that.

Random faces, both men and women—and more women— Larry's most obvious weakness. Lines of cocaine drawn alongside a small caliber weapon, high-speed boats, the inside of a yacht, music, nudity, orgies, the face of a man, sinister, impatient, and intolerant...

G released his grip and the ensuing mental images generated by the physical connection began to fade.

"Whoa, this doesn't mean we're making some kind of contractual obligation, young man. I just want to know if you'd like some temp work. Seems you may indeed be able to weld after all," said Larry in reaction to the extended handshake.

G returned an insincere smile as the mental images continued to linger.

"You're off the clock and on your own time. Go home and do whatever it is you do. Just be back here at 7:00 a.m. tomorrow ready to work."

A glimpse inside the mind and motivation of Larry showed G several things—among them that Larry was weak-minded and had become a hostage to his own greed. He was involved but wasn't a power figure in the food chain of illegal operations; he had put himself in the vulnerable position of front man on the receiving end for someone much higher in the supply chain. And Larry would easily roll if pressured or given the incentive. The information would have to be confirmed, but for the time being, G knew he was in the right place. Identifying Larry as a drug pawn was relatively easy. Protecting him as a source would be another matter altogether.

G took note of his surroundings as the men casually walked back to return their gear to Larry's office. The docks were tucked back into an obscure part of East Bay, centrally located to other industrial centers with convenient access to Causeway Boulevard—a main thoroughfare that ran north to Interstate 4 and southeast to I-75, both providing easy distribution routes for someone with the right high-demand product. An industrial rail yard was located two miles to the west, and the Peter O. Knight regional airport was just three miles to the southwest. The location had all the desirable elements to serve as a premiere drug hub. G's immediate concern centered on two pivotal aspects the DEA was unable to yet determine: who was actually in control of the hub, and who was supplying it.

As he returned his gear to the storage area, G noticed a padlocked door next to a restroom.

"Hey, I'm gonna hit the head before we leave," said G to his new friend. "I gotta use the facilities if I expect to make it back to my place without pissin' myself."

"OK. You need a ride? I'll wait for you."

"Nope, got it covered. I'll just catch up with you in the morning," replied G. "Thanks for everything today."

G took a quick glance around the area before he opened the bathroom door. Seeing no one around, he slipped inside. He flipped the light switch that simultaneously activated an exhaust fan and then locked the door. He looked up at the ceiling panels and quickly discovered the only thing separating the bathroom from the storage room next door was the wall and a low-grade construction tile ceiling.

Standing on the toilet tank, he reached up and pushed on a ceiling tile closest to the wall on the storage room side. The opening was just large enough for him to fit through once he got it loose and pushed aside. He grabbed the top of the wall and hoisted himself up through the ceiling. Bracing himself on a rafter, he carefully lifted a ceiling tile to the storage room and peered in. It was too dark to see anything. He had to get into the room.

He glanced at his watch. He'd been in the bathroom three minutes. He figured he had about five more minutes before anyone would be expecting him to emerge. That gave him two minutes on the front side and a minute on the backside to get in and get out of the storage room.

He carefully lowered himself into the dark room when his feet came to rest on something soft and unstable, so he moved aside slightly and found the floor. He activated a flashlight application on his cell phone and glanced at his watch—just under two minutes remaining.

G saw three black storage bags on the floor placed neatly against the wall. He knelt to one knee and slowly unzipped one of the bags and shined the light inside. The bag contained several small caliber handguns, each wrapped in soft-sided zippered cases. Several boxes of ammunition surrounded the weapons.

Time check—just over a minute remaining. He paused when he thought he heard someone outside the door. He slowly unzipped the next bag. It was packed full and tight.

Holy shit! he thought when he discovered the bag packed full of cellophane-wrapped white bricks. *Can't get better evidence than this.*

His heart skipped a beat when he heard a knock on the bathroom door.

"Anyone in there?"

He didn't answer. Instead, he quickly took two infrared camera shots and quietly zipped the bag.

Time's up...

Again he heard a knock on the bathroom door, followed by an attempt to enter.

"Hey! Anyone in there? I gotta pee. Besides, we gotta lock this place up soon! Hello?"

He recognized the voice. It was Larry. G reached the rafters and stuck his head through the bathroom ceiling opening, doing his best to throw his voice and answered.

"Yeah, be out in a minute!"

The French police transported Avigdor to an interview room in a regional police station in Saint-Tropez where he was held without immunity, pending an inquiry into the disappearance of his wife.

"I demand to speak to the Israeli consul at once!"

"He is on his way, sir. Meantime, we are trying to determine the whereabouts of your wife, Hanah. Can you tell me the last time you saw her?"

"I will tell you whatever you wish to know. But you must first tell me whether you are busy trying to find her this very second!"

"We have a team of experts—"

"You better have an *army* of experts looking for her!"

"Sir, please tell me, when was the last time you saw your wife?"

"It was the middle of the night sometime. She got out of bed to use the bathroom."

"Did you not see her return to bed?"

"No, I must have…fallen back to sleep," he said, trying desperately to recall anything after that, his words trailing as he fought hard to recollect what had transpired.

"How did you sustain your injuries…the cut on your shoulder and the bruise on your head? They are defensive wounds, no? Did your wife deliver those wounds while trying to defend herself?"

"I slipped on the bathroom floor…on the…floor," he said, recalling the scene in painful detail.

"Do you mean, on the blood? Is it her blood, sir?"

Malkinson looked at the interrogator with an ice-cold stare of defiance. "I don't know if it's her blood. That's what you should be busy trying to determine instead of wasting your fucking time asking me these questions. I have no information for you that will lead you to her. If I did, I would have provided that to you by now," he stressed.

G returned to the hotel with a bag of Chinese takeout, which he finished in no time, barely remembering just what it was he ate, only that his hunger was now satisfied. He pulled a computer tablet from his bag and synched it electronically with his smart phone, connecting it to a secure Wi-Fi stream and the NSA operations directorate. Once connected, he sent a short narrative of the progress he'd made and attached his photo evidence.

His findings successfully uploaded, G researched everything he could find on welding and the principles of metallurgy. Fascinated and a bit overwhelmed by the sheer amount of information available on the topics, he absorbed as much as he possibly could, knowing he would mentally extract it and continue to learn as he slept.

He opened an e-mail account connecting to a secure portal to a hub server for field agents to communicate with NSA regional offices. The hub server had the ability to process all electronic mail and remove any vulnerability, such as viruses, shadows, or malicious logic, and convert it to a secure state before sending it on to the recipient. The service, available only to those with the proper clearance level and access credentials, produced encrypted e-mail in a matter of seconds without third-party eyes ever having to examine or filter the contents.

While scanning his inbound mail, he discovered a message from someone he hadn't heard from in quite some time. It was from his old friend, Todd "T-Rock" Jordan. Todd had been instrumental in G's unorthodox rescue and recruitment process five years back when he was sequestered against his will by a rogue arm of the FBI.

What's happenin' G-money! the message began. *Sippin' a cool one, smokin' a fat stogy...only thing missin' is you! Hope all is well, bro. Holla!*

G smiled when he read the note and briefly thought about how he'd gotten to know the colorful Mr. Jordan, a self-made millionaire and highly proven operative. Jordan was several things to several people: an entertainment promoter, a politician of sorts, a con man, a businessmen, and self-employed "equalizer." He was good at choreographing an operation and eliminating evidence trails—a cleaner—and often prided himself on predicting the moves of his adversaries before even *they* had a clue. If time permitted, he would typically use his computer skills to learn everything he could about his marks and then decide whether or not to destroy them with a few simple keystrokes.

He powered down the computer tablet and turned on the news. A report caught his attention, and he turned up the volume to catch the details.

This is a Sky News alert! Reports are streaming in that the wife of the Israeli deputy prime minister is missing. The couple is said to have been vacationing in the French Riviera with their nine-year-old daughter when Hanah Malkinson simply vanished. Initial reports indicate that foul play may be a factor. French officials are currently questioning the husband, fifty-four-year-old Deputy Prime Minister

Avigdor Malkinson. In an unprecedented move, French authorities have ignored pleas from Israel for his immediate release pending confirmation that he is somehow involved. The decision by French authorities has reportedly increased tensions between the two countries...

A still picture of Avigdor Malkinson filled the TV screen, followed by a short aerial video clip of the area of the disappearance accompanied by the news narrative. G squinted slightly, his mind reeling as he made a mental connection with his dream. After the newscast, he powered on his computer once again and began typing.

Dream Notes: I've been trying to make a connection with a notably vivid and disturbing dream I had last night. I have to analyze it further, but I believe the connection may have just revealed itself to me through a television newscast concerning the disappearance of the wife of the Israeli deputy prime minister, who also happens to be the defense minister. Details to follow as I discover more information.

G worked best when he was evaluating dreams. It was the primary reason he had been brought into the agency as a deep-cover analyst. This particular analysis proved especially difficult however, because it required him to draw conclusions from a first-hand perspective of someone other than himself—in this case, quite possibly that of the deputy prime minister of Israel.

G's cell phone alerted him to an incoming text message.

El Sol has the best hand-rolled cigars!

4

anah awoke, her mind hazy. She became alarmed when she realized there was a blindfold tied around her head. Her pulse quickened as she suddenly realized her hands and feet were bound as well.

"What's happening? Where am I?" she nervously asked anyone within earshot.

Her lips were dry, and her hearing was muted, but she could make out subdued, mechanical engine sounds and could feel vibrations and gravitational forces acting upon her body. A well-traveled, intellectual woman, she concluded she was aboard an aircraft en route to somewhere—but where? Her head throbbed as she tried to recall the ordeal surrounding her abduction. Scant memories played out in her mind but not enough to make any sense of the moment. Panic set in as she realized she was now in the hands of her captors and completely at their mercy.

"I'm thirsty. Can I get some water, please?"

She gasped when she felt someone grab a fistful of hair at the top of her head and hold her steady while a paper cup was carelessly lifted to her lips. Despite the water being lukewarm, she was relieved to be given an opportunity to satisfy her thirst. She gulped as much as she could without choking, but a good bit of it escaped out the sides of her mouth onto her neck and chest.

"*Shukran*," she whispered, using the Arabic term for *thank you*, in an attempt to determine the cultural origin of her captors. She made sure, however, to pronounce the word hesitantly, not wanting anyone to know how fluent she was in the language.

The words no sooner left her mouth than she felt the unexpected sting of a firm slap across her face causing her to scream out in shock and pain.

"Do not defile our language, you Jewish bitch! Keep your mouth shut unless we permit you to speak."

Tears streamed down her face as she fought to hold back her fear. Her heart pounded with adrenaline as panic set in, and she began to fully realize the seriousness of her situation. She felt her body being pushed by the forces of gravity as the aircraft made a tight left turn.

The blindfold, coupled with the fact that she had been unconscious, had robbed her of any ability to determine how long it had been since her abduction. It had also played havoc with her equilibrium and she began to feel nauseated from the effects of the flight. She thought of her daughter, Rina, as she felt the aircraft begin its descent.

Tzofiya Kalev had grown up in a middle-class section of Tel Aviv where she was exposed to the rapid growth and popularity of the port city. She was given her first name by her father who, at the time of her birth, felt strongly that she would answer to a higher call of service—hence, the origin and Hebrew translation of her name: *the guardian.*

At twenty-eight years old, she was well-educated, attractive, and streetwise. She grew up in a mixed neighborhood where Arab, Russian, and Jewish residents had collectively and peacefully coexisted until the early 1990s when conflict began to surface between the Palestinian and Jewish people.

Some of her earliest and fondest memories were of visiting office buildings with her father, which she later found out were embassies of other countries that had moved into the city in the early eighties. The experience of "going to work" with her father remained with her and ignited a fascination for working with people from diverse cultural and international backgrounds.

She attended Tel Aviv University where her focus was Jewish studies with a minor in mechanical engineering and physics. Fluent in several languages, she had a knack for remembering the mechanics of linguistics. At twenty-three years old, she went on to pursue her Master of Science degree at the same institution where she took an elective course in International Relations and Conflict Resolution. It was there where she was successfully recruited to work for one of the world's most respected intelligence agencies, the Mossad.

She was immersed into a four-year intensive training program deep inside the walls of the Mossad that literally reshaped her from a college schoolgirl to a young woman and highly capable intelligence collections agent. She went on to qualify to become the first woman operative inside the Metzada—a highly secret clandestine operations branch within the Mossad.

Tzofiya lost both parents to an auto accident in 1995, shortly after the death of Israel's prime minister, Yitzhak Rabin. She had clear memories of the sadness she and her country felt at the time of Rabin's passing and could remember the discussion she had with her father immediately following the tragic event.

"There is no shame dying in the name of peace, Tzofiya," he said as he stared into her glassy eyes. "Rabin died doing what he loved for a country he so dearly cherished. What an honor for a man to answer to such a call."

The memory of that talk with her father filled her heart with joy and her eyes with tears every time she thought of it. If he could see her now…he would be so proud, knowing that she was in a position to serve the country she loved, just as he had predicted so many years ago. The *guardian* had finally come of age.

Ybor City was an historic district located just northeast of downtown Tampa. Established in the 1880s and populated mostly by Cuban, Spanish, and Italian immigrants, it became one of Tampa's premiere gathering places for entertainment and some of the best handmade cigars in the country.

G stepped off the trolley at the center of the historic city just after sunset. The humid air carried a mixture of scents ranging from various ethnic foods to the ever-present aroma of cigar smoke from nearby shops. The sidewalks were beginning to reveal an increasing crowd of people as he made his way toward El Sol, one of the oldest and most popular cigar shops in the city.

Pausing in front of El Sol, he looked into the storefront display window, and then stepped inside.

"Welcome to El Sol, sir! Looking for anything in particular?" greeted the cheerful associate.

"Yes, something hand-rolled and full-bodied please," answered G.

"Of course. Right this way."

The sales associate led G to a glass, walk-in humidor that housed the store's premium cigars. A small chime rang as she opened the door. An alluringly sweet blend of tobacco aromas greeted him when he stepped into the room. The associate showed G some of the more discriminating blends and explained the layout of the room, and then suggested he take some time looking around before choosing something he liked.

"If you have any questions, I'll be just outside. Feel free to look around, and let me know if you need anything at all."

Closely examining a particular blend, G heard the chime again and assumed the girl had left the room. Even so, he managed not to start with surprise when he heard a man's voice behind him.

"The selection on this side of the room is a lot better," the new-comer said.

"Better than what?" asked G without turning around.

"Better than the *shit* you're looking at over there."

G casually walked to the other side of the room where the man stood alone, keeping his eyes on the cigar display boxes.

"What's your recommendation?" asked G.

"My *recommendation*? My recommendation is to get out of Tampa as soon as possible," he casually answered, lifting a cigar to his nose to capture the aroma.

"*Your* recommendation, or someone higher in the food chain?"

"We're all on the same team, G. You may not realize it yet, but you're in the middle of a pending shitstorm."

"I'm not finished here."

"Suit yourself. If you change your mind, let me know. Meantime, try this one," he said as he looked at G for the first time, offering him a hand-rolled El Sol *Signature Dominicana Clasico*. "I particularly enjoy the Cameroon-wrapped smokes. I think you'll find this one interesting. The toothy leaf Dominican-blended filler holds a special surprise. Let me know if it piques your interest."

The man turned and exited the room.

G stood there holding the cigar, reflecting on the words of his elusive contact.

"I see you've found one. It's one of our best!" said the cheerful associate.

"I'll take it," said G, placing the cigar in his pocket.

"I've got a preactivation plan for you," said Lisa when she stopped Paul on his way back to his office. "It's going to require a bit of explaining though."

"That was quick. But that's why I hired you," said Paul with a smile. "C'mon into my office and show me what you've got."

Lisa followed Paul into his office and closed the door. She pressed a button on the wall that simultaneously dimmed the office lights and activated a heads-up display high-definition 3-D hologram positioned against the backdrop of a handsomely appointed paneled wall.

"May I?" she asked, gesturing to his computer terminal, clearly eager to begin her briefing.

"Please," answered Paul as he stepped aside and took a seat in a leather chair next to his desk.

"OK, I'm assuming you're completely informed on the political and historical background of the deputy prime minister, Mr. Malkinson. He and his wife, Hanah, have been married for twenty-two years and have one child: nine-year-old Rina. I've uncovered nothing to indicate that he would have anything at all to do with the disappearance of his wife. But as you and I both know, the *absence* of evidence doesn't always equate to innocence."

Paul's direct line rang.

"Want me to get that?" asked Lisa.

"I've got it," said Paul as he picked up the receiver. "Paul Harriman—"

"Paul, Jon McCoy. Our situation just got uglier. Can you go secure?" Paul activated the secure feature on his phone and held up one finger to Lisa, indicating the priority of the phone call.

"You want me to leave?" she whispered.

Paul shook his head slowly, indicating that she should stay.

"I show secure on this end, Jon."

"Secure here as well, Paul. Listen, French authorities are telling the Israelis that Mr. Malkinson will be remaining in custody until they recover his wife...or a body. The Israeli prime minister doesn't appreciate the decision and is pissed, to say the least. The PM wants us to engage in clandestine collaboration with them to do whatever's necessary to find her. Oh, and if we have the time or inclination, to assist the Israelis in delivering a punishing blow to whoever's responsible. There's just one problem."

"What's that?" asked Paul.

"We have no idea who the hell's responsible."

"Can I assume we have *top cover* on this?" asked Paul.

"No, not officially. That's why I called *you*. But, you know the drill, my friend. You'll get whatever you need to support the op, just not an open endorsement."

"I understand. I've asked for satellite coverage over the Mediterranean, and I'm in the process of selecting a team for the mission, Jon. But in order for that team to be effective I'll need everything you have. Send me the FBI forensics, foreign aircraft movements in and out of the country since the disappearance, personnel files, educated hunches, opinions, suspicions, and whatever the hell else you have that'll help. I'll have my analysts pore over the details. Once I receive your data, I'll have a better idea how to address this for maximum effect."

"Already ahead of you on that, Paul. I'm pushing the file to you as we speak."

Paul heard the audible notification of an inbound mail from his Secure Internet Protocol Router, or SIPR, computer.

"Just got it, Jon. Will let you know as soon as I have something we can work with."

"Thanks, Paul…there's just one more thing."

"I'm listening."

"We need to act fast because word has it that Prime Minister Levinson has scheduled a meeting with the leaders of the Mossad to select their team and formulate their plan. I know I don't have to tell you that the Israelis will move with or without us on this, and they'll do it quickly. I want to be prepared to respond in kind with the construct of our team when the prime minister is ready."

"Understand. We'll be ready. Out here."

Paul hung up the phone, hesitated, and looked at Lisa.

"Well, this continues to get interesting. Lisa, I'm gonna need you to reassess what you have, along with the files we just received from the State Department. Take a good look at 'em, along with what you've collected, and have our analysts determine whether we need to make any adjustments to the team you're prepared to suggest. Look hard at the details and see if there's any chatter from the field we can use."

"I can certainly do that, but I'm gonna need your endorsement on this preactivation plan."

"What preactivation plan is that?" asked Paul.

"The one I *unofficially* approved pending your endorsement."

"You have my attention. What is it that *we* have approved?"

Lisa placed a folder onto Paul's desk marked "Top Secret." In it were a few pages of personnel details on operative agents and a request for an action plan, loosely based on the assembly of a covert team of agents with an overall objective to find the deputy prime minister's wife.

Paul opened the folder while Lisa continued to speak. "Ian Wolfe has offered to put a team together—pending your approval, of course—to go to France and connect with the Mossad to find the deputy prime minister's wife," explained Lisa.

"I don't see a detailed plan," said Paul as he examined the file.

"I know you don't. All he's looking for at this point is your approval to assemble the team. You asked me to lean forward on this. As I was doing just that, Ian contacted me and presented his availability based on information he gained from open sources and his geographic and cultural knowledge. He's assembling a team as we speak and, as ironic as it seems, he's asking for the very same data we just received from Mr. McCoy at State."

"I've met Ian. He's a good operative," said Paul, still scanning the documents. "His request is reasonable. Send him the data and connect him with the analysis cell here. Tell him I want a detailed action plan in twelve hours, to include a team construct," concluded Paul as he endorsed the request.

"Will do. How do you want this classified?"

"'Top Secret—Disavowed.' I don't need a congressional inquiry coming back to haunt us should things take a bad turn. And make damn sure that's crystal clear to Ian and his team."

"I understand," said Lisa, nodding.

G returned to his hotel room, locked the door, tossed the cigar onto the dresser, and walked to the window to stare out into the night. Memories of the day's activities flooded his mind like the second wave of a tsunami, as thoughts of his dream overshadowed it all.

What the hell am I doing here? And why am I feeling this way? he thought. *And what is this about a "shitstorm"?*

He pushed his frustrations aside to give his mind room to fire away with the random images of his day mixed with the ever-present insistence of his latest dream. He watched as flashes of lightning in the distant sky accentuated the silhouette of the city skyline with each random burst. He could feel the stresses lift as the serenity of the scene reminded him to relax and allow the tranquility of the moment to add clarity to his thoughts. He closed the curtain and returned to the edge of the bed—the words of his contact echoing in his mind.

My recommendation is to get out of Tampa as soon as possible...

G picked up the cigar and held it close to examine it. He glanced at his reflection in the mirror as he lifted the cigar to his nose to savor the aroma. He held it out in front of him rolling it in his fingers as the words echoed in his mind.

The toothy filler holds a special surprise—

He interrupted the thought by breaking the cigar in half, revealing a micro SD memory card. He pulled the tiny chip from its hiding place, held it up close to examine it, blew off the tobacco remnants, and placed it into a chip reader connected to his tablet.

5

irajuddin Hammadi led an insurgent guerrilla network bound together by close tribal and clan relationships. Originating in Afghanistan in the late 1970s, the Hammadi network was principally financed and supplied with arms by the United States through the CIA and Pakistan's Inter-Services Intelligence for counterinsurgency operations against the Soviets in the 1980s, and was largely responsible for holding back the Soviet invasion during that time period. The Network eventually moved into neighboring Pakistan in a province near North Waziristan—a known Taliban stronghold.

Siraj grew up believing the ideals of intolerance that had become a way of life and embracing what he believed was the last remaining way for him and his people to fight back against the repeated attempts of oppression aligned against the historic sanctity of the Islamic way of life. History had shown that force showed promise whereas all other diplomatic means had failed. "If it is war they want, war is what they will get," he often heard his father say.

A scholar of his father's teachings and radical methodologies, when he was old enough, Siraj took over responsibility for the organization's military operations. He built several echelons of radical leaders inside the insurgent network. Sanctioned splinter cells scattered throughout the world stepped up their violence. The network became globally known as one of the most resilient and fastest-growing enemy networks and one of the highest threats to US-led NATO forces in the Middle East.

Siraj had the utmost respect and admiration for his father and had quickly come to support the ideals of the jihad as the movement expanded over the years. His methods had been instrumental in the disruption of diplomacy, proliferation of propaganda, and the outright cold-blooded deaths of US and allied forces and innocent civilians—casually and brazenly regarded as collateral damage in the name of the jihad. He had become classified as a tier-one interest by coalition nations and placed on the International Security Assistance Forces', the ISAF's "kill or capture" list. There had been several attempts to eliminate him with US and coalition weapons assets, including remotely piloted air strikes—all to no avail.

The Hammadi network's operations were principally carried out by small, semiautonomous units organized according to tribal affiliations under the direction and logistical oversight of commanders orchestrated and directed by Siraj himself. One of the more lethal Hammadi units, with possibly the widest regional reach and effect, was a core group operating out of Yemen, comprised principally of foreign militants, primarily of Arab, Chechen, and Uzbek descent. But the network's reach had increased over the years to Central and South America, Europe, the Dominican Republic, and had recently fostered devout followers inside the borders of the United States.

Siraj typically preferred highly specialized missions with an objective of profound impact; or situations requiring the use of creative and exploitative methodologies where traditional diplomacy was a feeble attempt overshadowed by its inevitable futility. His cause was simple: in order to perpetuate peace throughout the world, the world needed to comprehend the philosophy of Islam and allow it to be free of the encumbrances of Western influence. His approach was destructive: if the world refused to comply, he would do everything in his power to destroy it, preserving the very principles he deemed integral to restoring peace throughout the world.

Recent CIA reports indicated the Hammadi network in the Middle East was in dire need of weapons due to the increasing control of the battlespace by US and coalition forces after a series of precision airstrikes on vital areas of interest and Al-Qaeda strongholds in the region. Siraj had begun reaching out to the Iranians for relaxed border crossings, refuge support, and weapons resupply. In return, he offered the Iranians money they badly needed because of international sanctions, and he pledged his support to the Iranians in the form of diplomatic subversion and chaos within Israel. He promised his efforts would become a major distraction designed to reveal vulnerabilities in the Hebrew nation. What he failed to fully consider was the unbreakable will of the Israeli people and their determination to protect their own interests and to cover the wager with the backing of the United States with an objective to deliver a punishing blow to their aggressors without regard to time, distance, or political objection.

His relationship with the Iranians took a serious turn for the worse when a weapons-supply deal, covertly brokered by Iranian operatives, nearly imploded as a result of the network's overreaction to a decision by the Iranians to divert weapons to Syria instead of predesignated destinations controlled by the network. When Siraj discovered the change, he reacted by instructing a faction of Al-Qaeda operatives to move in and seize the weapons at a key transfer point inside southern Iraq. The attackers failed to intercept or acquire any weaponry but managed to destroy a CIA outpost in what was later determined to be a case of misdirected aggression. The attack backfired on Siraj's aggressors, ignited a political firestorm, and seriously delayed the transfer of weapons to the Syrian rebels. The Iranians reacted by shutting down one of the network's most lucrative arms-supply streams, forcing Siraj to consider other alternatives.

"Micah, good to see you," said Avigdor as the Israeli consul general closed the door of the small meeting room.

"And you as well, Mr. Deputy," the consul general said with a respectful nod. "I regret the circumstances are not more favorable."

"Thank you. Do you bring with you any hope of a release for Rina and me?"

"Regrettably no, sir. The French authorities are determined to retain you until they locate your wife or produce a solid lead on her whereabouts or circumstance."

"Then why are you here?" asked Avigdor with disdain in his voice.

"I'm here because you're a citizen of Israel who is in need of counsel in a foreign country—"

"Do not offend me with your insolence and trite consolations! Your time is better served by offering me *solutions* rather than petty services. If this is all you have to offer, get out of my sight. Otherwise, produce something I can use to move these French assholes into action to release me so I can find my wife."

"Mr. Deputy, *please*. Your temper is not helping you win empathy. Our visit is no doubt on someone's monitor this very moment."

"Empathy?" Avigdor scowled as he stood and glared at the consul general. "You know me well enough to know I don't give a *shit* about empathy, Micah. I want *action*...real action that produces real results. I am good to no one as long as I sit here in confinement. Find a way to release me!"

"My staff is doing everything in its power to secure your release. They are also doing everything to assist in the efforts to find your wife, Mr. Deputy. I'm doing the best I can under the circumstances."

Avigdor paused for a moment to collect himself. "I know you are, Micah. I'm sorry," he said, taking a slow, deep breath while he considered the tone of his intolerance. "I realize my incarceration poses a unique situation for you, given my political status. Please show me the initiatives taking place to resolve this."

Micah shared some surface information regarding the Israeli diplomatic and investigative initiatives seeking to address Avigdor's incarceration and then presented documents to him as to the process of international law. He had him sign a confidential power of attorney allowing the consul to represent him in personal and legal matters and offered him an Israeli newspaper so he could get caught up on the latest news from home.

"There's a particularly good article in the finance section you may be interested in, sir. I know how you enjoy watching the market. Word has it that the international market may see increasing volatility in the near future," said Micah as he handed the paper to Avigdor. "My office will continue to be in touch with you," he added as he turned to walk away.

"Thank you, Micah."

He was lost in thought when his secretary walked into his office. Israeli Prime Minister Doran Levinson sat at his desk in a high back leather chair, staring out the window at a near-perfect sunny day.

"Sir, they're here," she said softly.

"Show them in," he said without breaking his distant gaze.

The men filed in quietly and stood near a small conference table in the corner of the room. They comprised the three pillars of one of the most clandestine and effective organizations in the world—the Mossad department leaders: the intelligence collections director, the covert operations chief, and the counterterrorism director.

Levinson slowly turned his chair around and nodded to indicate his permission for them to take a seat. His stern expression matched his tone of voice as he spoke, looking each man in the eye to stress the importance of his message.

"Gentlemen, I refuse to believe the deputy prime minister is culpable in the disappearance of his own wife. It's the premise we must operate on until *and unless* we discover otherwise. But we must be certain of what we're dealing with. We have always been a nation whose people operate on certainties. It causes me grave concern to know our enemies would employ such tactics to destroy one of our own, but I'm not surprised. What concerns me most is how such a thing could happen, given the level of protection surrounding him and his family at the time. I want unbiased insight from each of you as to what happened, how it happened, and who is responsible. I need details on an appropriate investigation into the truth and, if appropriate, a covert counteroffensive once we have answers. I do not have the highest degree of confidence in how traditional sources are engaging with what I suspect are nontraditional tactics by the enemies of Israel. I don't need to remind you of the importance of accurate information and the perishable nature of time. We'll reconvene collectively or separately as your discoveries and plans materialize. Thank you."

The prime minister slowly turned his chair around to look out the window once again as the three leaders quietly departed.

The computer screen came to life as it accessed the SD card. G sat on the edge of the bed staring at the screen. A YouTube music video began playing. G placed the cursor over the video presentation and right-clicked the mouse, revealing embedded program options to look past the video and unlock the contents of the chip.

The screen went blank for one second and then presented a flashing cursor prompt.

He entered a unique, seventeen-character passcode. The screen went blank once again, but produced audio, revealing a vaguely familiar voice. G listened while continuing to stare at the empty screen.

Hello, G. I see curiosity managed to get the best of you after all. I know you're currently on assignment, and I can understand how you hate to leave anything untied before moving on, but your services are needed for a rather delicate and pressing international matter—if you're inclined to assist. We need someone who is able to look past the shroud of what appears to be the absolute. Someone with your skills can make a huge difference in the approach we take and the methods we employ on this mission. You know the rules—this is as far as I can take you on the information loop unless you commit to becoming an active member of the team.

G stared at the empty screen, allowing the words to sink in while contemplating his options. The message made sense. Despite his minimal but significant role in his current assignment, he despised the thought of leaving the docks at Barge Avenue—and his responsibility. He prided himself on finishing the job. And aside from the drugs and weapons he uncovered, he felt he was close to something more significant he could provide to the DEA that would help them discover the source of their problem. But he felt the tug of a higher call as he struggled with the choices now facing him. He needed to close the loop on his current assignment if he was to commit to move on with a clear conscience. He decided he'd return to the docks the next morning to take action on an exit strategy that would be useful to the DEA. His intuition on the pressing "international matter" concerning the disappearance of the Israeli deputy prime minister's wife gave him good reason to believe it had something to do with his next assignment. Accepting a mission blindly was always a gamble, but it was one he was willing to take, given the increasing reliability of his educated hunches and gut checks.

Satisfied, he simply pressed the Y key, indicating his acceptance.

Hanah awoke to the jolt of a hard landing. Still blindfolded, she could hear the roar of the reciprocating engines and could feel the forces of her seatbelt restraining her as the brakes were applied to slow the aircraft. She had arrived somewhere after an unknown period of time. The only indication of just how long it had been was the sheer exhaustion she felt. But even that was a poor indicator of the distance she traveled and the time it took to get there.

She gasped slightly when she felt the firm grasp of a strong hand on her right arm. She felt a tug on her seatbelt and heard a clicking sound followed by the release of its grip from her lap. Her foot restraints were removed but her hands remained bound.

The engines went silent as the aircraft powered down.

She was lifted to her feet and led to the aircraft door where she was greeted by a wall of heat and humidity laced with the distinct smell of jet fuel. She was led down a short set of extended stairs. The sounds of other aircraft echoed nearby—some taxiing, others in the distance taking off or landing. She worked hard to use the few senses available to her to orient herself and provide a clue to her whereabouts.

"Step carefully!" commanded an unknown voice, devoid of any kindness whatsoever.

She cautiously stepped forward, attempting to find each step with the feel of her previous one and the visualization her mind provided for her. She did well, despite the impatience of her guide.

"Step forward! Step—"

She misjudged one of the few remaining steps and began to fall forward. Disoriented, she was unable to correct appropriately for the miscalculation. Her instinctive reaction caused her to suddenly pull away from her guide's grasp as she raised her restrained arms in reaction to the fall. Struggling to find her balance, she fell down three remaining steps and onto the concrete tarmac.

Her pulse raced as the fall seemed to happen in slow motion. Her mind struggled to stay ahead of the momentum as her body twisted and turned to find equilibrium and correct the misstep. She found herself thinking of her daughter, Rina. She caught images of her as an infant, then as a young five year old, then she imagined what she'd look like as a teenager, and ultimately as an adult. She also thought of Avigdor. She missed them both.

Her shoulder hit first, and then her face hit the hot pavement of the tarmac. Thoughts of Rina and Avigdor faded as the reality of her plight quickly caught up with her. Consciousness faded as someone rushed to her side, turned her onto her back, and removed her

blindfold. She slowly blinked as she fought to maintain consciousness, squinting to avoid the bright sunlight. She felt the warmth of
the sun on her face and the moisture of a tear roll across her cheek
as she struggled to look into the eyes of her captor. An eerie peace
overcame her as she felt herself being lifted into an awaiting vehicle.
Blood dripped from her right nostril and oozed from a contusion
above her right eye. Then she lost consciousness.

Todd gazed out the window of the Gulfstream V as it passed
over the Dominican Republic. The fading orange glow of the setting
sun streaming through the small window reflected off his Oakley
Romeo sunglasses as he took a sip of his drink—Grey Goose on the
rocks with a lime twist. He casually pressed the intercom button to
communicate to his pilot.

"Yo, Monty, what's our estimate to Tampa?"

"One hour and twelve minutes, boss."

"Thanks."

Todd checked a secure computer smart pad and found an e-mail
from an undisclosed covert operative indicating he had invited his
old friend, G Weston, to join the small clandestine team. He smiled
when he discovered that G had opted to join them.

*Brother G has no idea where this is gonna take him. Hell, what
am I thinkin'? I have no idea either. I'm jes happy to know he's on
the team...*

Sitting beside Todd was a relatively new protégé of his by the
name of Leon Lambert. Todd met Leon during an agency investigation of alleged operational intelligence leaks coming from sources
inside Washington, DC, during the first year of the last Democratic
administration.

Todd and Leon collaborated on code-breaking strategies to
successfully penetrate some of the most secure networks on the
planet in an effort to find the source of the leaks. The operation was
laced with politically sensitive landmines and potentially danger-

ous blowback to anyone clumsy enough to be discovered snooping around. Together, the two were good enough to penetrate sophisticated security barriers and ultimately determined the leaks to be authentic, but they were never able to accurately identify a source before being locked out by smart sentries and active, multilayered security programs on the receiving end of their focus. The operation was terminated on short notice and immediately disavowed when a tracer-bot program began tracking and destroying their exit paths, resulting in the loss of several layers of critical agency data. In the end, they were able to destroy the tracer-bots, erase their trail, and eliminate the evidence of their operation. The nature of the operation served to drag both men into a shadow of secrecy that would never be disclosed and proved to be a learning opportunity that became a driving force in their determination *never* to be caught in a similar situation.

Leon reminded Todd a lot of himself in a number of ways. He was intelligent, creative, opinionated, and one hell of a smartass. The two would often clash over ideals, computer theory, and methodology but would consistently challenge each other to find solutions to strategic and tactical issues and complex system barriers that would otherwise confuse and deceive rivals and enemies alike. The two routinely verbally sparred—each attempting to outwit the other at every opportunity.

A relative newcomer to the agency, Leon was an avid PC-gamer and would often discover his best ideas inside the confines of virtual reality. He ascribed to the notion that if something was possible inside the walls of virtual reality, it was possible—even if not plausible—that it could be brought to fruition in reality. He'd often use the gaming environment to test his ideas, theories, and tactics, and selectively solicited the insight of other avid gamers inside his trusted circle of technophiles.

Leon was one of the original concept originators of next-generation remote-controlled drones, which the DOD later adopted and ultimately developed as the small unmanned aerial system program, or the SUAS platform. The program later evolved into one of the most sophisticated and successful intelligence and combat advantages for the US global war on terrorism, for which Leon was never given due credit. The lack of acknowledgement was just the incentive he needed to separate from active duty when he was recruited by the NSA on Todd's recommendation—not only for the talent he had, but for the potential he possessed. When asked about the source of his inspiration, Leon would often credit the lucidity of his dreams and the limitless potential of the human mind, especially on a collaborative basis, such as the interaction he enjoyed with his gamers and trusted operatives.

Leon was successfully recruited by the NSA with an offer to explore the limits of his creativity supported by an endless array of video games and programming opportunities designed to support the development of his ideas—one of which stemmed from his original unmanned design concepts "adopted" by the DOD. "These things can be made much smaller," he would often say. "There's so much more that can be done with a small system."

As the senior operative, Todd was as intelligent but used reality, logic, and street smarts as his guides to problem solving. He had an affinity for beautiful women and was especially fond of the South American flair. His streetwise approach was largely responsible for the position he occupied inside the agency—and the success he enjoyed on the outside as an entertainment producer and special-effects production consultant. He was well connected and well liked. Todd believed that in life, it's not so much about who you know, but who knows *you*, that mattered most. It was a delicate balance to live two lives, and no one pulled it off quite as smoothly as he did.

"What are you smiling at?" asked Leon.

"Hmm? Oh...just lookin' at the team roster. Good friend of mine has just joined in on the op," said Todd, taking another sip of his drink as he powered down his PC pad.

"So when do I get to meet this friend of yours?"

"Not sure," answered Todd.

"What's his specialty?"

"That one's kinda difficult to answer, but I suspect you'll be able to relate. He's good at just about everything. But you wouldn't know it just by lookin' at him. Don't get me wrong, the brother's almost as fit as me, but he also has some rather *unconventional* talents that give him—and us—an advantage. I wouldn't want to step out on an op like this without him."

Leon nodded politely as he tapped away at his PC pad.

"What are you doin' over there…playin' another one of your games?"

"No, not exactly," said Leon. "I'm actually reviewing the design specs for a new microbot I created."

"A micro-what?" asked Todd with a chuckle.

"Here, lemme show you…" Leon handed his PC pad to Todd and explained how he had designed a remote-controlled robot using the exact specifications and scale of a dragonfly.

"So this thing can actually fly?"

"Yup. And it can take full-motion hi-def video and pick up sound, too."

"Impressive. Where do we get our hands on these?"

"I'm hoping to have a couple before we head out. I figure they could be useful if we get into a *situation*."

Todd laughed. "We always seem to find a situation, don't we? It's finding our way *out* of one that can get a little interesting sometimes."

Both men chuckled, acknowledging the accuracy of Todd's statement as they recalled the ordeal of their last operation together.

"Remain in your seats, gents. We're on our initial approach into Tampa," Monty announced over the intercom.

Todd pulled his lap belt tight, took another sip of his drink, and looked out the window at the approaching nighttime landscape of the Florida coastline.

6

With a plan in place approved by Prime Minister Levinson, the three leaders of the Mossad issued an activation order for Tzofiya. Currently on assignment in Italy attending a meeting with Omani dignitaries, she was supporting an Israeli objective to open an embassy in Jordan. She was a tactical addition, assigned to read the details that invariably led to clues and opposing personal agendas hiding behind surface diversions and evidentiary distractions.

"Is one agent enough to do the job?" asked Levinson.

"Sir, you've met Tzofiya and have acknowledged that she can do what *five* good agents are capable of doing. We have provided cover for her as a criminal investigator for the Israeli parliament and have prepared a path that will mitigate any access barriers she may encounter."

"The *path* you have prepared is not my primary concern. It is the unexpected obstacles she is likely to encounter that gives me pause. But I agree she is more than capable of overcoming and adapting appropriately. What is the status of the American support team? Are they on board?"

"Yes, Prime Minister. We expect to have the construct of their team and their itinerary soon. They have assured us that they will be ready to do their part in support of this initiative."

Levinson nodded approvingly. "Keep me informed."

The leaders understood the prime minister's dismissal. They gathered immediately afterward in a secure room where they compared final notes and enacted the plan.

"It seems we have all the pieces in place, gentlemen," said the intelligence director.

"I will activate the Guardian," announced the covert operations chief.

G turned off the light on the nightstand and laid his head on the pillow. He drew in a relaxing breath, closed his eyes, and felt his mind gently slip from consciousness. Images began to randomly ignite his mind's senses. He was conscious enough to know he was in a transition, tired enough to fall asleep quickly, and aware enough to see that he was in for another active, dream-filled night. He often joked that he would entertain some of the most interesting people in his dreams. They seemed to know just when he stepped through the portal of alter-consciousness—most often before even he was fully aware of the transition.

G opened his eyes to see ominously dark-gray storm clouds building nearby. They were close enough to cause him some concern, so he stepped inside a nearby building for shelter. A few people scattered about in the room and paid him no attention—until a small boy approached him. He felt drawn to the boy, which he found odd considering he could not recall ever seeing the child anywhere inside or outside the realm of consciousness. The boy, roughly five years old with dark short hair and an olive complexion, made eye contact with G—a rarity inside the dimension of his dreams. The boy's vivid blue eyes were captivating.

The boy drew close and remained by G's side as the howling wind and the low rumble of thunder echoed just outside the building. Looking intently into G's eyes, the boy communicated telepathically.

It'll be fierce, but it'll be quick.

G returned a questioning look as the boy buried his head into G's hip and held on tight to the hem of his shirt. G turned his head to look out a nearby window to see a thin black tornado approaching. He instinctively reacted by shielding the boy in a protecting embrace and closed his own eyes tightly. The intense power and pressure of the storm filled the room and was quickly followed by a massive explosion as the entire room disintegrated around them, scattering debris in slow motion in several directions.

Silence followed.

G turned his head to check his surroundings and found himself crouching in a corner alone, inside a modern, well-appointed room. The chaos of the previous dimension had occurred just as the boy had warned—*fierce and quick.*

He slowly rose to his feet and looked around the room to determine his whereabouts. White marble floors adorned the area as far as he could see. Two columns framed a short flight of stairs leading down into a larger room just ahead of him. An elegant fireplace filled the entire wall on his right on the lower landing. A red-leather couch and chair were positioned to his left and flanked a large, black-and-gray Chinese Ming rug. On the far side of the room, directly in front of him, tall sliding glass pocket doors fully opened to the outside, the picturesque backdrop painted with the orange hue of a setting sun.

Silence eerily dominated the rich surroundings as G slowly made his way down the short flight of stairs and across the room to the threshold of a wide, open patio. Dim lights shone beneath the shimmering waters of a large swimming pool positioned between him and an elegant one-hundred-twenty-foot yacht moored alongside a dock.

G was startled by a sound, turned out to be a woman brushing by him. She laughed as two more women followed her. He watched as they strode right by toward the yacht. They were some of the most gorgeous women he'd seen since his days in Belize. One blonde, two brunettes—each wore a different-color bikini, leaving very little to the imagination. Their laughter carried on as they continued to make their way toward the yacht, oblivious to his presence.

The metal threshold separating him from the outdoors caught his attention for no apparent reason. He watched his leading foot as it slowly extended across the threshold as he took a step into the backyard. He blinked slowly and, as his foot came to rest, he suddenly discovered himself on the yacht watching the three bikini-clad women approach. A man emerged from a doorway to his left and diverted G's attention from the women. The man was of Hispanic descent, about five feet ten inches tall. He wore white linen pants and a matching short-sleeved, button-down linen shirt that contrasted with his dark skin. The salt-and-pepper color of his hair told G that the man was well into his late forties. The man displayed an air of arrogant confidence as he made his way onto the aft deck to greet the women and assist them in boarding the vessel. G had a reasonable sense that his presence was unknown, so he continued to observe without fear of being discovered.

"Welcome aboard, ladies," greeted the man in a heavily accented dialect, extending a hand to each of them, smiling and greeting each with a quick kiss as they reached him.

The man looked up toward the house while helping the last lady board the vessel. "You're late," he shouted in disgust.

A look of confusion appeared on G's face as he watched Larry, the Barge-Avenue dockyard superintendent, hurriedly making his way toward the gangplank of the yacht.

Just after sunset, a late-model, white BMW M6 coupe pulled up to the Hotel Eden in Rome. A valet opened the driver's door for Tzofiya. Her long, slender legs extended gracefully to the brick-paved entryway of the historic hotel.

Tzofiya was just returning from a meeting at the Israeli embassy where she had met with a representative from the Omani consulate to establish a dialogue that would lead to the reopening of an embassy in that country. The chances of a successful agreement were remote, but the talks were productive.

She emerged from the luxury sport sedan and paused to adjust the strap of her open-heeled Louboutin stiletto, the trademark red sole gracefully accentuating the black leather uppers of the shoes—a perfect accessory to her tailored, black-silk business dress.

Heads turned as she gracefully strode into the hotel lobby, the tailored cut of the rear slit of her skirt revealing occasional glimpses of her athletic legs. The confidence of her cheerful smile preceded her as she approached the reception desk.

"Welcome back, *signorina*," greeted the desk clerk as he handed her a room key and an envelope containing a message.

Tzofiya accepted the key and then paused to open the envelope.

Please join me for dinner at La Terrazza this evening at 8:00 p.m.

La Terrazza was a well-known, exclusive restaurant located on the roof of the Hotel Eden. Tzofiya had dined there once before, several years earlier, with a colleague whom she had later come to respect as a mentor inside the tightly knit clandestine circle of Israeli operatives. This message was vague and contained the subtle indication of an unscheduled meeting. Still, she had to be certain. She glanced at a clock on a nearby desk in the hotel lobby—6:30 p.m. She walked to the elevator, pressed the call button, and stepped inside as the doors opened.

The sound of water gently lapping against the side of the yacht kept time with the rhythmic rumble of the twin diesel engines as it motored into the Gulf of Mexico. G moved to the main salon where three six-inch lines of cocaine were neatly drawn on a glass table-top. Beside the lines was a tightly rolled one-hundred-dollar bill sitting in scattered residue—evidence of a partially consumed drug. The well-appointed room was finished in rich mahogany and accentuated with high-end burgundy leather furniture, brass accents, and nautical artwork. Above a large mirror hung a starboard-side picture of the yacht displaying the name *Pair-O-Docs* beneath it on a brass plate.

Muted sounds of laughter and conversation diverted G's attention. He closed his eyes to enter a second, deeper level of consciousness and found himself peering into a bedroom on a lower deck. Following the sound, he was able to discover the source. Unfolding before him was a scene involving all three women, now naked and fully engaged in a heated orgy with Larry in the middle of the action. G watched as the two brunettes took turns servicing the blonde while Larry straddled the blonde, happily accepting her oral services.

G continued to observe as Larry grabbed one of the brunettes by her hair, tossing her onto her back. She seemed to enjoy the aggressive move and responded by willingly spreading her legs before him. He positioned himself, grabbed her ankles, and pushed himself between her open legs, causing her to gasp involuntarily as she reached forward and dug her fingernails into his thrusting hips. The blonde and brunette watched as they continued to fondle each other.

G's focus was broken by a tug on his shirt. Surprised, he opened his eyes and found himself back in the main stateroom. Then he looked down to see the familiar face of the boy he had met in a previous dream. Gazing up at G, the boy had one finger placed against his lips to indicate that G should remain quiet. Then he communicated in a telepathic whisper.

It'll be fierce...but it'll be quick...

Suddenly, G heard the sound of a door bursting open, followed by the surprised and frightened screams of the three women. Two large men escorted Larry into the main stateroom where G and the boy stood as invisible witnesses, positioned behind a high-back leather chair, facing a set of stairs that led to the lower room. G shielded the boy's eyes when a naked Larry emerged from the lower level, his arms firmly grasped by the two larger men. Larry wore a puzzled and humiliated look as the men positioned him in front of the chair.

"Get his pants. I refuse to speak to a naked man," said a man in a heavily accented, raspy voice. There was a man seated in the high-back chair. G realized he was the same man he had seen earlier on the aft deck. He struggled to determine why he had not noticed him in the room earlier.

Larry sat in a chair adjacent to the man, accepted his clothes from one of the men, and quickly slipped into his pants. He was visibly nervous, making occasional eye contact with the man in the chair. He stood up to zip his pants and then sat back down.

The forces of the boat shifted forward slightly as the engines went quiet. An uneasy stillness took control of the room as Larry nervously waited for the man to speak. The two large men stood to the side of the room in statuesqu poses, obediently awaiting further instructions.

"I'll get right to the point, Larry. I brought you out here tonight to kill you," said the man. He paused for effect. It was working.

Larry's face froze. "I don't understand," he nervously replied. "I've done everything you have asked and more."

"It is precisely the 'more' I am most concerned about," interrupted the man. "The distribution of our product is working well despite some occasional interference by your government watchdogs."

"That's because we have easily handled just about everything the DEA has thrown at us and have made sure key agents have been eliminated or bribed. What have I done to warrant a death penalty?" asked Larry.

"I pay you well, Larry. I supply you with money, protection… women, and yet, all of this doesn't seem to be enough. You have *stepped on* a significant amount of our product and have cheapened it and are skimming money by inflating prices once they pass through the gates of your country—"

"I don't understand. How have I stepped on—"

"You idiot! I would have assumed you would have learned the language of the street by now, as long as you've been working with us. 'Stepping' on the product simply means you have been infusing your garbage filler into our high quality product to artificially increase the supply and convince unsuspecting buyers they are getting *more* of that quality product for a small increase in price. You're stealing from me!"

Larry sat speechless.

The man stood. His average height didn't mitigate the confident intimidation he wielded as he stepped toward Larry. The two men standing guard stepped forward and constrained Larry.

"You want it all, Larry? This is our purest product," said the man, holding a gumball-sized rock of cocaine in his hand. "Here's twenty thousand US dollars' worth of the best," he said as he grabbed Larry's hair, forced his jaws open, and jammed the rock into his mouth.

"Swallow it!"

Larry choked and coughed as he attempted to spit out the drug, but the man held his mouth closed while sternly looking into his eyes. "I said swallow it, asshole."

G shielded the boy's eyes from the drama and watched as Larry finished ingesting the lethal dose of pure cocaine.

"Take this piece of shit outside, and feed him to the sharks."

The two men escorted Larry to a portside exit. As the door closed, G looked up to see the man slowly turn in his direction. G instinctively reached down to protect the boy, but he was gone. He watched as the man took two steps in his direction and stop. G's pulse quickened as he wondered if he was suddenly somehow visible. He remained still and studied the man's face, more specifically, his eyes, committing it all to memory. G remained intently focused on the man's eyes when his cell phone began to sound.

El Rahaba Airport was a dual-use airfield containing several military and civilian aircraft, serving functional purposes as both Sana'a international airport and a major air base for the Yemeni Air Force. Although not a busy airport by world standards, commercial airline, cargo, and military aircraft routinely used the location as a principle hub of operations for the southernmost Middle East and East African regions.

"Quickly, get her into the van," commanded a voice, shouting to compete with the noise of a departing aircraft.

A dusty, nondescript van pulled alongside Hanah where she lay unconscious on the tarmac, two men kneeling at her side. The sliding side door of the van opened as it came to a stop. The men picked her up—one at each end of her body—and hurriedly placed her into the back of the vehicle. The van sped off as the door slid closed. An SUV followed, stopping only briefly to pick up two men waiting by the aircraft, and quickly continued in pursuit of the van.

Hanah's unconscious body bounced inside the van as it drove over bumps and pothole-laden dusty roads in the third-world country. Dried blood stained her nose and lips as the contusion on her head continued to swell.

Hanah...Hanah, can you hear me?

The words were a faint whisper, but subconsciously, Hanah clearly understood the question. She struggled to open her eyes but was powerless against the forces keeping them closed. She did her best to nod her head in a feeble attempt to answer the question.

Hanah...they can hurt you physically, but they cannot break your will. Stay strong and trust your instincts. I will find you and bring you back to safety. I love you...

Hanah's face revealed the slightest hint of a smile at that reassurance, even if it was a hallucination or the hope of her overactive subconscious. She slowly regained consciousness as the van came to a sudden stop. Stealing quick, calculating glances, she desperately tried to determine her location while trying to avoid tipping off her captors.

The side door of the van slid open.

"Grab her arms and legs. Quickly, carefully...hand her to Munahid," instructed one of the men.

Another quick glance by Hanah showed her a distinctive tattoo on one of the men's wrists: a serpent supported by two crossed swords. She quickly closed her eyes to keep from revealing the fact that she had regained consciousness as a huge man, twice the size of the others, placed his arms around her waist, draped her over his right shoulder, and carried her a short distance to a nearby safe house.

Her head throbbed as she felt her body being lowered onto a thin mattress in a dimly lit room. She kept her eyes closed as she felt a firm grasp on each of her wrists extending her arms above her head to be secured in shackles. The shackles were tethered by chains to an iron ring anchored in the concrete wall above her head.

"Shall I summon the doctor?" asked Munahid to an elder.

"Is she breathing?"

"Of course," answered Munahid.

"Then I see no reason to bother the doctor," he answered. "I will check on her in a few hours, *insha'Allah*."

Hanah stole a quick glance at the men, who were now speaking in the only doorway to the small room. She was able to make out only the vast differences between the silhouettes of the two men as they exchanged a few words. The larger Munahid easily stood a foot taller than the one she assumed to be the elder. Their conversation ended with the echoing sound of the closing door, leaving Hanah alone for the first time since her abduction.

7

The tires of the Gulfstream chirped as the wheels made contact with the runway of the Peter O. Knight Airport. It was a perfect landing. Todd and Leon felt the forces of rapid deceleration as Monty pushed the reverse thrusters forward and aggressively applied the brakes to safely turn off the runway.

"What's our layover time?" asked Leon.

"'Bout twenty-four hours," replied Todd as he checked his watch and then unbuckled his seatbelt. "We gotta check in with a local agent here to pick up some puzzle pieces and party favors for the op. He'll also be the one who'll connect us with the rest of the team."

"Shouldn't you keep your seatbelt fastened until we come to a complete stop?" asked Leon, one eyebrow raised to indicate he expected a response.

Todd returned a dumbfounded stare and quipped, "Really? Don't you have anything more important to focus on besides my safety and well-being? What…are you a flight attendant now?"

"OK," shrugged Leon. "Who's the local agent?"

"Beats me." Todd shrugged. "You know the CIA—they're a different breed, going by first name and last initial only. Makes ya wonder if they ever use their *real* names at all," he added rhetorically. "'Bout all I know is our contact is a man who simply goes by 'Dru.'"

"So I take it this Dru character is gonna connect us with your buddy—what's his name again?" asked Leon.

"Dude, are you for real? You seriously can't remember *one* initial? It's not like it's real complicated. It's the seventh letter in the alphabet. Brother goes by 'G.' Try to lodge it in that overloaded cranium of yours somewhere among all that micro-shit you got going on up in there."

Leon smiled as if he knew all along and was just toying with Todd.

Todd just shook his head. "Let's find someplace to eat. I'm famished."

Avigdor sat quietly in a secluded room staring at the folded newspaper left behind by his newly appointed state counsel, Micah Bachman. As he sat patiently awaiting an official visit from the investigation team, his thoughts drifted to Hanah and Rina. His frustrations continued to mount the more he thought of them. Taking a deep breath, he placed his face in his hands and tried to calm himself by mentally communicating with his wife.

Hanah…Hanah, can you hear me? Hanah…they can hurt you physically, but they cannot break your will. Stay strong and trust your instincts. I will find you and bring you back to safety. I love you…

Avigdor's thoughts were interrupted when he heard voices outside the room. He stood when the door opened. A French investigative magistrate entered the room. He was accompanied by an American, an Interpol agent, and the Israeli Consul General—Micah Bachman—Avigdor's diplomatic counsel.

"Mr. Malkinson, please be seated—"

"Do you bring news of my wife's whereabouts?" asked Avigdor anxiously, still standing.

"No, sir. This visit is to officially inform you of your rights under international law and to—"

"Micah, what is this?" asked Avigdor, concern in his voice, looking to his friend and counselor.

"Sir, if you'll kindly allow us to explain, you will learn that we are doing everything we can to find your wife," the French magistrate assured him.

"I'm listening," Avigdor replied impatiently, still standing.

The magistrate gestured for Avigdor to take a seat while he took the time to introduce him to the others in the room. Avigdor reluctantly played along and sat with his arms folded, looking expectantly at the magistrate and his guests while occasionally glaring at Micah as if he would reveal some insight or intervene.

"Mr. Malkinson, this is Agent Claude Chevalier of Interpol. He and his officers are principally serving as investigative coordinators among the various international agencies that are involved in finding your wife. Their role, as you may know, is to mitigate cross-cultural anomalies, language barriers, and international law interpretations."

Avigdor nodded to acknowledge the introduction.

"And this is Special Agent Nate McEwan, with the US Diplomatic Security Service. He is here at the request of your country to assist in the investigation and is empowered by the US State Department to direct US assets to exploit all aspects of this investigation. The DSS is a world leader in international investigations, threat analysis, cybersecurity, counterterrorism, and the protection of people across the world. We are fortunate to have him working on this investigation with us."

Avigdor took special note of the last introduction. It was the only confidence boost he felt since the abduction. He uncrossed his arms—a gesture noticed by everyone in the room with the exception of Avigdor himself. He looked the agent in the eye and seemed to respond to his confident nature.

Agent McEwan spoke with calming confidence. "Sir, I have just a few questions. After that, we've arranged for you to be moved to a more comfortable and secure location."

"You're moving me? To where?"

G awoke to the sound of his cell-phone alarm. He reached over to silence it and glanced out the window. The morning dawn was obscured by a gray overcast. He turned on the television to check the weather. Storms were forecast for the entire central Florida peninsula. The words of his contact rushed to the forefront of his mind when he heard the gloomy forecast.

...you're in the middle of a pending shitstorm.

He smirked at the irony, packed everything he had into his bag, and powered on his tablet to file a report. As the computer came to life, he began recalling remnants of his latest dream. Clicking on an obscure icon, he opened an encrypted file he used to log dream sequences and elements.

Storm...fierce...whoa! The kid...the boy. Who the hell is the boy?

His thoughts fixated on the boy in his dream. He struggled to make sense of the boy's role. Then he recalled more of the dream sequence.

The yacht, the women, the man who seemed to be in control...and Larry. What the hell—

A subtle knock at the door surprised him. Knowing it was too early for housekeeping to show up, he grabbed his weapon, chambered a round, and walked toward the door. He stopped in his tracks when he heard someone attempt to turn the doorknob. He took a position alongside an adjacent wall and listened to the sound of the door as it unlocked. As the door slowly opened, he quickly raised his weapon and stepped to the backside of the door and took aim, head-high, determined to get off the first shot.

G's adrenaline spiked as he waited for the door to close or for someone to step into the room so he could make a split-second decision on his next move. He secretly hoped the intruder would have a change of heart and just leave. Suddenly and without warning, the door burst wide open and crashed into him—a move he failed to anticipate. The door slammed into his extended arms, knocking the gun out of his hands. A man stepped forward, kicked the weapon away, and grabbed G by the collar to subdue him.

The man was good. G was better.

When the man grabbed his collar, G thrust his palms up and into the man's chin, causing him to break his grip and step back. G quickly spun his body and extended his right leg, connecting a full roundhouse kick to the man's chest. As soon as he connected, he noticed the familiar face of a fellow agent, Ian Wolfe. Ian's face contorted as he absorbed the explosive kick to the chest, his arms extending and flailing uncontrollably as he fell back toward a corner of the bed.

G rolled onto the floor, grabbed his weapon, and took aim at the agent, who was now sprawled out on the floor next to the bed, gasping for air, waving one hand in a gesture of surrender while clutching his chest with the other. G moved toward the door and kicked it closed while maintaining a steady aim on his intruder.

"What do you want? Why are you here?" asked G, breathing deep from the intense encounter.

He moved to the window and glanced out to see if Ian had set him up by placing reinforcements outside the hotel. Nothing tipped him off, so he waited for the agent to catch his breath.

"Talk to me, asshole," G demanded.

"You accepted the mission," responded Ian, a raspy voice that indicated he was still struggling to catch his breath. "I'm here to brief you on the details."

"You almost got yourself killed," said G.

"I could've taken you," responded Ian with a painful smirk.

"You overestimate yourself…or you *underestimate* me. Either calculation could've ended real shitty for you, Ian." G lowered his weapon, flipped the safety, and placed it into a concealed holster in the small of his back. "Get up. I gotta get to the docks. I'll meet up with you to discuss the details of the mission when I'm finished there," said G.

"You don't want to do that," said Ian.

G stopped and stared at Ian expectantly. "What do you know that I don't?"

Tzofiya lifted the hem of her skirt, placed one leg upon a small footstool, and securely fastened a concealed holster to her thigh. She pulled a Ruger LCP .380 handgun from her suitcase, checked the six-round magazine, pushed it into place, and gently slid the weapon into the holster on the inside of her left thigh. Although her unannounced date was located in a fairly well-known public place, she preferred the company and security of a weapon at her disposal should the situation require it.

She checked the time: 7:55 p.m.

Arriving at the La Terrazza dell'Eden rooftop restaurant just after 8:00 p.m., she approached the maître d', who smiled when she showed him the note.

"Right this way, signorina."

Tzofiya was escorted to a table with a breathtaking view of St. Peter's Dome, fully illuminated against the night sky and standing out among the historic architecture of the picturesque city. She sat alone for just a few minutes, until a man approached her table.

"I see you're seated at the very table we shared the last time we were here together. May I join you?"

A wide smile appeared on Tzofiya's face when she recognized the man.

Ezra Pennington had served in the Knesset with her father and had grown close to him and the Kalev family through the years. Tzofiya had always known Ezra as a friend of her father's until she entered the clandestine ranks and discovered him to be much more than that. From his position deep inside the Shin Bet, he had watched over her through every arduous phase of her training and would occasionally mentor her on the peculiar nuances of the profession.

"Very nice to see you again, Ezra. I must admit, this is a surprise," she said as she stood and embraced him with a fond hug and her signature warm smile.

"May I?" he asked, indicating his desire to sit with her at the table.

"Of course, please. I assume you're the one who arranged this meeting. I had no idea who would've been so bold," she admitted, smiling. "How did you know…wait." She chuckled. "Forget I even asked. When will I ever learn you just have a way of knowing such things?"

Ezra smiled. "So is it safe to assume you have prepared yourself accordingly?" he asked.

"If you're asking whether I am armed, you already know the answer," she said, returning a coy smile accentuated by a raised eyebrow.

"Indeed, the Guardian is always prepared," he answered.

Ezra took the liberty of ordering a bottle of wine—a 1983 Biondi-Santi Brunello di Montalcino.

"Excellent choice, sir," responded the waiter.

"So tell me, Ezra, is this meeting business or pleasure?"

"I was going to give you an opportunity to go back to the docks and finish your business, but the predicted shitstorm took place earlier than I expected," explained Ian.

"I'm listening," said G impatiently.

"Your 'boss,' Larry, down at the docks, had several bad habits that were incompatible with the drug profession. He had a deal with the DEA that required him to allow them to infuse the product with a trace element that helped them track the specific blend coming through the docks at Barge Avenue. The Feds nailed him a couple of years back, after they discovered he was involved with covering up deliveries, essentially assisting importers in exchange for a lucrative cut of the profits and few fringe benefits of the trade. From what I hear, the 'small cut' was triple his traditional salary at the docks, but the fringe benefits were what got him into real trouble. Anyway, the Feds subsequently convinced him to continue facilitating the shipments while working undercover for them. The decision was rather simple. His only alternative was prison. No way he was about to take that option."

"You said 'had.'"

"Yeah, so you see, your boss is no longer alive. Seems he had decided to play both sides of the fence once he discovered the trace element actually *increased* his overall supply and bottom line. He must have made a mistake he couldn't recover from somewhere along the line."

"But I just saw him yesterday," said G.

"These things are never static, G. You know that. Or are you *still* learning that part?"

"Who killed him? How did he die? How do we *know* he's dead?"

Ian shrugged his shoulders. "Washed up onshore this morning on St. Pete Beach. Some tourists found him. Initial reports say he OD'd on his own product. Details are unconfirmed beyond that. Besides, who gives a shit at this point?"

"Two things I don't particularly care for, Ian—surprises and loose ends. Hearing about this brings both elements together to form more questions than answers. Any idea where the shipments are coming from?"

"Dominican Republic," answered Ian matter-of-factly.

"You answer that as if it's public knowledge," queried G. "Who runs the show on that side?"

"Word has it that a Dominican by the name of Enrique Espinosa runs the operation. He's said to be in bed with powerful people on all sides. Only issue is that no one has seen him in over ten years… no one who's still alive that is."

G's thoughts drifted to the dream he'd had of the activities on the yacht. He struggled to recall the characteristics of the man he'd seen on the yacht, but the details had become obscured.

…no one has seen him in over ten years…no one who is still alive that is…

"Doesn't seem like much of a shitstorm to me. I mean, someone dies and all of sudden you define it as a shitstorm? What am I missing? And what, if anything, does all this have to do with why you've suddenly shown up in my life?"

"I'm getting to that. First of all, the Feds have locked down the docks at Barge Avenue, essentially shutting down the entire operation. There are agents crawling all over the place. They're asking lots of questions of lots of people. I know you only worked there one day, but I figured you'd probably like to avoid that place right about now," explained Ian. "No sense in pushing the limits of exposing your cover because you somehow feel compelled to 'punch out' on the time clock."

"What about this Espinosa character?" asked G.

"What about him?" returned Ian.

G stood in silence, contemplating an answer against the contrasting perspectives of the facts before him and the elements of his dream. Considering the circumstances and the ensuing shitstorm, he had no choice but to cut loose and focus on his newest objective, whatever that happened to be. Espinosa would have to wait, but G would not forget the man.

"OK, so now what?" asked G.

Hanah looked up at the ceiling, struggling to keep her tired eyes open, her mind quickly succumbing to the effects of sheer exhaustion—her arms uncomfortably extended above her head, still securely fastened to the rusty wall anchor. Exhaustion had ultimately taken the place of fear and pushed her into the only state that allowed her to escape her dire situation. The hint of a smile appeared on her face as the dream she entered opened her to a gradual awareness of her new peaceful surroundings. Gentle, soothing music emanated from nowhere in particular, and it was some of the most serene she had ever heard. Her emotions were electrically connected to the energy surrounding her as various forms of light danced around her in a symbolic embrace of affection. Her smile grew larger when she noticed she was free from the shackles that bound her in the makeshift prison cell. She extended her open hands and slowly moved her fingers while she watched in amazement at the way her movements manipulated the light and the changing colors.

Momma, whispered a familiar voice that seemed to move through her. *Momma, if you can hear me—*

"Rina?" exclaimed Hanah in surprise. "Is that you? I cannot see you—"

Shhh, it's OK, Momma. I am with you, even when you cannot see me.

An inexplicable peace washed over her as she listened to the whisper that stirred deep within the core of her soul. She closed her eyes, determined to find a way to the source of the love she felt emanating from the whisper.

"Please, I must see my child," she cried to no one in particular.

She opened her eyes as the colors surrounding her receded into thick billowy clouds of white, gray, and pale blue supported by the multitude of colors still emanating from the light just beyond her reach. She remained silent as the limits of her patience and determination were tested while she watched the scene develop before her. She heard faint sounds gradually drawing nearer. The clouds continued to slowly move about as she listened to the sound of a gentle rain overshadowed by footsteps quickly moving from right to left in the distance. Muted, concerned voices echoed on her left. The sound of a crying baby surfaced and quickly faded into the distance. Hanah's mind reeled, trying to comprehend the sounds while desperately trying to see beyond the shroud of thick fog. The random dancing of the colors slowed, their eclectic blend uniformly transitioning to a breathtakingly translucent blue as the sound of rain and voices faded into the more soothing sound of music. It was the most beautiful combined experience of sight and sound she had ever witnessed.

The clouds surrounding Hanah began to fade as she felt her feet come to rest on firm ground. She struggled to see past the subsiding fog as the sound of concerned voices returned, enveloping her in a low murmur. She watched as the colors surrounding her suddenly grew brighter and soon after, slowly began to fade. She felt an inexplicable emotional connection to the intensity of the light. As the intensity increased, she felt elation. As the colors and intensity faded, she became depressed. She struggled to disconnect herself from the negative effect as she helplessly watched the lights continue to fade until they were no longer evident. A scream echoed around her, followed by wretched sobbing. No longer able to control or contain the emotional toil, Hanah felt her tears well and fall from her eyes.

Silence followed as she continued to struggle to make sense of it all.

"Rina," she called out. "What is this?"

Shhhhhh…

The odd but peaceful response to her question calmed her.

She wiped the tears from her eyes as a bright light emerged from within the fog. As the smoke cleared, the silhouette of a small child appeared before her. Hanah's heart ached as her eyes caught the first glimpse of the child. Her mind raced to catch up with the enormity of what was happening. She squinted to bring clarity to her emotional struggle to comprehend.

It's good to see you, Momma.

"Ro'i? Is that you, Ro'i?" she asked, still uncertain.

Yes, Momma, it is I.

Hanah wept when she heard the voice of the child—her child—the one she had lost so soon after he was born. Her eyes glistened with joy-filled tears as she watched the child slowly appear before her.

Clarity washed over her in an overwhelming torrent of emotion as she recalled giving birth to the child and holding him in her arms, looking into his deep, translucent blue eyes. It was at that precise moment—when a mother completes the connection she has to a child—when he offered her his first and only smile before he closed his eyes for good and returned to the hand of God. Doctors tried to revive him but to no avail. Hanah's eyes continued to well with tears as she recalled the crushing moment she had lost the child.

She and Avigdor had struggled with a name for the boy for months before his birth. They both recalled the moment when they reached a decision. Hanah was in prayer when she discovered the name. She remembered hearing the voice of God tell her that the child would be a shepherd who would one day show the way to many people. It was not an answer Avigdor could argue with, nor did he care to, for he was at peace with the most excellent choice.

Hanah recalled the anger and resentment she felt toward God when Ro'i had passed. *How can he show anyone the way as a shepherd if he is dead?* Years passed as she continued to struggle to find an acceptable answer. The answer finally came, and was standing before her, bathed in a spiritual light of love that consumed her every emotion.

Are you lost, Momma? I can help you. I can show you the way.

"Sir, we believe that you'll be safer at the Israeli consulate in Marseille," explained Agent McEwan. "You'll be free to operate within the confines of the consulate while you're there, but you'll not be permitted to leave until we sort things out."

"I understand," answered Avigdor, nodding slightly in reluctant approval of the notion.

A man entered the room and approached Agent Chevalier who was standing in the corner of the room. The man whispered into his ear and waited for a response. Agent Chevalier nodded and gestured for the man to leave. Micah and Agent McEwan looked at Agent Chevalier expectantly when he asked them to step outside the room. Avigdor watched as the last man to leave the room closed the door, leaving him alone once again.

A short time later, Agent McEwan and Micah returned to the room, concerned looks painted on their faces.

"Ballistics tests conducted on your handgun are a match to the bullet found in the fatal shooting of one of the security agents found just outside your vacation villa," explained Micah. "There are two rounds missing from the clip in your weapon that match the rounds taken from the victim."

"So you think I shot this agent—a man there to protect my family and me? What about the other agents? Where are they? What about my *wife*? Has anyone bothered to investigate *that* aspect of this twisted bullshit? What kind of sideshow are they running here, Micah?" Avigdor demanded, pounding his fist on the table.

"Sir, I'm merely reporting the facts as I am commissioned to—"

"Fuck you, Micah! You're nothing but a weak, pathetic excuse for a counselor. It's the very reason you never ascended in the

Knesset." Avigdor turned his back and stepped to the back of the small room.

Agent McEwan stepped forward. "Gentlemen, dissention will get us nowhere. This obviously changes things, so let me see if there's anything I can do to unscrew this. Meantime, I need you to think real hard about whether or not you remember firing your weapon," McEwan said, directing the last part of his statement to Avigdor.

"I have to report in with a team construct and an action plan," explained Ian.

"Let me guess. You have twenty-four hours to provide the details," responded G, knowing the standard routine.

"Boy, you *are* disconnected, G. The *new* boss wants it in *twelve*. And I've already used eight of 'em. Here's the deal: we're scheduled to meet a CIA contact at noon. The contact will connect us with other specialists on the team—"

"You still haven't told me the objective, Ian. Your message indicated an international matter. Is this about Espinosa?"

"Who? Oh, you mean the Dominican badass that most likely greased your boss?"

G returned a look of impatience to Ian's poor attempt at sarcasm.

"Look, I'm not here to spend the taxpayer's money on chasing some ghost around the Caribbean to solve the DEA's hard-target problem," said Ian. "Besides, assuming the cat did eliminate what-sisname, I say he did the taxpayers a huge favor. No, we've got a much bigger mission that's taking us to the South of France."

"So does this have anything to do with the disappearance of the Israeli defense minister's wife, or are you just going to keep making me play guess-the-mission?" asked G.

"It has *everything* to do with it," replied Ian as if G had just won the prize.

"Perfect. Who's leading the op?"

"The Israelis have the lead. The State Department asked us to take a deeper look and to do it as inconspicuously as possible. We're to assist the Israelis however we can within the confines of our charter."

G paused a beat and then asked, somewhat naïvely, "We have a charter?"

Ian shrugged his shoulders. "Beats me. I assumed *you*, if anyone, would know."

G returned a blank stare.

"OK, look. DSS is already on scene and working alongside Interpol and the FBI collecting evidence and gathering leads," explained Ian. "We'll get more clarity on the operational details on our swim across the pond. Meantime, collect your shit, and let's get ready to meet up with our contact."

"So who's the CIA contact?" asked G.

"Dude by the name of Dru. You know the drill—they find us; we don't find them," explained Ian.

"You waste no time getting to the point, Tzofiya. It's an admirable trait—a focus and drive that I see too little of these days from most others. A meeting with you is *always* a pleasure, my dear."

The waiter uncorked the wine bottle, offered the cork to Ezra, and proceeded to pour a small amount into the crystal glass set before him. The deep red color contrasted with the white linen tablecloth as the wine gave off noticeable notes of roses, violets, and red fruit combined with slight hints of earthy minerals and aromatic herbs.

Tzofiya smiled politely while she waited for Ezra to approve the wine.

Ezra nodded approvingly to the waiter who poured Tzofiya's glass first, followed by a generous finish to Ezra's.

"To perspective and insight, and the advantage of maturity," said Ezra, lifting his glass as he offered the toast.

Tzofiya tipped her glass forward to lightly connect with Ezra's as she looked into his eyes, determined to extract the deeper meaning of his toast. The seductive notes of the wine greeted her as she brought the glass to her mouth for her first sip of the deep red Sangiovese.

"I assume you aren't merely referring to the wine," said Tzofiya. "Although, I must admit, it is one of the best I've tasted."

Ezra smiled. "Your perception for quality is noteworthy. Your intuition for the subtleties of the message is the very reason why you have been such an asset to your country."

"You didn't come here to give me a performance review, Ezra. Don't get me wrong, I always enjoy the pleasure of your company, but—"

"Indeed, your curious nature deserves an acknowledgement, dear Tzofiya." He paused. "I am here at the request of Prime Minister Levinson to redirect you to one of the most important tasks you may ever face."

Tzofiya looked deep into Ezra's eyes as he quietly explained the classified details surrounding the disappearance of Hanah Malkinson. Her mind reeled with possible ways to approach the case as Ezra continued to lay out the details of her cover and the expectations of the prime minister.

"Time is of the essence, Tzofiya," said Ezra as he slid an envelope across the table to her. "You're on the first flight out in the morning. Here are your credentials, your passport, and your airline tickets. Study your cover, and see what you can discover from the scene in Saint-Tropez. You must look for details others have overlooked and determine an appropriate response to take based on actionable intelligence."

"So I'm acting alone on this? You know I have no issue with that. It's just that—"

"You're never alone, Tzofiya. Not while I'm alive. But you *will* be the only Israeli special agent at the crime scene with orders from the prime minister himself. There is an elite team of American special operatives on their way to support you once your collection and analysis is complete. They are operating as US secret-service agents. You are free to arrange a meeting should you discover anything that requires their assistance."

"I understand," she said.

9

"Let's go," said Ian when he saw the taxi drive up to the front of the hotel.

"Where we headed?" asked G.

"We're supposed to take a taxi to the airport and rendezvous with this Dru character."

G nodded and donned a pair of sunglasses as they stepped outside the hotel.

"Where to, gents?" asked the driver without turning around.

"Airport," responded Ian, head down, looking at his phone.

"International or Knight?"

"Uh, good question. I actually have no idea," said Ian.

Well this is off to a fantastic start, G thought.

"Hold on a sec and lemme check," Ian added, sending a message to the home office.

The driver patiently waited. "You guys pilots or passengers?"

Neither man answered. Instead, G looked out the window while Ian continued to fumble with his smart phone.

"Reason I ask is that I used to fly with the 160th out of Hunter Army Airfield," added the driver, trying to find common ground.

G listened while continuing to stare out the window. If the driver really *did* fly with the 160th, he managed to get the airfield correct. Of course, anyone could *say* he was a part of an elite special operations unit and back it up with a few cool facts easily discovered on the Internet. G looked down at his watch and stole a glance at the driver to size him up. He was older, maybe in his fifties, balding a bit on the crown of his gray head. From G's angle, the man seemed fit for his age judging by the tone in his arms.

The driver continued to banter. "Yeah, those were the days," he said. "You just never knew when your last flight was *literally* gonna be your last," he added as he seemed to drift off in thought.

"OK, here it is," Ian reported. "Peter O. Knight Airport?"

"Know it well," reported the driver. "We're about twenty-five minutes away, depending on traffic, which shouldn't be bad this time of day," he said confidently as he pressed a button on the meter and hit the gas.

No one spoke for the first fifteen minutes of the drive, each lost in his own thoughts. The only sound breaking the silence was an occasional radio call from dispatch connecting drivers to various fares throughout the area.

"So when did you serve?" asked G, still gazing out the window.

"Hmm? Oh, '88 to '93," he said, his thoughts interrupted by the question. "You serve?"

"No," answered G.

"So what's *your* background?" asked the driver.

"He's a jack of all trades," interrupted Ian with a smile, finally looking up from his phone.

The driver chuckled as he merged onto Davis Boulevard, the main thoroughfare leading to the airport. "Aren't we all?" he answered as he drove past the main entrance of the small terminal.

"You can drop us off here," instructed Ian.

"OK, I'll just turn around up here," responded the driver as he slowed to make a turn into a side street adjacent to the terminal. He stopped the car next to a small building and rolled down his window, foot resting on the brake.

A man approached.

Ian slowly placed his hand across his waist to reach for his weapon. G sat still, watching and calculating the movements of all three men, his right hand near the release handle of the door.

The driver flashed an ID card at the man, who paused to examine it. He glanced into the back seat at Ian and G and then waved them through.

Ian glanced at G and then slowly turned his head toward the driver. "Sorry, I didn't catch your name," he said while looking for ID credentials noticeably absent from the visor or dashboard of the cab.

"No, you didn't," responded the driver as he pulled the car in front of a large hangar and placed the gearshift into park. "The name's Dru," he replied without turning around.

Hanah awoke to the intense beam of a flashlight and the forced opening of her eyelids. Gasping in shock and fear, she winced at the pain of her own reaction as she pulled against the wrist restraints that still anchored her to the wall above her head. She blinked and turned away to avoid any further examination from the doctor called in to check her injuries and vitals. She closed her eyes to find comfort in the ghost spot remnants the bright light had cast against the inside of her eyelids and rolled her body away from the man at her side. Warm tears rolled down her cheeks as she vividly recalled the alter-conscious encounter with her firstborn, Ro'i.

The man sitting beside her said nothing; instead he placed his hand against her injured shoulder in a convincing gesture for her to return to a supine position. She moaned slightly as she reluctantly complied, repositioning her body on the lumpy, stained mattress. She opened her tired eyes to see a bearded Middle Eastern man wearing a stethoscope around his neck. His features bore harsh evidence of a stressful life, with many creases on his face and a hardened demeanor. He placed his hand against her forehead for a moment and followed with a touch on the right side of her face to convince her to turn toward him. She recognized the familiar tattoo on his wrist. She had seen it before.

A serpent supported by two crossed swords.

Hanah closed her eyes when the man turned on the flashlight again, this time to examine the contusion on her forehead. She winced as he indifferently tested the tenderness of the wound. She gasped when he unbuttoned her blouse and placed his hand inside her shirt to place the stethoscope on her chest. Her heart beat faster than normal with anxiety as he moved the stethoscope to find the best echo of her heartbeat.

Hanah fought back tears of helplessness as she felt his hand release the stethoscope and begin to explore other regions of her breasts. She opened her eyes and stared at him in anger and disgust as his fingers reached her right nipple. He smiled at her menacingly, his teeth revealing brown stains of neglect and decay. She reacted defiantly by spitting in his face and pulling away as best she could despite the restraint of her worn wrists.

The man pulled his hand away to wipe the saliva from the corner of his eye and the bridge of his nose. Then he violently backhanded the side of her face. She turned and twisted her body away in fear and pain and began to sob. He climbed on top of her, straddled her waist, and grabbed her hair with both hands while forcing his pelvis into her hips. He lowered his face toward hers; the foul stench of his breath grew viler the closer he got.

"You spit on those who would take the time to care for you?" he said in a thick accent, angrily looking into her eyes. "Then you shall taste the sweetness of *my* saliva."

The man grabbed a fistful of hair at the top of her head with his right hand and firmly held her jaw with his left while he forced her clenched teeth apart and spat into her open mouth. He quickly released his grip and surprised her with another swift slap against the side of her face with his open palm.

Hanah struggled to push the foul saliva from her mouth when she felt his hands aggressively ripping her shirt apart. Ringing echoed in her left ear from the painful blow while her ability to resist continued to diminish. Her eyes slowly blinked while she fought to maintain consciousness and helplessly endured the savage assault of the monster on top of her. She had little fight left in her when she heard someone enter the room.

Tzofiya caught the first plane out of Rome bound for Toulon the morning after receiving her instructions from Ezra. The one-hour flight provided just enough time for her to mentally rehearse the remaining details of her cover and the intent of her objective she had studied throughout the night.

An American FBI agent and two Interpol officers waited for Tzofiya at the baggage claim area on the lower level. She spotted them almost immediately and stepped into a nearby restroom before they were able to see her.

Tzofiya had learned the power of perception and self-confidence early in her training. She had purposely chosen to wear a dark suit— a Marcela Rialto one-button blazer over a gray silk blouse accompanied by dark Tilana trousers and black Tori Birch flats. Pausing in front of a full-length restroom mirror, she glanced at her reflection, took a deep breath, gave herself a look of confidence, and turned to walk away. She watched as one of the officers noticed her walking toward them and alerted the others.

"Good morning, gentlemen," announced Tzofiya as she confidently strode up to the men, her hand extended. "Special Agent Cohen," she announced, introducing herself in a straightforward, professional manner. "I'm waiting for one bag, and we can be on our way," she added.

Tzofiya retrieved her luggage and followed the men to an awaiting vehicle—a black, late-model BMW 7 Series sedan. She declined an offer to assist her in placing her luggage in the trunk and took a seat in the back next to the FBI agent. The hour-long drive gave Tzofiya the opportunity to receive a rundown on known facts and relevant information pertaining to the case. Satisfied she had gleaned everything she could, she set her mind to analyzing the information until she could physically examine the crime scene. They passed a small airport just off the main route into Saint-Tropez, about forty-five minutes into the trip.

"Is that a private airfield?" she asked no one in particular as they drove past the airstrip.

"That's La Mole Airport. It's primarily a charter field, although there are a few commuter airlines that ferry passengers between the major hubs," answered the FBI agent.

"Has anyone investigated that airport yet?" she asked.

"Investigated it for what?" he answered.

"Turn the car around," she demanded.

Dru led the men inside the hangar through a side entrance. He flipped a few light switches that brought the overhead lights to life, revealing a sleek white Gulfstream V jet parked in the center of the hangar. G tilted his head slightly as he examined the familiar craft. Memories of former days alongside a similar plane filled his mind until he pushed the thoughts aside to focus on the task at hand.

"This way," said Dru, his voice echoing inside the hangar.

"G-money," exclaimed Todd when he saw his old friend enter the small office connected to the hangar. "Damn, brother. You're *jacked*. That's the fittest I believe I've *ever* seen you," he added. "What's your secret? Whatever it is, I gotta have some of it."

G just smiled.

"I see you managed to meet Dru. Did he try pullin' that stealth CIA bullshit on you too?" said a laughing Todd.

"I see you two already know each other," stated Dru, unfamiliar with the friends' history.

"Yeah, we're practically brothers. Can't you tell the similarities?" answered Todd sarcastically as he approached his old friend and offered a firm handshake and a man-hug. "Good to see you again, G," Todd quietly said during their quick embrace.

"Likewise, my friend."

"You men can get better acquainted once you're in the air. For now, we have business to take care of. As you know, an op like this would normally call for a stop at the home office for an in-depth mission brief and setup, but considering the compressed timeline you're on, I've been authorized to provide you with everything you need to get underway ASAP," explained Dru.

"Sounds good," answered Ian.

Todd glanced at Ian and then at G, seeking a sign of approval from his old friend on the *new* guy.

G returned a slight nod indicating his tentative approval and returned his focus to Dru.

Truth was, no one really knew much about Ian beyond the fact that he was responsible for putting together the best team for the task at hand—that and the home office trusted him, which carried weight with G. Despite that, however, Todd couldn't help but feel a reluctant skepticism as Ian stepped into an informal leadership role.

Dru opened a wall locker, retrieved a backpack, and placed it on a small table in the center of the room. "These are your credentials, gentlemen. You'll be operating as secret-service agents—"

"Cool," interrupted Leon with a smirk. "I've always wanted to play one of those," he added with a chuckle. "So when do we get to meet the president?"

"Dude, really? Are you done? Let the man at least finish his briefing," Todd warned with an intimidating look.

Dru waited for a break in the dialogue between the two men before he continued. "The State Department has agreed not to seek the assistance of *real* secret-service agents for this op," explained Dru with a glance toward Leon. "The ruse actually works in your favor because there'll be no confusion or potential for compromise. That and the FBI typically doesn't mind sharing information with the secret service for some reason. Seems even *they* think secret-service agents are pretty cool. Should make it easier to find out what they know from the start and help your team to begin the process of discovering what they *don't* know. You'll be minimally armed. Any additional firepower requirements will be handled on an as-needed basis."

Dru glanced at his watch and then looked directly at Ian. "As I understand it, you have a plan that's due to the director in just over an hour. I suggest you finalize that with the rest of your team and submit it. No one leaves here without approval from the home office. OK, which one of you is Leon?"

"That would be the smart ass who wants to meet the president," quipped Todd.

"Bashir! What are you doing?" Munahid shouted to the man sitting on top of Hanah.

"I am conducting an examination," answered Bashir. "Now get the hell out of here."

Munahid looked at Hanah who returned a fading, helpless stare, her eyes slowly blinking, marked by fear and overflowing with tears. Fresh assault marks on her face bore evidence that she was anything but all right. He looked at Bashir with contempt and began walking toward the smaller man.

"I said get the hell out of here, Munahid," warned Bashir as he grabbed Hanah's throat with his left hand and raised his right fist in a threatening gesture.

"I think it's time for *you* to get out of here," Munahid said as he ran the remaining few steps and tackled Bashir, aggressively grabbing his arm in midair and wrestling him to the floor. "You bring shame to our people, Bashir," shouted Munahid, now sitting on top of the subdued elder.

Bashir was livid. But considering the size difference between him and the much larger Munahid, he reluctantly conceded and opted to avoid a futile power struggle.

"This isn't over, Munahid," he said as he rose from the floor and brushed himself off. "You have disrespected an elder, and for that, you will pay," he shouted angrily before he turned and walked out of the room.

Hanah looked into Munahid's calming blue eyes and drew in a quick, frightened breath as he slowly approached her.

"It's OK," he whispered. "You are safe now." He carefully pulled her torn shirt together as best he could. "I will get you some water and something new to wear."

"Don't leave me," whispered Hanah as she faded off into unconsciousness.

10

Micah stepped out of the small interrogation room, leaving Avigdor alone with Agent McEwan.

"Sir, would you be willing to submit a saliva sample for a toxicology examination?" asked Agent McEwan in just over a whisper.

"I don't understand," answered Avigdor.

"Your counsel would most likely advise against it, but if we can determine why or *how* you managed to essentially sleep through your wife's abduction—"

Avigdor gave the agent a surprised look. "So you believe me?"

"I didn't say that. It's...just that little else makes sense right now. It may actually help us close the loop on looming questions surrounding your state of mind that night. Of course, it may also lead to more questions."

"I'll do it," said Avigdor. "But only if you can assure me that it will stay between us."

"Not sure I can—"

"Look, I don't trust a whole lot of people right now, so you'll have to agree, or it's not going to happen. It's the only way I'll consent," interrupted Avigdor as he looked to the agent, seeking an assurance of confidence.

McEwan offered a reluctant nod indicating his agreement when Micah returned to the room.

"I have filed papers requesting your transfer to the Israeli consulate," reported Micah. "Ordinarily, the request would be denied considering the circumstances—"

The men were interrupted when Agent Chevalier opened the door. He was accompanied by two uniformed French National Police officers.

"Gentlemen, my apologies for the interruption. Mr. Deputy Prime Minister, I regret to inform you that formal charges have just been handed down by the magistrate. You are under arrest for the murder of an Israeli Mossad officer who was assigned to your security team. Please stand up and come with me."

The two police officers grabbed Avigdor's arms and helped him to his feet. One of them brought Avigdor's hands behind his back and attempted to place him in handcuffs. Avigdor had a look of shock painted on his face as he looked at McEwan and then at Micah.

"Are those really necessary?" asked McEwan.

Agent Chevalier waved his hand to prevent the officer from placing the restraints onto Avigdor's wrists. "My apologies, Mr. Malkinson. Please come with us so we may affect your transfer to a more suitable location," said Chevalier.

"Micah—"

"Where are you taking him?" asked Micah.

"The magistrate has ordered that he be sequestered in a private villa in the city where he—"

"Exactly where *in the city*?" demanded Micah.

McEwan listened as the men continued to discuss the details of Avigdor's transfer with elevated emotions on one side and determined resolve on the other. Avigdor would be transferred without regard for the opinion or objection of diplomatic legal counsel. If McEwan wanted Avigdor's saliva sample, he'd have to be creative, and he'd have to be quick.

"Mr. Malkinson would you like something to drink. Water, perhaps?" asked McEwan conveying more of a message with his eyes than the content of the question.

The out-of-the-blue question took everyone but Avigdor by surprise as they waited for him to answer.

"That's very kind of you. Yes, please," answered Avigdor. "At least someone around here has my best interests in mind," he added, giving his counsel a look of disappointment.

Agent Chevalier gestured to one of the officers, who returned a short time later with a small plastic cup of water. Avigdor drank the water but not without leaving a sample of his saliva inside the cup.

"The DPM will be held at an estate in a Saint-Tropez marina. The conditions are the best we can offer, given the nature of the charges and the political sensitivities surrounding the case. He will be under house arrest and well-protected in accordance with an appropriate level of protocol, save for a few of the freedoms he is accustomed to," answered Chevalier as if Micah should have known.

"I want the specific name and location of this estate. I have to report the details directly to the prime minister. And I must know the limitations that will be imposed upon him," demanded Micah.

McEwan took note of Micah's questions and the responses of the French agent.

"Due to the sensitive nature of the situation and the status of Mr. Malkinson, we will reveal the exact location once we have completed his transfer. He will be free to move about but will not have unmonitored access to communications or computers. And that access will be limited," explained Chevalier. "Let me assure you that the arrest is a necessary formality to ensure he remains in country and under French control until the investigation is complete. This is for his protection as well as to preserve the integrity and delicacy of the investigation."

"Everything will be all right, Mr. Deputy," assured Micah. "I will continue to do my best and get to the bottom of this. I must fly out to Marseille this evening, but I will return as soon as possible with more information."

"I don't need *information*, Micah. I need *results*. Get me some results," said an aggravated Avigdor as the officers led him out of the room and to an awaiting vehicle outside the station.

McEwan followed the men out of the room but not before he passed by the table to inconspicuously grab the cup left behind by Avigdor.

Dru led Leon outside to the parked taxicab. He opened the trunk and turned to Leon. "I was told to protect these cases at all costs and to hand 'em over only to you. I have no idea what they are and don't really *care* to know. So if you'll kindly remove them from my rent-a-car, I'd be much obliged."

Leon smiled when he looked into the trunk to discover several hardened pelican cases of various sizes. He grabbed one of the cases and noticed it was locked.

"I take it you have the keys?" asked Leon.

"I saw a set of keys in the backpack with your creds," answered Dru. "I wondered why they were there but wasn't given any instructions about 'em. Sometimes it's best not to ask about such things."

"Well, I'm happy to take them off your hands if you'll be so kind as to help me bring them inside," said Leon.

Paul Harriman activated a secure voice line and computer connection to the four-man team in Tampa. Sitting beside him in the NSA operations center conference room was the operations center supervisor, Dennis Kinkaid. Harriman and Kinkaid served on active duty at USSOCOM together at various times during their careers. Each man respected the abilities of the other, and Paul was happy to have Dennis on the team providing big-picture analysis and operational oversight from a command and control perspective.

"All comms are secure, Paul," reported Dennis.

"Very well. Gentlemen, we show 'secure' on this end, over," announced Paul to the team.

"Secure here as well, sir," reported Ian.

"Copy, Ian. Thank you," said Paul. "I have Dennis Kinkaid with me here at this end. Some of you may know Dennis. He and his team will be running things in the ops center during this mission. Please confirm the members of the team at your end."

"OK, I have Agents Weston, Jordan…and Lambert, who just returned to the room. Agents Jordan and Lambert have the computers, comms, surveillance, and transportation covered while Weston has the psychological. I have the intel connection angles covered, and I've assumed the lead on the op. I don't believe I've met you, Dennis—Ian Wolfe here."

There it was—an open admission and an overt assertion that Ian was in charge. Todd gave an obvious sigh that made it clear he was *not* in complete agreement with Ian's presumption of leadership. Leon looked away to avoid the tension, while G sat stoically evaluating the cues and waiting for the call to continue.

Ian paused long enough to silently acknowledge Todd's wordless comment and continued. "I suspect you've already reviewed our 201 files, as well as all known details of the situation, so if there's anything you believe we may be lacking in terms of construct or capabilities, please let us know as soon as possible so we can address it. We've come up with a plan that'll allow us to easily respond to the needs of our Israeli partners in just about any capacity they require."

"Thanks, Ian," Paul acknowledged. "Gentlemen, welcome to the team. From this point forward you are activated for an operation that is highly classified and extremely sensitive. Your mission objective is *not* officially sanctioned nor endorsed by the US government. If there are any reservations, now is the time to step out with no effect to your reputation or usefulness to the agency."

Ian looked each man in the eye, including Todd, who gave him a chins-up gesture, indicating his readiness. The others offered quick, affirmative nods.

"We're all in, Paul," Ian responded with confidence.

"Understood, Ian. OK, gents, the objective of your mission is to investigate the disappearance of Hanah Malkinson. Hanah is the wife of Avigdor Malkinson, Israeli deputy prime minister and minister of defense. I'm sending two pictures of Mrs. Malkinson now."

Each member of Ian's team watched as the pictures of Hanah appeared on the screen.

Paul continued. "Hanah Malkinson mysteriously disappeared from a vacation villa in the South of France, specifically Saint-Tropez, approximately seventy-two hours ago. French authorities have DPM Malkinson sequestered for his wife's disappearance and have essentially ignored his political status pending the outcome of the investigation," explained Paul. "Under the circumstances, I can't say I blame them. I think it's their way of asserting control. At any rate, as far as we know, they're treating him well, despite their lack of evidence of his involvement. Investigators are scouring the villa and are busy examining and analyzing evidence. The last thing they're going to want to see is more investigators descending on their turf, hence the reason I sent secret-service credentials to make your access as painless as possible. It may also help remind the French of the importance the United States places on our relationship with Israel, the DPM's sensitive status, and the manner in which he's treated."

"We have the creds in our possession, Paul," confirmed Ian.

"Good. Gentlemen, your primary objective is to find Mrs. Malkinson. If the DPM is implicated in her disappearance, you are to *stand down* on that aspect of the investigation and allow due process to take place between the Israelis and the French. But if you can find anything that can exonerate him, it can only help reshape and refocus the primary objective of finding her. We're operating on the assumption that Mrs. Malkinson is alive and is more valuable to her captors as long as she remains that way. Once you discover her whereabouts, your objective will be to recover her and bring her home. Should you require special operations rescue intervention or top cover—and make damn sure you understand me crystal clear on this—your role will convert to a support and advisory status. There are a lot of moving pieces here. I don't need to remind you how this works, but for the sake of those who are new to disavowed operations, I will emphasize the fact that, should your cover be compromised, your government will *not* protect you. You will have no rights whatsoever. Are we clear?"

Once again, Ian looked at each member on the team and received a confident nod from each man.

"Affirmative," reported Ian.

"Good. Let me know if the secret-service cover creds I have preselected work for the plan you're prepared to brief," said Paul.

"The cover actually works quite well, Paul. We'll be arriving on scene to assist investigators as required, but we'll principally be analyzing evidence for clues that lend themselves to actionable intel. Jordan and Lambert will work offsite, crunching data, while G, uh, Weston and I will be working independently to identify and prosecute relevant leads, conduct interviews, and physically examine the evidence. The overall objective of *all* team members is to find the DPM's wife, pursue those responsible, and effectively deal with anyone who gets in the way of her recovery, assuming she's alive," said Ian.

"We're on the same page, Ian. Please continue," said Paul.

"As I understand it, the Israeli team has the lead on this, and our actions are subordinate to their requests. We're prepared to avail ourselves to that protocol but we want to make sure we're able to do so from an informed position, hence our desire to collect relevant intelligence from the start," said Ian.

"That's correct, Ian. The Israelis have the lead, but we must act with prejudice and keep in mind the sensitivities of this case. I will have to periodically inform the president of the generalities surrounding your actions because of the high level of international interest this has garnered. As I said, the only two countries aware of this covert operation are Israel and the United States," explained Paul.

"Understood, Paul. Knowing that doesn't change our plan," responded Ian. "Phase One calls for us to take a back seat on the formal investigation and approach this from an inverse angle to pick up on actionable intelligence," said Ian. "We'll interview the DPM and try to gain access to his daughter as well. G will be out front for the interviews while I work on opening some political doors and interact with your primary contact in the operations center. Can I assume that'll be you, Dennis?" asked Ian.

"That's correct, Ian. I'll be here throughout the operation," responded Dennis.

Ian continued. "I'm sending you an overhead satellite photo of La Mole Airport. La Mole is just south of Saint-Tropez and is the most convenient airport to the epicenter of the operation. We'll be traveling on Agent Jordan's Gulfstream, which will be overtly marked with the US blue-and-white markings, government seal, and registry—we'll need that to be washed in the diplomatic clearance process, of course. If we can get priority hangar space at La Mole, it'll help."

Paul nodded to Dennis, who was busy typing notes and coordinating the requests.

Ian continued. "The cover setup works well. US secret-service agents, commissioned by the president to assist the Israeli government, is a perfect play. We'll use that angle to its full advantage in order to obtain the information we need. Phase Two will be situation dependent and will commence as required. We'll keep you informed if and when we transition to the second phase via SITREPS through Mr. Kinkaid and the ops center floor, unless you have any objections to that course of action. Do you have any questions so far, sir?"

Paul glanced at Dennis, who returned a slow negative response.

"Negative, Ian, no questions. I *do* have some updated details, however," said Paul. "It's no secret to the French government that this incident has garnered international interest and will draw several collaborative international agencies into their backyard. They are *not* aware, however, that we've elected to send in a covert operations team. The last thing the French want is western gunslingers operating outside the span of their control. It's bad enough already that we're not well liked by the general populace. We don't need anyone making any mistakes along the way to inflame an already delicate situation."

"We understand," replied Ian, quickly glancing at each member of the team.

Paul continued. "The Israeli *team* you're expecting is actually *one* agent. Seems the prime minister wants to keep this part of the investigation as controlled and quiet as we do, and he's doing so by sending in one of his best. I'm sending you a picture of Agent Tzofiya Kalev. She's already on scene, operating under loose cover as an Israeli government investigations officer. She is going by the name of Agent Tzofiya Cohen."

Ian raised an eyebrow of intrigued approval when the picture of Tzofiya appeared on the screen. G picked up on Ian's interest and flashed a glance at Todd who was also admiring the photo, no doubt conducting his own personal assessment. Leon seemed somewhat distracted, almost anxious.

"You are to avoid making first contact with Agent Cohen. I suspect there will come a time when your paths will cross, either intentionally or coincidentally. Your first priority is to collect and prosecute actionable intelligence. Your methods are, of course, at your discretion in accordance with our charter."

Ian glanced at G and cracked a hint of a smile at the word "charter."

"The operations center will work on your diplomatic airspace clearances and landing permits and will notify you when everything's in order. Meantime, advise Dru that I'm authorizing your OPLAN with authentication *Operation Key Horizon*. Are there any questions, gentlemen?"

Tzofiya flashed her badge at a young woman behind a counter and asked to speak with the airport manager. A middle-aged man emerged from a corner office.

"Excuse me, madame. I couldn't help but overhear your inquiry," he asked.

"Hello, I'm Agent Cohen, and I'm conducting an investigation that may involve the use of this airport. Are you in a position to assist me?"

"I am. How may I be of service?"

"I'd like to know if you can provide me with all your flight logs for the past seven days. I'll need everything you have—times, aircraft type, registry, origin, and destination, any unusual requests from crews, manifests—"

"I can do most of that, madame. However, procuring manifests will be difficult as we rarely enforce that beyond the number of personnel on board an aircraft," he reported. "I'm sorry, whom did you say you represent?"

"I represent the prime minister of Israel," she said, handing him a card. "If you require French credentials, I can obtain those for you as well."

The man examined the card and looked at Tzofiya and glanced at the two men accompanying her. "Not necessary," he answered. "Would this have anything to do with the disappearance of the Israeli diplomat's wife? Tragic event that is," he added, shaking his head in disbelief.

"It does. And anything you can provide will be helpful. Your information is important, so I must have this as soon as possible. Please call me as soon as you have anything whatsoever," she said as she shook his hand and then turned to walk away.

Tzofiya closed the passenger door of the BMW and stared out her window, lost in thought as the driver merged onto the highway.

"Would you care to stop at your hotel before we continue to the villa, madame?" asked the agent.

"Where are they keeping the girl?" she asked, continuing to look out the window.

"She's in a foster home, staying with a wealthy magistrate and under the watchful eyes of the French child-protection system," said the agent.

She turned her head toward the agent. "That's our next destination. How long until we arrive?"

The men exchanged glances. Tzofiya picked up on the body language.

"Is there a problem with my request, gentlemen?"

"No, madame. It's just that we're to clear any access to the girl through the Israeli consul and the French magistrate before—"

"Then I suggest you get on one of those cell phones of yours and get to work…unless you need *me* to do it for you."

11

"We have proven just how serious we are. Now it's your turn," explained Siraj, speaking with an Iranian operative. "Our actions have successfully distracted the Israelis, just as we predicted."

"So you have seen this woman personally?" asked the operative.

"I can assure you, she is in a secure location and is well cared for. She will be useful for the long term," reported Siraj.

"You had better be correct. Otherwise, you will have succeeded only in igniting a powder keg of wrath from the Israeli ministry of defense."

"We have taken care of that as well. The defense minister has been implicated in her disappearance and—"

"You fool yourself if you believe that distraction will have long legs. Once evidence is revealed to exonerate him, he will do everything in his power to find his wife and make *you* pay for your actions with your life," replied the operative. "Unless, of course, you have *that* taken care of as well."

"Indeed we do," answered a confident Siraj, unaffected by the operative's hypothesis. "Can I count on you to resume our weapons supply?"

There was an extended pause.

"I'll see what I can do. I cannot provide much hope for anything inside southern Iraq at this time, given the history of your overreaction in the region. You can expect a resupply for your Afghanistan operations at the Zaranj border. Give me two days to divert the shipments," said the operative. "Meantime, I suggest you keep that woman well hidden. The Israelis and Americans have eyes everywhere and are very good at tracking their aggressors. And they are very patient. Once they discover who is behind her disappearance, they will pursue you with a vengeance."

"Let me deal with the infidels," answered Siraj. "You deliver the weapons we need, and they will be the least of our concerns."

"We're counting on it. Now, there is an unresolved issue of payment for our services."

"Your money will arrive as it always has, by electronic transfer through the National Bank of Dominica within forty-eight hours of the transfer."

The nine-hour flight gave the team plenty of time to get to know each other and to get a grasp on the details of their operation. G found a quiet corner near the back of the plane, lowered the window shade, and reclined his seat. He yawned and glanced down the aisle just long enough to catch a glimpse from Todd who offered a nod of reassurance. G felt the gravitational forces of the jet acting upon his body as it made a climbing left turn when he closed his eyes, intent on getting ahead of the time difference.

The sun quickly set, leaving the jet to fly into the darkness as it turned northeast toward Nova Scotia and Newfoundland.

REM sleep came suddenly for G as he felt himself gradually becoming aware of his new surroundings inside the dream state.

I have to take you somewhere, announced a voice from nowhere.

Surprised by the greeting, G furrowed his brow in an attempt to determine the source of the voice and the content of the message. He opened his eyes as soon as the small hand gripped his. He glanced down to see the boy he'd come to know in his most recent dreams. Random images flashed by much too fast to comprehend. Traveling at speeds he rarely experienced, he felt coldness as the air rushed by.

"Slow down," said G.

Sorry, but we have to hurry. She needs us.

Who? Who needs us?

Her...

The speed of the images slowed and quickly came into focus when the boy pointed toward the end of a darkened hallway where a small dilapidated table and chair were positioned just outside a single door. The sandy stone floor showed evidence that the path had been heavily traveled over the years. The door was solid but bore the characteristics of environmental stress and was secured by a single, rugged padlock.

Who's in there? G asked the child.

The one you seek. She needs you.

What is your name? asked G. *I don't even know your name.*

G's surroundings began to fade as the child looked up at him with concern.

Where are you going? You cannot leave! She needs you, the child pleaded.

I'm not trying to—

G awoke to an abrupt bang as the Gulfstream maneuvered through turbulence. He looked down the aisle to see Todd glance his way, once again offering a calm thumbs-up. G returned a look of irritation, tightened his seatbelt, and closed his eyes, determined to return to the dream he had been ripped from.

Hanah sensed the proximity of her firstborn and reacted by sitting straight up. Unaware at first that she was once again free of the constraints that imprisoned her physical body, she remained still, seated at the edge of her mattress, staring at the door to her cell. The dream provided fleeting sensory inputs as she struggled to gain clarity.

Ro'i, she managed, allowing her mind to project the call. *Are you there, Ro'i?*

I'm here, Momma, he answered in a whisper.

I cannot see you, Ro'i.

Don't worry, Momma. I can see you.

I can feel you, she said, closing her eyes to concentrate.

And now you can see me, he said, his voice echoing throughout her very soul.

Hanah opened her eyes to the familiar, deep-blue eyes of her firstborn less than six inches away. The sight of Ro'i stole her breath as she struggled to maintain her composure. The surprise and overwhelming emotion captivated her as she locked onto his eyes, drawn into a mesmerizing trance of love and spiritual connectivity. Her surroundings began to transform as she yielded to the sensual escape he orchestrated. Tears welled as she began to experience the changes taking place, all while never breaking her gaze from his captivating eyes.

Sweet scents filled her nostrils as a new scene developed around them. She reached up to touch his face and hesitated when he smiled.

How do you like it, Momma? he asked, referring to the scene wrapped around them.

It's lovely, Ro'i. Where are we?

We are simply, here, Momma. It is a place I designed just for you.

Hanah found herself beside a small natural pool surrounded by lush vegetation. She could make out the ocean just beyond the thicket of a palm mangrove at the base of a small hillside. The fresh salt air surrounding them was filled with the natural sounds of running water, birds singing in their territorial tongues, and the gentle wind winding its way through the trees overhead, delicately mixed with the ocean waves crashing in the distance. The scents were intoxicating. Eucalyptus, blackcurrant, and her favorite—jasmine—filled the air. The overwhelming combination was exquisite and provided just the escape she needed.

I am bringing someone to help you, he announced.

Who? Who are you bringing?

I have found someone who is connected to us. He is strong and is able to travel with me.

I don't understand, Ro'i. Who is this person?

*Shhh. Stay strong. Everything will be OK. You'll see, Momma.
Everything will be OK.*

He reached up to close her eyes, kissed her on her forehead, and
gently placed her back into a peaceful, dreamless sleep and, regrettably, back into the confines of her physical surroundings.

"Let's get some sleep," announced Todd, dimming the cabin
lights as the jet made its way across the northern Atlantic. "We've
got a big, fun-filled day tomorrow."

"Sounds like a good idea," said Ian as he reclined his plush
leather seat, draped a small blanket over his shoulders, and closed
his eyes.

Leon reached up and turned on an overhead light so he could
continue examining the contents of an open pelican case. Various
pieces and parts were randomly strewn about a small table in front
him.

"Is that one of your microbots?" asked Todd, sitting across the
aisle from him.

Leon looked up, lowered a pair of magnifying glasses from his
eyes, and smiled.

"Yup."

"Doesn't look like it's doing too well."

"Oh, it's fine. I'm just calibrating it," said Leon.

"Those things come with instructions?"

Leon smiled and pointed to his head. "Everything I need is right
in here, my friend."

"So where's the controller?" asked Todd.

Leon looked at Todd curiously.

"You know…the joystick? Where's the joystick?" asked Todd.

Leon smiled. "Well, the *controller*, or the joystick, is in my smart
phone. But it can be independently programmed inasmuch as it can
be manually controlled," explained Leon.

"So you can set it and forget it?"

"In a manner of speaking, yes," answered Leon. "But it's always a good idea to at least monitor it. We can even redirect its mission on the fly, so to speak."

"Damn thing sure is small," commented Todd.

"Oh, that's not small," answered Leon. "Now, *this* is small."

Leon pulled a pelican case the size of a cell phone from under his seat, and carefully held the open box in his hands for Todd to examine. The box contained a micro SD chip and a small device with six buttons situated next to what appeared to be a common housefly.

Todd returned a look of curiosity and skepticism. "OK, so what am I lookin' at? Oh, and I'm not sure if you see what I see, but it looks like your micro-device is *bugged*." Todd laughed.

Leon smiled. "Laugh all you want, but this system may save your life."

"Oh, so it's a 'system' and not a fly, huh? And it can save my life too? What's it gonna do, *bug* someone to death while I shoot 'em?" Todd had to stop himself from laughing in order to not wake the others.

His face registering his disapproval, Leon lowered his glasses and continued to work on the larger disassembled system. "Leave me alone, so I can finish this."

"All right, bro, just don't be up all night working on your *systems*. We're countin' on everyone to be rested and ready when we arrive in country."

"Sweet dreams, princess," answered Leon.

Avigdor looked out the window as he was driven through the narrow streets of Saint-Tropez. Agent Chevalier sat next to him in the back seat of a Range Rover SUV.

"I've arranged for you to stay in an exclusive area of the city. It is located in the center of the Saint-Tropez marina. The site is owned by someone very high in the British Petroleum Corporation who is sympathetic to your situation," explained Chevalier. "I hope you like water," he added, noting the fact that the location was a virtual island with only one point of access by land.

The Range Rover slowed as it approached an iron gate positioned beneath a brick archway connecting two adjacent buildings. The gate opened with the press of a button on the console of the vehicle, allowing access to the property. The SUV stopped in front of a large home about forty yards beyond the iron gate.

One of the officers opened the door for him, and Avigdor stepped out of the vehicle. The scent of the salt air mixed with fresh-cut grass and mature trees filled his lungs as he drew a breath and studied his surroundings. The home was too large to take in with one glance. A guard was positioned just outside the front door. The low rumble of yachts motoring past was a subtle counterpoint to the otherwise serene setting.

"This way, sir," said Chevalier, leading Avigdor to the entryway of the home.

The guard positioned at the door offered a quick glance as they walked into the residence. The inside of the home had been remodeled to include the latest modern conveniences and was a vast contrast to the early nineteenth century architectural construct of its exterior. Light filtered in through a number of windows positioned about the home.

Chevalier was leading Avigdor through the residence when the agent's cell phone rang.

"Excuse me one moment," he announced, holding up an index finger. "*Allo? Oui, c'est Agent Chevalier.*"

"Sir, there is an Agent Cohen representing the Israeli parliament, who is in country investigating the DPM case," reported the French officer.

"Yes, I am aware of her involvement. Do your best to accommodate her," said Chevalier.

"I understand, sir. The reason I'm calling is to inform you of her desire to see the girl."

"I see," said Chevalier stepping out of Avigdor's earshot and lowering his voice. "Tell her I will arrange a time for her to interview the girl tomorrow when it is more convenient."

The officer lowered his voice. "I will do my best, sir. But this agent is unlike any I've worked with in the past. She is not likely to accept—"

"Find out where she is staying. Then tell her it will be tomorrow. Insist if you must. If she has an issue with that, then I will deal with her personally. Otherwise, I will inform you of the time and place."

"Very well, sir."

Chevalier disconnected the call and returned to Avigdor who was waiting patiently in the parlor.

"My apologies. Where were we? Ah yes, you will have complete freedom to move about the home during your stay, but your primary residence will be on the yacht moored at the back of the home," he informed Avigdor, motioning for him to follow.

The sun cast its warm rays on Avigdor's face as he stepped into the backyard of the home. A single guard paused to acknowledge the men as Chevalier led Avigdor to the elegant, seventy-foot yacht moored alongside a dockside seawall.

"*Archimedes*," announced Chevalier proudly, introducing Avigdor to the yacht by name. "Your newest lodging."

"Not for very long, I hope," responded Avigdor as they boarded the yacht.

"It is better than your previous accommodations, no?"

Avigdor ignored the comment. Part of him wanted to rip the guy's head off for ignoring customary international diplomacy. The logical, more rational side of him knew there had to be an opportunity disguised among the trappings of his newest accommodations, something that would permit him to begin the search for his wife himself if he had to.

"This will do for now," he conceded.

"Very well. I will have your clothes delivered to you. Your host has graciously extended an offer for you to help yourself to anything you desire. There is food in the pantries and plenty to drink in the coolers. Unfortunately, you will not be permitted to be connected to the outside world without being monitored or supervised, and you are not permitted outside the vessel after dark, for your own safety, of course."

"Of course," responded Avigdor sarcastically.

"Please inform the guards if you need anything at all. I will keep you up to date on any progress we make in discovering the where-abouts of your wife."

"Where are you keeping my daughter?"

"She is being well cared for. She is under the protection of the French child protection serv—" answered Chevalier, but he was interrupted.

"I want to speak with her."

"I will arrange it at once. Will there be anything else?"

"How many guards do I have at my disposal?"

"None. There are four guards on the property. They are all at *my* disposal. Should you need anything at all, however, they will be sure to relay your requests," answered Chevalier as he turned and walked away. "I will be in touch. *Au revoir!*"

"Good news, madame. We have arranged for you to interview the girl first thing tomorrow," reported the Interpol officer.

"Is that the best you can do?"

"Yes, madame."

"Very well. How much longer until we arrive at the villa?"

"We are nearing the edge of the city now," responded the FBI agent.

Tzofiya watched as their drive along the winding road provided breathtaking views of the popular French Riviera vacation spots of Maleribes and Saint Bonaventure. Glimpses of the ocean randomly appeared between buildings on the north side of the road as the car navigated through the picturesque landscape. The officer turned the BMW into an exclusive area just off the main coastal road and parked inside the walls surrounding the large villa. The FBI agent showed his credentials to a French police officer who briefly challenged them at the villa entryway.

Tzofiya walked into the main entrance and stopped in the foyer. Her eyes were drawn to the winding stairway to her left. A bloodstain above the banister contrasted with the white wall at the stairway landing. She pulled a small flashlight from her pocket and drew close to the stain.

"Have you had this analyzed?" she asked the FBI agent without turning her head.

"Everything you need will be in the forensics analysis report," he confidently answered.

"I sure hope that's a 'yes.' So collection is complete then?" she asked.

"The forensics have all been collected, and the technicians are busy analyzing the evidence."

"And the scene remains as you found it?"

"Any evidence that has been collected has been identified with an appropriate marker left in its place."

"Very well," responded Tzofiya with a nod as she slowly began walking up the stairs.

The FBI agent stepped forward to follow.

"I can take it from here, thank you," she added as she slowly turned around to address the agent, now some three steps beneath her. "Why don't you leave me the keys to the car and catch a ride back with our hosts."

"I don't think—"

"It wasn't a suggestion," she interrupted, pausing for the order to sink in.

He nodded reluctantly and turned to one of the officers who tossed the keys to her.

"That'll be all, gentlemen," she said as she placed the keys in her pocket and turned to climb the stairs.

The agent glanced at the officers, rolled his eyes, and gestured for them to follow him out.

Tzofiya spent a good part of the day analyzing the scene, taking photos of things she determined to be significant, unique, or possibly overlooked in the normal course of evidence collection. While in the bedroom, she saw a forensics marker—#17—on the nightstand and checked the list she was given earlier. Number seventeen was a bottle of wine. She took a picture and made a note to follow up on the analysis of the wine that had been collected from the spot. There were other markers placed about the room that seemed appropriate or obvious to her as she continued to evaluate the scene.

The late afternoon sun began to cast shadows among the homes when Tzofiya walked out onto the balcony. Her eyes were drawn to a view of the ocean framed between two large white concrete homes beyond a stone wall surrounding the property. Her thoughts drifted for a moment as the scene provided a respite from the task at hand. She drew a deep breath of fresh salt air and forced herself to refocus.

How could such a tragedy occur in such a beautiful place? she thought.

She turned around to head back inside when she noticed a tiny object lodged in the corner of the wooden deck of the balcony. She knelt down to take a closer look, snapped a picture, and then poked her pen between the planks of the deck to retrieve the object, careful not to lose it as she manipulated it free from its position. She held it in her hand and studied the uniquely shaped rigid metal object.

Hmm, now what are you doing here? she wondered.

12

"**I** need a favor, and I need the results to be discreet," requested McEwan.

"It'll cost you," answered the young lab technician, peering over her glasses at the handsome American.

"I figured it would," answered McEwan with a smile.

They had met casually some three years earlier at a coffee shop just outside Paris, and a friendship had ensued. She had been a part-time coffeehouse waitress supplementing her income while attending college in pursuit of a chemistry degree, and he had been on his first assignment to France in support of a State Department site visit. The relationship developed over time into one of convenience and mutual aid on both a personal and professional level. They kept in touch and often connected when proximity allowed.

McEwan's assignment to Saint-Tropez had placed them as geographically close as they had ever been since they first met. She, now a full-time lab technician in Cogolin, was within an hour's drive of him, so she was delighted when he scheduled the lunch date.

"And as far as things remaining just between us…well, isn't that just how it is?" she added seductively.

"Of course…so can you run a toxicology test on a saliva sample for me and keep it anonymous?" he asked while trying to keep her focused on business.

"I can do that and *so* much more. You should press me on it sometime soon, Nate."

"I'll keep it in mind," he said, discreetly handing her the sample.

She gently grabbed his hand with both of hers and seductively accepted the sample.

"You sure you don't have anything else you'd like to give me? Do you have time for dinner later?"

"Another time perhaps," he said with a sincere smile. "You know how to get a hold of me when it's ready?"

"Indeed I do."

Satisfied she had seen everything on the second floor, Tzofiya made her way to the top of the stairs and paused to reflect on the information she had collected. Her mind played out several possible scenarios, none of which gave any credence to the DPM's involvement but *all* of which incrementally revealed the horror that Hanah must have endured.

As she descended the stairs, Tzofiya's eyes followed the blood traces on the steps and banister, each stain clearly identified with forensics evidence markers.

She stopped once again to examine the stains on the wall at the stairway landing. It was a unique mark that, at first glance, appeared to be a last attempt at resistance. Something about the mark intrigued her, however. She took another picture and wrote some notes then turned to examine the first floor.

Stepping across the foyer, she made her way into the study, her eyes constantly scanning for clues that would help provide insight to what took place the night Hanah disappeared. The room was a mess. At first glance, it appeared as if someone had been looking for something specific but didn't give a rat's ass about destroying the place in the process. Papers were strewn about, books were pulled from shelves and cast about on the floor, and very little was in its original place.

Tzofiya sat in a high-back leather chair at the desk and closed her eyes for a moment to connect with the energy of the room. When she opened her eyes, her attention was drawn to a stack of scattered papers and pages torn from books that were lying about the desk. She pushed the papers aside, randomly scanning their contents for clues, when she uncovered the end of a USB computer cable, the other end of which was connected to a nearby printer. She scanned the desk in search of a forensic evidence marker indicating the seizure of a computer, but she didn't see one.

She stood and examined the desk and the surrounding area for anything that would indicate the presence of a computer. Suddenly and with hardly a second thought, she aggressively pushed everything from the desktop onto the floor, scattering papers about. She knelt to the floor and looked under the desk. There she found what she believed to be the printer cable she had seen earlier. But what had first appeared to be a cable was in fact a power cord plugged into an electrical outlet in the floor. She unplugged the cord, placed it upon the desktop, and scribbled more notes onto a small note pad. Then she wrapped the cord tightly around itself and held onto it.

It was getting late, the sun was setting, and Tzofiya was satisfied she had what she needed to begin her analysis. An officer positioned just outside the front door of the residence greeted her as she left the residence.

"Good night, madame,"

"Good night, officer."

The officer called Agent Chevalier as the BMW left the property.

"Sir, the Israeli investigator has departed the villa. Shall I secure the building?"

Micah Bachman arrived in Marseille on the 11:15 p.m. flight. He confidently strode through the airport, gripping the handle of a small roll-aboard. A leather satchel hung at his side. Inside the satchel were papers relating to a number of cases—diplomatic files, visa applications, and clientele information. Chief among them was Avigdor Malkinson's information. Tucked neatly inside a separate pouch, beside the papers, was a laptop computer belonging to his client, absent its power cord.

After arriving home, he turned on a small lamp and placed the satchel on the floor next to the desk of his home office. Then he poured himself a drink—Scotch, neat. He placed the drink on the desk, lit a cigarette, pulled the laptop from the satchel, and sat down in a plush, leather executive chair next to an empty, soot-stained fireplace.

Staring at the black laptop computer, he took a sip of his drink and followed with a long drag on the cigarette as it hung precariously between his pursed lips. The fact that the DPM's laptop was sitting right in front of him was mind-numbing, even euphoric. It all seemed so easy, too easy in fact.

What is it that you have for me? What secrets do you hold that I can use? he thought as he continued to stare at the computer, cigarette smoke slowly escaping from the corners of his mouth.

Micah placed the cigarette into an ashtray, opened the laptop, and pressed the power button. A low-battery indicator immediately illuminated on the screen. He searched the satchel frantically for the power cord but found only the bulk of legal paperwork it contained. He opened his carry-on bag and aggressively pulled everything out, trying feverishly to remember where he had placed the cord, to no avail.

He needed the power cord. And he needed that *specific* power cord. The key-logger device attached to it was the only source that would reveal a history of key strokes that could provide the password he needed to gain access and provide insight on any activity that would be useful to him. The pressure mounted as he had little time, low power, and no clue how to access the device. He tried several obvious passwords—each attempt resulting in denial. So close…

"*Allo?*" answered the obscure voice on the receiving end of the call.

"I have a laptop computer with no power cord."

"What…who is this?" responded a groggy, tired voice.

"If I have no power cord, I have no way of deciphering any information whatsoever," said Micah in a stern voice.

"Do you have any idea what time it is?"

"Of course—it's time for you to deliver that damn power cord," demanded Micah.

"You asked for the laptop. The laptop is *exactly* what was delivered. It was difficult enough for me to get the computer out of the residence without getting caught."

"You idiot! Did you not place a keystroke device onto the power cord? Did I hire an imbecile?" shouted Micah.

"No, sir, I will retrieve it first thing tom—"

"You will retrieve it *now!*" he demanded.

"But it's the middle of the night—"

"Precisely why you should go now, before anyone else discovers it."

There was a short pause on the receiving end of the line, followed by an audible sigh. "And just how am I supposed to get in? The place is a secure crime scene now, complete with armed guards."

"It didn't stop you last time," answered Micah.

"So what do you expect me to do, walk right through the front door?"

"Figure it out. If this has suddenly become too difficult for you, then perhaps I should look elsewhere for *competent* assistance. Have you forgotten the long-term benefits of our deal?"

"No, sir. I'll see what I can do."

"Call me the moment you have it," instructed Micah, abruptly hanging up the phone.

Micah took a sip of his drink, placed the cigarette in his mouth, and gently closed the laptop.

Hanah awoke to the sound of the opening door. Stealing a startled breath while trying to quickly awaken from her restless sleep, she watched as a large silhouette of a man slowly approached in the dead of the night.

"Please, no, not again," she pleaded, her voice trembling.

"Shhh, it is OK. I brought you something new to wear," he assured her.

Hanah watched as the face of her savior came into view, his rare blue eyes projecting compassion as he approached her. Her eyes followed him as he carefully unlocked the shackles binding her wrists. He placed a white linen tunic at her side. The tunic was embroidered with a subtle, white kurta appliqué.

"The garment I promised," he whispered as he offered a subtle gesture for her to pick it up. "I also brought you some water."

Hanah stared into his eyes while rubbing her wrists. Unsure of just what to make of his kindness, she offered a hint of a skeptical smile and accepted the water. She quickly consumed the water and then grabbed the tunic and lifted it to her nose. The fresh scent of linen greeted her as she temporarily lost herself in the feel of the new material against her face. Then she looked at her strange benefactor expectantly.

"Oh, my apologies," he said, turning his back to her. "Please let me know when you are finished."

Hanah quickly removed her torn shirt, placed the new garment over her head, and slipped it on. Despite the circumstances, it felt good to be wearing something new. She cleared her throat as a subtle gesture that she had finished getting dressed.

Munahid slowly turned around, hesitating only slightly, and offered a sincere smile when he saw her wearing the shirt.

"It is a good fit?" he asked.

Hanah nodded her head as she timidly looked up at him.

"I must return you to your restraints," he said apologetically. "Please," he added indicating she should comply.

Hanah did as she was asked and extended her arms above her head, reluctantly allowing herself to be bound once again to the tethered chains. The pace of her heartbeat quickened as she heard someone outside the door. She and Munahid looked at each other and paused.

"What is your name," she whispered.

"I am Munahid," he whispered.

"The strong one," Hanah translated.

Munahid smiled curiously. "You know this translation?"

"I do now," she answered.

13

"Whatcha got there?" asked G on his way through the cabin.

"It's a microbot," answered Leon, purposely offering only a short answer to his new teammate.

G nodded. "I've read about those in *Popular Science*. I've never seen one up close and personal. Would you mind?" he asked.

"Certainly," said Leon handing the tiny craft to G.

"Pretty light. Looks *exactly* like a dragonfly."

Leon nodded. "The bulk of the weight is behind the eyes. It's actually a hi-def camera."

"No shit?"

"No shit. Here, lemme show you," said Leon as he typed a few commands into his smart phone and traded the device for the tiny drone G was holding.

G watched the smart-phone screen come to life with the images captured by the camera embedded within the tiny machine. Leon manipulated the craft to project a moving image of G holding the smart device as he watched himself on the tiny screen.

"Impressive," G admitted. "You design these things?"

"Yeah."

"Listen, we haven't had the time to actually get to know each other. You got a few minutes?" asked G, handing the smart phone back to Leon.

Leon chuckled. "I'm not going anywhere…unless you want to take that literally. In which case I'm headed somewhere *really* fast over the Atlantic."

"You're an intellectual. I like that," said G. "In fact, Todd told me you'd challenge us *all* to think deeper."

Leon smiled. "What else did Todd tell you?"

"He told me you'd be the most likely to accept my—shall we say—*unconventional* role on the team."

"So just what *is* your role, G?"

"I see things. Most often from the inside out, sort of like you do."

"So you're an analyst," Leon surmised.

"Yeah, but it's deeper than that actually."

Leon listened intently as G explained the details of his unconventional gifts.

"So you see, Leon, my insight is a lot like those drones you've created. They open the aperture of perspective for us *all* to make better decisions."

"This is all too much for the conscious mind to comprehend," admitted Leon.

"Let me ask you, Leon. Do you dream?"

"Don't we all?"

"I believe we do," nodded G, agreeably. "I want you to try something if you're open to it."

"Sure."

"I want you to close your eyes and try to remember the last thing you did consciously before I walked up to you."

"OK," said Leon, smiling as he closed his eyes. "I had just finished calibrating the dragonfly when you walked by..." he said, his voice trailing off as he thought more about what had really happened.

"No, Leon," G responded calmly. "I never walked by anyone. In fact, if you look toward the back of the plane, you'll see that I'm actually still sound asleep in my seat."

Leon opened his eyes and offered G a look of confused fascination. As he stood to look toward the back of the plane, his alter-conscious body separated from his conscious body, now slumped over, fast asleep in his seat. G picked up on Leon's confusion and tried to reassure him.

"It's OK. Don't fight it or attempt to overanalyze it."

"Or else?" asked Leon cautiously.

"Or else you could simply wake up and miss the experience."

"This is freaky weird," said Leon.

"Now that you realize you're not constrained by the limits of your conscious mind, tell me what you see," said G.

"I…see things I've never truly appreciated seeing. In fact, I've *always* seen them. I just never knew this could be so—"

"Real?"

"Yeah, real. So is *this* real?"

"I've learned that reality is relative to and among itself. So what's real to you is, in fact, reality. Embrace it," G offered in a calm whisper.

Leon awoke to a cabin alert tone initiated by the pilot, indicating their proximity to the destination. He lifted the window visor to catch a subdued orange light cresting over the horizon, an introduction to a new day. The landscape below crawled slowly beneath them on this last stretch of their journey. As he watched the expanse of land creep by, he recalled remnants of his dream and glanced over the seat to the back of the plane where G slumbered.

"Reveille, gentlemen. We're a little over an hour out from our destination. Would one of you be kind enough to bring me a cup of hot coffee when you get a chance? Straight black, please" called Monty over the intercom.

"Guess we're gonna have to physically wake *some* people," said Leon to Todd, insinuating that G needed further prodding.

"Trust me—you don't wanna do that," warned Todd.

Tzofiya called the front desk to have her car pulled around to the front of the hotel.

"Your car is waiting, madame."

"But I didn't ask—"

"There is an Interpol agent in the lobby waiting for you. He informed us you would be on your way down soon," responded the desk clerk, second-guessing his assumptions.

"How long has he been here?"

"About thirty minutes, madame."

"Very well. I will be along in a few minutes."

Agent Chevalier spotted Tzofiya as she made her way through the lobby.

"Bonjour, madame. How are the accommodations?"

"Bonjour. Agent Chevalier, I assume?"

"My sincere apologies for the lack of formal introductions," he said, his hand extended. "Agent Claude Chevalier, at your service, madame."

"I wasn't informed we would be meeting this morning," said Tzofiya offering the agent a firm handshake.

"I hope you do not mind. I took it upon myself to accompany you today. I avail myself to you as needed," he responded with a smile.

"That's fine. What time do you have me scheduled to meet the girl? Oh, and has the American secret-service team arrived yet?"

"We are scheduled to meet the girl at two o'clock. Is that acceptable?"

"Yes. And the Americans?"

"Assuming they are on time—"

Tzofiya returned a questioning glance.

"*Un moment, s'il vous plaît,*" he interrupted himself, unwittingly responding in his native tongue while pulling his cell phone from his coat pocket. Clearing his throat, he spoke into the phone in English. "Yes, this is Agent Chevalier with Interpol. I'm calling to inquire on the arrival estimate of the US secret-service flight. Yes…I see. *Merci.*"

"They are scheduled to arrive at La Mole in just over two hours," said Agent Chevalier.

"Perfect. Take me to meet them. I need to make a stop by the villa first, though. There are just a couple things I need to verify."

"Of course," said Chevalier.

"*Allo*?" he said, using his best French accent.

"Wow, you *are* getting good, Nate. Blending in well, I see. But you know I'll always be able to tell it's you," she flirted.

McEwan suppressed the smile he wanted to enjoy, but he was with an FBI agent and an Interpol supervisor.

"I think you owe me a date," she said, her sultry voice demanding his undivided attention.

Nate excused himself from his company and walked to a more secluded area where he could talk.

"Do you have the results?" he asked.

"Nate, my sweet Nate, is that any way to greet the woman of your *deepest desires*?"

He smiled when he realized how poorly he was handling the call. "I'm sorry. It *is* really good to hear from you. To what do I owe the *absolute* pleasure of this call?" he asked humbly.

"That's better, Nate McEwan. Yes, I have the results of your request. Ran it through as a routine lab test, hence the reason it took as long as it did. But it was the best way to keep it from inquiring eyes, if you know what I mean. Now, I was thinking, if you take me to dinner first, I'll wear that black dress you like…the one with the low-cut scoop neck you just can't keep your eyes off of."

"OK, I see you're going to make me work for this. The results of the test must be worth taking you to dinner—"

"No, Nate, results or no results, I can assure you, *I'm* worth it. Besides, you already know that. The question is, would you like the results now, or do you prefer to wait until you can coax it out of me?"

"As appealing as that sounds, I could really use the results now if you have them," he said, trying not to beg.

"OK, Nate," she conceded. "The sample you provided had small traces of zolpidem present. So if you're trying to bust somebody on drug charges, you're pretty much out of luck."

"No, it's not that at all. So what's zolpidem?"

"It's the active ingredient in Ambien. A single dose typically does the trick for a good six to eight hours of sleep. Now, about that dinner date…"

Hanah awoke to stifling heat and the sound of voices just outside her cell. Daylight filtered in through a small opening in a high corner of the room. She could hear the Islamic daily call to prayer—the *azan*—echoing outside the walls.

The loudspeakers outside went silent, offering a moment of peace that was suddenly interrupted when the door to the room burst open. Two men approached and removed her wrist restraints. A third obscured figure stood off to the side and quietly observed. One of the men commented in Arabic on Hanah's new shirt. She almost answered them but wanted to keep the secret of her knowledge of the foreign language to herself, so she remained silent, eyes lowered to the floor.

"They are puzzled by your new garment," commented the dark figure, now approaching.

The female voice took Hanah by surprise. She looked up into the eyes—the only part she could see—of a woman dressed in a black abaya and niqab, traditional conservative garment and head covering for local women.

"They want to know who gave you the new shirt. It's OK. You can tell them."

Hanah gave them a reticent glance then lowered her gaze to the floor and slowly shook her head.

"You do not know his name? Then you must describe him," said the woman. "I cannot help you if you don't say *something*."

The last thing Hanah wanted to do was to compromise the delicate connection she felt she had begun to establish with Munahid. This was no way to repay the kindness he had shown toward her in one of her most harrowing moments.

Hanah's heartbeat raced as she slowly raised her head and answered, "Bashir."

The two men looked at each other with surprise when they heard the familiar name of the doctor.

"Lisa, what can you tell me about Agent Weston that his 201 file doesn't?" asked Harriman.

"I know he was an unconventional hire—personal acquisition of the previous director, and that it had something to do with a highly classified scientific R&D project," said Lisa. "The file is intentionally vague and heavily redacted because of the nature of the operative's rare specialty."

"And you know this how?"

"Well, for starters, I have the same clearance level you do. And I've been here awhile. You do enough time inside these walls, they begin to talk. I'm a good listener."

"Where can I find more information?"

"Doubtful anyone would talk about him. You know how well we're trained to deny. Suffice it to say, however, it's a good thing he's on our side."

"You're alluding to something. What is it?"

"Just that you should trust your instincts—and your operatives."

"Can I at least assume his teammates have a good handle on his relevance to the operation?"

"Someone once told me—actually *a lot* of people around here tell me—never to *assume* anything. So, sir, with all due respect, you can rest assured that the team is comfortable with Agent Weston's capabilities and his role, or they wouldn't have recruited him for the op. The way I see it, the only one with any trepidation is you—once again, with all due respect. And I suspect that's only because the information you have is limited."

Paul sat listening to Lisa's wise perspective.

"I can say with a fair amount of certainty that Agent Jordan knows him best. I also know G—uh, Agent Weston—and Ian Wolfe worked together in the past, but I'd venture to say that no one really *fully* understands Weston's capabilities," said Lisa.

"So I have four operatives, each of whom are highly capable—three of whom have a fairly decent amount of background disclosure, and one I know almost nothing about beyond the details of his former life as a psychologist," Harriman summarized in a rhetorical statement.

"I'd say that about sums it up, with one caveat," said Lisa with an unsolicited response.

"What's that?"

"Without Weston, our chances of a successful outcome decrease significantly. He has an uncanny ability to see things most people miss. I'm not sure how he does it—that's the classified part—but I hear he's a real rock star. Completely shook up the psy-ops division when he first arrived. The walls still echo with the things he did and the lives he saved," she said.

14

"OK, gents, keep in mind we represent the personal interests of the president of the United States. Put on your game faces. This may call for a little more arrogance than you're used to. If you feel like you're laying it on kinda thick, then you're doin' it right," instructed Ian as the Gulfstream approached the VIP parking spot.

"Sounds like the voice of experience," murmured Todd to Leon. "By the way, you look *good*."

Leon smiled and put on a pair of Ray-Ban Predator sunglasses. "How 'bout now?" he asked.

Todd smiled and followed with a wink. "Even better."

Monty cut the power to the engines as Todd opened the portside door and lowered the stairs.

One by one the men deplaned onto the tarmac, each impeccably dressed in a dark suit and tie, sporting trademark sunglasses—mostly for effect but also against the intense French early morning sun. Ian emerged first, followed by Leon, then Todd.

"Where's G?" asked Ian.

"Not my turn to watch him," quipped Todd.

"Last I knew, he was still getting dressed," offered Leon.

The doors to the terminal slid open and three men walked toward the team. An outside observer would've easily confused the meeting as the beginning of a men's designer-suit conference. A light breeze blew the ties of all the men as each dealt with the small annoyance in his own way, some folding them into their jackets while others simply ignored the wind altogether. The three men greeted the team at planeside as they waited for G.

"Gentlemen, welcome to the French Riviera. I am Agent Claude Chevalier, with Interpol. This is Officer Dumont and Officer Pierre of the French National Police."

"Pleased to meet you," said Ian. He followed up with an introduction of the team.

"I was told to expect four members of your team," Chevalier commented.

"There *are* four of us—" responded Ian as he was interrupted by a distracting glance from Todd.

G emerged from the plane wearing an open-collar white button-down shirt, black sport coat, and matching tailor-made slacks, all finished off with Calvin Kline Barker Black leather boots. The wind whipped his thick dark hair and occasionally pushed the hem of his coat open to reveal the black-leather shoulder harness of his holster securing his Kimber Stainless II Pro .45 1911 handgun.

"Our fourth, Agent Weston," announced Ian to Chevalier.

Chevalier smiled and extended his hand as G approached. "Pleased to meet you, Agent Weston."

"Likewise, sir."

"Nice work, G," commented Todd discreetly. "You do that on purpose?"

"I do everything on purpose, TJ."

"Agent Wolfe, my men will assist your pilot in transferring your baggage to the vehicle. While we wait, would you and your team have a moment to meet the Israeli investigator?"

"She's here now?" questioned Ian.

"Yes. She has requested a short meeting and is waiting in the terminal," he answered, gesturing for the team to make their way to the terminal building.

Todd adjusted his posture when he heard they would be meeting Tzofiya.

"Settle down, big guy..." said G quietly as he casually walked by.

Tzofiya watched the arrival of the American team through the window of a small office inside the airport. She studied the personal interaction of the team with Agent Chevalier and quietly observed the body language of each man while she conducted an initial assessment of the team dynamics from a distance. She couldn't help but notice the difference of the last agent to emerge from the plane and how he stood apart from the others in mannerism and appearance.

She continued to gaze out the window even after she lost sight of the team as they entered the building. She slowly turned her head when she heard a knock and Agent Chevalier opening the door.

"Gentlemen, this is Agent Cohen, investigative agent of the Israeli parliament."

Ian was the first to greet Tzofiya, asserting himself as the team leader while the others waited to be introduced. He hesitated when he looked into Tzofiya's captivating green eyes until her firm handshake brought him back to reality. He introduced each of the members of the team.

"Hello, ma'am, I'm Special Agent Lambert," said Leon with a smile and a handshake.

Todd approached, removing the glasses still covering his eyes. "Pleased to meet you, Agent Cohen, I'm Special Agent Jordan," he said, offering his signature smile. Tzofiya politely returned the smile and immediately looked past him toward G.

"And you are?" she asked, slowly approaching G, her hand extended.

"Special Agent Weston...G Weston."

"Pleased to meet you, Agent Weston," she said, extending her hand.

G reached for her hand. Time slowed as he looked into her eyes while taking a slow deep breath. As their hands connected, G's mind stepped past the beauty and the façade of her tough exterior and right into a myriad of Tzofiya's innermost thoughts and experiences. The speed at which the images fired away provided a glimpse into the fullness of her life, the depth of her intellect, and diversity of her experience.

Attack drills, military experience, scholastic settings, father figures, political leaders, personal desires, dislikes, covert—

He disengaged when he felt he had begun to go too far. She returned a curious smile of subtle intrigue. It was the first time she could ever recall any kind of distracted hesitation on her part. She smoothly recovered with a request of their French host.

"Agent Chevalier, would you be so kind as to give us a moment?" she asked.

"Of course," he said, turning to walk out the door.

Siraj had received information from an informant that discord had erupted among those watching over Hanah and that she had been assaulted.

"You cannot trust them. They're a bunch of animals. And one of them has softened and has become sympathetic to her," said the informant.

"I'm not too concerned about sympathizers. They are easy to identify and even easier to deal with," said Siraj calmly.

"Indeed. Then perhaps you will be more interested to know that the Americans are now involved in looking for the woman."

"You know this how?" asked Siraj.

"The American press is reporting it as *leaked information* from 'sources' inside Washington."

Siraj contacted the elder holding Hanah, risking an intercept of the short call.

"If you cannot control your team, then I will have no choice but to replace you with someone who can," he said. "I have placed a great deal of trust and responsibility in your hands. Do not allow this to get away from you."

The elder listened as if his life depended upon getting it right from now on.

"Take the woman to location number six. Notify me when the move is complete," instructed Siraj and then abruptly terminated the call.

The leader hung up the phone and angrily summoned one of his lieutenants.

"Prepare to move the Jew. And assemble the team. We have some business to take care of before we transfer her," he instructed.

"Gentlemen, I hope you'll excuse the unannounced meeting. Time is *not* on our side. If we are to have any hope of finding Hanah Malkinson alive, I need to know if you are prepared to act decisively," announced Tzofiya in her first meeting with the American team.

"That's why we're here," said Ian. "We're hoping to find any information along the way that'll lessen the pressure on the DPM's culpability."

"To be honest, I could give a *shit* about his culpability at this point," Tzofiya confided bluntly. "Because, in the end, the fact still remains that we have a missing woman on our hands. Don't get me wrong—I actually like DPM Malkinson. But my mission is to discover clues that'll lead us to his wife. In the end, culpability will come to rest where it belongs. And it'll be up to the authorities to react appropriately."

"I like this woman already," said Todd.

"Let's get one thing straight up front," said Tzofiya shooting a glance at Todd. "I may be a woman, but I can stand toe-to-toe with the best of you, so—"

"Whoa, settle down. I didn't mean nuthin' by what I said. It was actually a compliment," Todd defended. "We Americans sometimes use humor and sarcasm to extend a compliment."

"I'm not sure just what kind of women you're used to working with. I just want to make it clear that I don't expect to be treated differently because of my gender."

"Understood. I think we can all appreciate that," said Ian. "So how can we help you?"

"Thank you for asking. OK, here's what I am thinking..."

Micah awoke to a ringing telephone. He glanced at his watch and realized he was almost an hour behind his routine schedule. The tension in his head reminded him of the hazards of drinking too much Scotch at his age.

"Sir, there's an Agent Cohen here from the Israeli parliament. She is said to be in country at the personal behest of the prime minister himself."

"Thank you for the report. I've been expecting her, actually. She is most likely a Mossad agent," replied Micah. "Has she requested to meet with Malkinson?"

"Yes, as well as his daughter. I hear Agent Chevalier has arranged for both meetings to take place today. And sir, the US secret service is also in-country."

Micah paused to reflect on whether the team's presence posed any potential problems for him and also to allow his mind time to process coherent thoughts.

"Very well. I see no issues with the secret service, but keep an eye on the woman. I will return to the area later this evening," said Micah. "Were you able to find the power cord?"

"No. I'm on my way to the villa to—"

"So you ignored the instructions I gave you last night to go right away?"

"I have most everything I need in terms of evidence from the villa—" said Tzofiya.

"The crime scene?" queried Ian sharply.

"Yes, the *crime scene*. You and your team should get settled in and begin at once to gather the information *you* need. You've been cleared to enter the villa to conduct your own assessment. I'm nearly finished with my analysis and will be ready to discuss my findings with you soon. We can reconvene in the morning to compare notes and formulate a plan of action based on what we've collected," offered Tzofiya. "We'll need a secure place to discuss our findings. I'm not convinced the French will provide a room they haven't rigged with a listening device—" said Tzofiya as Leon cut her short.

"You don't have to worry about that. If the room is bugged, I'll find it. And I can neutralize anything I find," he said.

"Good."

"I'll need to talk with the DPM," said G, "and his daughter too, if she's available."

"I'm scheduled to meet the girl today," said Tzofiya. "Would you care to join me?"

G nodded and glanced at Ian who returned a short nod of approval.

"Let's all meet up in the hotel lobby at 0700," said Ian. "Leon, let Agent Chevalier know we're ready to depart."

Agent Chevalier returned to the room with Leon and one of the police officers.

"Gentlemen, Officer Dumont will take you to your hotel. There are cars at the hotel available for your use. Just check with the reception desk, and they will accommodate you," explained Chevalier. "Madame, are you ready for your next appointment?"

"I am. Agent Weston will be accompanying us," she said.

"Very well," said Chevalier, holding the door open for the agents.

As they were walking toward the exit, someone called out from a short distance down the corridor.

"*Excusez-moi, madame?*" called the middle-aged man. "Agent Cohen?" he asked to be sure.

Tzofiya stopped and turned and immediately recognized the airport manager approaching. He had a folder in his hands. G and the two men stood by and watched as the man did his best to communicate in broken English in his thick French accent.

"Here is the information you had requested, madame. Seven days of flight logs to include aircraft type, registry, origin, and destination. It is incomplete but I am hopeful it will provide the information you need."

Tzofiya accepted the thick folder and commended the man for his diligence. He smiled as she turned and walked away.

"Looks like I've got some homework to do," she said, mostly to herself.

"Why don't you let me give that to someone who can crunch the numbers and pull out the details you're looking for?" offered G.

"And who would that be?" she asked.

G paused a beat. "Look lady, we brought in a *hell* of a lot of capability to help you. You're gonna to have to trust us and delegate some of the workload."

"You're right," she conceded as she handed the folder to him.

"I'll be right back. Don't leave without me," he said to Tzofiya. "Leon, wait up," shouted G as he walked toward his fellow agent.

15

G climbed into the back of the BMW and took a seat behind the driver so he could better communicate with Tzofiya, now seated in the front beside the French agent. Chevalier called ahead to notify the custodian they were on their way to see the girl.

Tzofiya offered some surface level information about Rina to G, some of which he knew from preliminary briefings conducted by the agency.

"We're not certain whether she was a witness to anything," explained Tzofiya. "She's nine years old, so we expect *some* details will emerge telling us whether she saw anything at all. Her father tried to explain that she was hiding when he found her. So she may have been unable to see much. Either way, we should be sensitive to any trauma she may have experienced. If there's anything to discover, I'll be able to coax it out of her. Young girls seem to relate to me well," she boasted.

G nodded as he listened, all the while trying to predict what his own reaction would be to seeing the girl outside of his dream for the first time. And what, if any, would her reaction be to him?

Chevalier turned east onto Route 98A and drove into picturesque Maleribes. The car approached a gate where Chevalier stopped long enough for the residents to confirm his identity via a remote camera. A moment later, the gate opened.

Chevalier rang the doorbell and then turned to Tzofiya and G. "Please remember to be sensitive to the girl's feelings. We have no idea what she's been through."

A well-dressed woman in her sixties answered the door.

"*Bonjour, madame. Je suis Agent Chevalier—*"

"*Bonjour.* I am well aware of who you are, Agent Chevalier. I have seen you several times on the news. Please come in," she said.

"*Merci.* These are Agents Cohen and Weston. They are assisting in the investigation."

"Pleased to meet you," she said, leading them to the living room. "May I get you something to drink?"

"Nothing for me," answered Tzofiya. Chevalier and G politely declined as well.

"Very well," she answered, pausing for an uncomfortable moment. "Please have a seat while I get Rina for you."

The woman returned a few moments later with the girl by her side. The agents stood out of respect for the hostess and her guest.

"Rina, these are Agents Chevalier, Cohen, and Weston. They are here to help and would like to speak with you for a few minutes," said the woman.

Rina looked at each of the agents as she was introduced but paused and returned a look of curiosity when her eyes met G's. The other agents took note of the subtle change in her demeanor as she seemed to become momentarily lost in thought. Tzofiya watched the connection take place between the two and allowed the process to take its own course. The girl seemed to be curious about G for some reason. Tzofiya rationalized it as an aversion to men, confirming her assumption that the young girl would most likely relate better to her anyway.

"I will be in the kitchen if you need anything at all," said the woman, her announcement interrupting the silence.

Tzofiya invited Rina to join them. The girl chose one of two single chairs positioned next to a small couch in the center of the room. Agent Chevalier sat in the chair next to her while Tzofiya and G took seats on the couch.

"So, Rina, why don't you start off by telling us how old you are," suggested Tzofiya.

"I'm almost ten years old," she said, tucking her foot under her leg to get more comfortable.

Tzofiya saw her response as a good sign and smiled. "Almost ten, you say? Well, I must say that you're certainly tall for your age. I thought perhaps you were *already* ten."

Rina smiled.

"And how is everything going here in this house for you? Do you have everything you need?" asked Tzofiya.

"It's fine, I guess. I miss my mom and dad. Will I be able to see them soon?"

Tzofiya glanced at Chevalier and back to the girl. "We're doing everything we can, Rina. One of the reasons we're here is to see if you can help us. We'd like to ask you some questions about what you may have seen the night your mother disappeared from your vacation villa. Do you think you can help us?"

Rina looked at floor and reluctantly answered, "Yes."

"OK, I need you to take us back to the night your mother disappeared. Specifically where were you in the villa at the time?"

"I was sleeping in the bedroom upstairs, across the corridor from my parents' room," she said, still staring at the floor.

"Were you awakened by something, a noise of some kind?"

"Yes. I heard the shower and had started to fall back asleep when I heard my mother yell out. It was more of a scream, actually. It scared me," she said.

"OK, and what happened next?"

"I heard something break, like glass maybe. Then I heard a lot of bumping on the walls and some voices."

"You heard voices? Were they familiar voices? Were they the voices of your mom or dad?"

Rina shook her head no.

Chevalier scribbled an occasional note on a small note pad. "Then what happened?"

"I sat up in my bed to listen closer because the voices got quiet. Then I saw flashlights shining in the hallway, so I got out of bed and hid on the floor."

"Did the flashlights shine into your room?"

"Yes."

"Did anyone come into your room?"

"Yes, a man."

"Did you recognize the man? Was he one of the security guards?"

"I don't know. I hid under a blanket in the corner of the room. I could see his light through the blanket. And I saw his shoes. Then I heard someone say '*yallah*.'"

"You heard someone say 'yallah'? Then did the man leave your room?"

"Yes."

Chevalier whispered to Tzofiya, "What is 'yallah'?"

"It is Arabic for 'let's go.'"

"You mentioned you saw his shoes," said Chevalier. "Can you describe the shoes?"

"They were black boots, sort of like hiking boots."

Chevalier made a note of her description.

"Did you remain hidden until they left the villa?" asked Tzofiya.

"No. I heard them going downstairs, so I followed them."

"You followed them?" asked Tzofiya, somewhat surprised by the girl's bravery.

"Yes. I came out of my room and stopped at the top of the stairs and saw the men carrying my mother," she said, tears welling up in her eyes. "I thought maybe she was hurt. She was crying…"

"It's OK, Rina. Take your time," consoled Tzofiya. "How many men did you see?"

"I don't know. It was dark—two, maybe three men."

"You're doing so very well, Rina. What happened next?" asked Tzofiya.

"The men stopped when they reached the bottom of the stairs. One of them shone a light back up near me, so I ducked really low. I thought they saw me, but I guess they didn't. When I saw the light was gone I looked up and saw they had opened the front door."

"So the men took your mother out the front door?"

"Yes, I think she saw me."

"You think your mother saw you?"

Rina nodded. "Yes, I think she saw me, but she didn't say anything. It was the last time I saw her," she said, tears welling in her eyes.

"You're a brave young woman, Rina. Thank you for the details," said Tzofiya.

"Rina," said G calmly, "how did you end up in the closet in the office?"

Tzofiya was intrigued at the detailed nature of G's question but allowed it to play out without interrupting.

"The men left the front door open after they left, so I crept down the stairs to see if I could see where they were taking my mother. I knew something wasn't right, so I thought maybe I could find my father or one of the security guards. I heard voices outside the open door, so I stood where they couldn't see me. Then I heard someone say something about *me*."

"What did they say about you?" asked Tzofiya.

"They said, 'Go find the girl.'"

"Did you recognize the voice? How did you react?" asked Tzofiya.

"No. I saw flashlights coming through the doorway, so I ran as fast as I could to the office. I hid under the desk at first. That's when I saw two men. One of them went upstairs while the other one waited near the front door."

"I'm curious, young lady. How could you see from under the desk?" asked Chevalier.

"There's a small opening between the side pieces and the top. I found it once when I was hiding from my father during a game of hide-and-seek. It's the best hiding spot because you can see when someone is looking for you."

"I seem to recall being able to see that when I was looking under the desk," offered Tzofiya. "Please, go on, Rina."

"I watched the one man standing near the front door while he waited for the other man who was upstairs."

"Would you recognize the man if you were to see him again?"

Rina nodded. "I think so. He was scary. Sometimes I see him in my dreams," she said.

"Can you describe him for me?" asked Tzofiya.

"He was big and had a beard and a tattoo. And he didn't look happy," she explained.

"What was the tattoo, Rina? Was it a picture of some kind?" asked Tzofiya.

"I don't really know. It looked like a spider. I'm not sure. It was dark," she said.

"Where was it located on the man, his forearm, like here or his hand?" asked Chevalier.

G sat quietly listening to the dialogue as he mentally evaluated the circumstances and the questions posed by the agents and the answers provided by the brave, young girl.

"I think it was on his hand, no, his wrist, like right about here," she said, pointing to her own wrist.

"Why did you go from the desk to the closet?" asked G.

"The man in the doorway—he had a gun. While he was waiting for the other man he flashed his light into the office. I thought he would come in and find me. So when it was dark again I ran to the closet and hid under my father's jacket. My feet were uncovered so I slipped them into a pair of his shoes and sat very still."

Tzofiya raised her eyebrows at the girl's ability to be creative under pressure.

"I got real scared when I heard someone come into the office. He was making a lot of noise. I heard things falling on the floor and papers being thrown around. I held my breath when the closet door opened and saw a light flashing inside. Then I heard the other man call out to him."

"Is that when he left?" asked Chevalier.

"I think so," she nodded. "I heard another man call out to him. Then I heard the front door close, but I wasn't sure they had left, and I didn't want to be found, so I stayed in the closet. It was quiet for a long time after that. Then I heard another noise."

"What sort of noise?" asked Tzofiya.

"It was a noise that came from above me. I tried to ignore it by thinking about my mother. Then I heard the front door open, and I was so scared that I may have cried out loud because that's when... that's when I was found," she said, slowly raising her gaze from the floor and looking directly into G's eyes.

Tzofiya watched as the girl connected once again with G. "So that's when your father found you?" she asked.

There was a silence.

"Rina?" said Tzofiya, pressing for a response.

"I think there have been enough questions for today," said the woman, surprising the group by her sudden presence. "You are welcome to return at another time perhaps. Rina, say good-bye."

The agents stood. Tzofiya extended her hand to the girl and thanked her. "You did a really good job today, Rina. You're a brave young lady," she said. "I may come back to talk with you again, if that's OK with you."

Rina smiled. "I'd like to see my father. Can you help me?" she asked.

"I will see what we can do to arrange that as soon as possible," answered Tzofiya, glancing at Chevalier.

Rina stopped in front of G, paused to look up at him, and extended her hand. "Will you tell my father I miss him?"

G nodded and smiled as he reached out to accept her hand. "Of course," he answered.

When their hands met, G's mind was drawn into a tornadic, first-hand perspective of Rina's experience the night of her mother's disappearance. He was unprepared for the overwhelming emotion of it all and found himself reacting by slowly dropping to one knee before her, staring into her eyes. Images flashed in his mind at speeds he was fast becoming used to as he mentally processed and stored them all. He made sure to note one of the images he was most curious about when it came into view—the tattoo Rina had noticed and described as a spider. To be sure, he would have to further evaluate the memory. For now, however, he knew he had captured that and so much more from her brave, descriptive account and the psychological glimpse she somehow knew he needed to help her mother.

Rina leaned forward and put her arms around G's neck.

"I believe in you," she whispered.

16

Tzofiya sat in the front seat of the car, lost in thought, quietly contemplating the information gained from her visit with Rina and the bizarre display of familiarity between G and the girl. The interview was productive. They had walked away with a great deal of information they could use to help determine Hanah's whereabouts through Rina's first-hand account and description of her mother's captors. The interaction between Rina and G left Tzofiya with more questions than answers, however. But now was not the time to confront G on the details of his exchange with the girl—not now—with Agent Chevalier present. Tzofiya was hopeful the next interview with Avigdor would prove even more useful as she would use her experience and intuition to determine his culpability as well as to discover any information that would lead to Hanah's whereabouts.

G watched the scenic landscape of the French Riviera pass by as they made their way to the temporary residence of Avigdor Malkinson. He used the time to pull the image of the tattoo to the forefront of his mind to determine if he could get a better idea of the elements, their meaning, and most importantly, the identity of its wearer, but the image was frustratingly unclear.

Chevalier parked the car in front of the large residence, the electronic gate slowly closing behind them. Tzofiya and G both surveyed the area, each assessing the security vulnerabilities and the conditions of Avigdor's sequestration.

"This way, *s'il vous plaît*," said Chevalier.

The agents made their way through the residence and into the backyard where the *Archimedes* was moored alongside the seawall. Tzofiya glanced at G and then back at the yacht.

"You're keeping him on a boat?" she asked.

"Yes. I must admit it is a bit unorthodox, but we feel it offers the best in modern accommodations and certain protection flexibilities," offered Chevalier.

"I can understand the accommodations, but I'm not sure I agree with the protective part of your assertion," she argued.

The remnants of G's recent dream aboard the *Pair-O-Docs* flooded his mind as the two boats looked eerily similar. Images from that dream flashed through his mind as he thought of the murder he had witnessed firsthand.

Chevalier smiled and politely chose not to debate the issue. He extended a cursory greeting to a plainclothes guard near the gangplank and led the agents aboard the *Archimedes*.

Avigdor entered the main salon from an adjacent stateroom when he heard the guests arrive. He recognized Tzofiya but didn't reveal his familiarity with the Israeli agent.

"Deputy Prime Minister Malkinson, these are Agents Cohen and Weston. They are here to assist in the investigation," said Chevalier.

Avigdor acknowledged each agent but remained silent.

"May we be seated?" asked Chevalier.

"Actually, Agent Chevalier," said Tzofiya, "we would prefer to spend some time alone with the DPM if you would be so kind."

"Certainly," said Chevalier. He extended a courteous nod and walked out of the room, leaving the agents alone for the first time with the deputy prime minister.

"Sir, we won't take a lot of your time—" said Tzofiya.

"Are you serious, Agent Cohen?" Avigdor interrupted. "I have all the time in the world, but my wife does not. What are you doing to find her?"

G remained silent, deferring to the dialogue between the two Israelis.

"May we be seated?" asked Tzofiya.

Avigdor gestured toward four overstuffed chairs situated around a large teak coffee table. Tzofiya and G sat while Avigdor remained standing. Tzofiya picked up on the fact that Avigdor's patience for delay was wearing thin, so she got right to the point, her pulse quickening with the first question she posed.

"Sir, I have to ask, did you have anything to do with the disappearance of your wife?"

Avigdor looked at G then back at Tzofiya. "No," he answered, impatiently waiting for the next question.

"How is it that you slept, or remained unconscious during her apparent struggle and disappearance?"

"You look familiar, Agent Cohen. You are Israeli, no?" asked Avigdor.

"I am, sir," responded Tzofiya.

"Are you operating on the assumption that I may have had something to do with the disappearance of my own wife? If so, what do I gain from such an act?"

Tzofiya sat quietly, attempting to follow the DPM's logic.

"I have no idea why or how I managed to essentially *sleep* through such a horrific event as the abduction of my own wife. Do I really have to answer these questions from such a seasoned agent? Let's change the course of this discussion, shall we? Because I'm quite sure by now you've already assessed whether or not I'm involved in her disappearance—"

"Sir," G interrupted.

Avigdor gave G a stern look for the interruption but gave him a chance to step in to improve the course of dialogue.

"I *know* you didn't have anything to do with her disappearance. I also know that this came as a complete surprise to you. My gut tells me that this is an attempt to distract or subvert. I think it's intended to exploit the vulnerabilities that may exist in the Israeli machine."

"Well, now you have my attention, albeit with skepticism since you have no basis for the confidence with which you make this declaration. Tell me again who you are? US secret service?"

G looked over his shoulder, quickly scanned the room visually, and lowered his voice.

"Special Agent Weston…G Weston, sir. I'm here at the request of the president and the Israeli prime minister in a cooperative effort with Agent Cohen to find your wife. My team and I work for an *undisclosed* agency."

Avigdor returned a stoic expression and paused before responding. "I am well aware of this 'undisclosed agency,' Mr. Weston. I have had the pleasure of employing some of your finest in the most precarious of situations. They have never let me down."

"Nor will I, sir."

"You still haven't told me how you know with such certainty that I'm innocent of any involvement in all of this. Something tells me, however, you may not be at complete liberty to do so," said Avigdor as he casually walked toward G and took a seat in one of the chairs directly across from him.

"When I find your wife, I'll be happy to tell you everything. For now, let's focus on finding her," said G as he stared directly into the eyes of one of the most powerful men in Israel.

Tzofiya watched the interaction unfold, secretly impressed at how artfully G took control of the conversation but still somewhat skeptical of the nature of his agenda.

"Tell me the first thing you remember," said G, still staring into Avigdor's eyes.

"OK, I remember the blood. My mind raced to catch up with the enormity of it all—"

"Back up a bit for me," G interrupted. "Back up to the point when you got out of bed and looked out beyond the balcony," he instructed.

Tzofiya furrowed her brow, wondering how G would know to ask such a question. Knowing Avigdor as she did, he would surely crush G for asking such a presumptuous question. She braced herself.

"I remember feeling very content," said a reflective Avigdor. "Why wouldn't I? I was vacationing in the French Riviera with my family and was caught up in the moment…"

"Tell me about what you *may* have heard or seen on your way to the bathroom."

Avigdor was fully engaged in his thoughts when he responded. "A closing door…the sound broke my concentration."

"Could you have possibly heard or seen anything else at that time?" asked G.

"I don't think so," he responded, slowly shaking his head.

"Where are you going with this, G?" asked Tzofiya softly.

G ignored her and continued to patiently stare into Avigdor's eyes. "Take your time, sir."

Tzofiya's frustration grew as she listened to G's line of questioning and the arrogant manner in which he asked his questions.

"Wait," Avigdor responded.

Tzofiya raised her eyebrows in surprise.

"I was on my way to the bathroom to check on my wife when…I *may* have seen a shadow pass just outside the bedroom door. I took a second glance thinking it might have been Rina, but the shadow was too large, and I didn't see anything after that, so I discounted it as lingering morning cobwebs in my mind," explained Avigdor. "After all, there was no need for concern or alarm at that point."

"Could it have been anyone from the security detail?" asked Tzofiya.

"No, they are not permitted inside the residence after we have turned in—unless there is an emergency," he responded, his words trailing off as he reflected on the past.

"OK, very good. I can work with that," said G. "What happened next?"

"That's when I entered the bathroom and discovered the broken glass and…the blood."

"Sir, how do you explain the bruise on your face?" asked Tzofiya.

Avigdor ignored her. Instead, he looked directly at G. "Can you find my wife?"

"Yes. In fact I'm close to doing *just* that," he answered.

"Do you know if she's alive?" asked Avigdor.

G nodded. "She's alive."

Tzofiya stood, purposely intending the gesture to interrupt and dissuade further conversation. She had no interested in creating false hope for the DPM. "OK, gentlemen, listen, we should be going. We still have to get you over to the villa to take your first look around, G."

G remained seated. "Do you have any reason to believe any of your team has anything at all to do with the disappearance of your wife, sir?" asked G.

"The entire team was vetted and personally selected by the lead security agent."

"The agent who was killed…was he the lead agent?" asked G.

"Yes," said Avigdor breaking his gaze for the first time and glancing at the floor.

"How many security agents were assigned to the detail on this trip?" asked Tzofiya.

"Three: two on duty, and one on shift rest at his quarters," answered Avigdor.

G turned to Tzofiya. "Do we have statements yet from the remaining two agents?"

"Yes. I can deliver the transcripts to you later," she responded as she gave G a look that demanded he terminate the conversation. "Sir, may I ask if you were working on anything official while on vacation? The reason I ask is because the office in your villa appeared to be ransacked. Do you have access to your laptop computer?" asked Tzofiya.

"I haven't seen my computer. I assume Agent Chevalier and his men must have it. Other than some routine documents, there are a few confidential files concerning recent initiatives of the parliament and some strategic executive strategy on how the prime minister and I planned to maneuver our way through the politics of it all. We were to discuss the strategy upon my return. Election season is approaching. There may be some personal correspondence that I cannot readily recollect," responded Avigdor. "There are no classified files whatsoever on the machine, and everything is double-layer password protected," he added.

"Can you describe the computer? What type of machine is it?"

Avigdor shrugged his shoulders. "It's just an ordinary black laptop, a Dell, I think. No, wait, an HP, maybe. I'm sorry I can't be more help."

"That's OK," answered Tzofiya. "Believe it or not, the color helps, even though most laptops are black. Oh, and I believe I may have the power cord that belongs to it. I'll be sure it gets back to you."

"Is there anything else you need us to know before we meet again?" asked G.

"Yes, the sooner you find my wife, the sooner I can help *you*," he said.

"How do you figure?" asked G.

"Think about it, Agent Weston. As a sequestered man I am essentially powerless. As a free man, I am the Israeli defense minister," explained Avigdor.

"Good point," admitted G.

"Have either of you been able to meet with my daughter, Rina?"

"Yes, and we can assure you, she is being taken care of. Agent Chevalier is working on arranging a visit for you both," explained G as he stood.

Avigdor stood and then hesitated. "Oh, Agent Cohen, speaking of my daughter…I almost forgot, there's a small pink sticker on the laptop. It's a flower. I left it there because it reminds me of her. I realize it is an insignificant detail, but it is a detail nonetheless, no?"

Tzofiya smiled. "Thank you, sir. That actually helps more than you know."

Avigdor stood and extended his hand. G hesitated but returned the courtesy by reaching out and accepting the gesture. The grip of the handshake pulled G's mind from conscious reality into synch with Avigdor's subconscious thoughts as fast as a bullet. Images from Avigdor's experiences overlapped G's memory of his dream of the recent ordeal. The dual perspective—G's personal account of the recent incident combined with the man's experience—gave G fresh insights. Images of Hanah and Rina flashed before him in an eclectic, emotional mix of mounting frustration and tireless determination.

What seemed like an eternal grip lasted for just seconds, but it was long enough for G to realize the extraordinary man he had just met. Enough of Avigdor's life flashed through G's alter-conscious mind for him to appreciate the diversity of Avigdor's responsibilities to his country and for G to honor the sensitivities of the secrets he held close.

Avigdor released G's hand and paused. "Why is it that I feel you and I have met sometime before? If not in this life, perhaps one of our past lives?"

G offered a respectful smile and spoke in Avigdor's native Hebrew , offering him an assurance that he and the team would find his wife and punish those responsible.

Agent Chevalier was waiting for G and Tzofiya at the back of the residence in a patio chair and stood when he saw the two disembarking from the yacht.

"Take us to the villa, please," instructed Tzofiya rather directly.

"As you wish, madame," answered Chevalier.

17

Two cars were in the driveway when Chevalier drove through the gated entryway of the villa. He recognized one of the vehicles as one of three he arranged for the secret-service team's use.

"It appears that one or more of your teammates are here," said Chevalier. "If you don't mind, I have some business to attend to."

"Certainly," answered Tzofiya, preferring the option. "We can take it from here. Thank you for your assistance today. We'll check in with you tomorrow after breakfast."

"Very well," answered Chevalier as Tzofiya and G stepped out of the vehicle.

Tzofiya stopped G as they made their way toward the villa. "OK, you and I have to talk."

G stopped and turned toward her.

"I'm not sure what kind of stunt you're pulling here, but it's apparent you know more than I assumed you did," said Tzofiya.

"If there's one thing I've learned, Agent Cohen, it's that assumptions have no place in our line of work. Maybe if you'd taken the time to just ask, I'd be more forthcoming. Once you get to know me better, you'll find that I despise 'stunts,' I am not prone to performing them, and I never operate on assumptions."

"OK, tell me what you know," she said.

"I know quite a bit. Care to be a bit more specific?"

"I need to know why...or *how* you know the things you know. The questions you asked both the DPM and his daughter are too coincidental and intimate. It's difficult for me to trust someone who holds back information," answered Tzofiya, her frustration clearly getting the best of her.

"Are you angry with me, Tzofiya?"

"What kind of question is that?" she asked, clearly frustrated by her own lack of sufficient information.

"Just answer the question."

"I don't have time for this shit," she said, abruptly turning away toward the villa.

"Hey," called G as she walked away.

Tzofiya paused and turned her head, sending him an unmistakable look of impatience.

"Meet me after dinner this evening in the courtyard of the hotel, and I'll answer all of your questions."

"Whatever," she quickly answered and walked into the residence.

Ian looked up from behind the executive desk in the office when the front door of the villa opened. He stood when he saw Tzofiya walk into the foyer.

"Hey, how are you?" he called out.

"Fine," she answered matter-of-factly, still feeling the sting of her frustrating encounter with G. "So how's everything going?" she asked.

The elder summoned Munahid and Bashir to a dusty room that served as a makeshift office.

"Close the door," instructed the elder.

Munahid's heart raced as he awaited the reason why the two had been called to the elder's office. Bashir offered only a smug smile as if he was there to witness the official punishment for the insolence and disrespect shown toward an elder, specifically by Munahid.

"I have decided to move the Jew," announced the elder. "Before we do that, there is a small matter I wish to discuss concerning action involving her treatment."

"Sir, I wish to state that I was performing a routine examination when—" said Bashir.

"Silence!" shouted the elder. "Munahid, I need you to supervise the transfer of our Jewish guest to location six. I'm holding you personally responsible for her safe transfer. You will report to me when she is securely in place."

"As you wish," replied Munahid.

Bashir sat seething in anger and resentment that the younger man had not only been selected to lead the transfer but he would not be scolded for disrespecting the religious elder.

"As for you, Bashir—the prisoner was not to show signs of physical mistreatment. Your so-called *examination* resulted in her clothes being torn and even worse, physical evidence of mistreatment. Your attempt to compensate with an act of kindness was—"

"Sir, I admit to accidentally tearing her garment when she resisted, but I did not replace it. In fact, it was Munahid who—"

"You are guilty of several things, Bashir. Lying well is not among them. There is *no* room for sloppiness in this organization. I simply will not tolerate one more misstep from you or anyone when it comes to the protection of this prisoner. Is that clear?"

"Yes."

"You are both dismissed."

Munahid and Bashir made their way to Hanah's cell to carry out the transfer order. A chill ran through Munahid's veins as he thought of how close he'd come to paying the ultimate price for his kindness toward Hanah and how her bravery had ultimately saved his life.

The door of Hanah's cell opened. Fearing the worst, she withdrew as best she could to avoid yet another so-called examination or interrogation. Three men approached. She was confused and frightened when she saw Bashir but was relieved when she saw Munahid. She purposely avoided direct eye contact with any of them.

"We are moving you to another location," explained the third man as he unlocked her wrist restraints.

The men helped Hanah to sit up and then lifted her to a standing position. She was weak, but she managed well despite the infrequent use of her legs. Her body was racked with joint stiffness and pain, but her mind was still sharp. She was fitted into a black abaya and led toward the cell exit.

The sun had set, and dusk had fallen heavily as the men led Hanah to an awaiting vehicle. They didn't blindfold her or cover her head as they had initially intended, so she took advantage of looking around as best she could while being moved toward the vehicle.

A single driver waited in the front seat with the engine running as Hanah was forced into the back seat of the four-door sedan. Two men climbed into the back with her, one on each side. Munahid slid into the front seat, his large frame taking up most of the allotted space even with the seat almost fully reclined. Bashir sat behind him, next to Hanah, and he was not happy about the lack of sufficient legroom.

"You big troll!" exclaimed Bashir. "How the hell am I supposed to breathe sitting behind you? Readjust your seat."

Munahid pulled forward a notch while the driver sped throughout the dirty streets of Aden, careful not to make any mistakes with the ferrying of his passengers. The men spoke in their native tongues, assuming Hanah wouldn't understand their conversation.

"Why are we moving this bitch anyway? And where the hell is location six?" asked Bashir.

"It's an abandoned engineering facility in Hafoon," responded the driver as he accelerated down a narrow street.

Bashir placed his hand on Hanah's thigh and offered a menacing grin. Hanah returned a look of defiance, pulled away as best she could and glanced at Munahid. Bashir persisted and began rubbing the inside of her thigh. "I'm looking forward to getting to know you much better—"

Munahid overheard the comment and, when the car hit a bump in the road, he took advantage of the momentum, releasing his seat lever and thrust his legs forward, pushing back hard and jamming Bashir's knees into his torso.

"Arrrgh. Hey!" he shouted, pulling his hand away. "You fucking beast. Push your seat forward. I can't breathe."

Hanah nervously looked out the front of the vehicle. She could see a hint of a smirk appear on Munahid's face as he glanced her way. Her eyes widened in shock as she watched Bashir pull a handgun from his waist and take aim at the back of Munahid's head. Hanah reacted swiftly and drove her elbow into Bashir's face causing him to pull the gun and the trigger simultaneously. The gun fired twice, sending one bullet through the windshield, barely missing the base of Munahid's skull, the other finding its way directly into the driver's right temple, killing him instantly.

Blood spattered against the windshield and dashboard. The car swerved sharply to the left and accelerated when the dead driver's weight fell against the steering wheel and his foot depressed the accelerator. Munahid grabbed the steering wheel in a desperate attempt to find a clear path while trying to pull the driver away from the accelerator. The car careened into a woman crossing the street and then crashed into a small retaining wall, slamming Munahid's massive body into the dashboard of the sedan. The sudden stop projected Hanah's body into Munahid's, softening the deadly blow she would've otherwise encountered. Her body twisted as she fell to the front passenger side floorboard in an inverted and contorted position.

Taking a deep painful breath, Hanah opened her eyes to the smoke-filled interior of the vehicle. She grabbed at the passenger seat, attempting to find balance. Blood covered her right shoulder and chest, but she quickly determined it wasn't hers. She coughed on the smoke. Her right ear rang with an annoying tone as she grappled with her equilibrium. She turned to check on Munahid. He was in pain but otherwise alive and slowly regaining his composure. Her eyes widened when she saw the handgun lying on the passenger side floorboard next to her head.

G stood in the front yard of the villa staring at the large residence. A French guard posted just outside the front door ignored him while he stood alone, thinking about his alter-conscious experience and just how far he'd come since learning about the significance of his dream. He glanced toward the driveway where the white Bentley was once parked, the Bentley he—Avigdor—drove to frantically search for Hanah.

He walked toward the front door, each step taking him closer to the real-life venue that held the truth of just what had happened to Hanah Malkinson. The guard opened the front door for G and stepped out of the way. G paused for a moment, took a breath, and then stepped inside.

The enormity of his dream descended upon him like a ton of bricks. Stepping inside the villa was like stepping inside an alternate dimension, only this was reality wrapped in a surreal déjà vu where the stakes were high and the discovery of the truth meant life or death. It would be a true test of his abilities to pull it all together and use everything he had to find her.

Tzofiya and Ian both watched from the office as G entered the villa. G never noticed them. Instead, he glanced up at the winding stairway, mentally retracing the steps he had taken once before. He turned toward the stairway and ascended the stairs, each step taking him deeper into the surreal scene he had dreamed of so vividly.

He stopped just outside the master suite, just across from Rina's room. The door was closed, so G opened it and stepped inside. Rina's room was a small, windowless area with a queen bed positioned at the center of the far wall. Stuffed animals and small, assorted toys were neatly positioned in a corner next to a crumpled blanket on the floor alongside a small chest of drawers to his right.

The door swiftly closed behind him, leaving him in the dark.

Where have you been? She needs you. I waited for you.

G recognized the boy's voice immediately. *I'm sorry, there are things I need to do here in order to help her,* explained G. *I planned to look for you soon,* he added.

Why did you leave me?

G struggled to find the right words to explain the differences of their dimensions. *There are just some things I simply can't control.*

But you and me, we're the same. You're just stronger than I am. You have to help her. I need you. She needs you.

We're not exactly the same, replied G. *I'm quite sure you'll realize that soon enough.*

They're moving her, he said without warning.

Where are they moving her to?

I can't say. I can only show you once the move is complete, responded the boy.

Then make certain to watch over her until the move is finished. I'll find you soon, and together we'll figure this out.

I'm watching her now, he said. *I can show you how.*

G felt a surge of curiosity, and the boy picked up on it.

I'll be waiting for you, said the boy as he disappeared.

"I know you will," responded G, speaking aloud.

"There you are," said Ian, opening the door to Rina's room. "You know they make these really cool devices called *light switches*. You should try 'em," he added as he flipped the light switch on the wall to illuminate the room. "There are better things to be doing than talking to yourself in the dark. Unless of course you were doing that thing you do. In which case, I'm sorry to have barged in."

The attention of both men was immediately drawn to a dark spot on the floor.

"What do you make of that, Ian?" asked G.

"Looks like a shoe print of some kind," Ian answered. "More like a boot print actually. I'll take a picture and see if it's anything that forensics has already analyzed. You 'bout ready to head to the hotel? I can give you and Tzofiya a lift," he offered.

"Almost. I want to check out the master suite before we leave. By the way, who else is here with you besides Cohen?"

"What do you mean?"

"There was another car here when we arrived," explained G.

"Oh yeah, that was one of the members of the Israeli security team. He dropped by to see if he could help with anything. He didn't stay long actually," said Ian.

"Those guys have all been instructed to stay away from the crime scene," G reminded Ian. "They're a party to the investigation and have no business here anymore. Did you get a name?"

"Actually, no, but he's easy enough to find. He's staying in a hotel in Sainte-Ame with the other agent until they're cleared to return to Israel. We can have Cohen follow up on it. Hell, she may even know the guy."

"Good call. Why don't you fill her in and see what she thinks while I finish looking around. I'll be along shortly," suggested G.

18

G stepped into the master suite and closed his eyes for a moment to concentrate on bringing the memory of his dream forward. He focused on the glimpses of Avigdor's recall and the sequence of his own dream, essentially transposing the two perspectives. The initiative was a stretch, but even G was impressed with his ability to pull it off. He opened his eyes and stood just inside the doorway and watched as his thoughts mentally replayed the event while pushing his mind to pick up on any subtle differences between the two perspectives.

The allure of the scene slowly drew him to the center of the room. Stopping at the foot of the bed, he watched as Avigdor approached the bathroom door, hesitating slightly before he entered.

Stop.

G mentally commanded the moving image to freeze. There, just outside the bedroom door, was the shadow of a man glancing back while hastily making his way *away* from the bedroom and toward the stairway. G walked toward the shadowy figure to get a better look, but the closer he got, the more diffused it became, despite his best efforts to concentrate on keeping the details from fading.

Frustrated, G decided to separate himself to an alternative aspect of the dream sequence and projected himself to the landing of the villa.

Go, he commanded, as his mind resumed the sequence of events from this new perspective.

Standing in the foyer, G watched the man descend the stairs. The closer he got, the more G was able to get a good look at him.

The experience and emotions were so real, he felt as if he could've decked the man where he stood and prevented the entire incident from taking place. The man stopped just before reaching the door. He seemed to look straight into G's eyes before turning to look back upstairs. He glanced toward the office and saw his partner. He called out for him. "Massii...Massii, yallah. We must leave *now*," he stressed in a firm whisper.

A large, menacing man emerged from the office. He wore a close-cropped beard and, true to Rina's description, didn't look very happy. He had a flashlight in his right hand and a handgun in his left. G's heart raced as he realized just how close the man was to finding the brave young girl. G took advantage of the opportunity to get a close look at the man and the tattoo emblazoned on his wrist.

A serpent supported by two crossed swords—or "a spider"—depending upon your perspective.

The men rushed through the door, slamming it behind them in their haste to leave the villa.

G stood alone in the momentary stillness, absorbing the entirety of it all until his focus was abruptly broken by the echoing slap of Avigdor's shoes hitting the wood foyer floor from their second-story fall. Looking up at the top of the stairs, G saw the barrel of Avigdor's gun followed by a quick glance from the distraught father and husband. He watched as Avigdor frantically searched for any sign of his family and patiently waited for the scene to play out until he and Rina were reunited before stepping away from the dream sequence.

"What can you tell me about Bachman?" Ian asked Tzofiya.

"Micah Bachman? Not much to tell, really," she said. "He and Malkinson have known each other for quite some time. They served in the Knesset together a number of years ago. Malkinson ascended through the ranks of government service while Bachman elected to serve abroad as an attorney in the hopes of becoming an ambassador. He's been working for the Israeli consulate for some ten years or more now. Why do you ask?"

"It may be nothing, but there's no record of a visit by Bachman to the villa. I find that odd considering the circumstances," commented Ian.

"Maybe he sent an investigator instead."

Ian nodded, contemplating the likelihood of her answer. "Oh, speaking of investigator, that reminds me—would you happen to know how we can get a hold of the two Israeli security dudes?"

"Certainly. They're staying in a hotel in Sainte-Ame. Did we need more information from them?"

"Maybe. G seems to think so. One of them was here today. He left just after you and G arrived. I'm surprised you didn't run into him, actually."

"He was probably avoiding me because I personally advised both of them to stay away from the crime scene during the investigation," she said. "That's troubling. I'll follow up on it and let you know what I find out."

"Follow up on what?" asked G as he approached the office from the foyer.

"Oh, hello, G. We were just talking about the security agent who was here earlier," said Ian. "So what'd *you* find out?"

Hanah's hand trembled as she grabbed the gun from the floorboard. The awkward position of her torso spread across the seat, her head down and left arm twisted between Munahid's legs, proved to be an uncomfortable disadvantage and gave her little room to maneuver. She panicked when she heard voices gathering outside the vehicle as she struggled to reposition herself. Her mind raced as she considered her limited options and the rare opportunity for advantage.

Munahid's legs pressed hard against Hanah's shoulder as he struggled to right himself. She was powerless under the weight of his muscular thighs. Her attention quickly turned to movement and noise from the back seat. Bashir was coming to. Her heartbeat quickened as she pushed hard against the weight of Munahid's legs to free herself from her contorted position. Bashir let out an angry scream as he attempted to free himself. Hanah could see his hands frantically grabbing the seat in front of him as he tried to break free.

Hanah winced when Bashir found her ankle and held tight, digging his nails into her skin. Munahid reacted by grabbing Bashir's forearm and forcefully pulled him into the seat in front of him, repeatedly banging his head against the headrest in an attempt to get him to release his grip on Hanah's ankle. Munahid's legs released their hold on Hanah's shoulder as he maneuvered to gain a better fighting position. He had to protect himself and the prisoner at all costs. His very life depended on it.

Her head and shoulders now firmly pressed against the floorboard, Hanah was finally able to grip the weapon with both hands. She aimed and fired three shots, sending all three rounds through the backrest of the front seat and into Bashir's torso. Bashir recoiled with each burst and stared at Munahid in shock as his eyes closed for the last time.

Hanah quickly took aim on the man in the back left seat of the vehicle. He froze, nervously glancing at Munahid and back at Hanah, his eyes wide with shock at the turn of events.

Breathing heavily, her head pounding with surging adrenaline, Hanah was now in control.

Flames danced from a gas fireplace in the center of the courtyard and served as a primary focal point on the peaceful hotel patio. G sat in an overstuffed wicker chair in a corner of the courtyard, and the smooth, rich taste of a Rocky Patel cigar slid across his palette as he savored the serenity of the mildly humid evening air.

Taking a slow sip of his drink, he looked up to see Tzofiya approaching from the far side of the courtyard. The warm glow of the fireplace on her olive skin gave him pause. He admired the effect. Her blue jeans were a perfect complement to her long muscular legs and the sensuous curves of her hips. Her white tank top captured his attention as the near-perfect lines of her figure drew subtle attention to the hourglass shape of her waist and the contour of her breasts. Her hair was pulled back, a style that served to enhance her high cheekbones. He considered standing to greet her as she drew closer but opted for an alternative approach by remaining seated.

Standing before him in silence, one hand delicately perched upon her hip, her green eyes connected with his with an expectant seriousness. He broke his gaze, taking the liberty of studying the long, slender lines of her shapely figure up close. The contour of her feet, toes slightly exposed in black leather sandals, the denim clinging to her long legs…

The standoff annoyed her yet intrigued her all the same. Her analyst side was busy calculating his tactics while her female instincts were captivated by the power of his dominant gesture of delay and presumptive visual encroachment. The analyst side resisted, even detested the tactic, while the woman in her longed for him to continue the visual investigation. She took a breath and summoned the courage to break free from the encounter.

"So are you going to ask me to sit, or are you just going to look at me all night?"

G reconnected with her green eyes, took a slow sip of his drink, and gave her a hint of smile. He gestured for her to take the seat next to him, the two now separated only by a small cocktail table.

A waiter approached. "Good evening, madame. May I get something for you to drink?"

Tzofiya looked at G. "What are *you* drinking?"

G spoke to the waiter, lifting his glass of wine. "*La même chose pour madame,*"

"Excellent, monsieur."

"What did you order for me?"

"I simply said, 'the lady will have the same.' I'm sure you'll like it." G smiled.

He's sure, *huh? Maybe a bit* too *sure. But then again...*

"Is it a French wine?" she inquired.

G responded in his best faux-French accent. "But of course. Besides, why drink anything else while we're in France?" he added, reverting to raw American.

Tzofiya smiled, quickly realized her nonverbal gestures might be revealing too much, and attempted to get back to business. "OK, so I'm here. Of course I'm sure you somehow *knew* I would be. Why don't you tell me how you seem to know so mu—"

"Your wine, madame," said the waiter, handing her a generous pour in a crystal glass.

G subtly raised his glass and looked confidently into Tzofiya's eyes. She returned a hint of a smile along with a shy tilt of her head and raised the glass to her lips.

"Very good choice of wine," she acknowledged. "OK, where were we? Oh yeah, you were about to tell me how it is you know all these details. I know you American clandestine types are good, but the level of your knowledge goes far beyond *good*. It's suspect, actually."

"I can assure you, Tzofiya, we're on the same team." G took another sip of wine. "I'm here because my specialty, or rather, my abilities give us an insight advantage the enemy isn't prepared for. It's not as difficult to explain as it is for some people to accept."

"So you're telling me you're some kind of clairvoyant?"

"Not exactly. I can attest to having an ability to *discern* things beyond normal sensory contact, which comes about as close to the definition as you'll get, but I'm not able to actually see the future. If I could, I'd probably be in a completely different line of work, or not working at all."

"So if you're not clairvoyant, then how do you explain it? Is it an extrasensory ability?"

G smiled. "Yeah, that actually pretty much captures the essence of what it is." He went on to explain the details of his perceptive abilities and how his dreams helped take him places and connect with people on the alter-conscious side of life. The more he spoke, the more intrigued she grew, although she remained skeptical.

The waiter approached. G gestured for two more glasses and glanced at Tzofiya who was now relaxed and smiling at him, subconsciously massaging the stem of her wine glass.

"OK, so aside from the fact that all of this is quite fascinating, what *value* do you add to the team? I don't mean to be so cynical, but I have to know whether or not I need to look out for you, or whether I can rely on you carrying your own weight should we ever get into a situation," she said. "Aside from the fact that you performed quite impressively during today's interviews, I have no idea whether you can actually do…whatever it is you do *and* protect yourself."

G smiled. "The *situation*. Why does that term follow me like the plague it seems to be?" he asked rhetorically.

"I don't follow," she said.

"It's nothing. Think about how easily I got into your head when you first approached me this evening. I have to admit, it was a first for me with someone so alluring. You don't have to respond to that because, as you said, I already knew you'd show up. What I *didn't* know was how you'd react."

"And?"

"Well, you're still here, so I must have done something right. But how did I know how to handle a woman like you without really knowing you?"

"Dumb luck?" she responded.

"I wasn't hired to operate on 'dumb luck.' I was hired for my ability to *know* things."

"Oh, so now you *know* me?" she said.

"I knew enough to know you'd show up. I also know how you're likely to react if we get into a *situation*," he confidently answered.

"Oh really? And how do you know this?"

G shrugged his shoulders and answered nonchalantly. "I took the time to get to know you without you even knowing it."

"You are way too deep, G. Anyone ever tell you that?"

G smiled. "Let's just say I've heard variations of that statement from time to time."

"OK, put your money where your mouth is. Tell me something convincing that no one else would know about me about how I'd react in a threatening situation," she challenged, careful not to ask him to reveal any personal insight he might have had into her.

G stared at her, pausing long enough to recollect the memories he gathered when he got his first glimpse into her subconscious.

"Your father…no, someone else…an older gentleman…someone you respect as much as your father, showed you at an early age how to use a weapon with either hand. Despite the difficulty and frustration, you practiced to perfection. Although your preference is to shoot right-handed, you are equally as lethal using your left. How am I doing so far?" he asked.

"Not bad. Impressive actually," she admitted. "So what am I thinking right now?"

G laughed. "It doesn't work that way."

"OK look, just tell me you know what the hell you're doing and can do it well enough to help me find Hanah Malkinson."

G nodded. "I can do all that and much more," he assured her and then took a slow sip of wine. Then he looked away for a moment, distracted by a distorted figure he saw through the flames of the fire pit in the center of the courtyard.

Tzofiya picked up on the distraction. "You OK, G?"

Ignoring her question, G squinted his eyes to focus on the figure beyond the flames. His demeanor changed. G slowly rose to his feet, placing his glass on the table next to him. As he stood, G connected with the eyes of young Ro'i. Fright and concern clearly shone upon the boy's face.

"G, what's the matter?"

"I have to go. I'm sorry." He paused to gently kiss her on the cheek. "I'll see you in the morning when we meet with the team."

"O…K."

Tzofiya sat in the chair as she watched him leave, slightly buzzed from the effects of the wine, partially puzzled by the manner of his exit. Her mind was caught up in the euphoria of the moment and her emotions were swimming in the pleasure of an encounter with a man unlike any she had previously ever met.

19

Munahid's eyes were wide and intently focused as he remained frozen, careful not to startle her. Hanah's hands trembled and her head pounded with pain as adrenaline surged throughout her body. Her contorted position proved to be a disadvantage as she considered her next move. A crowd of people who had witnessed the crash began gathering outside the vehicle.

"Give me the gun," Munahid said softly, slowly extending his hand.

Hanah quickly reacted by pointing the weapon at him.

He hesitated and raised his eyebrows in an expression that mingled surprise and compassion.

The man in the back shifted in his seat. Hanah retrained the weapon on him.

"Hanah, the only way we're getting out of this situation is if you give me that weapon," Munahid calmly explained. "The crowd outside will know you don't belong here. Worse, they may even discover that you are Jewish. I can only help you if you give me the weapon and wear this niqab, veiling your face," he said.

The crowd became angry and began shaking the vehicle. Hanah quickly turned her head when she heard an attempt to open one of the rear doors.

"I will protect you," Munahid assured her. "Just give me the weapon."

Hanah reluctantly handed the weapon to Munahid, second-guessing the move as he took it and reached for the niqab.

"Kill the bitch," yelled the man in his native tongue from the back seat. "She killed Bashir, she killed the imam. She deserves to die!"

Hanah clearly understood the man's demand that she die for the action she took to save their lives. Munahid handed her the niqab to cover her face and conceal her identity from the crowd, and then he extended his hand to help her up from the floorboard of the vehicle. Hanah placed the hood over her head. As she extended her hand to reach for Munahid's, the car door opened.

Several hands reached in and grabbed her. Hanah tried hard to fight them off and called out to Munahid, careful to use the local language. "Help me!" she screamed.

The two men watched as Hanah disappeared into the crowd. Munahid struggled to quickly get out of the vehicle while the man in the back seat called out once again, "Kill her, rip the limbs from her body. She kill—"

Munahid reacted swiftly, turning toward the man, and in one fluid movement, pistol-whipped the side of his head, crushing his skull and collapsing his eye socket. Blood splattered against the back and side windows of the car as he fell silent against the backdrop of the noisy crowd.

Munahid emerged from the vehicle into the crowd of people. The streets were dark, and he had lost sight of Hanah. His head moved frantically from side to side as he searched for her. His towering stature gave him a slight advantage over the average height of the crowd as he looked for clues. Suddenly he heard a distinct scream coming from a narrow alleyway. He placed the gun inside the waistband of his pants, inside his white thaub, as he forcefully moved through the crowd toward the sound. There he found several men gathered around a figure dressed in a black abaya.

Hanah was backed up against a wall at the end of the short and narrow alleyway. Several men surrounded her as she continued to resist their attempts to get close to her. A dog barked from a nearby balcony a few stories above. Sirens echoed in the distance. Munahid knew he didn't have much time to save her from the chaos of the crowd, but he was outnumbered, and his options were few.

Hanah's heart beat as fast as her mind raced. In her panic-stricken search for an exit, she looked past the crowd and saw Munahid through the shroud of her niqab.

G lost sight of Ro'i as he passed by the courtyard fireplace. Sensing urgency, he quickly made his way to his room where he knew he could focus without the threat of distraction. He stepped off the elevator and heard a whispered plea from the boy.

Hurry, she needs you.

G closed the door behind him, opened a small medicine bottle, and popped a 750-milligram Loritab into his mouth. He paused to look at his own reflection in a mirror above a small desk and then lay down on the bed.

Staring at the ceiling, G inhaled deeply through his nose and exhaled through his mouth—a method he used to enhance the effects of the medication and induce relaxation. He focused on escaping his consciousness in hope of finding the boy waiting on the other side. His eyes relaxed and began to close, finding sleep in no time.

The increasing volume of a contentious crowd of people was the first thing G recognized on his way into alter-consciousness. He heard the voice of the young boy even before his surroundings came into clear focus.

This way, he whispered.

Wait, said G, as he looked into the boy's eyes. *What is your name?*

I am Ro'i, said the boy as he firmly grasped G's hand and led him past several people and through a narrow alleyway where they came upon a smaller crowd of men.

G looked at Ro'i. *Where is she?* G asked as he forced himself to focus.

Ro'i pointed into the crowd.

G projected himself past the crowd and saw a panic-stricken woman, back pressed against a wall, clearly resisting any attempt by the crowd to make contact with her. G quickly examined the surroundings for options. To his right was a gate, secured by a lock. To his left was a closed door at the end of an adjacent short alleyway.

Ro'i, the door…I need to know if it's secure.

Ro'i projected himself to the other side of the door and saw that it was secured only by a flimsy, sliding bolt. He communicated with G by projecting the image directly back to him. G's mind went into overdrive trying to determine a way to help Hanah. Suddenly, a loud voice shouted over the cacophony of the crowd.

"Stand back. I said, stand back!"

A towering man stepped through the crowd. G watched as the man approached. There was nothing he could do but observe. G glanced toward the periphery of the crowd and saw Ro'i looking on with concern as the large man approached Hanah.

Hanah called out to him. "Munahid!" she said as she fell to her knees.

G and Ro'i looked at each other, sharing their confusion.

"This is my wife," shouted the man, stepping between the crowd and Hanah. "How *dare* you frighten her like this," he scolded them. "Stand back. I said, *stand back*," he shouted again.

The crowd relented. When the man bent down to console her, G could see the outline of a handgun in the small of the man's back. He wasn't the only one who could see it. When someone in the crowd noticed the weapon, he alerted the others.

"He has a weapon!"

The crowd erupted once again and a man jumped toward Munahid, going for the gun at his back. Munahid stood and swatted his left arm, easily knocking the man to the ground. Munahid reached down, grabbed Hanah's hand, and led her toward the only possible exit he could see, a door to their left at the end of a short alleyway. The crowd pursued them as the two ran toward the door.

Munahid tried opening the door. It was locked.

"Stand back," he instructed Hanah.

Munahid rammed his shoulder into the door, breaking away the sliding bolt and easily breaching the doorway. He grabbed Hanah's hand and led her into the building. G and Ro'i followed as did some of the men pursuing them.

The building was dimly lit and unoccupied for the most part, save for a few vagrants using the hallways and open rooms for shelter. The men pursuing Munahid and Hanah were close. Attempting to outrun them would be futile; they had to hide. They veered into a dim, shadowy room where Munahid gently pushed Hanah into a dark corner, telling her to remain hidden.

G and Ro'i were powerless to do anything but look on and hope that the man accompanying Hanah had her best interests in mind.

Munahid positioned himself behind a wall in another corner of the room, took a deep breath, and slowly exhaled. The men pursuing them scurried past the doorway of the room, leaving Hanah and Munahid to wonder if they had successfully eluded their pursuers.

Police sirens echoing outside the building bore a stark contrast against the eerie stillness of the room while Munahid waited long enough to believe he and Hanah had successfully eluded their pursuers.

A man walked into the room just as Munahid stepped from behind the wall, surprising them both.

Micah arrived on the red-eye commuter just before midnight. La Mole airport was quiet aside from the noise generated by the power cart connected to the aircraft.

A lone agent waited at the gate and offered to take Micah's carry-on bag as he approached.

Refusing the offer, Micah got right to business. "Were you able to get what I need from the villa?"

"No," answered the agent.

"You want to explain why, or are you merely amused by my questions?" asked a sarcastic Micah.

The men got into the car and headed north to Saint-Tropez.

"The Americans were on site, preventing me from spending too much time on the premises," explained the agent. "I have been ordered by Agent Cohen to stay away from the villa until I'm cleared. The fact that I was there *after* I was told to stay away puts me in a very precarious position. In fact, I had to slip out when she arrived on scene."

"Had you gone to the villa exactly when I instructed, you wouldn't have had to be so elusive," said Micah. "It appears I may have to do *some* things myself."

The two sat quietly during the remainder of the drive. The agent stopped the car to drop Micah off at his hotel.

"Pick me up at seven o'clock in the morning," instructed Micah, and he slammed the door without waiting for an answer.

A Yemeni police officer at the crime scene recognized Bashir in the back seat of the crashed vehicle and alerted the network leadership. Word traveled fast, even in *restricted* communications situations.

The network used a variety of reliable relays to transfer messages to key leaders within its ranks. Some were physically carried by courier; others were transmitted electronically via radio, telephone, or computer channels depending on relevancy, urgency, and importance. This specific information had to be reported quickly, and it had to make its way to the top, so it was transmitted directly to a key leader one echelon from the top, who would be responsible for delivering it to the Serpent.

Siraj became enraged as he read the communiqué reporting the escape of his most critical and valuable prisoner. The fact that she had been able to escape demanded his personal attention. The fact that she might have been responsible for the death of an entire escort team angered and frustrated him to his core.

He turned to a close personal assistant and demanded that travel arrangements be made immediately.

"Sir, the risks of travel—"

"I am well aware of the risks and do not wish to be lectured at this time. Make the arrangements," he demanded.

"As you wish," answered the assistant.

Siraj picked up the phone and dialed the elder responsible for Hanah's transfer.

"It has come to my attention that you have misplaced your prisoner," Siraj began the call.

"This is the first I've heard of such a thing, sir," he replied.

"Well I suggest you do a better job staying on top of things while you are charged with such responsibilities," Siraj yelled angrily into the phone. "I am on my way to straighten out the absolute mess you've made of this—"

"Sir, that is not necessary. I can assure you that I—"

"You can *assure* me? You cannot even assure me of your knowledge of the whereabouts of the prisoner. How can you assure me of anything else? Don't say another fucking word. Just listen very carefully to what I'm telling you. You will find the prisoner by the time I arrive, and when you do, I will consider whether or not you will pay for this with your life."

Siraj slammed the phone onto the receiver so hard that it fell onto the floor.

"Sir, your arrangements have been made. Your car is ready to take you to your aircraft."

The man froze and stared at the much larger Munahid. Without warning, he lunged toward Munahid and surprised him with a powerful strike to the chest. Munahid winced, fell to his knees, and held his chest as he gasped for air. The man quickly followed with a roundhouse kick to the face, his heel making contact with Munahid's jaw sending a splatter of bright red blood across the room. Munahid's head swam from the blow, as he fought to retain consciousness. He had to find an opening, and he had to find it quick if he was to survive. But the smaller man was quick and careful.

"Hanah," gasped Munahid. "Run. Run, Hanah," he managed to say between breaths.

The man set up for his final assault—an explosive kick to the face that would surely finish the giant. Ro'i watched in horror.

Help him, exclaimed the boy.

We can't. We're powerless, answered G.

Hanah stepped from the shadows long enough to distract the man.

What is she doing? asked a concerned Ro'i.

G watched the scene unfold, secretly wondering the same thing.

The man, clearly taken by surprise, stopped for a moment and stared at Hanah. "I will deal with you after I finish your husband," he said in his native tongue. He retrained his sights on Munahid, focusing his attack when Hanah boldly spoke.

"He's not my husband," she answered in Arabic. "He's my friend," she added in English as she removed the niqab from her head.

The man froze as he tried to come to grips with the woman's appearance. She was clearly not a local Yemeni. It was just the opening Munahid needed as he took aim and fired a single bullet through the man's neck. The gunshot echoed throughout the room and nearby hallways.

G looked at Ro'i and saw shock written all over his face.

Ro'i, go check the hallways, said G. *Ro'i!*

The boy, clearly shaken by the event, broke free from the grip of his shock and disappeared in order to comply with G's instructions.

Hanah rushed to Munahid's side. Helping him to his feet was difficult, but she summoned all the strength she had to accomplish the task. "We've got to go," she said leading him to the only exit. "The others surely heard the gunfire and will return soon. Come on, Munahid. We have to go," she stressed.

Munahid did his best to follow Hanah while maintaining a grip on the weapon, keeping it ready for anyone else who would attempt to impede their escape. Pausing before they left the room, he knelt next to the dying man and began searching him.

"What are you doing?" Hanah asked impatiently.

He confiscated the man's cell phone, checked it for a signal, and looked up at Hanah. "We need this more than he does."

Hanah peered into the dim hallway. "Let's go," she whispered.

"Wait," replied Munahid. "You may wish to wear this," he added, handing the niqab to her.

They're returning. The men are headed back toward the room, warned a concerned Ro'i from an obscure hallway.

They're on the move, answered G, assuring the boy that Hanah and Munahid were doing their best to evade the crowd. *Keep me posted on their location,* he instructed the boy.

Hanah stopped abruptly when she heard footsteps approaching. The two had made it far enough away from the first room, down one hallway and turning into another.

"We need to get to the street," she whispered.

"The street is not safe," answered Munahid, confused by her logic.

"If we can get to the street, we can blend in," she argued.

"Look at me. I'm a giant. I don't blend in well."

He had a point. She had to think of an alternative. She peered around the corner of yet another shadowy hallway. It was clear. They quietly kept moving away from the sound of pursuing footsteps, unsure of just where they were headed, or where they would end up.

Hanah stopped again when she heard the sound of footsteps coming from a new direction. These footsteps were different. There seemed to be more of them. She opened a door to her left and led Munahid inside to a dimly lit stairwell. Munahid carefully closed the door behind them. As the door closed, they heard the sound of several footsteps passing by the very spot they had just left. The muted sound of a radio crackled.

"The police," whispered Munahid, placing a single finger over his lips.

There are a lot of people in this place looking for them, warned Ro'i as he joined G's side. *Why isn't she calling out to the police?*

Because these police aren't the good guys you find most everywhere else, answered G.

20

"Sir, satellite comms have picked up a voice transmission I think you'll be interested in," reported an intelligence officer.

Dennis Kinkaid turned his chair toward the young officer and accepted the transcript. He furrowed his brow as he read it. As the NSA Operations Center supervisor, Dennis was responsible for vetting all raw intelligence and routing it to the appropriate department for validation. This specific report required the immediate attention of the operations director, so Dennis placed an immediate call directly to Paul Harriman.

"Hey, Paul, we have a Priority One COMINT on an HVT. Are you available for a decision briefing?"

Paul knew Dennis well enough to know that he would only enact the reporting protocol when absolutely necessary. The fact that he had new information regarding a high value target, or HVT, was enough to alert the director. The COMINT, or communications intelligence intercept, indicated that Dennis had a high probability of reliable information and knowledge on the whereabouts and intentions of a person of interest, or information leading to intent to do harm to the United States or its citizens. The highly sensitive and secret situation required Paul's immediate presence on the operations center floor.

"Absolutely," answered Paul. "On my way."

Dennis was working with an intelligence officer and a linguist deciphering the communications intercept on the HVT when Paul arrived to the operations center and approached the supervisor's desk.

"What do you have, Dennis?"

Dennis handed the transcript to Paul.

Time: 05:45:10Z

(Male voice, translated from Farsi)

You can *assure* me? You cannot even assure me of your knowledge of the whereabouts of the prisoner. How can you assure me of anything else? Don't say another fucking word. Just listen very carefully to what I'm telling you. You will find the prisoner by the time I arrive, or you will pay for this with your life.

Time: 05:47:22Z

(Inaudible "crashing" noise, no voice, some movement sounds)

Time: 05:53:33Z

(Male voice, translated from Farsi)

Sir, your arrangements have been made. Your car is ready to take you to the airport.

—END OF COMINT—

"What do you make of this, Dennis?" asked Paul.

"Voice analysis is a ninety-nine percent match to the Serpent," reported Dennis.

"Hammadi? Ninety-nine percent, huh?"

Dennis shot a glance at his intel officer for confirmation and nodded at Paul affirmatively.

"By what means was this collected?"

Dennis looked to the intel officer for the answer once again. "He won't bite you, Captain. Tell the director your source."

"Picked it up from *Misty*, which is currently in a geosynchronous orbit over the Arabian Sea," reported the young officer, assuming Paul knew the nickname of the highly classified reconnaissance satellite.

"Do we have a good location on him?" asked Paul.

"Southeastern Herat," responded Dennis.

"Well, that does us little good in a city that size," responded Paul.

"It's not as bad as it appears, sir," said the intel officer, asserting himself.

Paul and Dennis looked at the young officer expectantly.

"The satellite is still tracking the signal. Seems someone may have forgotten to hang up the phone," he said with a hint of a smile.

"Well that *is* good news, Captain," said Paul with a smile of his own. "So we're continuing to hone in on a precise location? Any idea on when we'll have that information?"

"Any minute now, sir," reported the young officer as he watched over the shoulder of an analyst typing feverishly on a keyboard.

"Any clues on who was at the other end of the line or where the call terminated?"

"Voice analysis turned up negative on recognition," answered Dennis. "Initial indications show that the call was routed through Saudi Arabia. That's as far as the trace got before we lost the receiving connection."

"*They* probably remembered to hang up," answered Paul sarcastically. "OK, Dennis, get a hold of General Montague at JSOC and submit a request for a team to pay a visit to Hammadi's safe house to see if we can collect any actionable intelligence or arrest any informants. And call Jason at CIA to put a drone overhead the Herat airport. If we can pinpoint Hammadi's safe house, we can look for vehicles approaching the airport from that origin. We've gotta move fast, gents. This is one slippery son of a bitch, but he may lead us to Hanah Malkinson if we can pick up his trail."

Tzofiya waited in a comfortable wingback chair in an obscure corner of the hotel lobby for the rest of the team to arrive when she recognized Micah Bachman approaching the front desk. She was able to get his attention as he made his way toward the front door.

"Hello, Micah," she said as he was walking by.

"Tzofiya Kal—" he said when she quickly held up her hand.

"Cohen," she said.

"Ah, yes. Agent *Cohen*. On yet another prime minister-directed assignment," he said with the smile of a salesman. "Do you mind?" he asked, indicating his intent to sit near her.

"Of course," she answered. "I see your disregard for the integrity of communications security protocol hasn't changed."

"I'm sorry, Tzofiya. It's just that I am used to referring to you by your *real* name," he quietly admitted while placing his satchel against the leg of a table situated between them. The satchel opened slightly when it came to rest against the table, revealing some of the contents of the leather bag. "It is good to know you are on this assignment, Tzofiya. Just a tragedy. I mean, who would've ever thought the DPM could be caught up in something so...well, tragic."

Tzofiya found Micah's comments somewhat odd considering he was the DPM's only legal lifeline. She steered the conversation toward surface pleasantries, careful not to reveal too much of what she and the team had discovered. Tzofiya was surprised when she saw the now-familiar Israeli security agent approach.

Micah picked up on Tzofiya's distraction when she looked toward the door. While doing his best to offer a courteous introduction, he turned in his chair and accidentally kicked over his leather satchel, partially exposing a laptop computer.

"My goodness," said Micah. "Looks like I could use another cup of coffee. I'm quite clumsy this morning."

Tzofiya leaned forward slightly to offer a kind gesture of assistance.

"I've got it, thank you," Micah nervously responded. When he grabbed the laptop to push it back into the satchel Tzofiya saw what looked like a pink sticker on its surface.

"Is there something I should know, Micah?" she asked, looking at him expectantly.

He laughed anxiously and said something about the antics of the people he worked with at the embassy. "Silly coworkers are always keeping me on my toes," he said, referring to the sticker. "I just noticed it this morning and haven't had time to remove it yet."

"Well, I think it's cute," she said. "May I see it?"

"Sir, we really must be going," interrupted the agent.

Tzofiya looked at the agent with disdain for the indiscretion of his interruption and poor attempt to distract.

Ian, Todd, and Leon strolled into the lobby. Micah watched as the men took a seat at a nearby table.

"Friends of yours?" Micah asked Tzofiya.

"Is it that obvious?" she retorted.

Micah extended his hand. "Pleasure seeing you again, Agent Cohen. I'm sure we'll be talking again real soon," he said.

Tzofiya returned the handshake. "You can count on it, counselor. And I'll need to have a follow-up word with you as well," she said, directing the last of her comment to the Israeli agent.

Chevalier arrived to meet the team in the hotel lobby just after 7:00 a.m. as planned. He was accompanied by Agent McEwan. Chevalier had arranged a small private conference suite in the hotel for the American team to discuss their findings and compile their reports. He was unaware that they had no intentions of filing anything, much less a report, but were instead there to collect enough information to exonerate the DPM and ultimately to pursue Hanah's kidnappers.

"Good morning, Agent Chevalier," greeted Ian with an extended hand. "Would you be so kind as to show us to the conference room?"

Chevalier led the group to a private room with a small conference table positioned in the center. Surrounding the table were six chairs.

"Sir, if you don't mind, I'd like to have one of our agents conduct a security sweep before we get settled in for the meeting," said Ian.

"Certainly," answered Chevalier.

"Leon, do your magic," said Ian.

"This won't take long," said Leon as he walked into the room and closed the door behind him.

Leon emerged a short time later. "The room is clean, but I caution everyone to refrain from getting too excited and raising their voices because, as I said, the room is *clean* but it's not soundproof, so it's not technically secure."

"Thanks, Leon," said Ian gesturing for the group to enter the room. "Tzofiya, would you like to lead the discussion?"

"Certainly. Agent Chevalier, would you please introduce your guest to the group."

"It is my pleasure to introduce Agent Nate McEwan, an American from DSS. Agent McEwan has been instrumental in helping to organize the many international organizations that are involved with this investigation."

Leon clicked away at a small laptop while Chevalier introduced each of the team members to McEwan. He accessed a government database and looked into the file of Agent McEwan while the others were engaged in conversation. He became so engrossed in the file that he failed to hear his name during the initial round of introductions.

"Leon?" said Ian.

"Huh? Oh, hi, I'm Agent Leon Lambert, SS crypto," he responded and then returned to the task of typing and analyzing.

"So the secret service is working alongside the Israelis who have the lead on this? Do I have that correct?" asked McEwan.

"That's correct," answered Ian, purposefully elusive.

McEwan nodded but sensed there might be more to the story as he had not heard of any collaboration taking place with other agencies involved in the investigation. So he remained quiet for the most part and opted to learn what he could about the dynamics of the group.

"OK folks, shall we get started?" asked Ian.

"Hold up. Am I the only one who's noticed that we're missing a member of the team?" asked Todd with raised eyebrows.

Ian looked about the room. "Anyone know where G is?" he sighed.

21

"**M**ad-dog two-two, this is Stingray, how copy, over?" The radio crackled in the SEAL team leader's earpiece as the team waited atop an abandoned apartment building near the perimeter of a small village at the edge of Herat, Afghanistan. Half a world away, the Joint Special Operations Command control center communicated directly with the highly specialized team, guiding them toward the safe house of one of the world's most dangerous and elusive terrorists. The conditions for a reconnaissance mission were near perfect. A slight, cool breeze blew from the north, the humidity was low, and the forecast was clear. The night was illuminated only by the sliver of a crescent moon, permitting the best use of NVGs, if and when required.

Paul and Dennis listened to the radio chatter as they waited for a satellite feed to connect to the NSA command center for full video.

"Stingray this is Mad-dog two-two, loud and clear," responded the SEAL team leader in a confident and quiet but raspy voice. "Two-two is prepositioned, awaiting instructions."

"Mad-dog two-two, we show you to be within one kilometer of the castle. You are cleared to launch the Raven for recon."

"Mad-dog two-two copies. Launch the Raven. Stand by for uplink and signal burst."

The team configured a small remotely piloted drone outfitted with an infrared camera and GPS signal emitter. The sophisticated electronics sent a signal to overhead satellites connected to transmitters, sensors, and cameras that projected a short-time-delay picture back to the JSOC command center in North Carolina. After a short time, the command center reported they had a good signal feed.

"Mad-dog two-two, Stingray has a good link and is assuming control. Stand by for orders."

"Mad-dog is standing by."

Static filled the video screens of the NSA command center as Paul and Dennis continued to wait on the video uplink.

"Where's the video, Dennis?" asked Paul.

"Should be any second now, boss," Dennis answered as he busily entered commands into a keyboard. The static was suddenly replaced with a green-hued picture of moving terrain from a bird's eye view. "There we go," declared Dennis.

The densely populated area of the westernmost city of Afghanistan came into view on the large NSA and JSOC command-center screens as JSOC took control of the remotely piloted drone. Comm officers worked alongside intelligence officers on the JSOC command center floor as they analyzed signal emissions that fed vectors to drone pilots and sensor operators. A real-time feed was transmitted back to the SEAL team who waited patiently for the command to proceed with the mission.

"Mad-dog two-two, this is Stingray. We show you to be positioned one-half mile east of the castle. Follow the yellow brick road and advise your ETA when able, over."

"Mad-dog two-two copies. Follow the yellow brick road. Will advise ETA when able," responded the team leader as he analyzed the data transmitted to him on his handheld device.

"OK, warriors, looks like we have a short hump to the safe house. Stay invisible and let's move."

"Let's discuss what we've got on this so far," Ian announced.

"I went over the FBI ballistics report," said Tzofiya. "Despite its apparent accuracy, something just seemed to be missing. So I took a look beyond the report and started asking questions about

Malkinson's personal weapon, his handgun. I found no mention of any analysis of the actual weapon specific to DNA, so I had it analyzed for trace DNA evidence," reported Tzofiya.

"And?" asked Ian.

"And there were elements of DNA present other than the DPM's on the grip."

"Any insight as to whose DNA?"

"No, the FBI is running it through their database. They're supposed to get back to me as soon as they have something conclusive."

"Do we have a toxicology report on the DPM yet?" asked Ian.

"On the advice of counsel, he wouldn't consent to one," responded Tzofiya.

"So lemme get this straight," said Ian. "His own lawyer advised him *not* to be tested? Any ideas on why that is?"

"Excuse me," interrupted McEwan. "I have a tox report, but it's unofficial."

"OK, we'll get back to the questionable legal advice in a minute," declared Ian. "You wanna tell me just how you were able to get an *unofficial* sample to submit for analysis? I'm no attorney, but I'd say your admission is putting you real close to breaking the law—"

"Actually, the DPM willingly submitted a sample for analysis," answered a confident McEwan.

Chevalier suddenly displayed a look of confusion and concern. "How and when did you manage to get the DPM to submit a sample while he was in my custody?"

"Oops, someone's pissed," said Leon in a lowered tone he didn't fully realize was audible to the entire group.

Ian glanced at Leon and quickly stepped in to cover for McEwan. "We Americans can be a creative lot," he said, discounting the apparent breach of protocol. "So what are the findings?" asked Ian as the group waited for McEwan's answer.

"The DPM's sample had small traces of zolpidem present."

"OK, I'll bite. What's zolpidem?" asked Ian.

"It's the active ingredient in Ambien and other powerful sleep compounds," Leon blurted, his pride in his intellect getting the best of him. He casually looked up from his keyboard when he noticed everyone staring at him in silence. "What?" he innocently asked.

"He's right," confirmed McEwan.

"So there's no way the DPM could've been coherent enough to be involved in his wife's abduction," Ian surmised. "Of course, had he *willingly* taken the drug to get a good night's sleep…"

"FBI pulled his medical records. I specifically looked for any prescriptions that may have had a zolpidem content and came up with nothing. He's never even been treated for insomnia," explained McEwan.

"OK, so what about the contents of wine bottle?" asked Tzofiya. "If we can tie a zolpidem trace to the wine bottle we can show possible involuntary ingestion."

"Listen, let's regroup. This is all productive discussion on how we can help the DPM, but I'll remind you that we should keep an equal focus on the facts that'll lead us to finding Hanah. Don't get me wrong, if we can help the DPM in the process, I'd like to do that, but we're consuming precious time we should be using to find his wife," admonished Ian. "Agent McEwan, perhaps you can follow through on the toxicology connection. Continue to work with the FBI and keep Agent Chevalier in the loop."

Ian redirected his focus to the Frenchman. "Agent Chevalier, I hope you are beginning to see where the facts are leading. It seems, to me anyway, that it's becoming increasingly clear that you may have the wrong man in custody. If there's any evidence whatsoever we can offer that helps you to consider a release of the DPM, we should do that. Meantime, my team needs to refocus on finding Hanah. What have *you* got for us, Leon?" asked Ian.

Leon looked up once again from his laptop and stopped typing long enough to answer. "I examined all of the flight logs and discovered one flight that paid the landing fee with cash. They stayed for five hours and departed without a flight plan."

"In other words, there's no paper trail that could lead us to the aircraft's origin or destination," surmised Tzofiya.

"Right," answered Leon. "But in *this* case, we may have gotten a lucky break."

"How do you figure?" asked Ian.

"Seems the airport manager insists on recording the tail numbers of every aircraft at his airport despite the lack of any law or regulation requiring him to do so. He has each pilot provide a tail number when they pay the landing fees. The airport manager discovered one particular pilot had provided a bogus tail number—"

"How'd he find that out?" asked Ian.

"He drives the parking ramp twice a day as a matter of routine. He discovered an aircraft on the ramp that didn't match up with any of the tail numbers he had in the registry, so he made a note of it and compared it against the numbers he had on file."

"He's thorough," commented Tzofiya.

"It's a small airport, so he can afford to be," answered Leon.

"So we have a verified tail number. How does that help us? Do we know what type aircraft we're looking for?" asked Tzofiya.

"Better than that, actually," explained Leon. "The airport manager took a picture of the aircraft with his cell phone, to include a close-up of the tail numbers. If this is our aircraft, we're dealing with an Antonov AN-140. It's a twin-engine all-purpose plane, Ukrainian made. It has a nonstop range of about thirteen hundred miles."

"Wow, that's money," commented Ian. "Now we're getting somewhere. Let's plug that into the database to see if we can cast a net that'll ping a location or, at the very least, a direction of its flight path."

"Already have. In fact, what I can tell you from our ATC radio communications intercepts and tracking data is that its last-known flight path was southeast. I can't speak to a final destination yet, but considering its range capabilities, I'd say it most likely landed somewhere inside Turkey to refuel."

"Good job, Leon. Stay on top of it and keep us posted on the details. If that's our aircraft, we'll need to know as soon as possible, especially if you can nail down a destination," said Ian. "OK, does anyone have anything else?" he asked.

Tzofiya spoke. "I have a question for you, Leon. And it may seem a bit off topic, but I found what appears to be a power cord at the villa. Only reason I bring it up is that it was plugged into the floor receptacle beneath the office desk, but it wasn't connected to anything. And there were no evidence markers indicating any kind of electronics were taken into evidence. Would you be able to tell me what kind of device it belongs to?"

"Probably. Do you have it with you?"

Tzofiya pulled the power cord from her bag and handed it to Leon.

"Belongs to a late-model Dell laptop," announced a confident Leon.

"That was quick. Are you certain?" she asked.

Leon smiled. "Aside from the fact that the transformer has the word 'Dell' printed on it, it's pretty much the same as most other laptop power cords. Except this one has an interesting added feature," he said, taking a closer look.

"What feature is that?" she asked.

Hammadi's safe house was an isolated building at the end of a row of similarly constructed buildings. Like most of the others in the area, it was protected by a ten-foot concrete wall, but it was slightly more illuminated than the others. A lone man smoking a cigarette stood outside the only gate on the west side of the compound.

The Raven quietly loitered high overhead a group of buildings at the edge of the city, its sophisticated electronics locked onto the signal of an open telephone line emitting from the safe house. The infrared black-and-gray display of the drone's night video provided an aerial view of the area that would alert the team of any potential areas of resistance—people or obstacles. The SEAL team took up strategic positions on adjacent buildings surrounding the safe house.

"Mad-dog two-two, this is Stingray. You are cleared to breach the castle. We show one warm body on the western perimeter. Be advised, you have a ten-minute window before the little birds arrive for extraction."

"Mad-dog two-two copies, cleared to breach, ten minutes shopping time," answered the team leader in a quiet but confident voice.

Two SEALS were positioned on the top of a nearby six-story building and took up sniper positions. The team leader, positioned in an abandoned room one floor below the snipers, fired a zip-line cable into the top of the three-story safe house. Common practice called for team members to cease all movement for twenty seconds after zip line impact to ensure the noise didn't alert anyone to their presence. Twenty seconds could sometimes seem like forever.

Fifteen, fourteen, thirteen...

The snipers scanned the area. All was clear and quiet.

Three, two, one...

"Go time," called out the team leader as he activated a small helmet-mounted microcamera outfitted with a night-vision lens. The feed was connected to all members of the team as well as linked to the satellite overhead and back to JSOC and the NSA command center.

The first member secured himself to the line. One last check of the area ahead from the snipers and the Raven overhead indicated they were safe to proceed. One by one, the team leader and two SEAL team members zipped from the adjacent building to the safe house rooftop.

"Mad-dog two-two *plus* two have reached the castle," reported the lead sniper into the team microphone as he continued to scan the area. "Mad-dog two-two, how copy?" asked the lead sniper as he scanned his night scope to reveal the team leader.

The leader pointed to his ear and returned a thumbs-up, indicating he had a good comm connection and that he was proceeding under radio silence. Two SEALs took strategic sniper positions on the rooftop while the team leader approached a rooftop door secured by a large padlock. He gestured to one of his teammates who approached with bolt cutters. He easily removed the lock. The team leader drew a silenced SIG Sauer P226 handgun and entered the building. One by one each team member disappeared into the building.

"Two-two is behind the curtain," reported the sniper lead.

Paul and Dennis watched the screen as the SEALs penetrated the safe house.

"It's a keylogger," explained Leon as he examined the small device.

"So what's a keylogger, and why would Malkinson place one on his power cord?" asked Tzofiya.

"That's the point, he wouldn't. But someone looking for hard-to-find information—say, a password or some sort of sensitive information, for instance—*would* place it there," explained Leon. "Keyloggers come in various shapes and sizes. This one, for example, is a small, battery-sized plug that serves as a connector between the user's power cord and the computer. Because the device resembles an ordinary plug extension, it is relatively easy for someone who wants to monitor a user's behavior to hide it in plain sight. It also helps that most power cords plug into the back of the computer where something like this is difficult to see."

"So how does it work?" she asked.

"As the user types, the device collects each keystroke and saves it as a text file on its own miniature hard drive. At some later point in time, the person who installed the keylogger has to return and physically remove the device in order to access the information."

"So let me get this straight," said Ian. "We have a power cord but no laptop? Agent Chevalier, would you happen to know whether your folks took a laptop into evidence?"

"I don't recall seeing one on the inventory sheet, but I can certainly verify that with the team," answered Chevalier.

"Leon?" queried Ian.

"There's nothing on the FBI's inventory list to indicate that *they* have it," answered Leon as he continued to tap away at his keyboard.

"Don't waste any more of your time, gentlemen," said Tzofiya. "I think I may know just how to handle this."

Agent Chevalier scribbled notes onto a small pad. "OK, so what have we learned from the Israeli security agents assigned to Malkinson? What are they telling us?"

"Two agents were on duty at the residence the night of the disappearance; one was on crew rest," said Tzofiya as she briefed the team on her findings.

"OK, so we know the agent posted at the front of the residence was shot and killed. Where was the other agent posted, and how does *his* role affect the events? What am I missing?" asked Ian.

"I interviewed him when I first arrived," explained Tzofiya. "He's the newest member of the security detail but has several years experience inside the agency. He claims he was taken by surprise and rendered unconscious. They nearly broke his neck when they subdued him. He's completely distraught over what took place, and he blames himself for virtually everything, including the death of his fellow agent."

"Does his story line up?" asked Ian.

"The transcript of his statement to the FBI matches my interview," explained Tzofiya.

"Understood. So his account is consistent. What about the agent who claims he was on crew rest?" asked Ian.

"There's no evidence to suggest he's lying," answered Tzofiya.

"Other than the fact that his teammate is dead and his boss's wife is missing," quipped Todd.

"Just because someone doesn't have an alibi doesn't implicate him," Tzofiya answered.

"Doesn't exonerate him either—" said Todd.

"OK, let's keep it together. The dialogue is good, but we don't need to be pissing on each other's theories," said Ian.

"I'm jes sayin'," said Todd in an attempt to have the final word.

"So what does all this tell us so far?" asked Ian, ignoring Todd's remark.

"Tells me they came in through the back and walked out the front door. When the last agent stepped up to confront them, they greased him," said Todd matter-of-factly.

"With Malkinson's gun?" asked Ian, somewhat skeptical.

Todd shrugged. "You asked for an opinion. I gave you mine. Don't shoot the messenger."

"The girl did say that the man with the tattoo waited in the foyer while another man went upstairs. He had time to return the weapon if it was used to kill the agent," offered Tzofiya. "What better way to keep Malkinson off their trail than to implicate him?" she added.

"But there's no report of forced entry," said Ian, pointing out the obvious.

They got in through a second-floor balcony using a tension tool," said Tzofiya. "I discovered it on a walk-through I conducted."

"Who uses a tension tool besides professionals?" asked Leon.

The entire team paused as they glanced around the room, as if expecting an answer of some kind from each other.

OK, we've covered the possibilities on how the bad guys managed to get into and out of the residence. We've learned from our interview with the girl that there were at least two men—" said Ian, attempting to summarize the facts.

"I believe there may have been three," interrupted Tzofiya.

"Listen, I'd love to stick around for *this* debate, but I'm gonna go check on G," announced Todd.

22

G had to think of something that would help Hanah escape her pursuers, and he had to act quickly. The building was crawling with an angry mob looking for retribution for the running-down of an innocent pedestrian, and the local police response unit was closing in.

G glanced at the stairwell. *Ro'i, look upstairs, and tell me if you see a way out. I'll look downstairs and do the same,* instructed G.

Both G and Ro'i closed their eyes and projected themselves to alternate locations to investigate viable escape options for Hanah and Munahid.

Ro'i was the first to report. *The roof is three flights up, but the door is locked. And there's no way out even if they could make it to the roof,* reported the dejected boy.

It's OK, communicated G encouragingly. *I think I found a way out.*

Ro'i appeared immediately at G's side, two floors down. G had discovered an underground corridor that connected the building with another across the street. The corridor was completely unlit and would require a courageous leap of faith for Hanah to take the dark path. Considering their life-and-death circumstances, G was confident they would take it…if only they knew about it.

This is their way out, exclaimed Ro'i, looking at G for confirmation.

G nodded, went down on one knee, and reached out to hold the boy by his small shoulders. Looking him in the eye, he said, *Ro'i, the only way she's going to know about this is if you show her. It's not an easy thing to do while she's awake. You've got to get through to her. I need you to concentrate and show her.*

I'll tell her—

No. Show her. You've got to show her. Do you understand?

Ro'i nodded. *I'll show her,* he said.

Good, I'm going to see if there's anything I can do about the crowd outside the door.

One of the video screens in the command center fluttered and suddenly changed to the first-person perspective of the team leader's helmet camera. Dennis pointed out the channel change to Paul. Both men were riveted to the screen as the scene played out.

The unsteady video depicted the extended arms of the team leader, both hands holding his handgun aimed into the stillness of a darkened hallway, illuminated only by the lime-green hue of the night-vision camera. The numerical icon on the lower left of the video screen was 22, indicating the feed was coming from the team leader. The camera scanned from right to left, consistent with the swivel of the team leader's head. The forward movement of the video stopped as the leader paused at a lower level landing and slowly scanned to the left to check on his teammates. The camera momentarily captured two SEAL team members in trail. The leader crouched and extended his hand and silently signaled to each member to take up defensive positions. The only sound coming through the speakers was the concentrated breathing of the team leader. Suddenly, the faint sound of voices and laughter could be heard, stopping the leader in his tracks.

The leader extended a corner scope and quietly peered around the edge of a wall at the base of the landing. He saw three men. Two were seated at a small table with their backs to the team, while a third stood facing the hallway the team would approach from. The team leader signaled to his team that the man standing was armed with an assault rifle. They had no choice but to take him out.

The team leader checked his watch: eight and a half minutes remaining. No time to waste. He crouched and took aim at his target while the two teammates stood over him with sound-suppressed MP5SD submachine guns at the ready in case the remaining two men resisted.

The team leader drew a breath and fired the silenced weapon with a slow, easy exhale, striking the man in the forehead. Blood spattered on the wall behind him as he fell in place. The SEAL team members charged the two men still seated at the table and subdued them before they even knew what happened. They quickly bound their hands and feet with zip ties and rendered them unconscious to prevent them from alerting anyone else who might have been within earshot.

The team leader approached the dead man and declared, "Dead check…two-two, confirmed kill."

"OK, Tzofiya. How do you come to the conclusion that there were *three* people involved in Hanah's abduction?" Ian asked.

"Well, I can easily see how *two* men could pull this off, but I'm still puzzled by the circumstances surrounding the murder of the agent posted in front of the residence," explained Tzofiya.

"How so?" asked Ian.

"I keep asking myself why the agent wasn't found *inside* the residence. There was enough commotion inside that any security guard worth his salt would've picked up on that and entered the residence to investigate."

"Maybe the intruders were really quiet. After all, most of the action occurred upstairs," said Leon, offering a plausible explanation.

Tzofiya nodded in agreement. "If that were the case, Leon, don't you think he would've at least had his weapon drawn when he noticed the assailants exiting the front door? Look, we all know Hanah's an intelligent woman. If the handprint on the wall is hers—"

"It's hers," said McEwan. "FBI was able to pull a partial finger-print and confirmed it's Mrs. Malkinson's. The blood turned out to be a perfect DNA match to hers."

"Then that only strengthens my theory," explained Tzofiya. "I think Hanah was trying to tell us something when she purposely left three finger swipes against the wall. It was a final attempt at resistance."

"Maybe she only had blood on three fingers," said Leon with a shrug, offering another dose of a logical consideration.

All eyes were on Tzofiya. "As I said, I think she's smarter than that. She saw something. And her life depended on leaving any clue she could," defended Tzofiya.

"We have no idea how coherent she was. For all we know, she could've been merely trying to grab something to keep herself from being abducted," said Leon. "She also could've ingested some of the very same drug-laced wine that we assume her husband drank. I'm not trying to poke holes in everything you say, but it just seems there's an alternate explanation for just about any theory we can come up with, dontcha think?"

"OK, how 'bout this? Ballistics shows the dead agent's gunshot wound came from close range," explained Tzofiya. "He was either asleep on the job or familiar with his killer."

Leon thought a moment. "Two inside plus one outside gives you three," he admitted. "But does the scenario fit your theory, or does your theory fit the scenario?"

"Not sure yet," said Tzofiya. "But I know how to find out."

G stood still, listening to the echo of distant footsteps in the quiet, dimly lit hallway. He cautiously began walking the long corridor in order to gain a better perspective of the threat when, suddenly, he noticed a silhouette of a lone figure pass the end of the corridor. G froze, his heart skipping a beat as he simultaneously re-alized he couldn't be seen by those in a conscious state. Breathing a momentary sigh of relief, he resumed his slow forward progression and retrained his focus on the task of finding the crowd of pursuers. The sound of footsteps grew louder with each step he took toward the end of the corridor. G froze once again when he noticed the lone, dark figure reappear, except this time, it stopped and turned toward him.

G squinted—partially to refocus and partially to gain a better understanding of the figure. Chills ran through his body when the figure spoke to him.

"You watched him shoot me, and you did nothing to prevent it," he said, the deep sound of his voice resonating through G's core.

Shit...

G knew right away that he was facing the spirit of the man Munahid had killed in the room. He also knew just how good a fighter the man was.

"I couldn't have done anything to prevent it if I wanted to. Seems one of you had to die, given the circumstances," G reasoned. It didn't matter. This ghost was looking for revenge, and G was the first *real* person he had encountered.

The footsteps of the crowd grew louder as G stood his ground, staring down his unexpected opponent. Suddenly, and without warning, the man lunged toward G with lightning speed. G instinctively reacted, crouching and twisting his torso just as the man reached him, narrowly averting a broadside body collision. Time and motion slowed as G watched the man sail above him in a feeble attempt to grapple with nothing but the empty space. At just the right moment and in one fluid movement, G thrust his fist straight up into the man's chest, sending him tumbling down the corridor.

G slowly rose to his feet, somewhat surprised by his own abilities. He turned to look at the man lying motionless on the floor as time returned to normal speed. Suddenly and unexpectedly, a small band of armed police flooded the corridor behind him, engulfing him in a crowd of people. The police began banging on doors throughout the corridor as they searched for Hannah and Munahid. The incessant banging was deafening.

"Ro'i, you've gotta get 'em out of there," shouted G audibly. "Get 'em out, Ro'i. Get them out now—"

Dennis and Paul watched as the operations center screen revealed a slow, easy scan of the room; two prisoners were subdued, lying unconscious on the floor, and one enemy KIA, bleeding out in a corner of the small room. The team collected the weapons, unloaded the ammunition, and quickly disabled them.

The leader signaled for the team to move out and then followed one of his teammates who assumed the lead while the last man took up a trailing position far enough behind to provide cover fire if needed.

The team quietly descended to the second floor, their night-vision goggles revealing the cluttered path ahead. Two doors were located on either side of a small hallway, one of which was slightly ajar. The leader reached into his vest and retrieved a small remote-controlled vehicle that he sent into the open room. He maneuvered the vehicle far enough into the room to conduct a quick threat assessment. Satisfied the room was safe to enter, he directed his teammate to enter and sweep the room. The teammate returned to the hallway and indicated with a slow swivel of his head that there was nothing to see.

The team leader reached for the doorknob of the closed door and slowly turned it until he heard it click. The trailing team member stopped him from pushing it open and indicated that he believed the door was rigged with an explosive device. As he looked down to type a message into his personal communications device he saw someone ascending the stairs from the first floor. Time and motion slowed as he dropped the device and drew his weapon.

"Down!" he commanded in just over a whisper as he took aim at the assailant. The leader kept his grip on the doorknob and held the door closed against its frame as he fell to the floor in response to the warning. The SEAL fired two quick silenced shots, sending one into the assailant's eye and the second one into his neck.

Dennis and Paul were riveted to the screen as they watched the close call and second kill take place. The trailing team member took over as leader and directed his teammate to clear the first floor. While he was gone, the new leader assisted his team member still holding the doorknob. He checked his watch: four minutes remaining.

"We have to abort," whispered the new leader.

"Negative!" demanded the teammate holding the doorknob. "We're at the threshold. We've gotta get into this room. Find a way."

The third member returned from the first floor. "The building is clear," he whispered.

Dennis directed Paul's attention to an adjacent monitor that projected a wide area satellite perspective that captured a five-mile radius of the safe house. Instructions from the JSOC command center could be heard on the NSA command center's speaker system.

"Have *Misty* cast a wider net please. We need more coverage," commanded an unknown voice. Suddenly, the picture projected by the satellite zoomed out to reveal a wider area surrounding the safe house. Very little movement was observed. Any movement that *was* detected was immediately analyzed and tracked.

Dennis and Paul could see three moving vehicles identified and tracked, red digital boxes surrounding their images. Three helicopters were moving in from the northeast, each identified with a blue digital box and associated alphanumeric designators—friendly forces inbound to retrieve the SEALs.

"Little birds are three minutes out," announced a voice over the loudspeaker in the ops center.

Digital text appeared on screen intended to provide an extraction notification to the SEAL team. They had to make a decision and move quickly to the rally point.

"Sir, we have to abort," whispered the SEAL to his teammate.

"Negative. I need you two to escort our prisoners to the rooftop and wait for your ride home. I plan on getting into this room and will join you in just a few minutes," he said.

"Sir—"

"Don't argue with me, Chief," he responded, looking intently into the man's eyes. "Now go!"

The SEAL reluctantly joined his teammate and left for the rooftop, picking up their prisoners on the way as directed by the more senior member. As they emerged from the building, the sniper announced their status.

"Two-three and two-four are clear of the castle with two in custody. No visual yet on two-two."

The chainsaw-like buzzing sound from the helicopters cut through the odd stillness of the night as the SEALs and their prisoners were extracted from the rooftop while the snipers watched over them. Two more helos hovered nearby and extracted one of the snipers from a nearby rooftop.

"Robin Hood Six, proceed to the little bird for extraction, over," commanded a voice in the last-remaining sniper's earpiece.

"Negative, Sting-Ray. Standing by for Mad-dog two-two, over," answered the determined sniper as he continued to scan the rooftop for his teammate.

"Proceed to the helo, Robin Hood. That's an order."

The SEAL conducted one final scan of the area before he acknowledged the order and reluctantly made his way to the helicopter. After he buckled himself in he conducted one more scan and saw the team leader emerge from the rooftop door holding a small box in his arms.

"Robin Hood Six has a visual on Mad-dog two-two," he reported. "Two-two is on the rooftop lookin' for a ride. Looks like he has some souvenirs."

G awoke to the sound of incessant knocking against his door. The sound grew to an intense banging as he dragged himself out of bed to answer the door.

"You look like shit, bro," said Todd as he pushed his way into the room. "OK, where is she?"

"What are you talking about? Who?" asked G, attempting to find some semblance of coherency.

"Well, the way I figure it, the only reason you—or I—would miss a prearranged team meeting is if you had some bad-ass broad up in this joint. So where is she?" he asked, finally standing still long enough for G to answer him.

G returned a blank stare and shook his head. "There's no 'broad' here. I just overslept," he admitted.

"Oh, I see, you were in one of your dream encounter things, is that it? Maybe I shoulda been more careful about waking you up. We both know what happened the last time I made that mistake."

G sat on the edge of the bed, staring blankly at the floor, ignoring most of Todd's rhetoric. A look of concern slowly appeared on his face as he began to recall remnants of his dream.

Todd picked up on the physical signs, stopped talking, and sat silently in a chair across from G to patiently wait for him to sort out his thoughts.

"I know where she is," G said, slowly looking up at his friend.

"You know where *who* is?"

"Hanah…I know where she is."

Todd leaned forward, placing his elbows on his knees. "How certain are you, G? Cause you know once we bring this to the team, they're gonna wanna know how you know this. So you better be damn sure."

"Todd, I know where she is. I just don't know *exactly* where."

"Damn, G, why you always makin' this so damn complicated? Either you know or you don't know. Which is it?"

"She's in Yemen. I'm just not certain yet on exactly *where* in Yemen."

"OK, that's more information than we currently have," said Todd. "We have to alert the team. Splash some water on your face to wake your ass up the rest of the way, so we can bring the news to 'em."

"She's in trouble, Todd."

"Yeah, no shit, dude. She's in the hands of terrorists. What are you trying to tell me?"

"I'm trying to tell you that she got away from her captors and is eluding them as I frigging tell you this. She's in the middle of some shithole city over there right now on the run."

"This is some heavy shit, man. You *gotta* take me with you on one of these dream encounter trips sometime. But for now, we gotta *move* on this. Get yourself together and I'll brew up some coffee. Make it quick."

"What do you mean we lost him?" shouted the JSOC director, a one-star general officer. "I place one of the most expensive and highly capable satellites over the area and we can't track a few roaming vehicles and nail this bastard? What about the airport he was supposedly en route to? Anyone come up with any activity there?"

"No, sir. No sign of him at the airport."

"Have CIA pay a hospitality visit to the two prisoners we picked up at the safe house. Tell them they have carte blanche on the interview process. I wanna know where that rat bastard is headed," he ordered. "Jim, call our friends at NSA and tell them the unfortunate news. But give them some reassurance that we're confident we'll be able to get something out of the guests we have in custody."

"Right away, sir."

Hanah began to panic as she heard the incessant pounding against the corridor doors outside the walls of her hiding place. She knew it wouldn't be long before someone would be opening the door just outside the stairwell—and then they would be discovered.

Munahid looked up into the stairwell leading to the roof. "We cannot stay here," he said. "We must find a safer place to hide."

Hanah was inclined to follow him. Anyplace else had to be safer. He grabbed her hand to lead her upstairs when she hesitated.

Momma...this way, Momma.

Munahid squeezed her hand in an attempt to encourage her to follow, but she stood her ground and listened as Ro'i did his best to *show* her the safest alternative they had.

You have to come downstairs, Momma. I will show you the way.

She looked at Munahid and pulled against him, slowly shaking her head. "We must go this way," she demanded.

"We have no way of knowing where that leads. There is no light—"

"Please," she said. "I can't explain it. I just know we need to go this way."

Hanah's heart quickened as she descended the dark stairwell, each step taking her and Munahid into darker surroundings. They came upon a landing with barely enough light to see each other when Munahid again expressed his reservations about moving forward.

"We have no idea where this will take us," he argued. "Besides, we cannot even see the path ahead."

"I know it'll take us away from certain danger and the risk of being captured, and that's all that matters," she answered confidently.

The two stared into the dark corridor, knowing their fate rested on the courage of their decision to move through the unknown blackness, away from the danger that pursued them. Intense banging began on the door one flight above them.

This way, Momma. I'll show you the way...

The sound of voices echoing behind them, Hanah grabbed Munahid's hand and boldly stepped forward into the blacked-out corridor, her hand extended before her in search of anything that would help her to better navigate the unknown. She stepped to one side of the corridor to allow her hand to make contact with the wall, and this helped them make slow and steady progress away from their pursuers.

Her eyes slowly adjusted to the lack of light. She glanced ahead and saw the faint outline of a small alcove. Munahid held onto her hand tightly and kept pace with her as they moved along the dark hallway.

"We'll pause here," she said. "Watch your head," she warned Munahid as he ducked into the alcove alongside her.

Hanah glanced back toward the stairwell to see flashlight beams scanning the area. She quickly ducked into the alcove to avoid the scan of random beams of light. Her heart pounded as she prayed her pursuers wouldn't enter the corridor to search for them. They were dangerously close. Voices echoed in the corridor as one member of the crowd considered the likelihood that Hanah and Munahid had taken the dark route.

Dust completely enveloped the small craft as the blades pushed the helicopter from the desolate, sandy earth. Siraj donned a pair of night-vision goggles and watched the ground grow distant as the tiny craft climbed into the night sky and departed the western outskirts of the city in a lights-out configuration.

The pilot pointed the nose of the helicopter to the west and pushed the throttle forward, staying in close proximity to the ground as they sped toward the western border with neighboring Iran. Siraj's men had precoordinated the border crossing to allow him to get into the tightly sealed country and ultimately to a little-used airport on the outskirts of the obscure city of Kariz, where a private jet awaited.

The thirty-minute ride seemed to take longer than usual as Siraj thought about the reason he was making the trip. He despised incompetence and was determined to find his prisoner before the news of her escape made it to the Iranians.

The pilot glanced over his left shoulder and displayed a look of concern as he returned his focus to the instrument panel and the terrain ahead. Siraj picked up on the troubled look and questioned him. The pilot pointed to the sophisticated onboard radar screen and indicated he might have seen something behind them in the distance. The area was known to host an occasional US or British patrol helicopter or unmanned aerial reconnaissance aircraft.

Siraj looked over his right shoulder into the dark night. Even with the assistance of his night-vision goggles he was unable to spot anything at all in the black of the night sky. He glanced back to the radar screen and saw the demarcation of the Iranian border—and relative safety—roughly fifteen miles ahead.

Todd held the door open for G. The entire group fell silent as they watched the two make their way into the room.

"I see you managed to find our missing—" said Ian.

"We're gonna need a private team meeting," announced Todd, interrupting Ian's comment and taking control of the conversation. "Agent Chevalier, would you excuse us, please?"

"Certainly," answered the French agent as he stood. "I have other tasks to attend to anyway. Please let me know if you need me for any reason," he said, directing the offer to Ian and Tzofiya.

"Agent McEwan, what's your current clearance classification?" asked Todd.

"TS/SCI," answered McEwan, citing one of the highest levels of classification.

Todd glanced at Leon who was busy typing away on his keyboard. "He's current."

"OK, you can stay. We may need you anyway," he answered while he waited for Chevalier to close the door. "Is the room secure?" asked Todd as he took a seat at the small table and lowered his voice.

"The room is secure," answered Leon.

Todd looked at McEwan. "What I'm about to reveal to you is top secret. I hope I don't have to remind you of the penalties of revealing any information that is disclosed from here forward, but if you make a bad decision and any harm comes to anyone on my team because of your indiscretion, I'll shoot you myself. Do you understand?"

"What's this about? Where are you going with this?" asked Ian.

"I'm gettin' to that. I just wanna make sure the agent understands and acknowledges the seriousness of the situation. The last thing we need is someone who misunderstands and ends up being responsible for one of us getting hurt or killed."

McEwan nodded. "I understand," he said, glancing at Tzofiya.

"You don't have to worry about her," said Leon, picking up on McEwan's concern. "Her clearance is higher than all of ours combined."

"All right, I'm good," said Todd.

"OK, proceed," said Ian with a slight hand gesture, still curious as to where Todd was headed.

Todd provided a brief synopsis of their mission to McEwan and Tzofiya, revealing the nature of their investigation and intent of their mission along with an admission that they didn't actually work for the US secret service, but rather, an "undisclosed" US government agency assigned by the highest authorities in collaboration of both countries to find and retrieve Hanah Malkinson.

"Consider yourselves read in," said Todd. "Do either of you have any questions?" he asked as he wrapped up the disclosure statement.

McEwan spoke up. "Just curious why you feel compelled to read me in on this."

"Because G is about to give us some important information that'll put us in motion, and we're gonna need someone who'll remain here to cover our asses and keep the DPM informed. I unilaterally voted for you. Any issues with that?"

"Nope."

"Cool. G, you wanna tell the group what you know?" asked Todd.

24

"**W**icked One, flight of three, returning to base," announced the pilot of the lead special-operations helicopter.

Three stealth-black MH-6 helicopters lifted off from the southwest corner of the city into the night sky, each carrying members of the elite SEAL team, the lead aircraft carrying two prisoners blindfolded and secured inside the cramped fuselage. As the pilot of the last helicopter maneuvered to join the flight, he detected an airborne target on his infrared radar.

"Control, Wicked Three has a bogey bearing two-seven-zero at five-hundred feet, traveling west. Request permission to break from the flight for a visual ID check."

"Wicked Three, control, that's approved. Wicked Two, accompany Wicked Three and report back when able. Remain within five miles and do not engage, repeat, *do not engage*."

"Wicked Three copies. Two, join left side," announced the lead pilot as the two helicopters leaned into the wind and sped off in pursuit of the target while the third proceeded back to the base of operations with the prisoners and two members of the SEAL team.

"Control, Wicked Three is approaching the target, currently trailing by three miles and closing."

"Control copies. Do you have a visual ID?"

"That's a negative for Wicked Three. Wicked Two, let's push it up and move in a little closer."

Suddenly, both crews heard the sound of metal striking the fuselage.

"Wicked Three is taking ground fire. Wicked flight, break away, break away," declared the aircraft commander of the lead aircraft as the two helicopters broke off the pursuit, simultaneously diverged, and executed an aggressive, high-angle evasive maneuver.

The aircrews began scanning the area using their forward-looking infrared radar while the SEALs aboard the tiny craft searched the area for the source of the ground fire through their NVGs. Overhearing their situation, the command and control center ordered them to return to the base.

"Wicked Three, control, return to base, I say again, return to base."

The flight commander of one of the helicopters saw a vehicle, marked by a dust trail, accelerating toward a nearby, isolated highway. "Wicked Three has a visual on a possible ground target. Request permission to engage."

"Negative, Wicked Three, return to base."

The flight commander glanced at his copilot with frustration, knowing that the assailant was literally saved by the order that kept the able crew from annihilating them.

"Wicked Three copies, returning to base," answered the flight commander. "Let's take it home warriors. ETA: twelve minutes."

The NSA control panel illuminated, indicating a call from the JSOC direct line.

"Operations, Kinkaid speaking."

"Sir, Chief Jenner at JSOC Ops. General Montague asked me to call and inform you that our HVT managed to successfully evade us. We're currently unaware of his whereabouts, but the general asked me to ensure that you are aware of our plan to conduct rigorous interviews with two detainees we have in custody. The general is confident we'll get something out of them."

"I understand, Chief. Please thank the general for the update. We're standing by to assist as required."

Dennis hung up the phone and looked at Paul disappointedly. "You're not gonna believe this. Seems Hammadi managed to get away, but we're told to stand by for information they expect to collect from the detainees."

"I know Montague. He'll get something useful outta them, but to be honest, we don't have time for this shit," said Paul. "Have we received a SITREP from our team in France, or are they just sitting on their collective asses on the beaches of Saint-Tropez?"

"The next SITREP is due in two hours. I expect to hear from Special Agent Wolfe on time."

"Keep me posted," said Paul as he turned and walked away.

Siraj tuned the airborne radio to a discreet frequency to alert his team of the successful border crossing and to provide an update on his estimated time of arrival. The helicopter pilot flipped a switch to illuminate the navigation lights shortly after crossing the border and put the tiny craft on a heading that would take it directly to the hardened-dirt runway at the outskirts of Kariz, Iran.

Four SUVs parked alongside a sleek, white Cessna Citation X at the remote airport. Several armed men stood by their vehicles as one man spoke into a handheld radio.

"Stand by, everyone. The khalifa is approaching," he announced. Turning toward the Citation he gave the order for the crew to start the engines. The navigation lights illuminated and preceded the high-pitched whistle of the engines as the crew brought the jet to life. He directed the drivers of the SUVs to tactically reposition themselves and to turn on their headlights to reveal their position adjacent to the runway.

The men watched as the helicopter touched down on the ramp and a man emerged from the passenger side. For some of them, it was the first time they had ever seen the elusive terrorist, and if they were lucky, it would be the last.

An admonishment to remain vigilant echoed in the earpiece of each man. The order served as a stark reminder of the serious nature of the transfer operation. Most had heard stories of others who had not done so well in protection details and ended up paying dearly for their complacency.

The pilots of the Citation were busy making last-minute adjustments and completing their checklist when Siraj stepped on board. He said nothing to them and took a seat in the back of the jet while the handler pulled the stairs, secured the door, and then poked his head inside the cockpit. The pilot pulled back one of the earphones to hear the handler.

"The door is secure, and the khalifa is ready for departure."

The pilot returned a nod, replaced his headphones, and continued making adjustments.

"Checklist complete," he announced to the copilot who acknowledged the same and followed with a thumbs-up signal to the pilot.

Two SUVs followed the jet to the departure end of the runway and stopped to watch it taxi onto the runway to power up its engines. The whistle of the engines transitioned to a roar as the pilot released the brakes sending the jet screaming down the runway and off into the night sky.

All eyes were on G as he began to brief the group on Hanah's situation.

"Excuse me," interrupted McEwan. "I don't mean to be the cynic in the room, but how do you know this? I mean, *no one* has been able to determine Mrs. Malkinson's whereabouts, and yet you sit here in complete confidence and report the details of her situation as if you've seen them firsthand," said McEwan. He looked around the room and saw everyone looking at him. Judging by their silent, stoic stares, he guessed no one shared his same viewpoint or opinion. "OK, so apparently, I'm missing something," McEwan conceded.

"First time is always the toughest, Nate," Todd said. "For the sake of brevity, let's just say that G has certain unorthodox gifts that allow him to see things most of us simply can't. Your reaction is normal, but for us to explain it to you would waste time we don't have, so we're gonna ask you to play along and trust us. Besides, I think you'll either pick up on it or simply accept it once you learn that G's never been wrong."

McEwan nodded, choosing to accept the evasive and brief explanation rather than debate the point. After all, he had just been granted a need-to-know elevation of his security clearance—something akin to a field promotion—on an operation he was never meant to be a part of. The last thing he wanted was to be ostracized before he ever got the chance of supporting such a pivotal mission.

G resumed his briefing. "As I said, I can't be certain of Hanah's *exact* location, but I can say with complete confidence that she's in Yemen," he said, glancing at McEwan. "For starters, I know the dialect. It's subtle but if you know what to listen for, there's no mistaking it. Oh, and the display of the national flag is a dead giveaway if you pay attention to the obvious."

"OK, that's all good. We know what country she's in, G," said Todd with raised eyebrows. "You got anything more specific we might actually be able to act on?"

"If I had to guess—and I hate to—I'd say she's somewhere on the coast near a port city," he said as he looked at Leon.

"So you can't be any more specific than that yet? Is it your guess that it's at least a major port city?" asked Tzofiya, searching for clarity.

G shrugged and slowly shook his head. "I think I may have already mentioned that I don't make it a practice to guess. Besides, I figured one of you analysts could answer that much better than I can. But I suspect it would come down to the simplicity of it being a good location in terms of a strategic perspective. Leon?"

"Actually, that makes sense, G," Leon agreed. "If I had to guess—and I guess more than I care to admit—it comes down to Aden. It's a strategic location for just about every reason imaginable, and there's a raw history there of extremist acceptance. Aden is predominantly controlled by the Sunni, a more radical sect of Islam. Who here doesn't recall the Cole bombing?"

"Any way you can confirm the location for us, G?" asked Ian.

"That was *my* next question," added Tzofiya.

"Sure, I can do that, but there are two distinct *disadvantages* to my doing that. One: it takes time we don't have."

"And two?" asked Ian.

G looked at each person in the room and stopped at Ian. "It'll take time Hanah doesn't have."

"In other words, the situation is not exactly stable," said Todd. "Give it to 'em straight, G."

"Hanah has managed to escape her captors, but the situation isn't encouraging," admitted G. "She's alone—well, sort of—in a city about as culturally different as it can be from her own city of Tel Aviv. Unless she has help, they'll find her soon, and they won't respond well to her insolence."

"What's your recommended course of action?" asked Ian.

Hanah breathed a sigh of relief when the flashlight beams disappeared, and the sound of the voices grew distant. She looked toward the distant end of the dark corridor and could see a faint outline of a doorway some thirty yards away. She hesitated and closed her eyes for a moment to say a quick prayer for guidance.

I can hear you, Momma. You're almost there. Keep moving.

When Hanah opened her eyes, she saw what quite literally appeared to be an illuminated path that would lead her and her companion to the end of the dark corridor. She reached out to grab Munahid's hand, surprising him.

"Where are we going?" he asked, resisting slightly.

"This way," she answered.

"And what way is that? How can you see anything *at all* in this darkness?"

She realized by his comment that, for some reason, she could see more clearly than he could.

"It'll be OK. We're almost there," she answered encouragingly.

The two came upon a gate at the end of the corridor. Faint light spilled in from an adjacent stairwell and shone against the backside of its frame. Munahid was encouraged when he first saw it.

"Good job," he declared, somewhat relieved. "Be careful. We have no idea what or who may be waiting on the other side of the gate."

"Our advantage is that no one knows where we are right now," she said. "So we have to move fast but cautiously."

Munahid stepped through the gate first and peered around the corner at the base of the stairwell. Nodding to Hanah, he stepped forward to take the lead to ascend the stairs. They had just reached a well-lit intermediate landing when the door to the stairwell opened just above them.

25

Siraj listened as a man shouted over the telephone. The satellite phone in the aft cabin of the sleek jet gave Siraj the freedom to communicate securely with anyone in the world.

"I want *every* man you've got searching *every* corner of that city. You will do whatever it takes to find that woman," stressed the agitated caller. "We cannot afford to lose her at this stage of our operation. There's just too much at risk with her on the loose."

"You just leave that to me and worry about your own ass. And don't forget who you're talking to," warned Siraj. He abruptly terminated the call and spoke directly to his handler. "Make whatever calls you have to in order to find that woman before we arrive. This bitch is beginning to irritate me."

The handler contacted the leader of a terrorist cell in Aden.

"I can assure you that we have several men searching every corner of the city for her," reported the cell leader. "We have narrowed our search to a three-block radius of where she was last seen and are confident it will only be a matter of time before we have her in custody."

"I hope you are as correct as you are confident," retorted the handler. "The khalifa has a personal interest in her capture, and he has no patience for carelessness. You are to report her capture or any changes at once."

"As you wish," answered the leader as he heard the click of the call termination.

"I think it's time we make a trip to Yemen," said G.

"Agree," said Ian. "But before we get into the details, I'd like to excuse Agent McEwan if there's nothing further for him.

"Of course," said G.

"Before you go, I have something I want you to deliver to the DPM for me," Tzofiya said to McEwan. She looked at Leon who still had the laptop power cord. Leon handed the power cord to McEwan while Tzofiya offered a brief explanation of her findings and how the pieces of her theory had come together. "My only regret is that I'll be unable to deliver it to him myself," she admitted.

McEwan smiled and assured her that he fully understood. "I look forward to presenting it to the DPM. And I'm quite sure he'll be equally as grateful for the opportunity to present it to his lawyer," he added with a wink. "I'm quite sure I'll be able to convince Chevalier to support us on a preliminary release of the DPM if we can get Bachman to cop to the unauthorized acquisition of the laptop," he added. "The pieces just seem to fit, if you know what I mean."

McEwan thanked the team for their trust and the cursory operational role and closed the door as he left the room.

"OK, where were we?" asked Ian.

"Uh, excuse me, but you don't just catch a plane and fly to Yemen. At least *we* don't," said Todd, stating the obvious, picking up right where G left off. "How do you propose we go about pulling this off, G?"

"Remember how we pulled off the Colombia extraction?" asked G.

"Yeah, I remember all too well," admitted Todd with a nervous chuckle. "I remember we convinced the bad guys to *let* us into their country. We didn't have to *sneak* in. I also remember how we almost got killed trying to get our asses outta there."

G listened patiently to Todd's concerns and then explained how his operational plan would call for similar deceptive practices but would also require additional creativity and even more precision.

"Leon," said G.

"Closest CIA outpost with a runway is located in Djibouti. The international airport hosts daily flights into Yemen," reported Leon. "There's also an embedded SOC FWD in Yemen we can count on in the event things get really contentious and we need firepower."

"SOC FWD is an acronym for Special Operations Component, Forward," offered Leon when he noticed the confused look on Tzofiya's face.

"Sorry, Tzofiya. Thank you, Leon," said G.

G looked at Ian to ensure he was still following. Ian nodded.

"I'd really like to avoid a firefight. And I believe we can pull that off under the construct of this plan," said G. "Leon, reach out to the CIA station chief on the ground in Yemen. Provide them with a guest list on who'll be on our commercial flight. Secure the necessary visas on foreign passports for our travelers—"

"Who do you want on the manifest?" asked Leon.

"Todd, Ian, Tzofiya, and yours truly," answered G. "Todd will go in on a Somali passport. Put Ian on a British passport under operational cover as a journalist. Tzofiya will be on a Yemeni passport returning to the country as a citizen from a visit abroad," instructed G.

"And you?" asked Leon.

"Put me on an Omani passport," said G.

Leon returned a curious look, as did Todd and most of the others.

"Do you even know how to speak the language and in an Omani dialect?" asked Tzofiya.

G shook his head. "Not yet, but I should have it down by the time I need it."

Tzofiya returned a blank stare while Todd placed a hand on his forehead and smiled.

"What's *my* role?" asked Leon.

"Orchestra director," answered G.

"Maestro," chuckled Todd.

Ignoring the sarcasm, G continued. "You'll operate from a safe distance in Djibouti at the US embassy. You'll be essential to our situational awareness through our eyes and ears and will keep the operations center aware of our status while we're on the mission. Can you control those drones of yours from that distance?"

Leon smiled. "All I need is discreet satellite bandwidth, and I can make 'em do whatever you need 'em to do from any spot on the planet. Oh, and I can preprogram them if you need me to."

"I'll clear that with the home office," offered Ian as he jotted some notes into a small notebook. "You'll have whatever bandwidth and frequencies you need."

Tzofiya was impressed as she watched each member of the American team formulate the precision plan on the fly, as if each one intuitively knew his role and responded in kind to each other's strengths.

"OK, we'll need an air carrier for our ride in," said G.

"I'll contact the bubbas in Djibouti to see if we can secure seats on a small commercial airliner, something that routinely operates in and out of Aden," volunteered Todd. "CIA should have intel and influence on that process."

"That'll work. We'll want to be among other passengers, so don't go over the top on anything like private conveyance. Just ensure we're covered on the receiving end if at all possible as we clear their immigration and security," explained G. "Everyone will meet at a predetermined rally point at the designated time to receive weapons and detailed instructions."

G glanced at Ian to ensure he was following everything.

"So far this sounds like a good plan to get us into the country. What I haven't heard yet, however, is just where we're headed once we get there, and just how the heck you expect us to get out once we have Hanah. It's not like we can just walk out holding her hand. We need an exit strategy," said Ian.

⊕

Micah hung up the phone and stared out one of the windows of the villa. His frustration was difficult to suppress as he contemplated the vulnerability of his position. The situation he had assumed would lead to a political opening in his native Israel was changing rapidly and beginning to reveal its flaws. His plan—which he had devised himself and on the basis of which he had garnered support from some of his country's worst enemies with promises that he would deliver upon his attainment of power—had begun to fray.

Micah had the misfortunate and unenviable distinction of being at a forced meeting with Siraj Hammadi some ten years earlier while on an official visit to the United Nations. While still serving as a defense attaché for the Knesset, Micah had presented his country's perspective and concerns on recent findings of Iranian nuclear power ambitions. Israel was understandably concerned about the implications of Iran possessing the knowledge to proliferate nuclear power and the very real possibility that the Islamic nation would develop nuclear weapons as a result.

After attending a long day's session, he stepped into the main elevator of the Benjamin Hotel, acknowledged a man in the elevator with a nod, and pressed the button that would take him to his fifth-floor suite. When the doors opened, both men exited the elevator and took the same path. Micah thought little of the coincidence until the man stopped behind him as he approached the door to his room.

"May I help you, sir?" asked a nervous Micah as he turned to face the man.

"Perhaps," answered the man with a nod. "May I come in and discuss just *how* you may help me?"

Alone on a quiet floor of a hotel, Micah had paused to evaluate any option or opportunity to refuse while doing his best to psychologically assess the stranger. Micah was no match for the confident and much-younger Siraj as his first attempt at a kind refusal did little to convince the man that he was disinterested.

"If you're here to discuss anything official, then you may do so with the delegation tomorrow. It's late, and I have business to attend to, so if you don't mind…" said Micah as he searched his pocket for a room key.

The man stood his ground and returned only the cold stare of someone who would not be easily dismissed or dissuaded.

"If it is sex you're looking for," said an uncomfortable Micah, "I'm not gay."

"We both know that is not entirely true, now don't we?" answered a confident Siraj.

Micah's mind went into overdrive in an attempt to determine the reasons for the encounter with the man standing before him. Few people knew of his sexual preferences. Those who did swore their lives to secrecy and were among the few choice partners he had encountered.

Siraj read Micah's facial expressions as they changed from nervousness to outright concern.

"Why don't you invite me in so we can discuss how we can help each other? If we come to terms, your secret will be safe with me," Siraj assured him.

"And if we don't?"

"If we don't, your secret will be the least of your concerns."

Avigdor was pacing the stateroom of the yacht when McEwan and Chevalier walked in, knocking on the door only as a courtesy. Chevalier stopped briefly to speak to uniformed police officers outside the doorway and closed the door behind him when he had finished.

McEwan placed a briefcase on the floor next to a table, asking the DPM to take a seat so they could talk. Avigdor glanced at Chevalier in an attempt to decipher the reason for their unannounced visit. Chevalier emphasized McEwan's request with a friendly nod and a soft open-hand gesture for Avigdor to take a seat.

Avigdor continued to assess the demeanor of the two men as he sat down, crossed one leg over the other, and expectantly looked into the eyes of Agent McEwan, now seated directly across from him.

"Sir, your attorney will be here soon to discuss some developing details concerning the case," said McEwan.

"Agent, my patience is growing extremely thin with due process and procedure. My only concern is, and continues to be, whether or not you or anyone else has discovered the whereabouts of my wife, and if so, what is being done to secure her release," stated an increasingly impatient Avigdor.

"Sir, I apologize for the amount of time it has taken for us to bring you the details, but we have all been working extremely hard to find your wife. In doing so, we have discovered other things that may in fact help you to become more actively involved."

Avigdor clasped his hands and sat back in his chair. "I'm listening," he said after a short pause.

"As I started to say, your attorney is expected to stop by today. We have reason to believe he may somehow be involved with the abduction of your wife—"

Avigdor quickly held up his hand, stopping McEwan from completing his statement. "I have known this man for well over twenty years," said Avigdor. "Before you give me theory and conjecture and take me on a path that is inconclusive, you had *better* have indisputable evidence that convinces me. Otherwise, it is *you* who will be on the receiving end of—how do you Americans put it—a *shitstorm*."

"Trust me, sir. I wish our findings had led us elsewhere," said McEwan.

A determined, focused, and increasingly angry look appeared on Avigdor's face. "Go on," he demanded.

McEwan placed the briefcase on a table between him and Avigdor and opened it with a simultaneous click of the clasps. He removed the power cord, placed it upon the table, and placed the briefcase on the floor.

"This is a power cord that was found in the study of the villa you were in. Can you identify it?" asked McEwan.

"No. It could be the power cord that belongs to my laptop computer. But I suspect you already know the answer. Have you found the laptop?"

"We believe we have," answered McEwan with a nod.

"OK, then where is it?"

"We're hoping you can help us with that," said McEwan. "It seems the very computer you described to Agent Cohen was seen, albeit from a distance, in the possession of your attorney, Micah Bachman."

"Why would he have it?" asked Avigdor.

"Again, we're hoping you would be able to tell us why he would have it," interrupted Chevalier. "The imperative question, however, is not *why* he would have it, but *how* he came to possess it," added Chevalier.

"Are you telling me there's no evidentiary paper trail—" said Avigdor when he saw the two men shaking their heads, indicating his conclusion was correct.

"You'll have to do better," said Avigdor to McEwan. "I'm not convinced that Micah would outright remove evidence without having my best interests in mind."

McEwan nodded understandingly, paused, and offered the defense minister a serious stare. He grabbed the power cord and pointed to the keylogger. "Sir, do you have any idea what this device is used for?"

26

Their faces revealed shock and fear as the door burst open and the young man stood before them, just as surprised to see them as they were to see him. Munahid spoke softly in the man's native Yemeni dialect.

"We are in need of assistance, young man. Would you have a safe route for us to find our way?"

The man looked at Hanah, her pleading eyes the only feature revealed by the black niqab. He looked back at the large stature of Munahid and quickly gestured for them to follow him. Munahid looked at Hanah, squeezed her hand, and led her to the door as they followed the man into a dimly lit hallway.

Hanah glanced out the window of an open office to see the building they had narrowly escaped from across the street. She did her best to keep up as the man moved quickly throughout the building.

Munahid pulled Hanah along aggressively as he tried keeping up with the man's pace when the man disappeared around a corner. Munahid and Hanah rounded the corner and found themselves completely in the dark. Pausing to assess their situation, Munahid quietly called out to the man.

No answer.

Hanah suddenly had a creeping suspicion they had been led astray and held tightly onto her companion's hand as he cautiously led her back toward the dimly lit opening to the room.

As Munahid stepped through the threshold he was greeted with a bullet to the head fired at close range. Hanah barely had time to process what had happened as Munahid let go of her hand and slumped to the floor. She felt someone grab her from behind and place a hand over her mouth, muffling her blood-curdling scream at the horror she had just witnessed. The last thing she saw was Munahid's body lying before her, blood beginning to ooze from his head, and a tattoo on the forearm of her captor…a serpent supported by two crossed swords.

Micah's trancelike stare out the villa window carried his thoughts back to that fateful day, some ten years earlier, when he had made a pact with the devil personified. Having little alternative, he had allowed Siraj into his hotel room, partially out of curiosity but mostly out of fear.

The terms laid out by the sinister Siraj provided Micah with a path to power and the allure of wealth in exchange for access to Israeli plans and tactics against its neighboring rivals. Siraj convincingly articulated how the information would be used to "promote peace" and assured Micah of his intent to facilitate an end to all land disputes and ultimately to foster peace throughout the region. Micah thought back to how sincere Siraj had seemed at the time. Even when he discovered Siraj was labeled a terrorist by the world's peaceful nations, including his own Israel, he refused to believe it. After all, he seemed so sincere.

"Sir, do you still need me to take you to the DPM's residence?"

Micah turned when the agent broke the focus of his thoughts. He glanced at his watch and nodded his head. "Yes. Any luck finding our missing power cord?"

"No, sir."

"OK, we're finished here then. Let's go see His Excellency, the DPM," said a sarcastic Micah.

"I've yet to determine an exact location, but I know I'm getting close."

"Well, we don't move out until we have that location, G. There's no way I'm leaning forward without it," said Ian.

"Understand. We'll have it," answered G confidently. "As for our exit strategy…that'll call for a bit of creativity," explained G.

Todd chuckled and rubbed his temples. "Creativity…that's G's way of sayin' we'll probably find ourselves in another one of those infamous 'situations.'"

Leon glanced at Todd, then at Ian who was waiting patiently for G to clarify his statement.

"Assuming we're successful in finding Hanah—" said Ian.

"We'll find her," interrupted G.

"OK, *when* we find her," said Ian, "then what?"

"Then we fly her out," G stated matter-of-factly.

"Uh, G, I think you may have overlooked the fact that we'll be flying her out of frigging Yemen? It's not like she's has a passport or an entry visa. She didn't exactly get into that shithole with state permission," retorted Todd.

"That's where we need to be creative," explained G. "Leon, we're gonna need some documents for Hanah. I need an Omani passport, valid visa, state papers, and a round-trip airline ticket from Aden to Dubai."

"Round trip, clever," said Tzofiya. "But why Dubai?"

"Yeah, the round-trip ticket won't tip anyone off like a one-way ticket would. Besides, she won't need the return trip once we get her outta there, no matter where we're headed," said Todd. "I like it."

"I selected Dubai because that's the best place we can position our people to have a state aircraft waiting for her," explained G. "I'm confident the UAE will work with us once we inform everyone that we're safely in the air with her."

"I'm still not following just how we plan to pull this off," admitted Ian. "What happens when the local authorities question her during the security screening process? I know for a fact they have extremely tight travel restrictions on women in the region."

"She's fluent in several dialects of Arabic," said Leon. "I just hope she can pull it off convincingly."

"If you recall," said G, "I asked to be placed on an Omani passport as well. My plan is to depart under the same last name, essentially with Hanah as my wife. I'm sure Hanah will do just fine with the language if she has to speak at all. Most women are not spoken to directly, especially if they're accompanied by a spouse," said G.

"I *told* you this man was the shit," exclaimed Todd to the team.

"We're really gonna need those mini drones of yours when we make our way back through the airport, Leon. We'll need to keep an eye on things from as many vantage points as we possibly can."

Leon nodded. "No worries."

"I have a pretty good idea where you're going with this," said Ian. "So far I like it, and I think it'll work...*if* things go as planned, which they rarely do. So tell me how we handle the bad guys who won't be ready for us to take their guest home early," said Ian.

"We do what we do best," said G. "We eliminate any and all threats and do it as quietly and as cleanly as possible. If we do our job right, the only bad guys we'll have to neutralize will be the ones holding Hanah. However, if word gets out that we're in country, we're screwed," G reminded the team. "If any one of us is compromised, we're essentially on our own."

G paused, partially for effect and partially to allow the statement to sink in.

"Our number-one objective is to get Hanah Malkinson home alive. I hope I don't have to ask if any of us here doesn't fully understand what it may take to make that happen," said G as he continued to look at each member of the team. "It's my intention to return with each and every one of you as well."

"Preferably with no bullet holes," quipped Todd.

"Todd, how soon can we have the plane ready to depart for Djibouti?" asked Ian.

"Lickety-split," shrugged Todd. "As quick as I can make the call and we get ourselves to La Mole."

"Awesome. Make the call," said Ian. "Leon, notify JSOC to have CENTCOM and AFRICOM work a diplomatic clearance for us to get into Djibouti. I need everyone to provide Leon with your weapons requirements so he can effect coordination with our contacts on the ground in Aden. Also, no one shaves from here forward. The last thing we need is to look like clean-cut Americans. Let's play the part and do it right."

"I'm on it," said Leon. "You want me to plan for SOF support?"

"Absolutely, but only on a quick-reaction-force basis. I don't want any overzealous general thinking he can assume command and control just because one of his aides is a good-idea fairy," said Ian. "So I see no harm in having a highly specialized QRF at our disposal should we require it."

"All right, everyone. We rendezvous at the jet in two hours," instructed Ian.

Siraj arrived in Aden just before sunrise. The sleek Citation X jet taxied to an obscure hangar where a man met him and led him to a nondescript sedan, per Siraj's request.

The handler frisked the man and asked him if the car was clean.

The man nodded. Siraj approached him confidently and asked a single question. "Do we have the Israeli in custody yet?"

"Yes."

"Very well. Take me to her."

A nearby observer alerted the network leader of Siraj's arrival. "Sir, Massii is on his way with the khalifa."

The sedan drove through the narrow streets of Aden and eventually onto a major coastline roadway on the outskirts of the port city. The twenty-minute drive provided enough time for the sun to rise fully over the eastern horizon, its heat beginning to push the humidity and temperatures higher.

"*As-salaam alaykum,*" greeted the local leader as he approached Siraj and his handler.

"*Wa-alaykum-salaam*," responded Siraj with a nonchalant wave. "Take me to her."

"Of course, right this way."

The leader led Siraj to a room where two guards were posted outside a closed door. The leader opened the door and led Siraj inside where a physician was attending to an unconscious Hanah.

"I gave her a sedative. She has been through a lot and was distraught by the execution of her friend," offered the doctor.

Siraj casually walked to Hanah's bedside and stared at the high-value prisoner. "So we meet at last," he said in a whisper. "How long until she wakes up?" he asked, raising his voice.

"Four hours perhaps," answered the doctor.

Avigdor removed his eyeglasses from a shirt pocket and accepted the power cord from McEwan. He examined the keylogger closely for a few moments and handed the power cord back to McEwan. "I've never noticed this device before now. Has it always been a part of the power cord? Why has it captured your focus and attention?"

McEwan explained the nature of the device to Avigdor.

"So virtually everything I typed into my laptop has been recorded on that device?" Avigdor watched as both McEwan and Chevalier nodded. "Well, then I am somewhat relieved because I rarely did much on my laptop while I was on holiday," explained Avigdor.

"Tell me, sir," said Chevalier, "does access to your laptop require a password?"

"Of course—" said Avigdor, pausing as he suddenly made the connection of how the device could be used against him.

"Sir, if you think about it, someone had to place that device onto your laptop. That act by itself is a serious breach of security," explained McEwan. "Is there anyone on your security team that you can think of with a reason to subvert the Israeli government in any way?"

"The entirety of my security detail was thoroughly vetted," explained Avigdor as he fought hard to recall each member of his security detail.

"As you know, there's been a collaborative investigation underway since the disappearance of your wife. Virtually everything has been examined and investigated by several agencies. The only thing we have been unable to gain access are the personnel files of each member of your security detail," explained McEwan.

"And now you want *my* help in doing that," surmised Avigdor.

McEwan nodded. "It's the only loop we have been unable to close. It may in fact help lead us to those responsible for your wife's disappearance. You can help her—and yourself—by helping us," he added.

"I'll need a phone and a secure computer," answered Avigdor.

Hanah awoke in her dream to find herself beside the now-familiar natural pool among the lush vegetation. The soothing sound of waves crashing against the shore echoed just beyond the thick canopy of palm trees and mangroves. The salt air filled her lungs with freshness and her mind with clarity as the gentle wind whispered its way through the trees overhead. It had become clear to her that this was a place lovingly and specifically designed for her to escape and find solace.

The breeze continued to carry the whispers of soothing voices until Hanah discerned a familiar one among them.

Momma…can you hear me, Momma?

I can hear you, Ro'i.

I led you astray, Momma…

No, my sweet child, no. You led me to safety.

I thought it was the right way.

It was…it was the right way. You'll see.

I'm sorry…

Ro'i, don't leave me now. I need you more now than ever.

I'll never leave you, Momma. But I have to find help. I have to find him so he can help you.

I understand, Ro'i.

27

The team received the necessary diplomatic airspace clearances and was soon headed to the East African coastline country of Djibouti. G sat alone in the back of the plane wearing a pair of noise-cancelling headphones while studying maps of Aden and committing the details to memory. He had an audio of the Yemeni dialect of the Arabic language playing through the headphones while he whisked through several pages of maps, airport diagrams, and cultural aspects of the foreign port city.

"Whatcha studying?" asked Leon.

G lifted one of the earpieces of his headphones. "I'm sorry, what did you say?"

"I asked what you're studying."

"Just a few things I'll need to know before we get to Yemen."

Leon offered a flash drive to G. "You may want to add this to your study list. It'll tell you most anything you need to know about the microbots. Most every platform in the inventory offers a surveillance advantage while there are two that are actually weaponized."

"So if I'm in a real jam, these things can actually shoot someone?" asked G.

Leon nodded. "Yup, and they're deadly accurate."

"Wouldn't the added weight impact their ability to fly?"

"Extremely small caliber and a limited number of rounds lessen the weight, hence the necessity to be highly accurate. They're programmed for headshots. It's typically enough to at least incapacitate the bad guy long enough for the good guy to gain an advantage."

"Nice," said G. "So how do you plan on getting these things into Yemen?"

Leon smiled. "Thought *you* might have that figured out, G."

G smiled and returned an expectant look.

"Most will be in a hidden compartment of some of the checked bags," said Leon. "An influential acquaintance of mine on the ground there has ensured the right luggage team will be handling the bags the day you arrive. It's amazing what can happen when you grease the palms of the greedy."

"So just how many influential people have you met during your career, Leon?" asked G.

"Literally? None. Virtually? *All* of them," he said smiling.

"You said 'most' of them will be inside checked bags. What about the others?"

"There'll be a few hitchhikers, as I like to call 'em. I plan on perching them on each of your shoulders or your backs," explained Leon.

G returned a look of skepticism.

"Don't worry they won't be hangin' on for long. I plan on maneuvering them as soon as I can, once you're in country."

G smiled, shook his head in disbelief and placed his headphones back over his ears and closed his eyes.

"Hello, Ezra. I need a favor," announced Avigdor.

"Whatever you need, my friend. Are you being treated well by the French?"

"Yes, I'm well, despite the circumstances, thank you. Ezra, I need the personnel files on each of the three security personnel who accompanied my family and me to France. I called *you* because I need it quickly, and I know you have always had a way of getting the right information from the right people," explained Avigdor.

"Of course," answered Ezra.

"Also, if you can look for anything on the selection process for this detail—"

"I know just where to look for that sort of thing. I will have my contacts retrieve the information at once. How do you want the information transmitted?"

"I have a secure e-mail address for you. And Ezra, this request is highly sensitive and must remain off the record," said Avigdor.

"I understand."

Avigdor hung up the phone and looked at both men standing before him.

"Now what?" asked Chevalier.

"Now we wait," answered Avigdor.

McEwan removed a secure electronic tablet from his briefcase, logged in to an e-mail account, and handed the device to Avigdor. "You guys have these yet?" he asked.

"Yes, but I am one of the holdouts, a dinosaur among the young and tech savvy who believed the new technology to be unnecessary…until now," admitted Avigdor.

Approximately twenty minutes later, the tablet emitted a muted alert indicating the receipt of an e-mail. Avigdor examined the inbound pane and saw that new mail had been received from *The Author*, indicating that it was a message from Ezra Pennington.

> My good friend,
>
> Attached you will find the unmasked files per your request. The selection process was based on seniority and personnel performance reports. An interesting fact I discovered during the records-retrieval process is how one of the agents was assigned based on the personal endorsement, recommendation, and outright request of a mutual acquaintance of ours: *Micah Bachman*. I believe he may be able to provide further details on the personnel and the selection process, should you require them. Good luck.

Avigdor handed the tablet to McEwan who read the message and then handed the tablet to Chevalier.

"Are you convinced yet?" asked McEwan to Avigdor.

Hanah awoke to the sound of the daily noontime call to prayer. She had been asleep for well over six hours when she opened her eyes to her new surroundings. Hardly a few seconds passed before the gut-wrenching memory of Munahid's execution gripped her entire being. He never saw it coming, which, in her rational mind, was the only good part of the ordeal. Tears rolled down her cheeks as she thought about how much she missed him already and longed for the connection of the only friend she had in her dire and unpredictable situation. Not since she was first abducted had she felt so alone and afraid.

Careful not to make any moves that would alert her captors, she carefully looked around the small windowless room for anything that would give her a clue to her whereabouts. A sink and toilet were positioned in the corner closest to the only door to the room. The walls were bare save for the peeling and faded white paint. A dilapidated ceiling fan spun slowly in the center of the room with a low hum. As she lay there watching the fan slowly spin above her, she realized there were no restraints binding her.

She closed her eyes to listen to her surroundings as the call to prayer ended. She furrowed her brow in a determined focus to concentrate on what she assumed was a gathering of children at play, periodically overshadowed by sounds of a passing vehicle. That concentration was severed when she heard the click of the door latch.

Careful not to open her eyes and reveal that she was conscious, Hanah reacted with a gasp when she felt a cold hand press firmly against her forehead.

"You must wake up now," a man announced. "Hello. You must *wake up,*" he rudely repeated.

The man assisted her to a seated position and steadied her at the edge of the bed. She stole a glance as he walked across the room, poured tap water into a plastic cup, and brought it to her. Careful not to make eye contact, Hanah accepted the water and drank most of it. She noted the tattoo emblazoned on his right forearm—two crossed swords supporting a serpent. The man took the cup from her and placed it on a nearby table. Her head pounded, keeping time with the rhythm of her heartbeat, quickened by the spike in her adrenaline levels.

"You must come with me now," he said, gripping her arm and hoisting her to her feet.

Hanah staggered. The sedative had not yet completely worn off, giving her some lingering effects of vertigo. She cringed when she felt the man's grip holding her steady as he led her out of the room and down a long narrow hallway. They passed three doors. The first two were closed. The third door was ajar and led to a small room like the one she occupied.

Hanah glanced into the room as they passed and caught a glimpse of a frail young man seated at a small table. He looked up at Hanah, and their eyes connected for a brief moment. Despite the young man's facial hair, Hanah sensed he was not a native Yemeni or of Arab descent. She also sensed a sad hopelessness about him and wondered if he too was being held against his will, and if so, whether anyone was doing anything to find him and secure his release. For that matter, she suddenly wondered whether anyone was doing anything about her *own* release. She was quite sure Avigdor would have the entire Israeli special operations defense force activated by now. But without knowing exactly where she was, any effort would be a futile, a proverbial stab in the dark.

"This way," commanded her guide as he led her into a room at the end of the hallway. "Sit here."

The room was illuminated by a single overhead lamp positioned above the chair, making it difficult for her to see to the full limits of the room. In front of Hanah, on the other side of a small table, was an empty chair much like her own. Thoughts raced through her mind as she sat waiting for what would come next—an inter-rogation, physical punishment for her escape, or maybe even death, retribution for her having shot and killed a man. Her heart pounded as she contemplated the uncertainty of her situation.

A man appeared from a dark corner of the room and casually took a seat in front of her. Hanah was careful not to make eye contact and said nothing as he approached.

"Do you know why you are here?" he asked in Arabic.

Hanah didn't answer.

"Do you know who I am?" he asked in her native Hebrew.

Hanah slowly shook her head to indicate she did not know him.

"It's OK. You may look at me," he said in English.

Hanah gasped when she felt his hand press against her chin and lift her face. She trembled as she looked into the stoic eyes of the forty-year-old Pshtun warlord, Siraj Hammadi.

"It is said that it is rare for an infidel to see my face and live to tell about it."

G gradually became aware of his surroundings as he detected the fresh scent of salt air followed by the muted, distant sound of crashing waves. He found himself sitting at the edge of a small pond, and he ran his hands through the grass around him while breathing in the freshness of the tropical air and admiring the vivid alter-reality of the lush green surroundings. It was all so…perfect.

What is this place? he asked no one in particular.

It is a special place I designed for her. It's her sanctuary.

Ro'i?

Yes, it's me.

G sat patiently waiting for the boy to reveal himself. *Why are we here?*

I failed her, said Ro'i as he appeared by G's side.

I don't understand, said G.

I showed her the way, but the way led to danger. And now she's sad…so sad.

What happened?

They have her. And her friend is dead. They killed him.

Take me to her, said G.

OK, answered the boy, looking into G's eyes.

Their surroundings quickly faded and dissolved as G felt accelerating forces acting on his body. No sooner had the acceleration begun than it slowed. Their surroundings dimmed until G and the boy found themselves standing in a dark corner of a poorly lit room. Ro'i slowly lifted his arm and pointed to the center of the room where Hanah sat facing them. A man was seated in front of her. He was speaking softly.

Stay here, said G as he moved closer.

Glancing to his right, G noticed a man behind a video camera. In the shadows near the door was another man, his arms crossed as he watched Hanah's interrogation. G positioned himself so he could get a good look at the man seated across from Hanah. He slowly moved closer, trying to confirm the man's identity. His mind reeled as he tried to recall where he had seen the man's face. His heart pounded with adrenaline as remnants of countless intelligence briefings fired through his mind.

G positioned himself directly behind Hanah and leaned in next to her while the man lifted her chin to force her to look at him. G listened as the man spoke to her.

"It is said that it is rare for an infidel to see my face and live to tell about it," said the man.

We'll see about that, asshole, G thought.

The man waved his hand in a slow, commanding manner. A light came on behind Hanah, illuminating a banner draped on the wall. Adorning it was an image of two crossed swords supporting a coiled serpent, and underneath was an Arabic phrase that translated to "The Swords of God." G realized it was perfectly positioned to be used to enhance the impact of the video message.

As G examined the sign, he quickly associated the image with the two crossed swords of Hamas, among other Arabian sects across the region, the blades indicating the extremist organization's belief in the use of force to achieve their ends. G's mind went into overdrive, first thinking of the founding leader of Hamas, Sheik Hassan Yousef. But this man was too young to be the sheik. G understood why a Palestinian might have abducted Hanah, but this man was no Palestinian.

G pushed his mind to recall everything he had learned about various extremist groups along with their known associations and ties to one another when it suddenly occurred to him that the man provided the very clue he needed when he first began speaking to Hanah.

It is said that it is rare for an infidel to see my face and live to tell about it.

There were only three known terrorists who had earned the distinction of complete anonymity. G had already successfully eliminated one of them five years earlier in an exhaustive pursuit ending in Costa Rica. That left only two: Enrique Espinosa, whom he'd encountered recently during his DEA assignment, and Sirajuddin Hammadi, whom he'd never seen...until now.

Gotcha, motherfucker!

28

"Y ou want me to wait outside?" the agent asked Micah.

"No, this may get a little contentious. So I'll need you to keep an eye on things while I speak to him. I especially want you to keep an eye out if any of the French goons decide to overplay their hand," answered Micah.

"What are you going to do, get him to *give* you the password?"

"You let me worry about that. You just stay on your toes and do the job I hired you to do."

Micah approached the boat dock with the security agent in tow, flashed his ID at an armed French agent, and proceeded up the gangplank of the yacht. He ascended a short flight of stairs from the lido deck to the main deck. A lone French agent stood as they approached.

"Micah Bachman," announced the counselor. "He's expecting us."

The agent nodded. "Yes, sir, I believe he is."

The French agent knocked twice, opened the door to the main room, and closed it behind Micah and the Israeli agent.

"Micah, so good to see you," greeted Avigdor. "I see you brought Levi," he added, nodding to the Israeli agent. "I'm saddened by the loss of your teammate, Levi."

"Thank you, sir," the Israeli agent answered nervously.

"Please, have a seat, both of you."

Avigdor took a seat perpendicular to Micah, separated from the consul general only by a small table. The agent sat across from

Avigdor and crossed his legs. Avigdor picked up on two things. One, a professionally trained Israeli agent never assumed a posture that compromised readiness; and two, crossing one's legs in the presence of dignitaries was an Israeli cultural sign of disrespect.

"So tell me, Micah, what news do you have for me?" asked Avigdor as he leaned forward in his chair.

"Nothing significant, I'm afraid," sighed Micah.

"Then why are you here?" asked a contemptuous Avigdor. "Is this a social call? Perhaps I should be *grateful* you're here to see how well I'm doing instead of actively pursuing Hanah's captors or working on—oh, I don't know—getting me released!" he shouted.

The Israeli agent rubbed the back of his neck as he became visibly nervous.

"Why don't you tell me the real reason you're here, Micah."

Micah nodded knowingly, leaned forward in his chair, and lowered his voice. "My visit concerns the whereabouts of your laptop computer," he confided.

"I'm listening," said an accommodating Avigdor, nodding patiently. "What is it about my laptop that brings you here?"

"It seems it has fallen into the wrong hands," said Micah.

"Well now, that *is* rather concerning, Micah. My mind is reeling with questions. For starters, why has this become a higher focus than finding Hanah? And how did you come to know of its absence? How do you know whether or not the missing computer is even mine?"

"I don't. That's why I brought this photo for you to help us to determine its authenticity," said Micah as he placed a picture of the laptop computer on the table in front of them. Avigdor examined the picture and noticed the pink sticker applied by his daughter, Rina.

"It appears to be my laptop," said Avigdor as he handed the picture back to Micah. "Do you know who has it? If you do, then perhaps we should alert the authorities."

"There's only one issue with that approach," said Micah. "It seems the people who have your computer claim to be connected to those holding your wife—"

"Stop. So let me get this straight, Micah. You have actually received word that Hanah may indeed be *alive*, and you come in here initially and tell me you have 'nothing significant'? Do you take me for a fucking fool?"

Micah returned a look of confusion and concern. Avigdor stood and began to pace the room when he noticed from his peripheral vision that the agent had uncrossed his legs and was beginning to stand up. Avigdor needed him to remain seated.

"Sit down," ordered Avigdor, stressing the order with a pointed index finger. He continued to pace while Micah and the agent watched and waited. Avigdor remained silent, giving them both time to continue in the lie they were perpetrating.

"I had hoped we could work together on a solution," said Micah, hoping to reduce the tension.

"So tell me, Micah, are the French or US authorities aware of your discovery of my computer?" asked Avigdor as he stared out the port side picture window.

"No."

"Why not? You must have good reason to keep it to yourself," he said as he turned to look directly at Micah.

"I wanted to present this to you because—"

Avigdor stood before him and waited for him to finish the statement.

"They said that if they didn't receive the password they would... kill her," he said, his voice fading as he finished the sentence.

"Well, now that makes perfect sense," said Avigdor. "Why didn't you just *say* that when you first came in here? Things would've gone a *lot* smoother wouldn't you say?" he asked Micah. "What about you, Levi? Wouldn't you agree that a lot of this *ass pain* could've been avoided had he just gotten right to the point?"

The agent sat silently, choosing not to answer. Instead, he glanced at Micah who was busy trying to figure out where Avigdor was headed with his sudden acceptance of Micah's story line.

"So assuming I provide the password," said Avigdor, "what then? Do these terrorist friends of yours simply release her? What are the details? Where will they fly her to conduct the release?"

"They're certainly no friends of mine, I can assure you."

Avigdor stood his ground in silence. The cold, expectant look on his face made Micah increasingly uncomfortable.

"I'm trying to help you, my friend," pleaded Micah. "Or rather, I am trying to help Hanah, which I'm hopeful will help you as well," he added. "After all, your situation isn't exactly what I would call 'resolved.'"

"My *situation* has never been the focus of my concern, you idiot. Don't pull that shit with me, Micah. The fact that you haven't shared this with the French authorities as evidence to exonerate me is puzzling to say the least. The fact that it may be connected to Hanah's life is infuriating."

"I'm sorry, but they said that if anyone discovered she was alive they would kill her," said Micah.

Avigdor took a deep breath. "So now you want me to keep *that* a secret *and* provide the password?" Avigdor glanced at the Israeli agent and then back to Micah. "I have to admit, Micah, this visit has taken me down a path I would never have expected. What do you believe these thugs are looking for? I have no compromising files on the machine. What if they don't find what they're looking for? What if the password I provide doesn't work? What then? Will they *kill* Hanah?"

"They promised to deliver Hanah as soon as they validate the password," said Micah.

"Excellent," exclaimed Avigdor. "Then let's validate it, shall we?"

Suddenly and without warning, the stateroom door opened, surprising Micah and the Israeli agent. McEwan and Chevalier walked into the room. McEwan approached Avigdor and handed him a laptop computer—his laptop computer.

"I believe this may belong to you," said McEwan to Avigdor.

"Thank you." Avigdor took a seat directly in front of Micah and stared at the attorney as he placed the laptop upon the small table separating the two men.

"Is this the laptop computer you were so concerned about, Micah?"

"I don't understand—"

"You don't understand? Give me the photo you showed me earlier," demanded Avigdor. "C'mon, hand it over. I don't have all day."

Micah handed him the photo.

"Agent McEwan, you have *heroically* discovered the whereabouts of my missing laptop. Tell me, did you personally pry it from a dead terrorist's hands?" he asked rhetorically. "Don't answer that. I think we all know where you discovered it," he said, looking at Micah with disgust.

Avigdor opened the laptop and pushed the power button. "Hmm, seems the battery is dead," he said. "Perhaps we should just plug the power cord in to see if we can get it running," he added as he pulled the power cord from a satchel leaning against his chair.

The Israeli agent squirmed in his seat, stealing a quick glance at the prize he and Micah had fought so hard to find. Shocked, Micah sat frozen as he watched Avigdor turn the tables on him.

Avigdor connected the cord and pushed the power button, bringing the computer to life. When the password prompt appeared, Avigdor turned the laptop toward Micah and paused before he spoke.

"I'm going to give you what you came for," he said to the shocked attorney. "It's a complicated password, so listen closely and enter it carefully."

"This isn't necessary," said a nervous Micah, looking at the floor while shaking his head.

"So suddenly it's not necessary?" asked Avigdor. "Is this not what you came here for? Will this not save the life of an Israeli, my wife? Look at me, you fool."

Micah looked at Avigdor, and for the first time, in their open stares of truth and disclosure, both men spoke volumes. The web of lies and deceit Micah created had suddenly caught up with him, rendering him defenseless in a scandal he had deviously perpetrated. Avigdor felt real hope for the first time since he had discovered his wife missing from their vacation villa. So many questions remained to be answered, but the shared moment gave both men a sense of closure to their diametrically opposed definition of friendship.

Without breaking his ice-cold stare, Avigdor directed Micah to enter the password. "Put your hands on the keyboard and type the following:

L-e-t-U-$-A-l-l-L-i-v-e-I-n-P-e-a-c-e. Enter."

Where are you going? asked Ro'i. *You can't leave now. She needs you.*

Stay here, said G as he projected himself outside the room.

Why do you keep leaving? asked the boy.

G reappeared at the boy's side, placed his hand upon his small shoulder, and looked him in the eye. He was about to explain how he had to investigate their whereabouts so he could bring help when the boy spoke first.

You don't have to explain, said Ro'i. *I think I know what you need.*

G silently communicated his uncertainty about what the boy meant.

I'll show you, said Ro'i.

Their surroundings began to quickly fade as the boy showed him how he could determine his position anywhere on the planet simply by projecting his mind from a point of origin and then essentially zooming out, in much the same way as any ordinary Internet map tool would allow, except *this* experience was more vivid and fascinating than G could have ever imagined. The entire experience was in real-time, or as real as it gets in an alter-reality state of mind. As the surroundings came into focus, G was thrilled to realize that he could see people actually moving about in the streets and alleyways of cities, cars in motion, and birds and airplanes flying. G witnessed what he could only describe as an ethereal blend of what was and what was possible.

Ro'i fed G's mind as their perspective began to focus and the terrain below them grew smaller as he was able to confirm what he suspected—they were in Yemen. Even better, he was able to determine their *exact* location within the country.

Good job, G praised the boy.

Micah watched as the computer prompt took him to the desktop home screen, its backdrop a family picture of the Malkinson family, all of them wearing expressions of joy, posing together at their home in Tel Aviv.

"What is it that you want from this computer, Micah? Is it worth the life of a fellow countryman, or in this case, the life of a sitting dignitary's wife?" Avigdor asked.

Micah sat silently, his mind blistering at high speed as he tried to figure a way out of his predicament. "I never intended for anyone to get hurt," he finally admitted.

"It has been said that the road to hell is paved with good intentions," answered Avigdor.

Agent Chevalier opened the door to allow four uniformed police officers into the room.

"Levi, please surrender your weapon to the authorities," instructed Avigdor to the Israeli agent.

The agent stood and placed his hand inside the left breast of his jacket. A uniformed French police officer drew his weapon and trained it on the agent. Chevalier placed his hand out to calm the officer but did not ask him to stow his weapon.

"I never should've listened to you," said the Israeli agent to Micah as he slowly drew his weapon from its holster.

"Place the weapon on the floor, sir," commanded the officer with his gun aimed at the agent.

Levi placed his weapon on the floor.

"Now step back," commanded the officer.

Two officers approached the agent, placed him into handcuffs, and then led him out the door.

Agent Chevalier approached Micah. "You are under arrest for conspiracy to commit kidnapping. You have certain rights that may be different from those you are accustomed to. Do you need me to explain those rights to you at this time?"

"No," answered Micah as he stood and voluntarily placed his hands behind his back to be handcuffed.

"Wait," instructed Avigdor as he stood.

Chevalier stood next to Micah with a firm grasp on his arm as Avigdor approached. "Tell me where I can find my wife."

"I can't do that."

"You *can't* or you *won't*?"

"What difference does it make? If I tell you, then she and I are both dead."

29

G opened his eyes as the plane gently touched down on the desert runway, and then he glanced out the window to take in the view. Various shades of tan dominated the landscape in every direction.

"Welcome to Djibouti. Local time is 1603," announced Monty from the cockpit.

G glanced at his Invicta Subaqua Noma IV watch and removed it from his wrist to readjust the time. As he watched the hands move across the face, he was reminded of the details of his dream and how he was finally able to pinpoint Hanah's location. He unbuckled his seatbelt and moved down the aisle before the jet came to a stop.

"I know where they're keeping her," he said as he took a seat next to Ian.

"You already told us, remember?" quipped Ian. "It's why we're here. What am I missing?"

"I know *exactly* where they're keeping her," explained G as he made sure to stress the point.

Ian raised his eyebrows. "OK then. That information will certainly help," he said. "Leon, make sure we have access to the latest maps when we huddle up to brief the team. Todd, we'll need to get an updated SITREP to the home office."

"I'm on it. I'll make it short and sweet," said Todd.

Leon acknowledged Ian with a quick nod and glanced at Todd who returned a hint of a cocky smile.

"*My* man," said a smiling Todd.

"What do you mean, 'you will *both* die'?" asked Avigdor.

Micah glanced at McEwan and Chevalier and then turned back to Avigdor with a defiant stare.

"Agent Chevalier, please dismiss your men momentarily and shut the door. *You* may stay," insisted Avigdor.

Chevalier did exactly as was he asked, which gave Avigdor an indication his credibility had begun to increase with the French agent. McEwan moved closer to the men.

"OK, Micah, you can count on these men to be sensitive to the delicacy of what you have to say, especially if lives are on the line, as you suggest," explained Avigdor.

"I want a deal," Micah stated. "I'll tell you where your wife is in exchange for immunity."

"Nice try, but you're in no position to bargain, Micah," said an enraged Avigdor. "You want a deal? The deal I'm prepared to offer you is simple. You talk and I won't rip your fucking heart out and show it to you before you die in front of me. What about Hanah? What kind of deal does *she* have at this very moment? I suggest you start talking right now and tell me what it is that makes you so important all of a sudden."

Micah returned a cold stare. "Because I'm the only outsider who knows where your wife is. I also know *who* has her. And if he doesn't hear from me when he next reaches out to me, then he will simply kill her."

Avigdor leaned in closer to Micah. "And if he kills her, then we know who will be next on his hit list, don't we? In other words, if *she* dies, *you* die. How do you think he will feel knowing you are in custody? Have you considered the fact that he may simply have you eliminated and continue to hold Hanah in order to meet his own objectives? After all, if you are no longer useful to him, then why should he risk the fact that you may expose him?"

Micah silently contemplated his quickly eroding options while Avigdor patiently waited for the logic to sink in.

"So what makes you think you're the only one who knows where Mrs. Malkinson is located?" asked McEwan.

Micah gave the agent an insolent stare.

"The reason I ask, and it's just a hypothetical assumption, if what you're telling us is true—that you're the only one who knows where she is—how are we to believe you're telling the truth?"

"Who is this American?" a defiant Micah asked Avigdor.

"This *American* is someone I completely trust. And he's put more time and energy into this case than you have. You may simply wish to answer his question…or not. Either way, you have a decision to make. I don't have all day, Micah," said an impatient Avigdor.

"Ya know what?" stated McEwan, "He doesn't have to answer because I already have the answer. We know she's in Yemen," he said confidently, as if it were common knowledge.

Micah tried his best to hide the dismay he felt as he learned others had discovered Hanah's location. It would only be a matter of time before they would be able to hone in on her exact location.

Avigdor glared at Micah. "Yemen? What have you done, you fool? You have delivered my wife to the pit of hell."

"You're correct," admitted a dejected Micah. "And now you know what I know."

"Except for *who* is responsible," quipped Avigdor.

"And that I'm afraid I must die with," answered Micah.

"As you wish," answered Avigdor. "Get him out of my sight."

Avigdor watched as Micah was led out of the room and the door to the cabin closed, leaving only him and McEwan in the room. He looked at McEwan after a contemplative pause.

"I haven't been completely honest with you, Agent McEwan."

"So am I to consider myself a dead woman?" Hanah bravely asked Siraj.

"You are very much alive at this time. Whether you remain that way is entirely up to you. Should you decide to repeat your recent 'heroic' behaviors, then I will have no choice but to prevent you from doing so. Do you understand?"

Hanah chose not to make eye contact. Instead, she remained expressionless and stared through the table in front of her.

"Do you know why you are here?" he asked.

"No."

"Look at me."

Hanah reluctantly raised her head just enough to make eye contact with the khalifa.

"You are my insurance policy," he said. "You are an important person inside your country, no? Would they not go to great lengths to have you back safe?"

Hanah returned a blank stare.

Siraj shook his head. "I don't ask much of my prisoners," he explained. "And I don't typically make a habit of keeping them around when they are no longer useful to my objectives. So if you cooperate, I give you my word that you will be treated acceptably and will be free from undeserved harm. Do you understand?"

Hanah offered a slight nod.

"Very well," he said as he reached his arm out to his side and opened his hand. The gesture was quickly answered by a man handing Siraj a folded newspaper. He unfolded the newspaper and spread it on the table. Inside the newspaper was a handwritten note—a script—for Hanah to read aloud. Siraj placed the script in front of Hanah.

"You are an intelligent woman, so I know you can read. When I step away, you will look into the camera and read this note. When you are finished, we will return you to your room where food will be waiting. You haven't eaten in some time. I'm certain you are hungry."

Siraj stood and walked away while two men with black scarves covering their faces from their noses down approached. The men stood to either side of Hanah, brandishing AK-47 assault rifles, ammunition belts across their chests. One of the two men picked up the newspaper and slapped it against Hanah's chest. In Arabic, he commanded her to hold it in place. The aggressive move startled her and made her gasp.

A red light blinked from the camera in the darkened corner.

"You will now look into the camera and read the note," commanded a voice from the dark corner.

Hanah's mind froze as she looked in the direction of the red light suspended in the dark corner. Tears streamed down her face as she did her best to hold her ground, fully realizing the price she might be required to pay for noncompliance.

"Read the note," the voice commanded once again. The voice... she would never forget the voice of the man she now knew was the chief architect of her captivity, the khalifa, a cold-blooded killer and terrorist.

She glanced at the note. The words didn't matter. She had decided not to comply with the order. She trembled, knowing her decision would cost her dearly, perhaps even mean her very life. She focused again on the red light. Setting her fear aside, she gripped the newspaper and flung it across the room in a defiant act of resistance. The cost was delivered swiftly.

"Massii," called Siraj.

The one-word command prompted the man to her right to drive the butt of his rifle into Hanah's head, sending her crashing to the floor in excruciating pain. Time slowed as her mind went numb. The remaining remnant of consciousness allowed her to experience what seemed to be a long-distance, slow-motion fall to the floor ending in a muffled thud as the chair and her body crashed simultaneously. She somehow remained focused on the red light of the camera until her head made contact with the hard floor sending her into unconsciousness.

⊕

"The personal laptop computer of a defense minister holds much more than simple family photos and ordinary office files," explained Avigdor to Agent McEwan.

McEwan returned a slightly confused look. "So you're telling me that there's a lot more inside that computer than you ever let on?"

"Yes. There are codes embedded in that computer that are connected to the Israeli central bank."

"Why would you have such codes?" asked McEwan.

"I am authorized to draw funds directly from the central bank's defense account in the event of imminent threat to Israel and only with direct authorization and knowledge of the prime minister. It is an authority granted to the prime minister as a failsafe against parliamentary delay and gridlock should we require large sums of money to defend Israel or pursue an enemy of the state. The prime minister may delegate that responsibility only to his deputy or the defense minister."

"And you happen to be both," acknowledged McEwan.

Avigdor nodded.

"Were you ever the least bit concerned when you discovered your computer was missing? Because you sure could've fooled me," said McEwan.

"Not until you revealed the keylogger device. As I said, the data was triple-layer encrypted, accessible by several passwords known only to me and specific to this computer."

"You think that's what Micah—I mean, Mr. Bachman was after?"

"I do. I'm just not certain why. So when do you expect the French to drop the charges against me?" asked an impatient Avigdor. "There is much work to be done."

Siraj pointed to Massii from the shadows. Massii didn't hesitate and began to speak to the camera, even as Hanah lay on the floor bleeding from her head wound.

"You have witnessed the result of defiant insolence. Such choices are foolish in the face of those favored by God. We have your precious Jewish jewel and will keep her until the terms of our demands are met," declared Massii.

The camera followed him as he knelt beside Hanah, grabbed her by the hair, and lifted her head while looking into the camera. "I have no problem whatsoever killing this bitch," he said as he retrieved a dagger from a sheath at his side and placed it against her throat. "If you wish to ever see her alive again, you will comply with the demands we have detailed in a letter accompanying this video. If you think you can send in your *special forces* to rescue her, you are welcome to try. Your attempts will be a useless waste of time that will only result in more infidel deaths."

"Shut it off," commanded Siraj as he walked toward Massii and an unconscious Hanah. "Will she live?" he asked.

"If I wanted her dead, I would've hit her closer to her temple," answered Massii as he stood to look at Siraj in the eye. "She'll live."

"Don't forget who's in charge here," said Siraj, detecting an arrogant overtone from Massii.

"In charge?" asked a defiant Massii. "Are you referring to the times when you are actually here?"

"Our blood ties do not imply a higher tolerance of insubordination from you, Massii," warned Siraj. "You are a valued member of the team, but you should be quick to remember to honor the integrity and structure of the network. I have eliminated men for lesser indiscretions."

Massii glared back at Siraj for a moment, but he decided not to push the envelope of insubordination. He turned and shouted at the other men. "Clean this shit up, and take this bitch back to her room. Attend to her wound, and make sure she's secure. And don't allow her to die…yet."

The team cleared airport security and was waved past the guardhouse at the perimeter of the American embassy in Djibouti, East Africa. A middle-aged man introducing himself simply as Jack met them in the embassy foyer.

"No last name," Leon whispered to Todd.

Todd flashed his familiar smile as Jack led the team down a long corridor to a secure room to be used for their team briefing and to make final preparations for the mission. Three uniformed Marines stood ready to deliver documents and support gear to the team.

"These Marines will provide everything you've requested. Each of them is a Middle East expert and can tell you anything you need to know about the nuances of your cover as well as everything you should know about Yemen," announced Jack. "When you're finished, we'll dismiss ourselves and inform the ambassador, who expressed a desire to stop by to check on you."

Leon found the computer-support administrators and got busy connecting equipment. He procured five cell phones and activated each to receive secure satellite transmissions. Then he embedded secure digital earpieces into ordinary radio headphones that were designed to easily slip past security screeners.

Each member finished with his or her respective area and reconvened around a small cherrywood table. G thumbed through a foreign-language booklet while he waited for everyone to settle in. Tzofiya placed a garment bag on the floor alongside her chair and examined an embroidered headscarf.

"Does everyone have what they need?" asked Ian.

"I could use a weapon," quipped Todd.

"Aside from that, I mean," said Ian.

Todd shrugged.

"OK, everyone, make damn sure you're familiar with every detail of your documents, especially your passports. Name, birth date, addresses…everything. We're all familiar with what we're likely to be asked at security, so be prepared to answer that in your alias's native language or in heavily accented English."

Leon stepped to the table and took a seat beside Todd.

"What's up?" greeted Leon in a whisper. "By the way, the whole beard thing works well for you," he added.

Todd smiled.

"What have you got for us, Leon?" asked Ian.

Leon cleared his throat with a quick grumble. "OK, first things first," he announced as he got right to work and began passing out cell phones to each team member. "This is your new cell phone. It's the only cell phone you should have with you on the op. It's equipped with the latest retina-scan technology and will *not* work unless you allow it to get a quick glance at your right eye."

Leon walked the team through the programming process that tied each phone to a specific team member. He went on to explain other features, including the phone's ability to connect via satellite to virtually any place on Earth.

"You'll notice your phone also comes with a wired earpiece," Leon pointed out. "Once you get past security, break open your earpiece and remove the smaller wireless digital earpiece and place it into your ear canal. It's more of a comm device. It has transmit and receive capability and is the one device that'll keep us all connected, no matter what."

"Is it tied to the cell phone?" asked Todd.

"No. It'll operate independently of the cell phone," answered Leon.

"That's good 'cause I'm always losing my phone."

"I know…that's one of the reasons I opted for the earpieces."

"Really?" asked Todd.

"No," answered Leon, a look of sarcasm on his face.

"Thanks, Leon. Is there anything else?" asked Ian.

"No, I just need to meet with G to discuss the deployment options of the drones should the team see a need to use them."

G acknowledged Leon with a quick nod while Todd remained preoccupied with the features of his new phone.

"G, you wanna tell us where we're headed now?" asked Ian.

"Sure. Leon, can you bring up a map of Aden, please?" asked G

"So it *is* Aden," Leon proclaimed with a smile.

"Yes, most likely for every reason you cited," said G.

Onto the screen at the far end of the room, Leon projected a map of the peninsula city of Aden, Yemen.

"We land at the north end of the city at Aden International, here," explained G as he identified the area with a red laser pointer. "Don't let the small size of the land mass deceive you. Aden is densely populated, and once you're in the city, it's very easy to become disoriented if you make even one wrong turn. Stay sharp and be firm with the local drivers. If you're not, they'll either take advantage of you or be onto you. Either way, you'll be late to the party and may end up endangering the mission.

"CIA will meet with us to issue weapons per your individual requests. They'll be stationed at a barge storage area here," explained G as he aimed the laser at the map. "Pay your driver, and make sure he drives away before you enter the building. Once you collect your weapon, a vehicle will be provided for you to drive to your assigned destination. Your vehicle will most likely be a piece of shit so it blends in with the rest of the cars there, so don't expect a Mercedes," he said, glancing at Todd.

"Damn," whispered Todd.

"You're to make your way to the Al Ma'ala district, adjacent to the shipping port. Todd, you'll post at the shipyard to facilitate a water approach should we require SOF reinforcements or an alternate exit strategy. I'll need you to join Leon and me when we huddle up in a few minutes to discuss the microdrones. I may call on you for deployment if we need it. Tzofiya, you and Ian will rendezvous with me here, two blocks from the target compound where we'll stage the vehicles.

"Because I know *exactly* where we're going, this will be a quick, hard-hitting, covert extraction. We'll be in country for no more than twenty-four hours. We get in and out as quickly and quietly as possible. Ian and I will breach the safe house first and take care of any unfriendly. Tzofiya, you'll cover our backside and enter the compound when Ian and I clear you in.

"I have each of you on the first flight out of Aden the following day. Hanah and I *will* be on that plane with you. I don't plan on leaving without her. If things go south, you're to be on that plane, with or without us. As previously briefed, you're to board Qatar Airlines flight 2106. It'll be bound nonstop for Dubai. I'll brief any changes tomorrow before we step for the airport. Any questions?"

No one spoke. Each one knew the role they had to play in order for the mission to succeed.

"One more thing," said G with some hesitation. "The people holding Hanah are not afraid to die and are very good at what they do. You should also know they work directly for Sirajuddin Hammadi himself," said G as he looked at Todd.

"Is the son of a bitch on site?" asked Todd without looking up.

Ian and Tzofiya both detected the possibility of an issue and were puzzled by Todd's comment. They exchanged a troubled look. "What's this about?" asked Ian.

Todd sat silently, clearly struggling with some kind of demon from the past while G explained the circumstances.

"A group from the Hammadi network executed Todd's brother after he was captured and held as a prisoner of war in Kunar, Afghanistan, four years ago," explained G.

"Todd, is this gonna present an issue?" asked Ian.

"No issue," he answered coldly. "But if there's any way I can get a crack at the motherfucker, I'd appreciate the opportunity."

"Noted," acknowledged Ian as he glanced at G. "All right everyone, once we leave this building, we operate independently. Trust your instincts and your training. If there are any updates, Leon will provide them to us via secure comms before we step out in the morning. After that, proceed with the plan and react to updates on your communications devices," he added before dismissing the group.

Shortly after the meeting Ian pulled G aside. "Any reason for me to be concerned about Todd, G?" asked Ian.

"No, he'll be all right. Can't blame him for wanting a crack at the man who killed his brother. I'd think any one of us would feel the same, actually," said G.

Ian nodded. "I just want to make sure he won't allow his emotions to get in the way of our objectives."

"That won't happen," said G reassuringly. "At least not before we know we've secured Hanah."

Avigdor looked at McEwan when he heard a loud knock on the door of the stateroom. Four Israeli security agents entered the room. One of the men handed him a cell phone.

Avigdor glanced at McEwan and accepted the phone from the agent. "*Allo?*" he answered.

"I have just spoken to the French prime minister," announced a familiar voice. "You have been cleared of all charges, and your privileges have been restored."

Avigdor recognized the voice as that of Doran Levinson, the Israeli prime minister.

"It seems you've made quite an impression on your French hosts with your patience," said Levinson. "For that, I thank you. Now, I believe it is time for you to get back to work. I have dispatched several field agents who will provide you with the proper level of security and the tools you need to be read-in on the operation already underway to find your wife. Let me know if I can provide anything at all."

"Thank you, sir," answered a grateful and reinvigorated Avigdor Malkinson. Avigdor hung up the phone and glanced at McEwan. "Time to get to work. Thank you for everything."

"Just doing my job."

"How would you like to continue doing your job alongside me? Seems we have some unfinished business to take care of together," said Avigdor.

Leon handed two small eyeglass cases to Todd and G.

"You're giving me eyeglasses?" asked Todd skeptically.

"You heard of Google Glass?" asked Leon with raised eyebrows. "Where do you think *they* got the idea?"

"OK, so these are super-cool, secret spy glasses of some kind?" asked Todd with a chuckle.

"Uh, yes," answered Leon. "These glasses will allow you to see your drones, no matter how small. If there's a fly in the room, and it's one of mine, you'll know it. If you want to see what it sees, just call it up by pressing right here on the corner of the frame. Of course you can also control any of these with your phone using this app," explained Leon to Todd and G. "You can also release control to me at any time," he added.

Todd stared at Leon for a moment. "Bro, they just don't pay you enough," he chuckled.

"Can you override and take control if we get into a jam or need the help?" asked G.

"Yes."

"OK, the glasses are cool. And I dig the frames too. But where are the actual drones?" asked Todd.

Leon smiled. "The small ones are everywhere. There's one on the back of your shirt right now."

Todd squirmed. "G, is there anything on my shirt?"

G looked closely and, with Leon's assistance, discovered the tiny drone clinging to Todd's collar. "Damn sure is, brother. Wow. OK, so how are we supposed to get these past security…wait, you don't expect us to just allow these things to hitch a ride on our shoulder and walk right in, do you?"

Leon answered him with a smile.

"Brilliant," said G. "So you'll effectively control these things right through security. What about the scanners? Will they detect the electronics? Any issues controlling more than one at a time?"

"No issue at all. The technology is called swarm intelligence. It allows me to control more than one element simultaneously. Each drone receives a slightly offset altruistic algorithmic input command that keeps it separated from every other drone but together as an equal part of the whole group. So I can effectively control them individually or collectively," explained Leon.

"Heavy," whispered Todd.

"As for the airport scanners, once I see you approaching security, I'll simply fly them around the threat, effectively maneuvering them away from the scanners," explained Leon. "All you gotta do is carry them in unwittingly. Hell, even Todd can accomplish that task," he added with a wink.

"So these things are always…awake?" asked Todd.

"Pretty much. Oh, and you'll really like this…wish I could take credit for it but someone else beat me to it…I can recharge them anywhere I can find an electronic emission. Power lines are the best sources, but I can also park 'em on a power outlet and draw electromagnetic charges from there as well. It's the simple concepts that really impress me."

"I see," said G. "What about the larger drones? The ones you were telling me were weaponized? How do we get those in?"

"Anything you need in terms of an armed drone is already in country waiting on you. We fielded a couple of systems a while back and put 'em in the hands of some special operators who are highly proficient, should you require their assistance. We're really hoping we don't have to deploy those for this op. After all, you did say you wanted to keep this as covert as possible."

"OK, so back to the glasses," said Todd. "How do I turn 'em on?" he asked, examining them at half-an-arm's distance.

"They're activated automatically when you put 'em on," said Leon.

"Whoa! So what I'm seeing on the screen now—"

"—is the back of your head," interrupted G.

"You should have everything you need between the glasses and the earpiece," explained Leon.

"Well, not everything," answered Todd. "Nothing's complete without my weapon."

G glanced at Leon who rolled his eyes.

31

The tiny hand gripped hers as she became increasingly aware of her surroundings. A smile naturally appeared on her face as she realized she was in her favorite place with her firstborn at her side. Everything was just as she last remembered it, right down to the gentle breeze and tranquil nature of the entire sanctuary. She looked down at the tiny hand in hers and felt the energy and bond of the purest love and compassion.

"Oh, Ro'i, I don't think I wish to ever return," she said softly as she lifted her tearful gaze from her hand to the boy's eyes. "I'm so tired."

But they need you, he unselfishly whispered to her mind. *You can't give up now. There are people coming for you. He is coming—*

"Who? Who is coming, my son?"

Ro'i slowly turned his head to look across the tranquil pond and pointed to a lone figure of a man in the distance. Hanah strained her eyes as she tried focusing on the slowly approaching figure. She glanced at Ro'i with confusion and turned to watch as G came into view and gently knelt beside her.

I told you he would come, Momma. He has come to show you the rest of the way home.

Hanah quickly looked away from G and into the captivating eyes of her son. "I don't want to leave you, Ro'i, not now, not after all this. I don't want to ever again be without you."

Ro'i smiled. *You've never been without me, Momma. I have always been here…and I always will be. This is not the end, Momma. It's just the beginning.*

Ian was the first to notice the US ambassador when she walked into the room. He immediately stood and approached her with an extended hand.

"I trust that everything is in order?" asked the ambassador.

The rest of the group turned when they heard the exchange and noticed that the American official had entered the room.

"Ladies and gentlemen, the ambassador," announced Ian, not quite remembering her name.

"Pleased to meet everyone," greeted the ambassador who kept her remarks brief in an effort to avoid getting to know any of them personally. "I want each of you to know that you have the full support of the embassy while you're here. Should you need anything at all, please do not hesitate to call upon my staff, as they have been instructed to support your requests. Has everything been satisfactory so far?"

The group nodded.

"Good. We have provided rooms for each of you inside the compound. This should make it easy for you to prepare for your mission and get a good night's rest before you get underway tomorrow."

"Thank you, Madam Ambassador," said Ian, speaking for the group.

G turned in early, determined to get some sleep. He sat in a chair in the corner of his small but comfortable room, drew a deep breath, and closed his eyes. Each deep breath he drew gave his mind clarity of thought and purpose for the mission he was about to begin. As he sat quietly in the chair, he began to focus on Hanah, setting aside for a moment the details of the plan to rescue her from her captors. He trained his focus solely on the woman, determined to get close to her somehow to assure her that everything would be OK, doing his best to prepare her for the rescue.

He wasn't certain whether he was awake or asleep at this point. It didn't matter. His breathing slow and deliberate, his body in a meditative state, he began to feel a complex mix of emotions surround him. Sadness, desperation, love, hope, acceptance…fear. He felt he was close to her, but nothing had yet been revealed to his mind's eye. He could feel the emotions swimming around him yet still he couldn't see anything. Then he heard the whisper of a voice he had become so familiar with throughout this journey.

I told you he would come, Momma. He has come to show you the rest of the way home.

G watched as his surroundings took shape, placing him at the edge of the tranquil pond Ro'i had created for Hanah. He looked across the water and saw two people sitting beside each other, the small boy pointing a finger directly at G. The gesture drew G to them. As he approached, he could see Hanah looking up at him, confused by his presence but comforted by her son's reassurance. Gently kneeling beside her, G looked into her eyes and, without communicating a word, assured her that everything would be OK.

Hanah's eyes glossed over with tears, as she seemed to suddenly realize how her son had kept his promise to bring someone to show her the rest of the way home. She quickly turned her attention away from G and back to the boy.

G looked at the sky to see the sun shining brightly through a tall palm and drew in a deep breath. He closed his eyes as he concentrated on the warmth of the sun against his face, allowing his mind to return him to the solace of his room, reassured that he had made the connection he had been hoping to make.

Avigdor was surprised to see an old friend walk through the door.

"Ezra, what a surprise—"

Ezra smiled and then glanced suspiciously at McEwan.

"Agent McEwan, this is Ezra Pennington," said Avigdor.

"Pleased to meet you, sir," said McEwan as he stepped toward Ezra and offered his hand.

"Agent McEwan has been instrumental in securing my release. I'm confident he'll continue to provide value to our efforts in securing Hanah," explained Avigdor.

Ezra nodded, paused, and extended his hand to McEwan. "Pleased to meet you then, young man. You'll forgive me for the hesitation and my suspicious nature. The betrayal of one's own countryman can have these effects on some of us more than others. Seems I may still have some things to learn in the customs and courtesies department," he admitted.

"No worries," answered McEwan with a sincere smile, secretly humbled by the presence of the two powerful men.

"As soon as I learned you had been officially cleared, I took the liberty of putting some things together you can use to monitor the progress of the initiative to secure Hanah's release. I hope you approve," said Ezra as he nodded to the agents making their way into the room. A group of men were busy carrying various electronic devices: computer screens, keyboards, wires, transmitters, secure telephones, and small satellite dishes.

"I know it isn't ideal, but since you're already here, I think this will be an acceptable location for our purposes. As they say, sometimes the best location is out in the open. Besides, the exclusive, gated community does provide a level of protection we would otherwise have difficulty finding. I have posted the necessary security at the gate as well as on the grounds outside. The men here in this room are at your disposal and are able to collect and relay information or assets at your direction."

Ezra briefed Avigdor and McEwan on the details of the mission, the timing, and the operatives as the other men set up the communications and surveillance equipment throughout the room. McEwan sat silently as he watched how quickly the makeshift command center was assembled and listening intently to the two powerful Israelis speak about the details of the delicate mission to save Hanah Malkinson.

"We have received varying accounts of her brief escape," reported Ezra. "But it was not long before they were able to track her down and recapture her. As you know all too well, these people are serious, and they will kill her if they even think we're close to confronting them. Intelligence reports reveal a sympathetic accomplice of hers was executed right in front of her."

"She's a strong one," said Avigdor, knowing his wife's defiance and strong will.

"We have a high degree of certainty that she is now being housed in an obscure facility in Aden, Yemen," reported Ezra. "The team is preparing an immediate rescue operation to commence as soon as all the players are adequately prepared."

"Sounds like a good plan," said Avigdor, clearly contemplating the details presented by his old friend. "I was privileged to meet Agent Weston when he came through with Agent Cohen," said Avigdor. "I have confidence in his ability to deliver."

"You can be sure of one thing, my friend…we have assembled the best possible clandestine team for this operation. I personally trained Agent Cohen and have watched her develop over the years. I can assure you she is every bit as capable as I used to be in my younger days—*better*, I think" asserted Ezra. "As for Weston, I don't know much about him, but he comes highly regarded and with a skill set so unique—and so unorthodox—his own government has not openly associated itself with him."

McEwan took note of the comments about the agents, particularly G. He found it intriguing that their own US government had distanced itself from the agent and his unique abilities, whatever they were. He considered himself privileged to have met the man and to witness the confidence produced by those abilities during a recent briefing. He wondered just what it was the government could be so afraid of associating itself with.

"Tell me, Ezra, When do you believe the team will begin the mission, and what can we do to help?" asked Avigdor.

G opened his eyes to the somewhat familiar surroundings of a foreign hospitality room. Frozen by the images of his latest dream, he continued to swim in the emotions he felt during the encounter and called forth everything he had to bring the forces of a successful outcome to him and the team. The tempo of his heartbeat increased as his active mind painted a picture of the scenario he envisioned against the risks they were taking to pull it off.

No matter what, we're gonna find you and bring you home…

A knock at the door brought him out of his reflective state.

"Come in."

G watched as the doorknob slowly turned, and the door opened slightly.

"You asleep?" called out a familiar woman's voice in just over a whisper.

G smiled. "Yeah, I'm actually answering you from my dreams."

The door suddenly stopped its inward motion. Silence followed.

"I'm…just joking, Tzofiya. Please come in," said G.

Tzofiya walked into the room, glanced at the bed, and then noticed G sitting in a chair next to a lamp perched upon a small table in a corner of the room. She smiled as she closed the door.

"I wasn't sure whether or not to take you seriously after everything you explained to me about your unique gifts."

G stood to greet her. "Please, have a seat," he said offering her a chair next to his. "So what do I owe the pleasure, T?"

"T?" she asked curiously.

"Sorry, I do that sometimes. It's a 'street thing' I learned from Todd some time ago. What's on your mind?"

"Nothing really, just checking on you."

"Checking on me, or checking *up* on me?" asked G with a smile.

"OK, so let's assume I'm checking *up* on you then. So how are you doing?"

"Calm, cool, and collected," said G with a smile.

"Bullshit," she declared. "You may have some pretty unique superpowers or whatever you call it, but I'm trained to see past façades. This kind of thing excites you but scares the hell out of you as well. How am I doing so far?"

G returned an expressionless stare.

"It's OK really. In fact, I'm actually relieved to know you haven't become immune to your emotions and that inner voice of calm. It's the one thing that'll keep you alive when everything else falls to pieces. I get it; you're a perfectionist, like me. You tend to overevaluate and rehearse every detail until you find perfection. Well, I've got news for you. I've been doing this a long time and have never found perfection. Something *always* goes wrong. The real truth lies in how you handle it when it does go wrong."

"So do you still trust me now that you've made this discovery?" asked G.

"With my life," she confidently answered as she rose and turned toward the door.

G stood out of respect and followed her with his eyes as she made her way toward the door. Her long slender legs were wrapped in tight-fitting, well-worn blue jeans riding low on her hips, accentuating her thin waist and an ass to die for. It wasn't *her* life he was concerned about. He would die for *any* fellow agent. It's what agents did. For her however, he'd die for just a few more minutes alone with her.

He followed her to the door and watched as she reached for the doorknob, hesitated a moment, and locked the door from the inside. He approached her as she slowly turned around and looked up at him with inviting eyes, giving him that look...the look he had secretly hoped for...the look he never expected he'd *ever* get from her.

"How is our guest?" asked Massii of the man watching over her.

"She took a pretty hard hit. She'll be out for a while but I suspect she will recover over time."

"Good. Have you been able to get the video to our contact at Al Jezeera yet?"

"Yes. I'm told it will be streaming within the hour."

"Very well," answered Massii. "Are the terms of our demands embedded into the software?"

"Everything is as you have instructed, sir."

Massii nodded. "I would love to be a ghost in the room when the fools see the video for the first time. This plan is brilliant. They will do anything to secure her release. And once they do, they will effectively be funding their own destruction when their emotions take over to save the life of one in exchange for the destruction of the many." He sighed with satisfaction. "Keep me aware of any changes in her condition and notify me when she regains consciousness."

Massii left the room and made his way down the hall to the next room where Siraj was interviewing the young man Hanah had briefly seen earlier.

"*Assalamu alaykum*," greeted Massii as he entered the room.

The young man looked up nervously when he noticed Massii.

"It seems the US news outlets have received the most recent picture we are circulating about you," reported Siraj in a calm, arrogant manner. "The initial word is that your nation is happy to know you are alive. We have offered to return you to your country as a gesture of our goodwill should they provide for the safe return of just four of our fellow countrymen who have been wrongly imprisoned in the Guantanamo Bay prison facility. We consider it to be a fair trade. You know—a warrior for a warrior. You should consider it an honor that your release is worth four of ours."

32

eon sat busily banging away on the keyboard making last-minute adjustments when Ian, dressed in a dusty photographer's vest, a loose-fitting, hunter-green, button-down shirt, and khakis, walked into the room. Multiple computer screens displayed various forms of secure data, video camera feeds, maps, clocks and timers, schedules, frequency displays, and satellite feeds.

"How long have you been up?" asked Ian using his best British accent, practicing the role he would assume as a UK journalist.

Leon glanced his way and smiled. "You shoulda practiced that accent more," he said sarcastically. "But you look the part." He rubbed his eyes and took a sip from a cold cup of coffee. "Never went to bed. Been up all night making sure everything is set for the op," he answered, turning his attention to one of the screens.

"Appreciate that," said Ian. "So how's everything working so far?"

"Got your earpiece in yet?" asked Leon.

"No, thought you said to wait till we're cleared through security."

"Well, let's see if anyone else does," answered Leon while tapping on his keyboard. He adjusted the wireless earpiece connected to a clear plastic microphone boom situated on the right side of his face. "Testing, one, two, three...radio check. How do you hear me?" he said speaking into his microphone boom.

A long pause ensued, causing Leon to begin to think some adjustments were required or that everyone had actually *listened* to his instructions to wait until after they cleared security to connect with him. Then he heard what sounded like someone handling his communications device.

"Hello? So tell me again…am I just supposed to talk out loud and you'll hear me?" asked Todd.

Leon chuckled. "Now why did I know *you'd* be the first one to ignore my instructions to wait until *after* you clear airport security to activate your comm device?" asked Leon.

"Maestro, is that you?" asked Todd using a newly designated call sign for Leon.

Leon glanced at Ian with a look of confusion. "Oh, I remember," admitted Leon as he suddenly made the connection. "Since G designated me the orchestra director, now I have a new call sign. Nice. I actually kind of like it."

"Loud and clear, Maestro. Sorry about the instructions breach. I was just messin' around, checking out the cool gear, and suddenly heard a familiar voice," Todd attempted to explain.

"OK, since you're the only one I'm in direct contact with so far, I'll run some checks with you," said Leon as he glanced at one of the screens. "I show you already positioned at the Djibouti airport, confirm?"

"That's correct," said Todd. "What else can I help you with?"

"Stand by," answered Leon as he turned to Ian. "I think we're off to a good start, Ian. Unless you have any last-minute alibis, I should probably get back to work," he said.

"Cool. Thanks for watching over us," said Ian.

"You can thank me when all this is behind us," he said as he turned his attention back to the screens.

"Sir, you're gonna want to take a look at this," said a young man who directed Dennis's attention to a video feed. "We intercepted an Al Jezeera prebroadcast video. I'm sending it through to your terminal now. Just a heads-up—it's graphic, sir."

Dennis directed his attention to a monitor as he watched the direct feed from Al Jezeera. The news agencies commonly mark their prebroadcasts with a test pattern to indicate its preedited status, so Dennis knew he was watching raw video footage.

The video began with three seconds of static. The next thing Dennis saw was Hanah Malkinson holding a newspaper. Two armed men, each wearing masks, stood behind her. Dennis remained glued to the broadcast, trying to analyze it as it played out.

He watched as Hanah defiantly flung the newspaper to her side, and he braced himself for the inevitable price she would pay. In all of his years of dealing with such experiences, he knew he could be watching the very footage that depicted the graphic death of Hanah Malkinson. He had seen it before. He recalled the shock he felt when he first saw the Daniel Pearl execution and that he felt again when he analyzed the top-secret Benghazi cell-phone video of a CIA operative who survived the terrorist attack. Those and many other experiences had not desensitized him to the true cost of freedom and the fragility of life. Watching this video brought each of the others to the forefront of his mind as his pulse quickened and his breathing grew shallow.

The price came swiftly, just as Dennis had predicted—a rifle butt to the side of Hanah's head. It was delivered so quickly that even Dennis was surprised. He winced as he witnessed the tilt of her head and the reaction of her body as it fell to the floor.

He heard a faint command as one of the masked men began his angry rhetoric.

"You have witnessed the result of defiant insolence. Such choices are foolish in the face of those favored by God. We have your precious Jewish jewel and will keep her until the terms of our demands are met," declared one of the masked men.

The camera followed the masked man as he knelt beside Hanah, grabbed her by the hair, and lifted her head while looking into the camera. "I have no problem whatsoever killing this bitch," he said as he slowly retrieved a dagger from a sheath at his side and placed it against her throat. "If you wish to ever see her alive again, you will comply with the demands we have detailed in letter accompanying this video. If you think you can send in your special forces to rescue her, you are welcome to try. Your attempts will be a useless waste of time that will only result in more infidel deaths."

Dennis moved closer to the screen to pick up every detail he could. Questions loomed. His biggest concern was whether she had survived the blow. *Is she breathing? Is she alive? Move, dammit. Show me a sign of life, Hanah. Breathe, dammit...*

Just before the video ended, he heard the Arabic command to "shut it off." Then the screen returned to static.

"Tell me we're already busy analyzing this," said Dennis to the young man who brought it to his attention.

"On your authority—"

"Approved. I want a *full* analysis report as soon as it's available. The boss is gonna want to see this, and he'll expect the facts. And see if you can find out if she's still alive."

Dennis pressed a button on the communications panel and connected to an NSA signals specialist. "Jack, Dennis Kinkaid. I have a signals-suppression request. Can you send someone to the ops center right away?"

"Certainly. I know just who to send," he said.

Five minutes later an escort led a man into the ops center to meet with Dennis.

"Dennis Kinkaid," he said with an extended hand. "Thanks for the rapid response. I have a video that's in the hands of Al Jezeera that I need to suppress just long enough for an operations team to conduct a rescue op. Is that something you can help me with?"

"Depends. There are number of variables I may have to overcome depending on what we're looking at," the new man explained.

"What kind of variables?"

"Well for starters, how old is the video? And how long do you want it suppressed. I'm good, but nobody can keep a video suppressed forever, even if I manage to shut down their entire operation. So why don't you show me what you've got so I know what I'm dealing with?"

"You're right. Not trying to do your job. The analyst in me is always trying to help. OK, here's the video…" said Dennis as he explained all that was known about the video and provided a suppression timeline he required.

"OK," said the man. "I'll need a secure terminal and unrestricted access to your grid."

Dennis took a deep breath. "We normally don't—aw, hell, gimme a second," he said. Dennis pressed a button on the communications console. "Captain, open up a full access credential for—what did you say your name was?"

"I didn't. But you can call me Pat," he said, intentionally omitting his last name.

Dennis nodded knowingly. "Open up a full access credential and label it 'Pat.' Yes, just Pat. Put my name on as the CO," he said as he waited for the active-duty Air Force captain at the other end of the line to respond to the request. "Yes, I'm still here. Good to go? OK, thanks."

Dennis turned to the specialist. "You've got full access, Pat. Terminal three right over there. The sergeant will help you with anything you need. Let me know when you've got the signal suppressed."

The intercom console rang. "Ops center, Kinkaid—" he attempted to announce his full title when Lisa, the deputy director of operations cut him off.

"The director would like to know if you're ready to provide an update on the Key Horizon operation."

"Yeah, we're ready," reported Kinkaid.

"Can you meet in his office, or do you need more space?"

"We can meet him wherever it's convenient for him. We don't need a lot of space."

"Very well, I'll put you in at 1430. That's thirty minutes from now."

Kinkaid hung up the phone and alerted his deputy. "Scott, do you have an open line to Agent Lambert?"

"Leon Lambert? Sure do," answered the deputy.

"Great, grab whatever updates he has to the minute and be prepared to present them to the boss in thirty…make that twenty-seven minutes."

The desert landscape crept beneath them as the airliner made its way across the southern coast of Yemen. Each operative contemplated his respective role as the plane began its descent into Aden International Airport. The final approach brought the aircraft in over portions of the Arabian Sea as the topography of the coastal landscape grew closer to the descending aircraft.

Passengers gathered inside the terminal and found their way to the security processing stations. They formed various lines inside the immigrations area of the terminal, each according to whether or not they were a returning citizen or an outside visitor.

G glanced about the crowded room as he stood in the visitor's line waiting his turn to clear Yemen security and immigrations. If ever there was a nearly inescapable bottleneck in the entire operation, this was it. His mind raced as the stress of the moment continued to build. He casually glanced across the room once again and noticed Tzofiya standing in the line designated for returning Yemen citizens. A subdued yellow-and-white headscarf covered her hair, and her pretty face seemed poised and confident, her posture relaxed. Her training and years of experience had prepared her well for the stressful and pivotal situation. G envied her.

The line inched forward as he continued to anticipate the encounter with the security official behind the processing booth. G watched as the official took his time examining the papers provided by each passenger. He read the official's lips as he asked a series of varying questions to each passenger. *Are you here on business? What is your purpose in Yemen? How long is your stay? Where are you from? Where will you be staying?* Each question reassured G that he and his teammates had adequately prepared themselves. But the question of whether they had time to prepare well enough for the unexpected remained unanswered. They would each know the answer soon as G stepped to the line and received the nod from the security official.

Ian and Todd made sure to space themselves out in line far enough apart not to be associated with each other. They watched as G approached the security checkpoint and handed his papers to the official. The official examined G's papers and tapped away at a keyboard hidden from view behind the counter. The official seemed to be taking more time than usual as G patiently waited for his papers to be processed. A look of concern appeared on the official's face as he looked up at G and spoke to him.

Todd was uncertain of the dialogue between G and the official, and he didn't have a good feeling about the delay. He instinctively reached into his breast pocket, opened the eyeglass case, and re-moved the glasses Leon had given him. Activating automatically as soon as he placed them onto his face, Todd immediately saw what everyone else couldn't—lime-green target displays of the position of the microdrones positioned about the room. He picked up another target hovering near the immigration booth where G was being screened. Todd suppressed a smirk as he watched one of the drones land on the shoulder of the immigrations official and knew that Leon was essentially peering over his shoulder to investigate. What seemed like an eternity passed when the official finally looked up at G and smiled and followed with a swift immigrations stamp into G's Omani passport.

Todd watched as G disappeared into the crowd on the other side of the immigrations processing stations. He glanced toward the returning Yemen citizen's line and was relieved to see that Tzofiya had already processed through, apparently without any issues.

Two down, two to go, he thought.

His fingers tapped feverishly on the keyboard as he entered commands to maneuver the tiny drones to survey the terminal for electronics scanners as the team deplaned and entered the terminal. Sensing only two security screening devices, he maneuvered them to circumvent the scanners to avoid detection. He saw no evidence of scanners inside the customs and immigration area. Leon decided he'd take a casual look around anyway. He positioned several drones strategically throughout the room to increase his overall situational awareness. He watched as Tzofiya slipped right through without an issue and wondered whether or not it was her experience or pretty smile that paved the way for her.

Everything seemed to be going well until G's immigration processing seemed to be taking longer than average. Leon maneuvered one of the drones to see if he could get a closer look at the immigration official's computer screen. He needed a good vantage point, so he boldly decided to land the tiny drone on the shoulder of the immigrations official. The landing was easy. He just picked a spot with his cursor and the drone flew directly to the spot. The only risk was whether or not the official would notice the drone and see it as a nuisance.

Leon worked fast. As soon as the drone was in position he scanned the computer screen for possible anomalies or flags that might have been associated with G's papers. He could plainly see G's Omani photo and data associated with the passport on the computer display but noticed it had not been properly activated when he departed Djibouti.

The keys clattered as his fingers moved across the keyboard with lightning speed as he hacked the system and sent an activation update, ending the command with a hard strike on the "enter" key. He held his breath and hoped the immigration official had enough patience to see the update flash before he passed G off to another agent, increasing the odds and likelihood of exposure, and quite possibly impacting the overall operation. Leon breathed a sigh of relief when he saw the computer screen indicate a green flag. He followed the official's movement with the drone's lens while he watched him stamp G's passport.

- 280 -

Two down, two to go, he thought as he breathed a temporary sigh of relief.

Leon noticed the direct line to the operations center was flashing. "Operator, how may I help you?"

"Leon, Scott from the home office. I need an updated SITREP for a brief to the boss."

As he expected, G was greeted with a barrage of taxi solicitations as he stepped outside of the terminal. G resisted as one of the drivers grabbed at the bag on his shoulder in an attempt to win the taxi fare. He saw a man standing alone beside his taxi just beyond the crowd. He pushed his way through and approached the man.

"Taxi fare, sir?" he asked in Arabic. "I charge good price and will take you wherever you wish to go."

"*Shukran*," answered G, thanking the man.

The driver closed the door for G, made his way to the front, and activated the meter. G's head swiveled around, his eyes moving about scanning the area and the crowd for anything unusual. The heightened state of alertness made him keenly aware of his surroundings as he listened to the driver report the pickup of a fare. He secretly wondered how the rest of the team would handle the overwhelming insistence of desperate drivers outside the terminal. He ignored the driver, who tried making small talk with him along the way, and stuck to the basics of telling him his destination as the taxicab sped through the crowded city streets.

Ian cleared immigrations without issue and loitered inside the terminal to be certain Todd made it through. He casually moved about the terminal looking at various shops and merchants while he waited for the final teammate to clear the hurdle. While he waited, he opened his earpiece case, casually inserted the device into his right ear, and then activated his cell phone. When the cell phone came to life, Ian looked at the screen to ensure it was able to capture a good scan of his eye.

"As long as you're out in public, I don't expect an audible response," said the familiar voice of Leon in Ian's earpiece. "Just look at the cell phone and scratch your nose if you can hear me clearly," he instructed.

Ian casually lifted his hand and scratched his nose while carefully looking at the cell phone.

"Awesome. I assume you're waiting for Todd. He just cleared immigrations and should be walking past you from your left at any moment. You're the only one I have on comms right now so, until anyone else comes up, I'll be chatting with you if you don't mind."

Ian looked up and saw Todd walk past, pulling a large suitcase. The two exchanged a quick glance—their only acknowledgement as Todd slipped out the front door.

"OK, Ian, everyone is inside the gate. Good luck," said Leon as he sat back and watched the GPS tracking the signals of each operative.

Harriman motioned for Dennis and his deputy to enter his office and sit as he finished a phone call with Jon McCoy at the State Department. "Yeah, Jon, they're here now. Appreciate your continued involvement in this. I'll be in touch."

Harriman remained seated and asked for the door to be closed. Scott was closest, so he closed the door and then sat down.

"What do we have, gentlemen?" asked Harriman, eager to get to the point.

Dennis spoke first. "Boss, we've confirmed Hanah Malkinson is located in Aden, Yemen."

"And how do we know this for sure?" asked Harriman.

"Direct observation, sort of," said a reluctant Dennis.

Harriman crossed his arms, his impatience apparent, but allowed Dennis to continue.

"Sir, I take it you're fully briefed on the rather unusual manner by which one of our very own operatives *discovers* certain things? I'll spare you the long version, but I can report that the latest SITREP confirms Agent Weston's direct knowledge of her *specific* location. The Aden location has actually been corroborated by one of the two detainees captured at Hammadi's safe house. Seems General Montague's men were able to convince one of them to roll and reveal the city."

"The old bastard actually got one of 'em to talk, eh? Nice. So how specific of a location do we have?"

"Agent Weston claims to know the *exact* compound she was in as of two hours ago."

"Two hours can make a hell of a difference here, gentlemen. What else do we know?"

"I realize it's been a while since you've received an update on this but quite a bit has happened the past few days," he said.

Dennis briefed Harriman on the known details of Hanah's abduction and provided a timeline to include her escape, her sympathetic accomplice, his ensuing execution, and her recapture. He explained how Agent Weston's unconventional insight helped to keep the team on pace to catch up to her captors, and he provided details of the team's plan to arrive undetected and to bring her home. "Without Weston, the team wouldn't be where they are now."

"OK, so the team gets to Aden. Then what?"

"They're actually *in* Aden now, Paul. Four operatives—three of our own and one Israeli—have all successfully made it past customary security barriers. As I said earlier, they know *specifically* where she's located. The team will rendezvous at a CIA checkpoint to gear up and collect their weapons. They'll proceed separately to the compound and execute a breach when the conditions are right."

"What's the backup plan?"

"Our preferred method is to do this as quietly as possible, hence the primary plan. Should the team require reinforcements or an alternative action plan, SOF is standing by to assist," explained Dennis. "Not taking anything away from the surgical capabilities of our SOF warriors, but as we both know, they tend to make a bit more noise."

"Understand. We're not trying to start another war but we *are* determined to achieve an objective nonetheless. What's her current condition?"

"All we know at this point is that she's alive."

"What do you mean, that's *all you know*? This Agent Weston can't provide any insight beyond that? Seems he's gone well beyond that in other areas. Why not now?"

Dennis explained the latest details surrounding the injury Hanah sustained as a result of her defiance to cooperate with her captors. "Fair warning, Paul, this is graphic," said Dennis as he played the video of Hanah's encounter with the rifle butt of Massii's AK-47.

Paul was noticeably agitated as the video came to an end. "I have to admit, that stirred an emotion inside me that is seldom moved anymore. I'm inclined to get on a plane and confront this bastard myself," said Harriman, clearly affected by the brutal nature of her mistreatment. "Who else has a copy of this, and what are we doing to keep this from getting out to the world?"

"To our knowledge, the only copy resides with Al Jezeera and the terrorists, of course. I've got a specialist working on suppressing it for us as we speak. But even he tells me he can only squash it for a finite period of time," explained Dennis.

"Will that 'period of time' be enough for our team to conduct the op and get out of there safely?"

"The specialist seems to think he can do that for us."

Harriman contemplated the gravity and delicacy of the situation for a moment. "I just received word that the Israeli deputy prime minister has been cleared of any culpability. They're constructing a mobile-ops center for him to watch over the operation from Saint-Tropez. The Israelis want to know what we know so they can bring him up to speed. Send a message to the DPM that his wife is alive but don't send the video. Reassure the Israelis that we have a high degree of confidence that this will end with her safe return."

Dennis nodded. "I understand."

"Does the team have everything they need? What's the exit strategy?"

"Scott has the latest, up-to-the-minute SITREP for you," said Dennis. "I'm confident it'll answer the rest of your questions."

G watched as the taxi disappeared into its own dust trail. He slung the satchel over his shoulder and began walking down the coral-ridden road to the abandoned marina scrapyard. He pushed aside the large rusty gate at the entryway of a large empty lot. Stopping a moment to look around, he saw a large white building at the far end and made his way to the entrance. He pulled on the front door handle but it didn't budge.

"You wanna give me a clue as to where I'm supposed to go now, Leon?" asked G as he stepped back to get a better perspective of the building.

"Far northwest end. Round the corner and stand on the concrete pad in front of the steel door. They're expecting you," instructed Leon. "By the way, once you're inside I'll be unable to communicate or track you."

G followed the directions and was greeted by the click of the door lock—his clue to step inside.

"Welcome to the hospitality suite," greeted a CIA operative who seemed overly happy to see someone. "So you're the one who's gonna go in and pull this off, are you?"

G didn't answer. He just stood his ground and waited for the man to do his job. Sometimes agents would test each other. They're unpredictable because of the very nature of the job they did, so G wasn't interested in trying to win the man over.

"Grab a set of keys from the board. If you're lucky you'll pick a car that'll actually work," he said smiling. "Just kidding. Hey, we don't get much outside company here in these parts. Anyway, your weapons are in the locker at the end of the table."

Both men turned their heads toward the front of the building when they heard a car drive across the coral just outside the building. "Enjoy your shopping experience. Let me know if you have any questions on the weapons. I gotta go answer the doorbell for the next contestant," said the operative.

G was impressed with the layout of the weapons. He picked up the Sig Sauer P938, examined and cleared it. He was happy to see that there were four preloaded clips, each with seven rounds of hollow-point 9mm. He grabbed all four clips, placing two in his pants pockets and two in his satchel. He also picked up a Benchmade tactical knife and placed it in his pocket. He stuck the Sig into the waistband of his pants, at the small of his back, and picked up a Bersa Thunder Pro Ultra Compact .45ACP for an added measure of protection, strapping it to his right calf. As he grabbed a set of car keys, he heard a familiar voice as his teammate, Todd, entered the room.

"Good to see you made it safe, G," he said as he placed his suitcase onto the table. "Let's see if the toys made it in good condition. You know, I'd really hate to file a claim against the airline if anything happened to them," he said with a smile.

Todd pulled out various garments and threw them aside until he reached the pelican cases housing the microdrones. "Man, I hope I don't have to actually control one of these bad boys. I'd crash it for sure. Good thing Leon can pick up the signal and give us what we need if we need it. Know what I'm sayin'?"

G just looked at him. "You talk too much sometimes, Todd."

"What are you so uptight about?"

"Oh, I don't know. Maybe it's just the op we're on, or maybe it's just me."

"Yo, G, look at me. We're gonna do this. You know we're gonna do this," he said nodding.

"Damn straight," agreed G.

"Yo, G."

"Yeah."

"I want a crack at him…the big dog…if he's still hanging out, that is."

"I'm not compromising this op to ensure your vengeance is served. Besides, we both know it won't bring back your brother. Grab your weapons and a set of keys so we can get moving."

Todd glared at G. "It may not bring him back, G…but it just might prevent someone else's brother from becoming another victim. I don't think you understand. I keep hearing the words play over in my mind."

"What words?"

"All the words I should've said to him before he died."

G nodded and figured he should allow Todd to have the last say. Besides, he was probably right. If Siraj was still sticking around, Todd was probably best suited to eliminate him if the situation allowed.

"Where're Ian and Tzofiya?"

"Ian's right here," announced Ian unexpectedly. "Haven't seen Tzofiya. Figured you guys may have seen her since you got here before I did."

"Yo, Brutus, young female operative show up here yet?" asked Todd, giving the CIA operative a new call sign befitting his large size.

"Yeah, she left about ten minutes before he arrived," he said pointing to G.

"Put your earpieces in," said G as he turned toward the garage bay housing the three remaining vehicles. "Ian, I'll meet you at dusk at the perimeter of the compound. Todd, check in once you're in position at the docks."

"G…we're gonna do this," reiterated Todd.

G paused and offered a confident, affirmative head nod and turned the ignition key.

The daily call to prayer began echoing throughout the area as the sun found its way below the artificial horizon cast by the surrounding buildings.

"The Jew is conscious," reported Massii to Siraj.

"Good. I had hoped to speak with her again before I leave. Hamad, bring the car around; we're leaving. And call ahead and have the jet ready to depart in one hour."

Hanah had barely regained consciousness when Siraj approached and sat next to her bedside. Her head pounded with pain as Siraj leaned in close and looked her in the eye. "This will be the last you see of me. If you continue to resist as you have, your stay will be a long and arduous one. You should rest, knowing that in the end we all die. Until then, we all live. I have left explicit instructions for you to be kept alive so long as you are useful to me. The quality of that life is a choice you must consider while you are a guest here. So far your choices have not been wise. I beseech you to consider alternative choices. Doing so will improve the quality of your life. You might take a lesson or two from the young man next door. He has been here since 2009 and has conformed quite well."

Siraj rose and walked slowly toward the door, stopping a moment to speak to Massii. "A word of advice to you," he said to Massii, "Don't leave any visible marks on her face. The infidels get so testy when their people, especially their women, show signs of physical abuse. I will find my way out. You make sure she is comfortable," he said with a chuckle and a wink.

Siraj made his way to the next room where the young man sat in a corner. He arose when he saw Siraj enter his room and watched as he closed the door behind him.

Massii closed the door and approached Hanah with determined lust. Hanah's heart pounded as she contemplated how to handle the lethal man. She moved and placed her back against the wall as she watched the man disrobe without looking away from her eyes. Hanah cried out and kicked wildly as he knelt on the edge of the mattress. He easily brushed her flailing legs aside and grabbed her by the hair and violently flung her onto the floor. Her head pounded with pain as she watched him grab a rope intended to bind her hands. She screamed and fought as hard as she could against his attack as he laughed at her feeble attempts to fight him off.

The street was void of any moving vehicles as he positioned the car one block to the east of the compound, turned off the lights, and removed his muzzar turban. He checked his weapon, chambered a round, and exited the vehicle as he replaced the gun in the small of his back.

"Approaching the compound from the east," G quietly reported.

"Copy," reported Ian. "I'm positioned just outside the front entrance, waiting for you."

"Recommend you post at the back of the residence," answered G as he looked up and saw a dark figure casually walking toward him from the front entrance of the residence. "Approaching the entrance. There's a woman in a black abaya walking toward me," he reported as he reached behind his back and wrapped his hand around the pistol grip.

"It's me, G," reported Tzofiya.

G breathed a temporary sigh of relief until he received a warning from Tzofiya.

"Car approaching from your six o'clock position, G. Looks like it's slowing. Recommend you keep walking and double back. I'll let you know if it's anything to be concerned about," warned Tzofiya.

The car caught up with G and slowed as he walked past the gated driveway to the compound. The man activated the electronic gate and stopped the car to wait as it opened, rolled down his window, and called out. G ignored him and kept walking as if he hadn't heard him. Tzofiya saw a need for a diversion and quickly intervened by knocking on the man's passenger side window. She distracted the man just long enough for G to step into the shadows and wait for an opportunity to slip into the compound.

"Leon, if you can hear me, I need you to launch one of your drones. I need a look inside that compound as soon as anyone opens the door," said G.

"I'm on it and ready when you are," reported Leon.

G placed the computer glasses on his head and picked up two drone targets maneuvering in the area. One hovered near the entrance while the other landed on the roof of the vehicle attempting to enter the compound.

The man in the car rolled down the passenger window and began shouting at Tzofiya. "Bitch, get away from my car. What's wrong with you? What are you doing on the streets after dark? Are you defying the law, or are you selling something you shouldn't be?"

"I'm sorry, sir. I had assumed you were someone I was waiting for," said Tzofiya as she placed a tiny GPS transceiver inside the door of the car as she leaned in to speak with the man, distracting him long enough for G to slip into the open gate.

"I said, get away from my car," he shouted as he rolled up the window and drove into the driveway.

Tzofiya followed the car onto the property. As the man got out of the car he noticed her approaching. He walked up to her. "What is wrong with you? I don't have time for this," he said as he cocked his arm back to strike her.

G appeared from the shadows and drove his fist into the man's lower spine. As the man was falling to his knees, G placed one hand over the man's nose and mouth and the other at the back of his head. A quick twist snapped the man's neck; he went limp and slumped to the ground.

"Impressive," said Tzofiya admiringly.

G dragged the man's body to a dark side of the building. When he returned to the vehicle, he and Tzofiya heard a muted scream coming from an upper level of the compound.

"Ian, are you in position?" asked G.

"Affirmative."

"OK, I'm going in. Gonna see if they left the door open for visitors," said G as he ascended a short flight of stairs and slowly tried turning the doorknob. "Locked…Tzofiya, I need a favor."

Tzofiya instinctively knew that G needed her to knock on the door to get someone to open it. G positioned himself just out of sight next to her as she stepped forward, knocked on the door, and waited. They both heard another muted scream while they waited for someone to answer the door. Suddenly, a light illuminated above her head. She knew enough not to make eye contact when the man opened the door.

"Good evening, sir. I seem to be lost. Will you kindly help me?" she asked in Arabic using a Yemeni accent.

The man stood silently for a moment and then reached out to gently lift her chin. As he did, Tzofiya looked into his eyes innocently. He smiled as he did his best to assess the potential possibility of a conquest. Then he looked up past her and noticed Siraj's car that had been driven into the gated compound. His demeanor changed from personal desire to personal preservation as he pushed Tzofiya out of the way and stepped into the entryway past G and down the steps to the vehicle. Tzofiya turned to look at G who flashed a signal for her to follow the man and immobilize him. G turned and quietly slipped into the residence undetected.

34

Ezra was speaking to one of the men responsible for the overall construct of the makeshift, floating operations center when his phone rang. "Hello," he answered. "Yes. I see. Yes, we are nearly set to go live with a full suite of communications and information systems. Yes, we will be able to monitor the situation from here," answered Ezra as he looked for confirmation from the man he had been speaking to earlier. "I will relay your message. Is there anything else? Very well then, thank you." He hung up the phone and returned to his earlier conversation. "How long before we are ready?"

"We're ready now, sir."

"Let's go live then," ordered Ezra as he turned and walked toward Avigdor.

Six people sat typing in front of laptop computers and communications consoles, sending and analyzing data inside the main room of the yacht as the remote Israeli operations center went live. Some people focused intently on the task at hand while others sat and collaborated, quietly awaiting for orders from Avigdor. Each knew the importance and highly sensitive nature of the operation and the rarity of being under the direct operational command of the minister of defense.

"The system is up and running, the resources are not ideal, but you and I have both operated under worse conditions, no?" said Ezra to Avigdor. "Before you become overly involved in the process, I want to let you know that I just received a phone call from the American National Security Agency. They wanted me to tell you that your wife is alive and they have a 'high degree of confidence' in the operation to return her safely."

"Thank you, Ezra. What do you make of the message?"

"My friend, you know me well. I instinctively mistrust everyone. My cynicism has served me well over the years and is largely responsible for keeping me alive. While I truly believe Hanah is still alive, I cannot help but feel the Americans may be holding something back. Time will tell, but it may indeed be time Hanah does not have. Trust your gut and watch over the rescue team. They are risking their lives to bring her home."

Avigdor always appreciated the candor of his friend and trusted confidant. He was also encouraged upon hearing that Hanah was still alive. A deep sense of determination welled within him as he took a deep breath and immediately went into action with all of the power and influence of his authority as defense minister. He barked out his first command. "I need eyes over Yemen. Reposition the Eitan drone over the city of Aden and tap into the US satellite signal. I want a picture on our screens now."

He heard laughter coming from an adjacent room as he quietly crept through the residence, his eyes darting about in search of cameras or anything or anyone unexpected. He could hear the men laughing at the "noise" coming from upstairs. "Massii must be teaching the bitch some new exercise moves," one of them laughed.

"Leon, get those drones of yours moving," whispered G.

"Already ahead of you, Big G," echoed the response in G's tiny earpiece.

Peering around a corner, G saw four men seated at a small kitchen table eating and joking with one another. A closer observation revealed a shotgun perched in a corner of the kitchen and two ammunition clips lying on a small table next to the stove—.45 caliber, he guessed. He looked to his right and saw a way he could quietly make his way to a small, unlit room. There he found the back door of the residence where Ian waited to be let in. As he approached the door, he heard footsteps heading his way.

No time for the door, he thought as he quickly assessed his options.

In the distance he heard the men spewing vulgarities about having to watch over the prisoners and how their time would be better spent on whores or in the battlefield.

G was crouched behind a butcher-block table when the light came on. The man walked to a nearby cabinet and started busily rummaging through it, his back toward G. Then he heard the click of G's knife as it popped into place. He turned around and was met with G's overwhelming speed and power. G's firm gaze was the last thing he saw before G drove the blade into his throat, killing him quickly.

G tried his best to prevent the man's body from falling to the floor under the collapse of its full weight. In doing so, he inadvertently knocked over a porcelain cup sitting on the counter top. G watched as the cup fell to the tile floor as if in slow motion, ending in a crash that echoed into the adjacent rooms. He removed his knife, dropped the man's body onto the floor, and quickly moved to unlock the back door.

A man called out from the other room, joking about how a man could not be expected to do the work of a woman with any kind of finesse. Clearly, he had no intention of investigating the sound of commotion and crashing porcelain. The men continued laughing as Ian made his way inside the compound.

"Leon, what've you got for us?" asked Ian in a whisper.

"Three men just off to the right of your position, all currently seated. At least one of them is armed. There's a shotgun in the far right corner of the room. You have to get to the shotgun if you wanna keep the noise level under control. There's a long corridor on the upper floor with several rooms. I'm unable to look past them as all the doors are closed. At least one man is posted at the top of the stairwell to the immediate left."

"Copy. We're on the move," whispered Ian as he signaled G to move out first.

G held up a finger and cocked his head to listen as Ian wondered why. G got to his feet, folded his knife, and winked at Ian. Then he turned out the light to the small room and simply walked into the kitchen area where the men were gathered.

What the hell is he doing? wondered Ian as he watched from a dark corner of the room.

"*As-salaam alaykum,*" greeted G as he walked into the room, taking the men by complete surprise. "How's it going?" he continued in their native tongue. "I'm wondering if any of you can help me with something," he said as he looked around the room at the three men staring at him in complete disbelief. "I seemed to have lost my way and am looking for a man who was supposed to meet me here," he said as he continued to walk closer to the men, his palms open. "Perhaps you can help me?"

One of the men pushed his chair back and stood. "Who are you looking for, and what is your name?"

Ian pulled his weapon and slowly rose to his feet as he watched the situation play out from the next room.

"My name? My name is not important—"

"But if the one you're looking for is here, then I should know who it is that wishes to meet with him, no?" asked the man as he stepped toward G.

A scream echoed above the men as the tension mounted.

"I think whoever you're looking for may be busy," said the man as he glared at G with a menacing grin.

"I'll wait," answered G when he noticed one of the men seated at the table slowly draw his hands from the table.

"Suit yourself," said the man as he turned slightly and drew his weapon.

G reacted with a swift kick to the man's extended arm knocking the weapon from his grip. He crouched and coiled his body, spinning tightly into close proximity and released a powerful close-range punch to the man's sternum sending him to his knees. The man clutched his chest and gasped for air. G felt a hand grab the back of his collar as he fell backward onto the floor. He had learned early on never to resist the energy of a fall, so he used the momentum to his advantage and swung his legs out into a powerful spinning scissor kick that easily took the legs out from under his attacker. The man fell hard and fast, banging his head against the edge of the table on his way down. He was out before he hit the floor. Realizing there was one more man to deal with, G quickly rose to his feet and assumed a fighting stance. He was surprised to see the man slumped over onto the small table, blood oozing from a bullet hole in his forehead.

G quickly looked over his shoulder to see Ian approaching holding a smoking Walther PPK with a silencer. G glanced at the weapon.

"What are you, James Bond all of a sudden?" asked G.

"I hope we're at the right place, G. 'Cause we just greased four dudes," said Ian.

G knelt down by the man still gasping for air and quickly snapped his neck. "*Now* it's four," he responded. He pulled the sleeve back on the man. "If we're at the wrong place, then we just eliminated four members of the serpent's inner circle," he said revealing the mark of loyalty most members displayed on their bodies somewhere. "Looks like a spider to me," he sarcastically admitted as he stood to assess the situation.

Both men looked up as they heard the muffled sound of footsteps traveling across the floor above them. Ian saw someone appear out of the corner of his eye.

"Down!" said Ian as he pushed G aside and took aim.

"Hold your fire, Ian. It's Tzofiya."

"Thanks, G," said Tzofiya as she quietly approached glaring at Ian.

"Did you eliminate the threat outside?" asked G.

"Yes. He's no longer an issue. What's the situation here?" she asked looking at the four men lying about.

"Four kills. We gotta move quickly. I need you to post outside and eliminate any squirters," instructed G. "Ian and I are headed upstairs to get Hanah," he added.

Ian stepped toward the stairwell and took the lead.

Leon posted three drones in the hallway on the second floor and spoke to Ian as he ascended the stairs.

"One enemy on the second floor, seated. Wait…he just stood up…looks like he's talking with someone. Moving in for a closer look," said Leon.

Ian stopped when he reached the top of the stairwell, crouched low, and peered around the corner of the wall. G remained standing to ensure a covered shooting position and took a deep breath.

Paul received a direct call from the ops center floor. "Paul Harriman," he answered.

"Sir, excuse the interruption," said the man. "I'm looking for Mr. Kinkaid. We have a developing situation here he may wish to see."

"Thanks for the call. We're on our way," answered Harriman, looking at Dennis.

Arriving on the operations center floor, Dennis and Paul saw full-motion video streaming on two large overhead screens.

"What are we looking at?" barked Kinkaid.

"Sir, we have eyes on the inside of the Key Horizon operation," reported the young operations officer.

Paul and Dennis watched as the scene depicted a bird's eye view of the operation play out.

"Not sure I completely understand how we're seeing this perspective," announced Dennis.

"We intercepted an encrypted signal when we scanned the area and discovered this. It appears to be a signal from microdrones, sir," reported the operations officer.

"Do we have audio?"

"Negative, sir, video only."

Harriman looked at Dennis to see if he could determine whether or not Dennis had authorized the use of the tightly controlled cutting-edge technology. Dennis just stood staring at the screens as the scene continued to play out. Judging from Dennis's reaction, it appeared this was the first time he'd even seen the technology at all.

"Who's operating the drones?" Harriman finally asked Dennis.

Dennis glanced at the operations officer for an answer.

"We traced the signal back to the embassy in Djibouti, sir."

"Get a hold of the ambassador at DJ and transfer the call to me when you connect," ordered Dennis while he and Paul continued to watch the details on the screen unfold.

Two minutes later, an operations officer alerted Dennis that the ambassador was on the line waiting to speak with him. Dennis picked up the phone without taking his eyes off the screens.

Hanah sobbed as Massii subdued her and tied her hands behind her back. The more she continued to resist the more he seemed to enjoy himself as he tore at her clothes and ripped her shirt. Careful not to leave any evidence of abuse on her face he grabbed her by the hair and tossed her onto the mattress. Hanah squirmed and cried out as Massii drove his fist squarely into her sternum causing her to gasp for air and silencing her cries. She desperately fought to catch her breath while he removed her pants and tossed them aside.

Massii stopped suddenly when he was distracted by sounds coming from outside the room. He opened the door slightly and caught the attention of a guard who stood when he saw thee shirtless Massii.

"What is all this commotion I'm hearing? Go take care of things and—"

Massii's tirade was abruptly cut short when he watched as a bullet pierce the side of the man's head, snapping it violently to one side as blood and brain fragments exploded from the exit wound.

Massii froze momentarily as he watched the man's body crash to the floor in front of him. Time slowed as he willed himself to snap out of the shock and surprise that had a grip on him.

He quickly slammed the door shut and ran toward a corner of the room to retrieve his weapon, a Desert Eagle .44 Magnum. He chambered a round and listened carefully while trying to catch his breath. Hearing footsteps just outside the room he quickly moved toward Hanah and positioned himself behind her while taking aim on the door.

35

eon took advantage of the opportunity to get a microdrone into the room when Massii had the door open. His fingers swept across the keyboard as he entered the commands to maneuver the tiny drone for the best vantage point in the room while simultaneously monitoring the video feed from all three drones. He watched as Ian took out the guard in the hallway, essentially declaring the full commitment of their lives to completing the mission.

"I'm in," declared Leon to all four operatives listening in.

"Confirm you have eyes on Hanah," asked G as he waited for a response that seemed to take forever. Just knowing Leon had the ability to see inside the tiny room was reassuring.

Leon manipulated the tiny drone's highly sensitive camera. He had trained it on the enemy combatant and followed him as he positioned himself behind someone in the only bed in the room. Leon zoomed in.

"It's her, G. I have eyes on Hanah," he reported. "But the situation is extremely delicate…"

Ian turned to look at G and indicated with hand signals that he would step out of the way and allow G to breach the room first. He indicated he would provide covering firepower.

G peered down the corridor and counted three closed doors. "Leon, confirm last door on the right?"

"Affirmative…be careful, he's got her at gunpoint and is using her as a shield," reported Leon.

"Understand," replied G. "Just tell me exactly where he is, and I'll take it from there."

"Got your glasses on?" asked Leon while he feverishly typed away.

"Yeah, why?" asked G as he made his way down the corridor with Ian on his heels.

"One of the amazing things I programmed these little guys with is an ability to *sparkle* a target. All you gotta do is aim for the bright green dot. Just don't miss."

Ian and G took up positions on either side of the door and waited for Leon's signal. G crouched low while Ian stood ready to kick the door in and jump out of the way in anticipation of being fired upon.

"The target is green," reported Leon as he held his breath and watched the monitors.

The Israeli drone circled overhead. Code-name *Eitan*, the reconnaissance drone was equipped with all of the sophistication money could buy, including a full electronics suite of high-powered day, night, and infrared cameras and sensitive listening devices.

Avigdor watched the aerial video as the drone loitered high above the area of interest. A bird's-eye view of an obscure group of buildings slowly panned across the monitor as the drone entered an easy left-hand orbit above the city.

"Are these the coordinates provided to us by the Americans?" asked Avigdor.

"Yes, sir," answered one of the specialists manning a computer terminal.

"Ezra, do we have a way to contact any of the operatives?"

"Yes, but I don't recommend it at this point. Is there something you need from the team?"

"Just an echo-burst location confirmation."

Ezra smiled. "Well then, that I can do without interrupting them," he said as he pulled his phone and entered a code onto the keypad. He waited a few seconds and retrieved a set of coordinates to deliver to Avigdor. "Give these coordinates to your sensor operator, and you will have the location of our operative. Keep in mind that it is a snapshot in time, and she may be on the move."

Avigdor provided the coordinates to an operative who fed the information to the sensor operator. Avigdor and Ezra watched the video screen as the camera angle changed revealing a small blue ring around the coordinates he provided. Avigdor looked at Ezra who returned a slight nod of affirmation. The blue circle was positioned just outside of an obscure building at the edge of a block of similar structures.

"Zoom in to that location and use the IR camera," ordered Avigdor.

The drone camera zoomed in to reveal a single figure identified as a ghost white silhouette standing outside the building. An even closer view revealed clues the figure could possibly be a woman.

"Is that one of ours?" asked Avigdor.

"I believe it may be," answered Ezra.

"Sir, I have eyes open from the inside of the building," reported one of the operators.

Avigdor and Ezra rushed to the terminal to see an intermittent picture captured by the microdrones inside the tiny room. Avigdor's adrenaline spiked when he caught a glimpse of Hanah for the first time. His mind moved at an amazing speed as he tried to come to grips with what he was seeing for the first time.

"Is that Hanah?" asked Ezra. "Avigdor—" He stressed the name, trying to snap his friend out of his momentary trance. "Is that her?"

"Yes," he simply answered. For the first time since her disappearance, Avigdor was speechless as he remained glued to the screen with an underlying sense of helplessness. The man holding her at gunpoint would be forced to act soon, as would those just outside the room waiting to kill him.

⊕

G looked up at Ian and offered a quick nod indicating he was ready. He hoped the man holding Hanah would react by shooting at the door before the thought occurred to him to sacrifice his prisoner. It would give him just the fraction of an opening he'd need to get the shot off he'd hoped would match perfectly with the green mark designated by Leon.

Time slowed as Ian positioned himself in front of the door, risking his own life to save another. G watched as the heel of Ian's foot made contact with the door as it broke loose from the frame and burst open. Pieces of wood flew into the air as the latch breeched the frame and the door broke away and swung inward. Ian maneuvered his body to fall away from the line of fire he was sure would be coming his way.

G pushed his arms into the doorway with a firm two-handed grasp of his weapon and concentrated on looking for the green sparkle as he fell onto his left side. Waiting for his shoulder to make contact with the floor before taking the shot, G watched as Massii took his first shot—an indiscriminate and desperate attempt at self-defense.

G made eye contact with Massii as his left shoulder struck the floor. He could clearly see the green laser sparkle just above the bridge of his nose as Massii glanced down to see him taking aim. It was the last thing he saw before G squeezed the trigger, taking the fatal shot.

Siraj listened intently to the sounds coming from the hallway just outside the room. He walked to a boarded window and carefully removed a small section allowing him to peer into the courtyard. He saw the rear corner of the car that would take him to the airport. He knew if his driver had not summoned him by now, it indicated he probably wasn't going to. Siraj had little information on what was happening, but he had enough experience to know that something wasn't right. He pulled a handgun from his waistband and used it to summon the young man to his side.

"Time for us to leave," Siraj said to the young man as he placed the gun in his lower back, leading him to the door.

Siraj stopped when he heard the loud noise of a door being kicked in at the end of the corridor.

"Open the door, slowly and quietly," he ordered the young man. "Look out and tell me what you see."

"Nothing…wait, I see a man lying on the floor at the end of the hallway."

Siraj grabbed the young man by the back of his collar and pulled him back into the room. "Here's the deal. You will accompany me to the car outside. Once we make it that far, I will release you. Understand?"

The young man nodded.

"You get me to that car, and you will find freedom," Siraj stressed. "There may be some people here who wish to bring harm and see to it that we fail to reach that goal. I'm counting on you to help me get to that car. Understand?"

The young man nodded once again.

"Good. Let's go."

Avigdor and Ezra watched as the video footage revealed the fatal shot Hanah's captor took as he still held the final loose grip pose he had with one arm around her neck and the other relaxed at his side, his weapon still in his hand. Avigdor celebrated with a hearty "Yes!" when he witnessed the moment his wife was freed from immediate danger.

The men watched as G carefully approached Hanah and reassured her. The absence of audio was a bit frustrating but both men knew enough about these operations to know that what they saw G and Ian doing was textbook.

"Any idea who the assailant is?" asked Avigdor of no one in particular.

"No way of knowing without a closer look, sir," responded an operator working one of the computer terminals.

The men watched as Hanah reached out to G as if she knew him while Ian pulled the dead man away from her. Ian stepped out of view as G helped Hanah into some clothes.

Ezra placed a hand on Avigdor's shoulder. "She's in good hands now, my friend."

Dennis was about to pick up the secure call with the ambassador in Djibouti when the pace of the operation on screen significantly changed. "Tell the ambassador to stand by," ordered Dennis while he and Paul watched the exchange of gunfire take place resulting in the killing of one of Hanah's captors.

The elated look on Paul's face told Dennis that he was relieved to have not only found Hanah but to know that she was now in the hands of a highly trained team of operatives who were determined to get her to safety.

"Looks like you can take that call now," said Paul reminding Dennis the ambassador was still waiting on the line to speak with him.

"Damn, that's right. Things got so exciting I almost forgot," he said with a wink and smile.

"Madam Ambassador, Dennis Kinkaid here. I understand you hosted our team there recently…yes ma'am, they have everything they need. I just wanted to follow up with a phone call to thank you for the support you've shown them. Can you tell me if any of them are still operating out of your embassy there? I see. Yes, ma'am. How many? One? I see. No, ma'am, if I need anything else, I'll reach out to you. And thank you once again for your support."

Dennis hung up the phone and turned to Paul who was still watching the video screens.

"One thing I can't figure out, Dennis," said Paul as he analyzed the scene still playing out before him.

"What's that, boss?"

"This other camera angle," he said pointing to the empty corridor view. "Is that a separate drone feed?"

"I believe it is…yeah, that's the corridor they came through to get to Hanah," explained Dennis.

"It may just be me, Dennis, but where's the cover?"

"Sorry, boss, I don't follow," said Dennis trying to determine Paul's concern.

"We have two operatives in one room with Hanah and an empty hallway behind them. Where are the other operatives?"

Dennis suddenly realized the oversight as he watched Paul's concerns materialize before their very eyes when they saw Siraj emerge from the room with his human shield.

Her heart and mind raced as Massii draped his arm around her neck from behind, using her as a shield. Hanah wondered if her life had come down to how this moment would play out. She was prepared to die if she had to because she knew without a doubt that Ro'i would be waiting for her. She was determined to live if she could, however, because of the love and life she had with Avigdor and Rina. For the first time she literally smelled the stench of fear emanating from her cowardly captor. She enjoyed the conflicting sense of righteous indignation she felt from it.

Hanah closed her eyes and ducked her head when she heard the sound of the door breaking away from the frame. She held her breath as Massii took his first and only shot. The sound of the gun at close range pierced her ears and muted her hearing.

Massii's grip increased around her neck as his head jerked back and struck the wall behind him. Warm blood and brain matter splattered against the wall and onto Hanah as things suddenly went quiet.

Stealing a glance, she watched as a man slowly approached her with open hands. Her hearing still affected by the sound of gunfire, she couldn't hear his words, but she knew his face. Tears streamed from her eyes when she recognized the one who was there to follow through on a promise her own son had made to her. She reached out to G as he pulled her from the grip of her assailant. She held him close as Ian covered Massii's body with a bedsheet to shield her from the gruesome sight.

G cleaned the blood from her face and helped her to get dressed while Ian stood by the door waiting for them. The three of them quickly made their way into the hallway with Ian leading the way when Leon picked up movement at the opposite end of the hallway.

"I've got movement at the far end of the corridor," he shouted.

36

The warning came too late as Ian and G had already committed to traveling most of the length of the corridor when they came face-to-face with Siraj and his prisoner. Ian quickly trained his weapon on the men when Hanah spoke up.

"Don't shoot!"

G positioned himself in front of Hanah as he looked into the eyes of the two men. He had not recognized the young man, but he knew right away who the other man was. Moments before, he had tucked his weapon away in its holster in order to help Hanah and now wished he hadn't.

Siraj nervously positioned himself near the stairwell of the building at the end of the corridor, one arm draped around the neck of the young man and the other extended, his gun aimed directly at Ian.

G spoke to Siraj in his native tongue. "Drop the gun, and we can all leave here alive and able to fight again one day."

Siraj returned a sinister smile. "I don't know who you are, but I know an American when I see one, even one who has learned the language as well as you have. You want to live to fight another day? Hand over the girl, and I'll put my weapon aside—and we will all walk away alive," offered Siraj.

"What's he saying?" asked Ian.

"Tell your friend to shut the fuck up before I shoot him," said Siraj. "I don't trust him anyway, and I'm not known for my patience."

"Give me a second, Ian," said G without taking his eyes off of Siraj.

"How about we make a trade?" offered Siraj. "You hand over the woman, and I'll release this American prisoner to you. You will be a hero for his safe return."

The young man being held by Siraj listened as the two negotiated the intense standoff. Concern showed in his eyes as he struggled to comprehend the dynamics of the situation. Hearing Ian and G converse, he detected right away they were Americans. He looked at Hanah who gave him an intense look of concern as G and Siraj continued to engage each other.

Leon maneuvered the microdrones to capture three vantage points and did his best to choose the right time to announce how he could help. "G...I've got a good close-up on the bad guy. I can easily distract him with a laser to the eyes. Give me a signal if you want the help," said Leon.

"Stand by, Leon," G announced aloud as he weighed his increasing but delicate advantage.

Siraj's suspicion clearly grew at G's open declaration.

Dennis and Paul watched as the screens revealed a close-up of the high-value target, Siraj Hammadi, a.k.a. the Serpent. They both stood staring in near disbelief at who they were seeing.

"Get me a confirmed ID on that man," barked Dennis to his intelligence officer.

"Sir, you have a priority-one call," announced the operations officer.

Dennis was about to answer the call when the operations officer interrupted him. "Sir, the call is for Mr. Harriman. It's the director."

Paul gave Dennis an inquiring look and then answered the phone. "Paul Harriman. Yes sir, we just discovered that. We're watching it right now. We're waiting to see how this plays out... No, sir, we don't have a confirmed ID yet, but we're as sure as we've ever been. No, sir, we have not yet identified the man with him. Who? Please spell...yes sir, I remember, active-duty soldier missing in action in 2009, assumed to be a prisoner of war. You think that's him? Copy. Bergantz, Private First Class. Copy. Say again, sir? I'm not sure I completely understand. But sir…no, I'll take care of it."

Paul hung up the phone and looked at Dennis with grave concern written all over his face. He brought Dennis aside, leaned in close, and lowered his voice. "We need to get the team out now. They have less than ten minutes to get out of that compound," said Paul.

"What are you talking about, Paul?"

"You see that young man next to the Serpent?" said Paul as he looked at the video screens. "That's Private First Class Dale Bergantz, American prisoner of war since 2009."

"Holy shit! Well that's a *good* thing. The team can get him outta there—"

"Not so fast, my friend. Seems someone much higher in the food chain isn't ready for the young man to return home," explained Paul.

"That's preposterous! Who would make such a decision and why?"

"Not sure, but this operation is being terminated, effective immediately."

"What? You're not gonna allow that to happen, are you? What about the team? What about the Israeli? This mission is damn near complete," he said as he realized he was beginning to shout at the operations director.

"Do what you have to do to shut it down, Dennis," said Paul as he did his best to communicate otherwise. "I'll engage this from my perspective and keep any heat from finding its way back here." He turned and walked out without bothering to see how the situation played out on screen.

"You may not know who I am, but I know who you are," G said as he continued to engage Siraj in his native tongue. "Now I'm going to ask you one more time to lower your weapon and agree to everyone walking out of here alive."

"I cannot allow you to take her with you," said Siraj as he pointed his weapon at G.

"Leon," said G.

As soon as Leon heard the command, he flashed the lasers into Siraj's eyes distracting him long enough for Ian to get off a shot. Unfortunately, he missed, and Siraj returned fire, hitting Ian in the chest. The young man dropped to the floor while Siraj broke away and dove into the stairwell rolling down to the first floor and out the front of the residence where he found Tzofiya waiting for him. With no time for a warning from G, Siraj had come upon her so quick Tzofiya had little time to react. As soon as she saw him exit the building she reacted with a right cross to the temple, his weapon breaking loose from his grasp and flying some twenty feet away.

Siraj quickly recovered from the surprise punch and engaged his aggressor, throwing her to the ground and landing on top of her. Tzofiya was no match for the strength and power of the battle-hardened Siraj, but she was not about to die by his hand. He raised his fist to strike a deadly blow to her face, but she moved her head at the last possible moment, causing him to drive his fist into the pavement. He winced in pain and pulled back. She grabbed him by the collar, drove her elbow into his chest, and then rolled out from under him.

Siraj managed to get to the car before Tzofiya got to her weapon. She shot, but she was too late. He ducked as he started the car, put it in gear, and pressed the accelerator.

G rushed to Ian's side to help him and realized he had failed to warn Tzofiya.

"Tzofiya!" G cried

"He got away," the embittered Israeli operative gasped out.

"Todd," shouted G. "We have a squirter. He's all yours. Tzofiya, we need transportation."

"Already on it. Waiting on you outside the compound," reported Tzofiya.

"Just tell me I'm in pursuit of vengeance," inquired Todd, confirming exactly whom he was chasing.

"That's affirmative, my friend; you are indeed in pursuit of vengeance," said G as he continued to fight the emotional turmoil of seeing Ian unconscious before him.

"Leon, I need eyes," shouted Todd as he pushed his vehicle to perform.

"I've got him, Todd. Tzofiya marked the vehicle, so I've got a good lock on him. Looks like he's headed northeast, toward the airport. You can literally run into him if you go north at the next opportunity. It'll be your next left turn. You should merge in thirty seconds. He's in a white BMW sedan," reported Leon.

"Great, motherfucker gets a BMW, and I get this piece of shit," said Todd as he made an aggressive left turn and accelerated through the narrow city streets while he counted the seconds. He was quickly approaching an intersection when Leon confirmed the merge.

"Fast-approaching target coming up on your right," announced Leon.

"Got a visual," reported Todd as he accelerated to make contact with the rear bumper of the late-model BMW causing it to fishtail and nearly veer out of control. Tires squealed as Todd swerved but quickly recovered, turned the wheel, and hit the accelerator in pursuit of the faster vehicle.

The narrow streets proved to be an advantage for Todd keeping with the larger, faster vehicle as he powered through a hard right turn followed quickly by another sharp left and a slight fishtail. Todd accelerated, once again making contact with the vehicle as Siraj slowed to make a turn.

Siraj soon found his way onto the main coastline thoroughfare leading north toward the central district of Aden where most of the city was still fast asleep in the predawn. The BMW easily pulled away from Todd as it merged onto an adjacent main highway.

"There's no way I'm gonna catch that Beemer, Leon. I need a different, shorter route to the airport," shouted Todd.

"Copy. I'm sending you a direct route that'll take you to the runway threshold. There's no legal access from there, but at this point I'm thinking we need to improvise if we want to beat him to the tarmac," said Leon.

"Just get me to the edge of that airport, and I'll make it work using whatever means I have to."

"OK, I just pushed the route to your glasses. Just follow the map," said Leon.

"Copy, it just came up on the glass. Good job, Leon."

"Good news is that I can see your buddy is taking the long way. It should give you about a nine-minute advantage on him, assuming you don't run into any issues breaching the perimeter of the airport. Gotta run and cover the team. Good luck."

"What's your name?" G asked the young man.

"Dale."

"Dale, I need you to help me get this man outside so we can get him someplace safe. Can you help me do that?"

The young man nodded and rushed to help G lift Ian. Hanah followed closely behind.

Tzofiya stood beside the vehicle with the rear doors open, anxiously waiting for G to arrive.

Leon's fingers sped across the keyboard as he continued to communicate with G. "I'm pushing the most expeditious route to the CIA annex to you. It's the same place you picked up your rental vehicle. You can find medical attention there," he said as he hit the enter button.

"Copy that. We're stepping outside the building now."

Leon was distracted when he heard the door to the room open behind him. A man he had never seen entered, accompanied by two armed US Marines. Leon looked up momentarily but kept entering commands into the keyboard.

"Excuse me, but this is a restricted operation," announced Leon as he glanced at the Marines who he assumed were there to protect the mission and the room.

"Your operation is terminated," said the man. "Shut it down."

"You obviously have the wrong room," said Leon as he continued to type. "This is a priority-one mission so unless you have a trump card, you can just take your happy ass right outta here. I'm busy."

The man approached Leon and pulled the plug on one of the monitors. "Either *you* can shut it down," he said as he pulled the plug, "or *I'll* shut it down for you. Either way, you're finished here."

"Hey!" Leon shouted as he stood to defend himself and his equipment. The Marines stepped forward, causing Leon to think twice about how serious the man was.

"Really, dude? Do you have *any clue* how many lives are at risk if this op is terminated?"

"Take him into custody," said the man.

"OK," Leon reluctantly conceded. "I'll shut it down, but there's a process…"

The man pushed Leon aside and proceeded to shut down the power to his computer and communications systems. Leon watched helplessly as the man cut off the only support lifeline the team had. With everything powered down, he turned to Leon. "The guards will show you to your quarters. You'll be on the first plane out tomorrow."

37

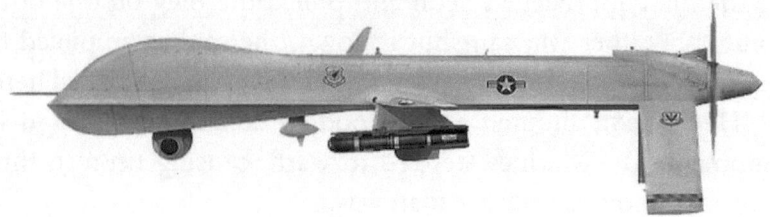

"**D**ragon One-One approaching the area, ETA two minutes," reported the drone operator as it approached the southern port city border.

"Copy Dragon One-One, confirm systems status green," echoed the voice of authority from an undisclosed location.

"Affirmative, systems status green."

"Dragon One-One, report target acquisition."

"Dragon One-One, WILCO."

The Predator flew high overhead the city, on an inbound trajectory from the northeast, its sensors searching for the building where Siraj and the team were last known to be located.

"Jon, Paul Harriman, can you go secure?"

"Sure, Paul, going secure now."

"I show secure on this end, Jon."

"Secure here, Paul. How can I help you?"

"Jon, you and I have known each other for a while now, so I need you to cut past all the bullshit and tell me what's going on with respect to our operation."

"Uh, well look, I don't like it one bit, Paul, so I know for a fact you certainly won't like it—"

"What I don't *like* is what I cannot understand, so help me understand why the op has suddenly been disavowed."

"The operation to rescue Hanah Malkinson has indeed been officially disavowed, Paul. That much I can confirm. The new development has put the entire operation at risk. I'm not at liberty to completely disclose—"

"The lives of five operatives are at risk, for God's sake! You'll have to excuse my impatience, but I'm in no mood for your non-disclosure rhetoric. What new development are you talking about? And who the hell made the decision to redirect?"

"Look, Paul, I'm clearly sticking my neck out by discussing this with you, but you're right, I do owe you an explanation. The unexpected discovery of Private First Class Dale Bergantz put the primary mission on its heels. The fact that Hammadi was even in the same room with him *and* your team spooked certain people. The simple explanation is that your operatives got too close to something that's in someone else's wheelhouse. Answering your other question would be suicidal, so I can't or *won't* even go there. I will tell you this much—there are powerful people who are not ready for Bergantz to be repatriated."

"Hold on a second. So you're essentially telling me our own government has purposely and knowingly allowed this young man to remain in captivity? Are you trying to tell me that this is political? Is that it? What about the fact that we never leave anyone behind?"

"Open your eyes, Paul. This is bigger than both of us put together. I can't disclose anything else. I can only tell you that your operatives are in *grave* danger if they even think of bringing that young man home. In fact, I'd go so far as to say they're already in grave danger. I wouldn't put anything past these people to eliminate any trace that this mission ever took place."

"What are you saying, Jon?"

"I'm saying the entire op is terminated. It's time to disavow and look ahead."

"They have the DPM's wife in their hands, for Christ's sake! The mission is all but complete. What about our allies, the Israelis? If you—or whoever it is calling the shots—even think about following through on this, you'll be the ones looking over your shoulders, not me."

"We're not going to have to worry about that. This conversation is over, Paul."

Paul listened as the line went dead. He slowly hung up the receiver, placed his hand to his forehead, and gently massaged it while he played the conversation over in his mind. He realized the orders he was dealing with could only come from the highest levels. Speculation on who made decisions or why they were made was enough to send a cold chill down his spine. But he was not about to sit idle while the lives of five operatives—four of his own—hung in the balance of someone's political motives.

"Dragon One-One, flight level two-zero-zero, target acquired. Request permission to release the weapon," reported the Predator operator as it executed an easy left orbit high above the city.

"Dragon One-One, release the weapon," came the command.

"Dragon One-One, weapons away, weapons away," reported the operator as he released the Hellfire II precision missile.

The command authority watched as the satellite acquired the weapon on its way to its intended target. The Predator took up a new heading to return to its undisclosed orbit at approximately 150 to 300 meters after the launch of the weapon. At the same time, the drone operator confirmed the weapon would do what it was designed to do by dutifully confirming the status. "The weapon is armed."

"Copy, the weapon is armed," answered the command authority as it continued to track the trajectory of the weapon.

"Thirty seconds…"

The command authority watched as the weapon hit with lethal accuracy and destroyed the compound, leaving little collateral damage to the surrounding buildings. The infrared return depicted a white-hot image of an explosion limited to the compound but no doubt having a shocking second-order effect on the surrounding area and the city of Aden.

Tzofiya helped G and Dale get Ian into the back seat of the car. She was about to get in the back seat with Hanah to attend to Ian when G asked the young man to take over responsibility for watching him.

"Tzofiya, I need you in the front with me in case we run into any opposition. Dale, I need you to ride in the back with Hanah and watch over our friend. Can you do that?"

Dale hesitated.

"What's wrong?" asked G.

Dale looked back at the residence.

"You don't have to stay here anymore, brother. We're gonna take you home with us, *all* the way home, understand?"

Dale nodded and climbed into the back seat. G closed the door behind him and climbed into the driver's seat, fired up the engine, glanced at Tzofiya, and sped off into the city.

"Leon, we're en route to the CIA annex. Make sure someone is standing by to give Ian medical attention. He's semiconscious and took a shot to the chest," said G as he called out to his teammate for top-cover assistance. He glanced at Tzofiya when he didn't hear an immediate reply.

"Leon, how do you hear me?" he called again. "Tzofiya, see if you can raise Leon on the satellite phone."

"Sat phone's dead, G."

G activated the map file displayed on his glasses. They had driven about a block and a half when an explosion rocked the area. He immediately pulled the car over, glanced at Tzofiya, and got out of the car to investigate. He looked back to see a huge plume of smoke coming from the area they had just left. Chills ran down his spine when he quickly got back into the car, put it into gear, and sped off toward the annex.

"What's going on, G?"

"Not sure," he answered. "Leon, if you can hear me, I could really use you right now," said G desperately.

Still no reply.

"That's certainly going to wake up the neighbors," said Tzofiya.

"See if you can get a hold of Todd."

Tzofiya tried making contact with Todd to no avail.

"Just when you need a technician, they're both suddenly out of commission," said G to no one in particular.

"I may be able to help," revealed Tzofiya.

"What the hell just happened? What happened to the internal video feed?" Avigdor demanded.

"Sir, you're going to want to see this," announced an operations specialist.

Avigdor and Ezra leaned over the shoulder of the specialist to watch an Israeli satellite video feed of the smoking results and devastation of the detonation at the exact coordinates of the building last occupied by Hanah and her rescuers.

"No," whispered Avigdor as he realized the gravity of what he was seeing. He went numb as Ezra took him aside and sat him in a chair.

"Allow me to give you a break, my friend. All is not lost. We'll see this to its end," encouraged Ezra with a calm and determined nature.

Avigdor nodded, clearly distraught over the enormity of what he had seen.

Ezra took over and began barking commands. "Access the archives and bring up the playback on this. I want to know how this happened, who is responsible, and if there is any chance our team made it out before this occurred. Place *Eitan* in an orbit over the airport and put the satellite lens over that compound. I want a report on any live infrared returns—people moving about. If we so much as *think* the Serpent has anything to do with this and has made his way to the airport, we will blow him out of the sky for the entire world to see."

Ezra stepped aside and entered a code into his secure cell phone, hoping to discover the whereabouts of his most-trusted operative. He hit "send" and held his breath for a second, hoping...and praying he would receive an indication that she, at least, made it out before the blast.

"Leon, I made it to the airport perimeter," announced Todd. "Need you to recommend the best access points in terms of security. And speaking of security, I need you to tell me if you can see anyone or anything I need to be concerned about."

Todd pulled to the side of the road and turned off the engine and the lights. The road wasn't heavily traveled, especially at the early hour so he still had the advantage of darkness. His heart skipped a beat when he saw a vehicle approaching with its emergency blue lights flashing. His mind raced as he thought of ways he would handle a confrontation with the local law enforcement. He watched the vehicle as it approached his position and sped past him, heading south. Breathing a momentary sigh of relief, he stepped out of the vehicle into the darkness, making his way toward the airport perimeter and examining the eight-foot fence in front of him. Fences surrounding airports weren't typically tall because of aviation restrictions, so scaling the fence would be easy. Getting over the barbed wire at the top would be a bit cumbersome, but he had done it before. It was the unknown security protocols he feared most. How often did anyone check the airport perimeter? Was there video surveillance he had to be concerned with? All unknowns he had no choice but to face in pursuit of the target.

"Leon, I really could use you right now, bro. I hope you're not taking this time for a piss break. If you are, I'm so gonna kick your ass when I see you next," he said as he examined the fence and began climbing.

Getting caught breaching an airport in his *own* country brought penalties that would make him think twice before committing. Getting caught in Yemen would make the US penalties pale in comparison. The inside of a Yemen prison was the last place on Earth he wanted to see.

He scaled the fence and dropped to a rolling crawl as he surveyed the area. Seeing the immediate coast was clear, he started running toward the tarmac. Todd could see the tarmac lights in the distance and was discouraged at the amount of ground he'd have to cover at his current pace if he were to beat Siraj to the hangar.

"Leon, you up yet?" Todd managed between deep labored breaths. "I ever tell you how I despise running? No? Remind me to tell you sometime. Why do they have to make airports so damn big? They certainly don't *look* this big from the jet. I'm so gonna kill someone tonight."

"Sir, I'm not exactly sure if this is something that concerns us, but it appears someone just breached the border of the airport. This person is on foot and running toward the terminal," reported the Israeli operator as he pointed out the infrared drone feed to Ezra.

Taking a closer look over the operator's shoulder, Ezra gave the order to follow the target. Avigdor snapped out of the shock that had gripped him and moved in to take a closer look at the screen.

"What do you think, my friend?" asked Ezra in an attempt to reengage Avigdor.

"Any activity such as this is unusual at best. I recommend we keep an eye on his progress."

"And I recommend you assume command of this operation," said Ezra as he gave Avigdor a confident look.

Avigdor nodded and went about the business of catching up on the details from each of his operators in the room while Ezra stepped aside to check his secure phone. The absence of an acknowledgement from Tzofiya began to weigh on him.

38

The coral crunched beneath the tires as he drove down the unpaved road to the CIA annex. He turned off the head-lights as he entered the abandoned lot and pulled up close to the building. G asked everyone to stay in the car and then got out of the vehicle to ensure someone was home before committing the group to carrying an injured man for no reason. He approached the door and knocked twice before he tried the doorknob. The door opened with an easy twist causing G to hesitate, step back, and draw his weapon. The inside of the building was dark, so he pulled a small Sure-Fire LED tactical flashlight from his pocket and looked for a light switch.

Tzofiya leaned toward the back seat to check on the passengers, especially Ian, and noticed he was beginning to regain conscious-ness. It was a good sign, but the last thing she wanted was for him to overreact, as some patients would when they experienced severe trauma.

G found a power panel and pushed the lever up, bringing power to the building and illuminating enough lights to see that the entire building had been abandoned, leaving no trace whatsoever that anyone had ever occupied the place. He shook his head in disbelief at how fast a building could be cleared out. He made his way outside to alert the others and helped the group bring Ian inside where they placed him upon a table and elevated his legs slightly.

"Wow, this place looks totally abandoned," observed Tzofiya. "Not that it was ever the Taj Mahal, mind you. But you would think someone would've left a note or something."

"Yeah, I don't like it one bit. I'm not sure what's going on, but something isn't right," said G glancing at Ian lying atop the table. "OK, first things first. Take my flashlight and see if you can find anything that'll help stabilize Ian. Dale, Hanah, either of you squeamish at the sight of blood?"

Both Dale and Hanah indicated they were ready to help do whatever it took to save Ian.

Tzofiya returned a short time later with a first aid kit, surprising G.

"You find that in here somewhere?"

"No, but I remembered we never looked in the trunk of our government rental car, so I took a chance and found this. It's not much, but it does have some wound dressing and antiseptic," she said.

"OK, hold that flashlight while I see just how serious this is," said G as he unbuttoned Ian's bloody shirt. "What the hell? He's wearing a vest."

"Then why all the blood?" asked Tzofiya as she manipulated the flashlight in search of the wound.

"Shine the light here, a little more to the right," said G as he continued to pull away at Ian's shirt. "There, right there," he said as Ian began to moan.

"Looks like the bullet hit the edge of the vest and penetrated his ribcage. Turn him to the side so I can see if there's…yup, the bullet went clean through. That's the good news," said G.

"What's the bad news," asked Tzofiya.

"The bad news is that I don't have anything to stitch him up, so we're gonna have to pack as much of that field dressing into the wound as we can and seal it with enough of that tape you've got there to keep it intact. It's the best we can do for him until we can get him to a doctor," said G as he placed a cloth on Ian's open wound.

"Dammit, Leon, where are you?" said G to no one in particular. "Tzofiya, didn't you say something about being able to help with our technical difficulties?"

"Yes, let me try again. You OK here?" she asked.

Ian groaned once again as G attended to the wound with the assistance of Hanah and Dale.

"We'll be fine. Just fix our comm issues, and see if you can find out why everything suddenly went quiet," he said.

Hanah watched as Tzofiya stepped away. "She's very pretty," she softly said.

G, taken aback by the comment, glanced at Hanah and offered her a faint smile as he grabbed her hand. "Put your hand here and hold it tight while I apply a bandage."

Hanah smiled knowing she was truly in the company of someone remarkable, someone who would die to bring reality to the promise of bringing her home safely.

The video playback from the Israeli satellite feed depicted a shadow entering the field of view from the northeast. Its track loitered over the southern city when a trace infrared heat trail suddenly revealed itself. A large white return from the detonation revealed itself approximately thirty seconds later.

"Play that back slower," Avigdor instructed the intelligence officer at the computer terminal.

The intelligence officer replayed the video at half speed and watched as the shadowy figure entered the field of view from the northeast. Ezra approached as the men were analyzing the footage.

"What do you make of this?" asked Ezra.

"Freeze the playback right there," instructed Avigdor. "Do you see that silhouette?" he asked both men. "That's an American drone, a Predator perhaps."

Ezra was puzzled by Avigdor's analysis and questioned the intelligence officer to be sure. "What is *your* analysis, young man?" asked Ezra.

Avigdor was clearly unhappy by Ezra's question, but he understood the gravity of the revelation if his initial assessment proved to be true.

The young officer, clearly not wishing to come between the two high ranking officials, offered his careful analysis. "I cannot clearly discern the aerial platform as well as the DPM, but if I may," he said, fast-forwarding the video to the detonation, "I am an expert on munitions characteristics and can tell you that this blast has all the signs of a Hellfire II missile. The only platform that would have been able to sneak in and deliver this weapon is the MQ-1 Predator remotely piloted aircraft."

Ezra looked at Avigdor, both men simultaneously coming to the realization that they were facing an extremely deep subversion for some reason.

Avigdor leaned in close to the intelligence officer. "Do everything you can to find out the origin of that Predator. I want to know all details, including who owns it, who controls it, and who gave the order to release the weapon. You do that, and I will promote you myself," he said as he glanced at Ezra and crossed to another operator in the room. "What's the latest on the airport breach?" asked Avigdor.

"He made his way to a hangar, here, where an aircraft is being prepared for departure."

"Reach out to our aviation contact there and find out what you can about that plane," instructed Avigdor. "I don't want to see any aircraft movement until we have heard from our inside source."

Ezra's phone vibrated. He pulled it from his pocket and smiled when he read the message.

He was nearly out of breath by the time he reached the first tarmac. He looked out into the distance and saw the private jet some one hundred yards away being prepped for departure. The gray-black sky revealed the slightest hint of dawn's illumination on the distant horizon.

About a hundred yards to go. Hell, I can do this. Jordan has the ball…and he could go all the way…he will go all the way, he thought as he pushed out the final paces to the edge of the next tarmac.

"Leon, just in case you're listening in and somehow can't respond, I've reached the edge of a tarmac where I can clearly see a sweet Cessna Citation X preppin' for departure. I may be goin' out on a limb here, but I'd bet *money* that's the plane I'm lookin' for. I'll keep you posted as I figure out the puzzle."

Todd approached the edge of the lighted tarmac where a lone technician was connecting a power cart to the aircraft. He could see someone in the cockpit going through a preflight checklist, occasionally reaching up to an overhead switch panel. He scanned the perimeter of the immediate area and didn't see a reason not to move in. He waited for the lone ramp technician to return to his truck and made his move.

Tzofiya stepped outside to check her phone and noticed that the echo-burst transmission she had sent to Ezra, her trusted friend and mentor, had failed on the first attempt. She figured the failure might have been caused by some sort of magnetic distortion caused by her close proximity to the detonation. Whatever the cause, she needed him now more than ever, so she made a second attempt to contact him. As she hit the send button, she looked up at the clear, predawn sky and said a short prayer, hoping that her call would reach him this time.

As she stood alone outside, looking at the stars, she sensed something wasn't right. Without overreacting, she reached for her weapon, holding tightly to the grip as she turned around toward the annex. As she turned, she noticed a dark figure standing near the entrance with his hands in the air.

"Please, don't shoot."

Tzofiya drew her weapon. "Down on your knees," she commanded as she cautiously approached. "Who are you, and what do you want?"

"I didn't want to leave, but they came in and forced me out. I pleaded with them as they totally gutted the place..."

"Look at me," she ordered him.

He slowly raised his head and looked directly at her.

"You're—"

"Yeah, I'm the guy that issued your equipment and transportation earlier. Did everyone make it out before the blast? I hope so because it wasn't my idea. I felt like shit when I knew they actually went through with it. I mean, Jesus, why would our own government want to do such a thing?"

"On your feet. Keep your hands where I can see them. Step inside the building. You make any sudden moves, and I'll shoot you where you stand, you got it?"

G was wiping the bloodstains from his hands when he heard the door open. Seeing the man instead of Tzofiya took him by surprise. He immediately reached for his weapon, but then he heard Tzofiya call out even before he noticed her right behind the man.

"Hold your fire," she called out.

"What's going on?" asked G.

"Found him loitering outside. Take a good look, and see if he isn't familiar to you," said Tzofiya.

G lowered his weapon, holstered it, and approached the man. "Why are you here?"

"Seems he has a guilty conscience," said Tzofiya, her weapon still trained on the man.

"Have a seat," said G.

"I'm good," he responded.

"It wasn't a request," said G.

The man took a seat at a small table while Tzofiya stood behind him.

"Answer my question. Why are you here?"

"I had some visitors about an hour after midnight. Said they were here to help me move some things out. I demanded to know who they were when a couple of 'em informed me of my right to live should I decide not to ask any more questions."

"And?"

"And I chose the living option. These guys are no joke, even for a big guy like me."

"So you returned here knowing they may even have someone waiting to show you Option B, the dying part?" asked G.

"Doesn't typically work that way. These guys follow orders, intimidate, and move on."

"OK, so they intimidated you, and you chose to live. Why are you here?"

"Because I overheard what one of 'em was sayin'…about something unexpected coming up and them having to scrub the mission you guys were on. Pissed me off, actually. I mean, I have no idea what the unexpected factor was, but there's absolutely no reason to whack your own people or worse, leave 'em behind. I was Army Special Forces. Hell, we even made sure to bring back the shitty officers because they were one of us. No one means *no one* in my code, know what I'm sayin'?"

G paused to reflect on everything the man revealed and looked him squarely in the eyes. "Give me your hand," ordered G.

The man extended his hand, and G quickly gripped it in an arm-wrestling-style grip, holding the man's eyes with his intense gaze. Tzofiya retrained her weapon on the man, wondering what sort of alpha-male stunt G was performing. The man returned the intensity of G's grip as he too struggled to determine the reason for the exercise. The encounter lasted for a mere fifteen to twenty seconds before G released his grip and took a deep breath.

"Lower your weapon, Tzofiya," said G, continuing to look at the man. Tzofiya was reluctant to follow through with G's request until he asked once again. Nodding affirmatively and glancing at Tzofiya, G reassured her. "It's OK, he's telling the truth. Lower your weapon."

Tzofiya slowly lowered her weapon, a stunned look on her face as she learned a bit more about G and his mysterious gift.

"What's your name?" asked G.

"Earl."

"So how can you help us, Earl?"

Sweat dripped profusely into his eyes as he reached the jet. Careful to avoid catching the eye of the ramp operator outside the jet, Todd made his way to the port side of the aircraft, staying in the shadow of the aircraft until he had an opportunity to board. He slipped inside undetected, collected his composure, and boldly stepped toward the pilot, smiling as he approached.

"Lemme see your papers," Todd said in English, using his best Somali accent.

The pilot gave him a questioning look and hesitated.

"Your papers, let me see your papers," said Todd doing his best to communicate across language barriers by using hand gestures.

The pilot reached down to retrieve some papers from his flight bag when the lights from an approaching vehicle momentarily flashed through the cockpit window. Todd looked away briefly as the pilot reached down and pulled a small caliber handgun from his flight bag. Todd's eyes widened as soon as he saw the weapon. He reacted instinctively with a swift strike to the base of the pilot's skull, sending his face into a sharp edge of the forward console, killing him instantly.

"I just wanted your papers," he said sarcastically. "I'll take that, thank you very much," he added as he pried the handgun from the man's hands. "Let's see what you've got in that bag of tricks of yours?"

As he rifled through the pilot's flight bag, he heard voices outside the aircraft. Todd looked up to see a man talking briefly with the ramp attendant and then turn to make his way toward the aircraft.

Shit. Gotta find a place to hide.

He took a quick glance around the small cabin and decided to squeeze himself into the forward lavatory. His adrenaline spiked as he anticipated the encounter he'd have with Siraj but despised the fact that he'd have to kill him in such tight quarters.

"Sir, there's a private jet that's been pulled onto the tarmac at the airport in Aden," reported the operator to Avigdor.

"And what of our airport-fence jumper? Where is he now?"

"I followed him to the jet I spoke of. It appears he is now inside the vessel."

"Have you been able to establish contact with our aviator insider?"

"No, sir, but I've accessed all of the pending departures that are lining up for the day. There are three private jets—two Citations and a Gulfstream."

"Do you have insight on destinations for each of them yet?"

"The Gulfstream is headed to Germany. One of the Citations is headed to Greece, the other to the Middle East."

"The one headed to the Middle East is the one we want. What time is it scheduled to depart?"

"It has an open departure time until 0600Z or about 8:00 a.m. today."

"That gives us about four hours, but we should be ready for an early departure. OK, keep an eye on any Citation moves within that time frame, and let me know as soon as you see any movement whatsoever involving a Citation," instructed Avigdor.

Ezra approached with an encouraging look.

"Tell me you have good news, my friend," said Avigdor.

"I do indeed. Keep in mind it is incomplete but encouraging nonetheless," said Ezra.

"Well, don't keep it to yourself, tell me."

◈

"I can help you maneuver around the land mines that exist here on both sides," said Earl in an offer to help.

"Both sides?" asked G.

"Theirs *and* ours. When you started this op you had the full faith and support of the good guys on your side. All of sudden you've found the good guys aren't so good. I can help you navigate around that…at least until you find a way out of the country," explained Earl.

"Can you fly a plane?" said Ian, surprising everyone as he painfully struggled to sit upright. Hanah and Dale helped him to find a comfortable sitting position on the edge of the table.

"Welcome back, Ian," said G. "Good to see you coming around. Where are you going with your question?"

"Look, I only heard some of the conversation as I was coming to, but the way I see it, things have changed. There's no way we can follow through on our original exit plan of a commercial flight out. Whoever wants this mission terminated will do whatever they can to stop it—and stop *us* from leaving. We need to find a charter or another way to get out of the country. I was just thinking we could possibly 'borrow' an airplane somehow. Only thing we need is a pilot. I'd fly it myself if I were in better shape but as you can see—" said Ian as he took a painful deep breath and looked at G.

"Yeah I can fly," said Earl. "Like I said, I was Army Special Forces. I flew little birds and fixed wing C-12s as a warrant officer. I still hold an FAA certification in multiengine—"

"Works for me," interrupted G. "What's your recommendation?" he asked Earl.

"Lemme make a call," said Earl.

"No calls," interrupted a suspicious Tzofiya.

"Just trying to help—"

"Excuse me for interrupting again," said Ian, "but where's Todd?"

"Shit, I got so caught up in making sure we got you someplace for first aid that I almost forgot about Todd," answered G. "Last we knew he was chasing Siraj. Then all our comms went dead."

"Who's Todd?" asked Earl.

"Teammate. He's the African-American you inprocessed along with the rest of us," answered G.

"OK, I remember him now. So you sent him to run down a squirter? Any idea where you lost contact with him?"

"G, didn't Leon say something on secure voice about helping Todd get back to the airport when we all lost contact?" asked Tzofiya.

"Yeah, that's right. That's gotta be it. Siraj was most likely headed back there to get out of the country. He's gotta have his own plane. Earl, any way you can look into this without compromising yourself?"

"Or us," quipped Tzofiya.

"Certainly. As long as I'm *allowed* to make a phone call," he quipped right back, glancing at Tzofiya.

Siraj called out to the pilot as soon as he boarded the aircraft. Todd heard footsteps walk past the lavatory door as Siraj made his way to the cockpit to speak with the pilot. When Todd opened the door, Siraj was leaning over the pilot making the grim discovery. He didn't have time to react before feeling the cold steel of Todd's barrel press firmly against the back of his head.

"Lemme see your hands. Nice and slow," said Todd as Siraj slowly raised his hands and stood with his back toward Todd.

"I don't know who you are, or why you are here," said Siraj as he complied with Todd's instructions. "But whatever it is you want, you may certainly have it."

"Oh, I have exactly what I want," he said as he struck Siraj in the head with the weapon, rendering him unconscious.

Siraj awoke a short time later. He opened his eyes to see Todd sitting across from him, sipping from a crystal glass. Siraj tried to adjust his position in the plush leather seat, and he quickly realized he was unable to move freely. He looked down to see his arms secured to the armrests, and his lap belt over-tightened against his waist.

"I took the liberty of strapping you in," said Todd, relaxing the emphasis of his phony foreign dialect. "You should always wear your seatbelt on an airplane. You never know when it'll be a rough flight."

"What do you want?" asked Siraj.

Todd took a sip from the glass. "As I told you before I knocked your ass out, I already have what I want. But that's not really the entire truth, you see, because what I *really* want is my brother's life back. But you already took that from me. I'm sure it's difficult for you to remember him from among the many you've killed. His death wasn't the huge news story that I'm quite sure you were hoping for. Not anything like the time your buddies beheaded the US journalist in '02."

Siraj returned a stoic look of confusion, choosing to remain silent.

Todd continued. "I'm just curious, Siraj—you don't mind if I call you by your first name do you?"

Siraj didn't answer.

"I'm just curious how it feels when you kill an infidel. I mean, to have such an amazing amount of power to rid the world of anyone standing against your personal beliefs must be a frigging rush. Does it get you off, do somethin' for ya sexually?"

"You're an American," Siraj surmised, making the connection with Todd's new dialect. "Let me guess, CIA?"

"You're good," said Todd. "Didn't take you long at all to figure that out," he added, glancing at his watch.

"So now what?" asked Siraj. "You bring me in to your authorities, and I get to join my compatriots at your tropical, all-inclusive resort?"

Todd laughed. "Oh you mean GITMO? Nah, I've got a much better deal for you."

"Deal?" questioned Siraj.

Todd nodded, his demeanor changing from a sarcastic smile to something deadly serious. "Yeah...*deal*."

Tzofiya stopped G just before he led the others outside to the car.

"I don't trust him, G. I don't trust this Earl character," she said.

"What choice do we have at this point, Tzofiya?"

Tzofiya's phone chirped.

"What's that?" asked G.

"Incoming call."

"From who? I thought all comms were disabled," said a curious G.

"All *American* comms were disabled. My country still thinks we have a fighting chance," she said as she stepped away to answer the call.

"You coming?" Ian asked G as he watched Tzofiya step away. "What's she doing?"

"New development. Hang on a sec, Ian."

Tzofiya returned a short time later. The group was waiting on G to make a decision when he deferred to Tzofiya for the latest.

"I've been able to establish communications with some very influential people from my country," she announced to the group, pausing to offer a special glance to Hanah.

Hanah smiled and offered an encouraging nod to Dale.

"They're concerned about our situation and have vowed to assist us in any way they possibly can. They're trying to collect the facts surrounding our sudden isolation by the US government, but it is secondary to helping us get out of Yemen safely.

"I gave them the details on Todd, who was en route to the airport to pursue the Serpent. They believe they may have spotted both men approaching the same aircraft on the ramp at the airport, but until my phone call, they had been unable to confirm their analysis."

"So where does this leave us? What are we to do now?" asked Hanah.

"Good question, G," said Ian looking for G to take the lead.

"Earl, think you can fly a multiengine turbojet?"

"I'd have to see exactly what kind of jet we're talkin', but I can fly it. Just have to become familiar with the instrument panel."

"I can help him, G," said Ian.

"You're in no shape to fly, Ian."

"I can talk him through it enough to keep things safe," said Ian defensively.

"Can you get us onto that ramp?" G asked Earl.

"Yes."

"OK, until we can reestablish communications with Todd, we need to act on what we know in order to stay ahead of things," said G. "We need to move. Sun will be up soon."

"So where are we headed?" asked Ian.

"To the airport. We have a flight to catch," said G with a wink.

"So here's the deal, Siraj. I cut you loose from that chair, and you get to defend yourself from the biggest ass-whippin' you'll ever face. If you survive, you can continue wreaking havoc around the world in the name of your so-called "gee-had" and send me to meet my brother in heaven. If *I* survive, I'll arrange it so you can personally meet Allah, and he can introduce you to your forty virgins. The way I see it, it's a no-lose situation for both of us."

Siraj clenched his fists and furrowed his brow. "Why would you cut me loose and take a chance on losing your life?"

"Because we Americans aren't cowards like you," said Todd as he pressed the button on the Benchmade pocket switchblade knife, momentarily surprising Siraj. "Besides, I don't plan on losing."

Todd stood over Siraj and drove the knife into the seatback beside his head. He pulled the handgun from the waistline of his back and showed it to Siraj. "I'm gonna place this weapon on a table at the front of the aircraft. If you think you'll need it to kill me, I suggest you get to it quickly."

Todd returned from the front of the aircraft holding something in his hand and approached Siraj. "This is picture of my brother, Daniel. He's gonna watch over me while I kill you. Don't even *think* you'll have a chance to see him where you're headed, you son-of-a-bitch," he said placing the photo into his own shirt pocket.

Siraj watched as Todd pulled the knife from the seatback next to his head. He was busy calculating his first move when he felt the restraint on his wrist give way. Then the blade sliced through the belt securing his left arm. As soon as his right arm was cut free he lunged forward attempting to send a head butt Todd's way, but Todd anticipated it and stepped back into the aisle.

"Don't forget to undo your lap belt," Todd said with a smile as he closed the knife and placed it into his pants pocket.

Siraj unbuckled his lap belt and stepped into the aisle. The bones in his neck popped as he moved his head from side to side in an attempt to loosen up while he looked intently at the towering American.

"Don't let the size fool ya, Siraj. I'm pretty quick," bragged Todd as he raised his fists and gestured for Siraj to step forward.

Siraj lunged forward, stepping into a powerful right cross, delivered by Todd. The terrorist crouched low as he tried to avoid the powerful first punch. Todd failed to make the connection he was hoping for but connected solidly with a knee to the man's face sending him into a table between the seats.

Siraj recovered quickly, shaking his head to clear the dizziness and repositioning himself for a counter attack. Todd continued his relentless pursuit and left an opening for Siraj to take advantage when he stepped in to grab him from his precarious position. Siraj delivered a swift kick to Todd's groin setting the American back on his heels doubled over in pain. Siraj followed through from a lying position with a kick to Todd's face sending a spatter of blood across the aisle.

Fighting to right himself from an awkward position, Siraj fell into the aisle and realized he had to get to the gun Todd had placed on a table in the front of the aircraft. He quickly rose to his feet and stepped forward just as he felt a firm grasp to the back of his collar. He clawed at the seat backs to get away from Todd, but the American's grip was firm and determined.

Siraj twisted his body and turned toward the American—a miscalculation that placed his face squarely in the path of Todd's clenched fist. Siraj winced in pain and blinked uncontrollably as he attempted to retain consciousness. Blacking out would mean certain death. Siraj was determined not to die that way.

40

Ezra looked into the eyes of his friend and placed a hand on his shoulder as he revealed to Avigdor that he had reconnected with Tzofiya. "I didn't want to say too much before I had a complete picture on the well-being of the team, especially Hanah," he explained.

"And?"

"And I am happy to report that Hanah is alive and well, my friend."

"Thank God," said Avigdor breathing a sigh of relief. "And what about the team, what is their status?" he asked.

"They need our help," he said in a serious tone.

Ezra explained the details of the team's plan to get to the airport to secure a way out of the country. He confirmed the man they had followed from the perimeter of the airport was indeed a member of the team and that the aircraft they had isolated belonged to Siraj Hammadi.

"We have confirmed the American made it onboard the aircraft," explained Avigdor. "We also observed a vehicle approach and one man boarding the jet shortly after the American made it aboard."

"So what do you make of it?" asked Ezra.

"Not sure just yet. There's been no noticeable activity for us to analyze. My suggestion is to direct the team toward the aircraft and hold them out until we confirm it is safe for them to proceed." said Avigdor. "Do we have anyone in-country who can help us?" he asked.

"We used to," responded Ezra as he thought of the American operatives he could no longer count on or trust.

Ezra's phone rang. "Hello?" he answered as he stepped away to take the call.

"I'm gambling with my very life by calling you," said the man.

"Who is this?"

The security at the airport had increased due to the blast south of the city. Earl convinced G to use two vehicles to avoid tipping off the guards he suspected would be posted at the airport perimeter. He called ahead to determine which access point to use based on whom he could bribe to gain access.

The sun had nearly crested the eastern horizon when the team approached the checkpoint. Earl lowered his window as he stopped the car to speak with the lone guard posted at the gate.

"*Kaef halek*, I am transporting important people to the hangar," said Earl as he extended his hand to the guard and indicated the car behind him would follow.

G sat nervously as he watched the armed guard approach the car in front of him. Ian did his best to sit upright in the front seat while Hanah and Dale sat nervously in the back seat. All four of them waited expectantly for Earl to get them through the perimeter checkpoint.

The guard accepted the handshake and the money cleverly disguised in Earl's palm. He bent down low enough to look inside the window to see Tzofiya seated beside Earl. She wore the traditional headscarf and looked straight ahead, careful not to make eye contact with the guard but keen enough to know whether to react to anything out of the ordinary.

The guard smiled at Earl and commented on how fortunate he was to have someone so pretty sitting beside him. Earl returned the smile and waited for the guard to wave him through.

- 342 -

G released the brakes as he watched the guard wave Earl through. "Here we go," he said as he approached the gate, expecting to see the guard continue to wave him through. His adrenaline increased the closer he got to the gate, and it spiked when the guard lifted his hand and signaled G to stop.

Ian reached down beside his seat to ensure his weapon was still within reach.

"Easy," said G to Ian as he rolled down his window to speak with the guard.

Earl stopped the car when he noticed in his rearview mirror that the guard had unexpectedly stopped G.

"*Kaef halek*," greeted the guard. "Can you tell me your purpose here today?" he queried in his native Arabic.

"Did the man in that vehicle not already inform you of that?" asked G, answering in perfect Arabic. "I suspect that if you require *another* explanation, it may not sit well with your supervisors."

The guard bent over to look at the other passengers in the vehicle but was distracted when he noticed Earl getting out of his vehicle. "Get back in your vehicle," he shouted to the American.

"This can't be good," said Ian in a whisper.

"Relax," said G as he waited to see how it would play out.

The guard approached Earl and began shouting. Earl shouted right back. The guard eventually turned away and reluctantly waved G through the gate as Earl returned to his vehicle and led him to an obscure parking spot on the ramp.

G pulled alongside Earl's car and instructed the others to wait a moment.

Earl, G, and Tzofiya convened at the back of the vehicles where they had a good view of most of the airport-parking ramp. Earl handed G a pair of binoculars.

"I believe that may be the aircraft you're looking for. We tracked it when it first arrived," explained Earl as G peered through the binoculars contemplating just how he'd get the others aboard.

G continued to observe when he noticed a man waving off the fuel truck that had just completed refueling the jet. "At least we know it's full of gas," he said as he watched the man climb the stairs to the jet.

"Shit!" exclaimed G when he watched in shock as the man suddenly jerked and fell away from the jet, tumbling down the stairs.

G pulled the binoculars from his eyes and glanced around the airport to see if there was any indication that anyone else might have witnessed what he'd just seen. The stairs were on the blind side of the control tower, so it was likely no one would notice such a thing right away. He knew they had to move quickly to take advantage of the situation, or they would have no other ready alternative.

"This is a voice from your past, Ezra. As for specifics, you'll understand why I'll be purposefully vague. Suffice it to say that you have already no doubt witnessed the desperation of a nation unwilling to follow through on its promises. I'm embarrassed to have been even remotely associated with such a calamity," said Paul Harriman, purposefully avoiding any use of his own name.

As he continued to listen, Ezra identified the man's voice. He and Paul had worked alongside each other on several occasions when ties between the two nations were on more solid footing. Ezra moved to an empty room just off the yacht's main room where he could express his consternation more freely.

"If you're calling me to apologize—"

"I am. And I'm calling to express my regrets for the DPM's personal loss. I'm calling to pledge my support in whatever way possible, albeit with limitations imposed by those who have chosen to see to it that the mission fails."

Ezra suddenly realized Paul had no knowledge that his team had made it safely out of the compound before the Hellfire missile destroyed it. He questioned Paul to determine his knowledge on why the mission had been suddenly disavowed when he learned of the team's accidental discovery of the American POW. He was angered by the thought that such utterly absurd politically motivated behavior would take precedence over the lives of others.

"I fear your nation has succeeded in turning an ally into an enemy and is creating a monster in the form of an angry group of highly capable, clandestine operatives," said Ezra.

Paul paused as he allowed the statement to sink in. What was Ezra trying to tell him? Had the team made it out alive? Should he break the code and come right out and ask? What did he mean when he described an *angry group of operatives*?

"What would you like me to do?" asked Paul with resolve in his voice.

"What I would like you to do is to simply watch the news. Word has it there will be a developing story that should capture the attention and interest of your nation and its politicians very soon," said Ezra as he disconnected the line.

Todd drew his fist back in an attempt to deliver another explosive right-hand blow when Siraj broke loose from his grip and fell back into the aisle. He watched as the American stepped forward in pursuit as he stumbled toward the front of the airplane. Todd's eyes widened when he saw just how close Siraj was to the weapon he had placed on the table at the front of the cabin.

Siraj felt the full force of Todd's bodyweight crash into him as he reached for the weapon. Both men violently fell to the floor adjacent to the portside opening of the jet when Siraj surprised Todd by revealing that he had indeed been able to reach the weapon.

The weapon now in full view and in Siraj's grip, Todd was suddenly at a disadvantage. He grabbed the terrorist's forearm, and he tried swinging it around to take aim at him. Siraj, determined to take a shot at the American, fired the weapon, sending one round into the head of a man who had just ascended the stairs to deliver a fuel requisition to the crew.

Both men paused as they watched in shock as the man's head snapped back and his body fell away from the jet toward the tarmac. Todd sent his right elbow into Siraj's face as he pounded the terrorist's arm into the floor until he released the weapon.

Gripping Siraj's shirt collar, Todd stood to his feet and kicked the handgun toward the door, watching as it sailed out onto the tarmac below. "That's the last man you'll ever kill," he said as he tossed Siraj onto the aisle floor.

Siraj looked up at the American towering over him as both men continued to breathe deeply, attempting to catch their breaths. Todd leaped onto Siraj and began to profusely punch him, unleashing years of anger, raining punishing blows on the man who had killed his brother. Siraj did his best to protect himself and managed to pull Todd closer until he was able to reach into the American's pocket. Siraj let out a blood-curdling yell as he grabbed Todd's shirt collar, looked him in the eyes, snapped opened the blade, and pushed it into Todd's rib cage. Todd yelled out in pain and quickly backed away from the terrorist, holding his bleeding side.

Stumbling to retain his balance, Todd fell back onto the aisle floor while struggling to catch his breath. His lung was punctured, and he knew it. He blinked slowly while he looked at the ceiling of the aircraft, contemplating the fact that he had given the terrorist a fatal opening. Siraj approached and straddled the wounded American. Todd looked at the bruised and battered Siraj holding the bloody knife in his hands. He took a painful, helpless breath as Siraj reached into Todd's pocket and retrieved the picture of his brother, placing it over Todd's heart. Siraj leaned in close to Todd and whispered in his ear. "This time, I will make sure you both die together."

Time slowed to a crawl as Todd contemplated whether or not he'd feel any more pain as the terrorist placed his left hand against Todd's chest and drew his right hand back, ready to drive the blade into his heart.

Todd's thoughts began to drift. He had led a good life, more privileged than most in fact. And for that, he had no regrets. He was in a dangerous business that consistently meant his very life hung in the balance. He had sometimes wondered how it would all end. He barely heard Siraj yelling his battle cry when an overwhelming sense of peace overcame him. He had approached the precipice of death and had accepted the fact that this was his end. He looked up to face the inevitable when he saw Siraj's head unexpectedly snap back, spraying him with warm blood as a bullet penetrated the terrorist's forehead.

Tears welled in his eyes when he realized G had pulled him back from the edge of certain death without a moment to spare. G yanked the dead terrorist's body away from him and threw himself down at Todd's side telling him, *commanding* him to hang in there.

Avigdor watched the intelligence monitor as a vehicle approached the Citation X on the Aden airport tarmac. The sun was stretching its morning rays across the landscape as the population came to life for the day. So far, the team had avoided the detection of anyone powerful enough to stop them.

"Zoom in on that vehicle," commanded Avigdor.

The picture grew larger on the monitor as the sensors zoomed in on the vehicle. One man emerged, heading onto the aircraft. Soon thereafter, five others emerged from the vehicle and made their way to the jet. Avigdor called for a closer zoom as the people boarded the aircraft. He was unable to get close enough to make a clear determination of who the people were but was convinced he was watching the group they were all looking for. He had to believe Hanah was among them.

"I want two armed F-16s on ready alert to escort that jet to Tel Aviv as soon as it enters the sovereign waters of the Red Sea," ordered Avigdor to an operations specialist.

Ezra's phone chirped. It was an incoming message from Tzofiya that confirmed what they had hoped to hear. Everyone had made it aboard the aircraft, and they were awaiting clearance to taxi. They would leave with or without it, but clearance would bolster their chances of a successful outcome. There was one more bit of unexpected news from Tzofiya....

The Serpent is dead.

41

G picked up the picture from Todd's chest, looked at it, and then showed it to him.

"Is this your brother?"

Todd nodded slowly.

"He'd be proud of you. Don't let him down by dying, understand?" G said softly to his friend, stressing the command. "Earl, get this plane started, and let's get the hell outta here. Where are the others?"

"They're stowing a couple of bodies in the fuel truck so we're not exposed," explained Earl as he busily flipped switches and turned dials in an attempt to quickly familiarize himself with the cockpit layout.

G looked out onto the ramp to see Dale driving the fuel truck far enough away to gain the required clearance. He stopped the vehicle and ran back toward the jet when Tzofiya appeared in the entryway, helping a stumbling Ian aboard, Hanah was right behind her. G rushed to assist the women with Ian and sat him in the first seat available.

"Help me reconfigure these seats so we can put Todd into a lying position. No way he's gonna be able to travel in a seated position," said G to Tzofiya.

Hanah waited by the door to ensure Dale made it safely aboard while Ian struggled to make his way to the cockpit on his own.

"You're gonna need an extra set of eyes and ears up here," Ian announced to Earl. "I'll take the right seat if you don't mind," he added as he painfully maneuvered his way into the copilot's seat and placed a headset over his ears.

Dale made it onto the aircraft and poked his head inside the cockpit to announce that everyone had made it on board.

"Awesome. We're gonna need someone to disengage the power cart once we start the engines. Can you do that for us?"

"Yeah, just let me know when," Dale answered.

Earl and Ian flipped a few switches and looked at each other. "Ready on one?" asked Earl.

"Ready on one," answered Ian.

"We have engine start on one. Ready on two?"

"Ready on two," reported Ian as he watched the dials and indicators come to life.

"OK, Dale, we're ready for the power cart to be removed. Be careful, and let us know once you're back safely aboard. And don't forget to pull the wheel chocks, or we'll never leave here no matter how prepared we are," instructed Ian.

"I'm on it," he said.

The powerful jet roared to life as both engines powered up to idle. Ian watched as Dale pushed the power cart away from the jet. *So far so good,* he thought.

"We have a vehicle approaching from the right," announced Ian.

Earl picked up a pair of binoculars. "This isn't good," he announced.

"What's up?" asked Ian.

"They look like Americans...ordinarily that would be good news, but under the circumstances..."

"Let's get that cabin door closed," Earl announced over the intercom. "G, we need you up front when you get a chance."

G poked his head into the cockpit and looked at Ian, surprised. "What are you doing up here?"

"Never mind that for now," answered Ian. "We may have some company that we need to be more concerned with at the moment," he said as he directed G's attention to the approaching vehicle.

"OK, everyone act normal and be cool," instructed G. "Let me make sure the cabin door is closed."

G activated the door handle, which simultaneously retracted the stairs and brought the heavy door close enough to pull closed. He secured it with the safety latch and returned to the cockpit. "Where's the vehicle?" he asked.

"No longer a factor," reported Ian. "Dude just drove by when I waved at him and smiled."

"Cool, let's go," urged G.

"Tower, Citation Two-Niner Alpha Whiskey ready to taxi to the active runway for departure," reported Earl.

Hanah placed her hand on Dale's and smiled at him when she felt the jet inch forward and begin to taxi. G checked with Todd once he was secured into the makeshift litter.

"Yo, G, did you make sure he was dead?"

"He's dead, Todd. Those frangible bullets…they make a helluva mess, but I didn't want to take a chance of compromising the cabin with a bullet hole."

Todd smiled painfully. "Good call," he said as he breathed a sigh of relief and closed his eyes to get some rest.

It had been a long day. Paul was one of the last people in the building, and now he sat alone in his office, getting ready to head home for the evening, when his office phone rang. The caller ID simply read "unavailable." He thought a moment about allowing it to go to voicemail but decided to answer it, considering the day he had just had.

"Paul Harriman," he answered.

"Paul, Jon at State. Can you go secure?"

"Sure, Jon, going secure now," he said as he pressed the button on his secure phone.

"I show secure here," announced Paul.

"Secure here as well, Paul. Listen, I'm sticking my neck out by calling you, but I wanted you to know that there was no evidence of any American or allied casualties on scene in Aden."

Paul purposefully didn't answer, imposing an uncomfortable pause on the State Department agent. Secretly, he was relieved to hear the news of his team's survival but he knew enough about the twisted world he operated in to know this was not merely a phone call to provide a status update.

"You still there, Paul?"

"I'm still here," he answered. "What do you expect me to say?"

"Well, we were *hoping* you could help us smooth out the back end should you reestablish any communications with your operatives," explained Jon.

"You've got to be kidding me. You and your cronies try to literally eliminate my entire team, including an agent from one of our closest allies, and you want *me* to sort it all out for you? I warned you when you were contemplating this decision that it wouldn't be *me* who would have to look over my shoulder."

"There are people who are willing to play nice as long as your operatives cooperate with the game plan that'll be neatly laid out for them," explained Jon without admitting he or any of his people had anything to do with the compound bombing in Aden.

"First of all, I can't assure you of *anything* until I establish communication with my team," said Paul hoping to pull more details out of Jon. "And until you clearly define what you mean by 'playing nice,' then all I have is conjecture and empty rhetoric. Because I know you well enough to know that you'll deny that this conversation ever took place. You clearly insinuated that when we began this chat. So I'll ask you again, what the fuck do you want from me?"

"I'm told that if we can get your assurance that you'll do your part to control your team, your communications will be reestablished. We want you to personally meet us in Saint-Tropez when the team returns from Yemen. We'll have someone there to take custody of the POW, after which we'll arrange for high-level press coverage on the return of Hanah Malkinson to the loving arms of her husband. We'll cite the cooperation of both nations of course. International relations between the two countries will be strengthened, and everyone will move on."

"Everyone except for our POW," said Paul sarcastically. "What about him?"

"There will come a time where he'll be repatriated. These situations are a matter of timing and political prowess," explained Jon.

"You know me well enough to know what I think of political prowess, Jon," said Paul as he bit his tongue. "As for my team, I can only assure you that they'll listen to me. After that, they'll make up their own minds about what's in their own best interest."

"I guess that'll have to do at this point then," said Jon. "I need you on a plane to Saint-Tropez right away then."

"I'll be on a plane once I'm able to talk with my team and I know they're safe from any more of your interruptions and not a moment before that," answered Paul.

"I understand," said Jon. "I'll be in touch soon."

Paul hung up the phone and sat back in his chair to contemplate what he had just heard. He knew that his presence would help to alleviate tension when the team arrived in Saint-Tropez, but he couldn't even begin to guess how he'd go about explaining or defending the actions of the government against its own people to cover a political maneuver. Those chips would undoubtedly have to fall where they would. Convincing the team to turn their backs on a prisoner of war would be another contentious matter altogether.

Unless he could think of a clever way around the ordeal.

The Citation X soared toward the western sky when Earl announced to everyone they had passed ten thousand feet, and they were free to move around if they desired. Hanah unbuckled her seatbelt and found her way to an empty seat beside G.

"We're not out of danger yet, are we?" she asked.

"Why do you ask?"

"I can see it written all over your face. You are concerned," she said.

"It's my nature to be concerned. I'm concerned about completing my mission of reuniting you with your family and of getting him the medical attention he needs," he said nodding toward Todd. "We're high enough and far enough away from Yemen for that aspect to be behind us. It's what's ahead of us now that concerns me most."

"G, need you to come up front," announced Ian.

"Excuse me," he said to Hanah.

Ian looked over his shoulder and handed G a pair of headphones. "Need you to put these on and listen in," he said, wincing in pain.

G donned the headphones in time to hear the air-traffic controller demanding the plane return to Aden. "Citation Two-Niner Alpha Whiskey, return to Aden at once. This is an order of the Yemeni sovereign authorities."

"What do you make of it?" asked G.

"Sounds to me like they may have found the carnage we left behind," said Earl.

"Have we responded?" asked G.

"Negative. Don't plan to either," said Earl.

"What's our position?"

"Turning right as we speak to a three-five-zero heading over the Red Sea, climbing through twenty thousand feet," said Earl as he entered the coordinates for Saint-Tropez and La Mole Airport.

"Not answering may be problematic," stated Ian.

"How do you figure?" asked G.

Ian pointed to the cockpit radar. "Well, for starters, there appears to be two fast-movers headed our way out of Yemen."

"So I take it we're not technically out of Yemeni airspace over international waters?"

"We're out of Yemeni airspace but not quite far enough out over international waters to be safe," answered Earl. "That should happen in about twelve minutes."

"About the same time it should take those fast-movers to reach us," said Ian as he squeezed out a painful cough. "Don't believe they'll have any issues blowing us right out of the sky at this point," he added.

"OK, you guys do the best you can to push up our speed. I'll see what we can come up with from the cheap seats and will be back to check in soon. Call me forward when those aircraft get close enough to see or if things change significantly," said G.

42

"**S**ir, the team is airborne!" announced an operative on the floor of the makeshift Israeli operations center aboard the yacht.

Ezra and Avigdor rushed in to witness the progress of the team as the sleek jet sped away from the coast toward the waters of the Red Sea. Avigdor felt an encouraging pat on the back from Ezra as he watched the jet inch away from the Yemeni coastline. Their enthusiasm was short-lived however when another operations specialist pointed out the fast-moving targets originating from Yemen that seemed to be in pursuit of the small jet.

"Sir, two fast-movers headed into the Red Sea from Yemen on the same course as the Citation. Time to intercept: eleven minutes."

"Launch the F-16s," commanded Avigdor. "Provide them with coordinates on the Citation. I want to know the frequency they are operating on and the estimated time of intercept for our fighters. Ezra, if you are in touch with our operative, now would be a good time to inform her of our intent to assist and divert."

Ezra nodded and stepped away to make the call.

Leon had arrived at La Mole airport just after sunrise to find Todd's Gulfstream V still parked in the hangar. He set his bags on the floor and walked into the silence of the empty planning room.

"Didn't think I'd ever see *you* guys again," said Monty, suddenly appearing behind him, surprising Leon.

"Damn, you scared the hell outta me, Monty," said Leon. "Why are you still here?"

"Son, I've been in this business for quite a long time. If there's one thing I've learned, it's never to make assumptions, especially *quick* assumptions. Figured I'd hang out long enough to make sure no one was coming back. Besides, I can think of worse places to hang out while I pull four hundred dollars a day in per diem. How the hell you holding up?"

"Not good, I'm afraid—"

Leon's satellite phone sprang to life with an incoming alert, interrupting his chat with Monty.

"Thought I powered this thing down," said Leon as he picked it up to answer.

"Domino's. Will this be take-out or delivery?"

"Agent Lambert, your privileges have been restored. You may reestablish contact with your team. Good luck."

"On whose authority? Hello?" Leon looked at Monty like he'd just heard from a ghost. "Son-of-a-bitch just hung up on me," he said as the reality of the situation hit him. "Shit, they're alive! They're alive, Monty."

Leon hit "send," hoping to connect with anyone on the team via satellite phone while he rushed to get his laptop computer powered up and connected to an open satellite channel. He figured it would be monitored, but he was so anxious to establish communication with his teammates it was of little consequence.

"Sabre Two-Three passing flight level one eight zero, turning south over the Red Sea, mission to intercept Citation Two-Niner Alpha Whiskey. ETA, fifteen minutes," reported the lead pilot of the two-ship Israeli F-16 flight.

Avigdor monitored the progress of the Israeli fighters along with that of the Citation and its pursuers. Despite the rapid rate of closure, it was becoming apparent that the Israeli jets would arrive just after the Yemeni aircraft would catch up with the Citation. Avigdor hoped the pilot of the Citation could hold his own until the F-16s arrived.

"Ezra," Avigdor called out, trying to determine the flights' progress.

"I am communicating with her now," he reported, as if knowing the nature of the DPM's hail.

"Sabre Two-Three has the target acquired on long-range radar. Secondary targets acquired as well. Sabre flight; push it up. ETA: six minutes."

"Ezra, I need to get to Israel. Please have someone bring Rina to La Mole airport and find a way for us to get out quickly," instructed Avigdor.

"As you wish."

G motioned for Tzofiya to follow him to the back of the cabin to have a private word.

"I need you to know we're not out of danger just yet," he explained.

"What's going on?" she asked.

"There are a couple of Yemeni fighters pursuing us. They'll surely catch us before we get much farther. Without some kind of assistance, we'll be forced to comply or get shot out of the sky. We both know we can't count on my side to cover the wager on this one, considering our most recent experiences. I need to know if you can think of anything that your people may be able to do to help us."

"G, we need you up front," announced Ian.

He made his way to the cockpit, jet noise filling the cabin. G paused to look out of a starboard window to see a Russian-made MIG-29 pull alongside the right wing. He looked out the portside window and saw another one. *This is not a good sign,* he thought. He quickly made his way to the cockpit.

"I see we have company," said G. "Have they hailed us yet?"

"Oh yeah, they're hailing, but we're not answering," replied Ian. "They want us to follow them back to Aden. And they're getting pretty damn adamant about it. Watch out, Earl," he said as the one on the right nudged closer.

Earl did his best to remain on course when he noticed two more fast-moving targets headed straight for them off the nose. "Aw damn, we're screwed. There's two more inbound off the nose, closing fast," he said.

Almost as soon as he finished his statement, the two Israeli jets soared just overhead, filling the fuselage with the deafening sound of jet noise.

"Shit!" exclaimed Earl.

"They're Israeli!" exclaimed Ian straining his neck as he watched the jets. He turned to look at G as if they had just won a multistate lottery.

"Hold your course, Earl," said G as his satellite phone began to vibrate.

G turned around, distracted by a tap on his shoulder.

"My people have sent reinforcements to assist us."

"Yeah, I see that. They just arrived," he said directing her attention to a starboard window.

"They want us to divert," she said.

"I'm sorry, what did you say?" said G.

"They want us to follow them to Tel Aviv. The DPM is on his way there now. He's expecting us to deliver his wife to him in our home country. All things considered, I assured him you would agree with the arrangement."

G looked out the window as he watched the MIG-29s peel away and the Israeli F-16s take their place. For the first time since the start of the mission, he felt a sense of pending accomplishment. He stepped back toward the cockpit for a moment to speak with Earl and Ian.

"Gentlemen, set a course for Tel Aviv. Our escort is compliments of the Israeli Air Force."

"Tel Aviv it is," replied Earl. "Copilot, set a course for Tel Aviv." He smiled.

Both phones rang simultaneously. Tzofiya and G looked at each other at the rare coincidence. Each picked up the phones and moved to separate parts of the cabin.

"I am arranging transportation for the DPM to meet you in Tel Aviv shortly after your arrival. He will have their daughter, Rina, with him. Please prepare Mrs. Malkinson accordingly," requested Ezra of Tzofiya.

"I will, Ezra. Will the DPM be taking the state aircraft?"

"Unfortunately, no. It has yet to arrive, so we are arranging a charter as we speak."

"Hold on a second, Ezra," said Tzofiya as she placed her hand over the mouthpiece.

"G, would you happen to know if your Gulfstream is still at La Mole? If so, is it available to transport the DPM and his daughter to Tel Aviv?"

Tzofiya smiled when she received a thumbs-up from G, who happened to be on the line speaking with Leon, who was in the flight-planning room with Monty.

"Ezra, I have a faster way home for the DPM, if he is interested."

43

The Citation jet transporting the DPM's wife and her rescuers was led to an obscure area of Ben Gurion Airport at Tel Aviv, where the plane was quickly ushered into a large, empty hangar. The silence was almost deafening once Earl shut the engines down and the doors to the hangar were closed behind them. A medical team was the first to board the aircraft to attend to Todd and Ian.

G grasped Todd's hand and looked into his tired eyes as the medical team prepped him for transport. "You made it. You have *no* excuse for dying. We have way too much living left for you to check out now. Do it for me. Do it for your brother. I'll see you again soon, my friend," he said as the emergency medical team carefully removed Todd from the airplane. Two more medical team members assisted Ian as he maneuvered his way out of the cockpit and into the aisle, where he collapsed under his own weight.

"Easy, big guy," said G as he stepped forward to help the EMTs maneuvering Ian to his feet. "I'll see if I can get you a room right next to Todd," he said with a wink and a smile.

"Please don't do me any favors," Ian responded with a wince. "Seriously though, I appreciate everything you did to save my life. I owe ya."

G nodded and smiled. "You can buy me a cigar." He winked again.

Tzofiya finished sending a text to Ezra informing him of their safe arrival when Hanah approached her and gave her an unexpected hug. During their extended embrace, Hanah whispered into

Tzofiya's ear, "I will never forget the sacrifices you have made for me and for our country. I couldn't be more proud to be associated with someone of your caliber. You put many a man to shame. I am happy to know you and will always be grateful."

A man boarded the plane and introduced himself to the remaining passengers on the aircraft. "Greetings, I am Michael, a member of the Mossad and personal security of the prime minister. If you will all please follow me."

Michael led Hanah, G, Dale, Earl, and Tzofiya to a well-appointed room where they were surprised to be met by the Israeli prime minister himself. He approached Hanah first and extended a warm and hearty embrace.

"It is so very good to see you, Hanah," he said. "Are you in need of any medical attention?"

She smiled the most beautiful smile and graciously refused.

"Please introduce me to your friends," he requested.

Hanah introduced each one, ensuring that she introduced G as the American team leader, and as the person who deserved the most recognition for being able to find her. G, while honored to meet a man of such importance, quietly stepped away after having been introduced.

"I am certain you are all weary and anxious to get something to eat and freshen up, so I will bid you all farewell," the prime minister said. Then he stopped to speak to Dale. "As for you, young man, I am more than certain you are ready to return home. I believe you have gone above and beyond in terms of service to your country and its allies. Please know that I am humbled by your sacrifice, and we are doing everything we can to return you home quickly," he said as he extended his hand.

The group stood as they watched the prime minister leave the room. Michael spoke to the group immediately thereafter. "The DPM's plane will be landing in one hour. We have facilities for you to freshen up if you desire. There is also food and drink in the next room. Please feel free to partake while you wait. Ma'am, we have taken the liberty of bringing you some fresh clothes should you desire to meet your husband in something fresh and clean," he said, directing the last part to Hanah.

Hanah looked at Tzofiya, who returned a smile and a slight shake of her head to indicate her opinion that Hanah looked just fine.

Hanah smiled and politely refused the offer. "I believe I will meet my husband and daughter just the way I am," she said. "I would rather spend the time I have left with my new friends."

G sat alone in a corner, carefully contemplating the details of the mission while Tzofiya watched Dale approach him to share a private moment.

"Incredible man, he is," said Hanah, surprising Tzofiya with her comment.

Tzofiya smiled as if she were just caught doing something she shouldn't. "Yes, he is."

"May I ask you something, sir?" the former POW asked G.

G looked up into Dale's glassy eyes. "Certainly, have a seat," answered G.

"Why did you bring me back with you?" he asked.

G returned a confused look. "Why *wouldn't* I?"

"I know you didn't come for me. And I know my country didn't send you to look for me," he added.

"And yet I still found you despite all that," said G with a sincere smile. "Would you rather I left you there to die? Would you not have done the same if you had found me?"

"I just wanted to say thank you but...that somehow doesn't seem to be enough," he said as a tear escaped from his eye.

G smiled. "Look at me. You have to believe me when I say that your thanks are all I'll ever need. Because of you, I now understand the meaning of *honor*. So maybe it's me who should be thanking you." G stood to extend a hand and a warm embrace. "Don't look back. *Now* is all you've got. It's time for you to enjoy the rest of your life."

Michael announced the arrival of the DPM's plane. Hanah knew she would soon be reunited with her family, but she also knew she might never see her savior again, so she made her way to where G was sitting. He stood when he saw her approach.

"You're such a gentleman," she commented with a smile. "Please," she added, gesturing for him to sit with her.

They sat quietly together in the isolated corner, G patiently waiting for to her to speak when she was ready. He watched as she stared at the floor, perhaps searching for the words or taking a moment to collect herself. Then she looked into his eyes—her own, full of emotion.

"The entirety of this experience has been surreal to say the least. I have no idea who you are, yet I feel as though I've *always* known you," she said. "I cannot begin to thank you enough for bringing me home. Although I wish never to repeat the horrid circumstances surrounding the experience, the encounters I've had will remain a part of me for the rest of my life. *You* are an important part of those encounters. I cannot begin to explain the reasons behind these things. Perhaps I never will. I am humbled and sincerely grateful to have met you, my gifted friend."

"You're a survivor and a damn good one at that," said G. "Your children—both of them—are fortunate to know you as they do. *I'm* fortunate to have met them both," he said with a sincere smile. "A lot can be learned from children, if we'll just take the time to listen to them. Something tells me you've learned new ways in which to do that. The honor and pleasure of getting to know you are mine. I *only* regret the circumstances."

"Excuse me, ma'am. The DPM has arrived and will be with us soon," said Michael.

Hanah and G stood and looked into each other's eyes. She stood up on her toes and embraced him in a grateful hug. He hesitated and uncomfortably returned the gesture. "I must go and meet my family," she said, fighting back the tears. "Perhaps I'll see you again, if only in my dreams."

G nodded and smiled. As he watched her turn and walk away, a whisper rushed through him.

Thank you. I knew you'd save her.

Michael led the group to an adjacent hangar where they watched the large doors close behind the sleek white Gulfstream jet as the engines powered down.

The team watched from a respectful distance as Hanah waited for the portside door to open and the stairs to extend to the floor below. Rina was the first to appear. The smile on her young face lit up the entire room as she made eye contact with her mother. Avigdor followed closely behind as Hanah approached her daughter and scooped her into her arms. Both were crying tears of joy when Avigdor reached his wife and embraced his entire family as he too shed tears of joy and relief.

Michael ushered the family toward a vehicle waiting to return them to their residence when Avigdor stopped and said something to him. Michael nodded and gestured for G and Tzofiya to approach.

Avigdor stepped away from Hanah and Rina for a moment to speak with the two operatives.

"Thank you both, and thank every member of your team for the sacrifices you have made to reunite my family. I will never forget it and am forever in your debt," said Avigdor. "There is some contention surrounding the fact that you brought home a bit more than your mission initially called for." He looked at G. "As you know, this did not sit well with your government, hence their attempt to sabotage the entire operation."

G listened as he learned the truth for the first time, reaffirming his own suspicions on why the team had been suddenly abandoned.

Avigdor continued. "In an effort to help remove the focus from you and your team, the prime minister and I have decided to cite Israel as the state who discovered and rescued your American POW. We will provide enough international press coverage to ensure America has no choice but to immediately repatriate and reunite him with his family. *My* family was separated for a short while. And although the experience was a living hell, I cannot imagine having to endure the amount of time this brave young man has. We will do everything we can to force the United States to discontinue using this man as a pawn to advance their political agendas. I trust this is a suitable arrangement for you?"

"Yes, thank you," said G as he looked over Avigdor's shoulder to see Hanah smile and nod.

"If you're ready for a holiday, I know where you can find a very nice luxury yacht in the South of France. I hear it has just been vacated. It's rather well appointed," said Avigdor with a wink and a smile. "I have ensured its availability if you're ready for some peace and quiet."

Tzofiya and G watched as Avigdor rejoined his smiling family and helped them into the awaiting limousine.

"It is *really* good to see you two," said a familiar voice approaching from behind them both.

"Leon," said G with a smile as he turned around to see his teammate's face.

"So how are Todd and Ian doing?" asked Leon.

"They're both gonna be just fine. Any issues with you hanging out in-country until they're well enough to travel?" asked G.

"I can do that. What about you? Where are you headed?"

"I think I'll get Earl to take me back to Saint-Tropez where I'll stay aboard the yacht for a few days. I could use the downtime to sort some things out," answered G. "What about you, Tzofiya?"

"Actually, my schedule is currently clear. Why do you ask?"

G smiled.

EPILOGUE

He watched her through the dark lenses of his Wiley-X sunglasses as she basked in a lounge chair, taking in the warm Saint-Tropez sun on the open deck near the bow of the expansive seventy-foot yacht. His vantage point at the helm gave him an elevated perspective on the scenic beauty and rich cultural backdrop of the French Riviera. The stark contrast of her naturally dark olive skin against her white bikini and the colorful lounge chair in which she lay, arrested his attention as he casually brought the ice-cold drink to his lips while savoring the experience of it all. Seeing her in this frame of reference provided an added element of satisfaction to the already relaxing allure of the picture-perfect vacation paradise.

Activity abounded as vessels of all sizes casually cruised by, each appealingly distinct from the next. Few other places on the planet provided as much nautical variety as the French Riviera. In every direction were beautiful people in a beautiful place enjoying a high quality of life and the opulence of success.

He picked up the binoculars to casually scan the area, pausing as he captured an up-close view of her athletic body as she adjusted her position slightly. The sun played on every sensuous glistening curve and feature as he visually caressed her body with a slow, easy pan of the lens starting at her manicured toes and slowly traveling to the curve of her ankles, along the lines of her calves to her slender, powerful thighs, pausing momentarily to examine the point where her hip met the hem of her bikini bottom…

"Not a bad spot for a little downtime, eh?" came a voice from below and behind him. "I bet the view is even better from *that* perspective."

G lowered the binoculars, turned around, and looked over the rail to find a man on a lower deck standing next to one of the security guards who had escorted him onboard. The security guard offered a slight nod, indicating the man had the necessary credentials to be aboard and to interrupt G's otherwise peaceful hiatus.

"Who are you, and what are you doing here?" asked G, anxious to get to the point.

"Mind if I come up and join you?" asked the man.

"Do I have a choice?" answered G as he turned his back on the man and raised the binoculars, once again examining the surrounding landscape.

The man climbed the ladder and made his way to the upper helm. "Man, this *is* a great view," he said as if G needed the confirmation.

G set down the binoculars and looked at the man standing before him. "I'll ask you once again," he said. "Who are you, and what do you want?"

"We've never met, not in person anyway," he answered. "It's by design, actually. My name is Paul Harriman. I'm your boss."

G allowed the words to sink in as he stared at the man—a man quite possibly culpable in selling out G and his team during their last operation—a sellout that nearly killed them all. G glared at the man, unsure whether he wanted answers or the satisfaction of seeing him suffer the consequences of his decision.

"Give me a good reason not to kill you where you're standing," said G as he stared directly into Paul's eyes.

"I'm not your enemy," answered Paul.

"Then who the hell *is* my enemy?" asked G.

"We don't represent a perfect country, G. There are a lot of moving pieces that are constantly in play in virtually every conceivable corner of the process—"

"The *political* process," interrupted G.

"Yes, the political process," confirmed Paul with a nod.

"And you're a central part of that political process?"

"We're *all* a part of the political process, G."

"That political process nearly got me and my team killed," G said angrily. "Not to mention the lives of an innocent civilian and a frigging US prisoner of war. I don't particularly enjoy the part I played in the so-called process, Paul. How do you explain the details surrounding *that*?"

"I can't."

"You *can't*, or you won't?" asked G.

Paul paused, turning on G a poker-faced stare.

"Look me in the eye and tell me you had nothing to do with the decision to disavow," G pressed.

"I had nothing to do with it."

"Then who the hell wanted the op scrubbed so badly they were willing to risk creating an international incident to prevent us from bringing home an allied diplomat and one of our own warriors?" asked G.

"I'm surprised you don't already know," said Paul.

G returned a look of confusion.

"It's just that...I had heard you had some kind of ability to discern these things," said Paul.

"Well, I appreciate the vote of confidence, but I'm only as good as the clues that lead me," explained G. "Unless that's the reason you traveled all this way." He looked at Paul for any sign of a confirmation.

"I'm not at liberty to say—"

"That's the beauty of my abilities, Paul...you don't have to *say* a word," explained G.

"G, everything OK?" called Tzofiya from the lower deck.

Both men looked down over the rail to see Tzofiya standing in a colorful sarong wrapped low around her slender waist. She wore a stylish, oversized, floppy hat and designer sunglasses, her tanned skin glistening in the sunlight as she looked up at the men.

"Can I get you guys anything?" she asked, closely watching G for a sign that he needed her for more than guest services.

"No, thanks," answered G. "In fact, we'll be down in a minute. Would you mind waiting for us in the salon? There's some new business we need to discuss."

The men made their way to the salon on the main deck.

"Who knows you're here, Paul?" asked G as Tzofiya walked into the room. She had changed into a conservative, floral-print dress.

Paul glanced at Tzofiya and smiled politely.

"Tzofiya, I'd like you to meet my boss, Paul Harriman. Paul, this is Tzofiya," said G.

"A pleasure, ma'am," said Paul, nodding politely.

"Is this business or pleasure?" asked Tzofiya of no one in particular.

"Technically, he's not even here," answered G.

"So business it is then," said Tzofiya matter-of-factly. "G, can I talk with you privately for a second?"

"Excuse me," said G to Paul.

Just out of earshot, Tzofiya expressed her suspicions of the man waiting in the next room. "What does he want?"

"He can't say."

"Then why is he here? How do we know we can even trust the fact that he's here right now? How do we know there aren't agents honing in on us as we speak?"

"I plan on finding all of that out if you'll give me a chance. Relax! We've done nothing wrong. And stop being so cynical," he said.

"I'm alive because of my cynicism, G. Don't ever forget that," she said as she walked away.

G returned to the room to find Paul looking out the window. Detecting G's presence, he spoke while continuing to stare out toward the horizon. "In my entire military and civilian career, I've never had the good fortune to have traveled here before this." Turning toward G, he asked, "So how does this work?"

"How does *what* work?" He suddenly realized what Paul was asking. "Oh, that. Have a seat," said G, gesturing toward a chair.

G took a seat directly across from Paul and immediately began asking direct questions.

"Why are you here?" asked G.

"I'm here to offer you your next assignment."

"Why did you feel compelled to deliver it personally?"

"So you know without a doubt that I'm not your enemy," responded Paul.

"Did you carry out an order to disavow my last mission?" asked G, ignoring Paul's assumption.

"Yes."

"On whose authority?"

"I cannot say."

"Am I an enemy of the state?"

"Not officially."

"Is my next mission sanctioned by the US government?"

"No."

"Does my life depend on a successful outcome or predetermined objective?"

"Yes."

"Look at me," instructed G. "I want you to extend your right hand. I'm going to grip your hand as if we're engaging in a friendly handshake. I don't want you to fight me until I let go, understand?"

ABOUT THE AUTHOR

Gary Westfal is a freelance writer, artist, and educator who developed a passion for writing purely by accident. A frequent and lucid dreamer, Gary began recording his dreams on paper in order to better understand the alter-conscious phenomenon and his self on a deeper level. What began as an exercise in self-prescribed therapy through documentation turned out to be much more than he expected, and eventually led to the creation and publication of his first novel—*Dream Operative*—an Amazon #1 Best Seller in the thriller genre.

Gary's website (http://garywestfal.com/) provides visitors with examples of his diversity across several media as an artist and his creativity as a writer/novelist. His personality and charisma are contagious attributes, whether in casual one-on-one conversation or speaking to a large audience. His lecture and presentation skills can best be described as confident, engaging, and articulate.

He is the creator and chief contributor to *Introspection* (http://gwestfal.blogspot.com/), a periodic blog that provides thought-provoking topics and seeks to enrich the lives of his readers by challenging them to think deeper, look within themselves for answers, and be mindful of the present moment. The blog offers a fresh perspective on personal empowerment and a wide range of human interest and self-awareness topics. He frequently speaks to audiences about human motivation, inspirational narratives, and practical business applications. *Key Horizon* is his second novel.

www.ingramcontent.com/pod-product-compliance
Lightning Source LLC
Chambersburg PA
CBHW030652120726
47905CB00001B/169